DEADLANDS

BONEYARD

NOVELS IN THE DEADLANS SERIES

Deadlands: Ghostwalkers
Deadlands: Thunder Moon Rising
Deadlands: Boneyard

•

BY SEANAN McGUIRE

*Dusk or Dark or Dawn
  or Day*
Sparrow Hill Road

The Wayward Children Series
Every Heart a Doorway
*Down Among the Sticks
  and Bones*
Beneath the Sugar Sky
In An Absent Dream
  (forthcoming)

The October Daye Series
Rosemary and Rue
A Local Habitation
An Artificial Night
Late Eclipses
One Salt Sea
Ashes of Honor
Chimes at Midnight
The Winter Long
*A Red-Rose
Chain*
Once Broken Faith
The Brightest Fell

The Incryptid Series
Discount Armageddon
Midnight Blue-Light Special

Half-Off Ragnarok
Pocket Apocalypse
Chaos Choreography
Magic for Nothing
Tricks for Free

The Indexing Series
Indexing
Indexing: Reflections

AS MIRA GRANT
The Newsflesh Series
Feed
Deadline
Blackout
Feedback
*Rise: The Complete
  Newsflesh Collection*
  (short stories)

The Parasitology Series
Parasite
Symbiont
Chimera

Rolling in the Deep
Into the Drowning Deep

Final Girls

DEADLANDS

BONEYARD

SEANAN McGUIRE

TOR

A TOM DOHERTY ASSOCIATES BOOK
NEW YORK

DEADLANDS: BONEYARD

Copyright © 2017 by Pinnacle Entertainment Group, LLC

Deadlands, The Weird West, and all related content is trademarked and copyright owned by Pinnacle Entertainment Group. Deadlands fiction is exclusively licensed and managed by Visionary Comics, LLC, with prose fiction published by Tor Books.

Deadlands created by Shane Lacy Hensley

Interior art by Steve Ellis

All rights reserved.

A Tor Book
Published by Tom Doherty Associates
175 Fifth Avenue
New York, NY 10010

www.tor-forge.com

Tor® is a registered trademark of Macmillan Publishing Group, LLC.

ISBN 978-0-7653-7531-5

Our books may be purchased in bulk for promotional, educational, or business use. Please contact your local bookseller or the Macmillan Corporate and Premium Sales Department at 1-800-221-7945, extension 5442, or by email at MacmillanSpecialMarkets@macmillan.com.

First Edition: October 2017
First Mass Market Edition: November 2018

Printed in the United States of America

0 9 8 7 6 5 4 3 2 1

For Jay Lake

Didn't I always promise you a midway?

DEADLANDS

BONEYARD

———◆———

Chapter 1

The plains of Idaho seemed to stretch from here to Heaven in the moonlight, if such a place existed, and the Blackstone Family Circus rolled over them as silently as a wagon train can roll, which was to say, not silently in the least. Wheels creaked. Oxen lowed quiet protest about being forced to work when they would rather have been stopping to graze in the low, patchy brush. Horses whickered, their hooves striking hard against the stony ground. A few still bore the painted stripes of their last show across their rumps, transforming them into half-zebras for the amusement of the townsfolk. The roustabouts who'd drawn the evening's short straw walked alongside the wagons, checking the snugness of wheels and the fastening of harnesses even as the train moved on. A show like this required constant maintenance, whether stationary or in motion.

"A circus is like a shark," said Nathanial Blackstone, whenever he was given the opportunity to do so—which was surprisingly frequent, even in places like this, where it seemed no human foot had trod since the West was won. "If it doesn't keep moving, it dies. So we move onward, ever onward, buy a ticket to see the bearded lady, and your children will thank you in the morning."

Sometimes the children thanked their parents by stowing away in the open wagons, hiding behind boxes or nestling themselves down in the cored-out hearts of old straw bales. Most of those runaways found themselves summarily dumped back on the road and ordered to go home, best of luck to you, young sir or madam, but we are not in the business of kidnapping, and we are not willing to risk ourselves on the likes of you. And to be fair, most of those runaways were glad to go. The glitter and lure of the circus was a night-thing, strongest by moonlight: it was, in its own way, a werewolf, transforming only when the sun went down. The circus by day was a different beast, less alluring, less attractive. It smelled of wet horse and rotting wood, of unwashed bodies and aging canvas, and it was hard to reconcile with the idea of the shining wonderland that had tempted them in the first place. But for some . . .

Oh, for some, the roustabouts or handlers who found them nestled in the hay or sleeping behind a costume rack needed only one look before they were going for Blackstone to report, in low, urgent voices, that his attention was needed. For some, who came with ribs that stood out like pickets in a fence, or with black bruises blooming across their cheeks—the kind that found a way to show through, no matter the color of their skin—a place could always be opened up. They might be doing manual labor, shoveling horseshit until the sun set or helping with the endless touch-ups the wagons required, but at least they'd be fed, and as safe as anyone could be in this world, which wasn't safe in the slightest.

A stranger could be forgiven if, seeing the show from a distance, they took it for a profitable target, and the Blackstone Circus had weathered its share of raids and stickups from people who didn't understand that circus gold is never true, that circus diamonds are always paste, and that circus beauty is at best a sham to fool the townies. At worst it's an outright lie, and that was true of most of the wagons, which were held together by hope, baling wire, and sheer cussed stubbornness. If the wagons fell apart, the circus would stop moving; if the circus stopped moving, it would no longer be a circus. Simple as that. So they slapped paint over cracks in the wood, and they repaired what could be repaired, and half the time when raiders came riding down out the hills, set on making mischief, the bold highwaymen somehow found themselves with hammers in their hands, helping to repair a broken axle.

They were paid, of course, in food and entertainment and whatever small riches the circus had been able to scrape together since the last time it had been attacked. And sometimes a man new to the highwayman's trade would burn a wagon out of an odd sense of obligation, filling the air with the smell of burning mold and blistering paint. But the quietly reproachful eyes of the circus folk seemed to have an extra weight by firelight, and rare was the man anywhere in the West who would harm a traveling show twice. The world was dark enough. Why darken it further by destroying one of the few amusements that served rich and poor alike?

So the circus rolled on, the lookouts keeping a weather eye on the hills while most of the show seized the rare opportunity to sleep between towns. Even if the human dangers would let them be, there were always things to fear out in the open. Cougars and wolves, and worse, to hear some of the roustabouts mutter in the night.

At the head of the wagon train was Nathanial Blackstone himself, owner of the show, reins in his hands as he guided his horses down the trail. Some people believed he never slept at all; that like his circus, he was a shark, and that if he stopped moving, he would die. Others knew that he was flesh and blood like any other man. A born showman, yes, who had no trouble encouraging his own mystique even among the people who worked for him, but still a man. He slept when the show was stopped. He slept in the early afternoons, when the crowds had yet to come in but the work of setting up had been finished. He slept in the space between sentences, where no one needed him to make their decisions for them, where, for good or ill, he could rest.

Rumor was he had a wife somewhere on the coast, in one of the green places where neither man nor beast came a-preying; that he had a child, or two, or as many as four, and that one day, when gray strands started to appear in that great black mustache of his, he'd be sending his trusted right hand to ride for Oregon and bring his eldest back to the show, ready to begin training his heir in the ways of the road.

Rumor *also* was that he was a clockwork man built by the master of another, fancier show, and that he'd run away from his creator the same way those occasional foundling children ran away from *their* creators, choosing freedom and uncertainty over captivity and a life where all their choices would come from someone else.

Nathanial Blackstone encouraged the rumors, all of them, no matter how ludicrous. If his people believed him to be a monster or a madman or a maestro, that could only enhance his reputation—and hence the reputation of the show as a whole—in the small towns they rolled through. Their route was a cartographer's masterwork of trails, roads, and semisafe paths, all connecting the settlements they served. A circus's map was one of its greatest treasures. Some of these routes, no other show in this part of the country knew. Without maps, the wagons couldn't get place to place fast enough to make a profit.

Keep moving. Stay alive.

Behind his wagon came the hulking shapes of the equipment wagons, largest in the train, which hauled the upright posts of the various tents, the collapsed game booths, the vast, billowing canopy of the big top. When Nathanial thought of the tent, he always saw it in silken stripes, high enough to beat its banners against the moon. The truth was tamer, fifteen feet at its highest point, patched canvas painted in irregular zigzags, but oh, it was still beautiful when the lights were strung around the edges, when the aerialists put on their spangles and their sequins and learned how to fly. How could something like that be anything *but* beautiful? And that, in a word, was the power of the circus, and the reason it had been able to pass unscathed through territory he'd been told, time and again, was too dangerous for any man to navigate. No matter how ugly the world outside the tent got, the world inside would always be beautiful, and people would always want beauty. No matter how bad things got, people would always want beauty.

Behind the equipment wagons came a scattering of smaller wagons, most privately owned, some barely worthy of the name. The Visali twins slept in an open cart, on a bed of hay and old carpet, their arms tangled around each other until they seemed like a single body split in two, the long white shapes of their borzoi hounds surrounding them in a hairy curtain. They refused to sleep in a closed wagon unless it was snowing, claiming the heat from their dogs made any enclosure unbearable. Half the show called them "the Russian werewolves," and untrue as the name was, it played well on the broadsheets they put up to advertise their performances.

Half the wagons were dark, their teams roped to the backs of the wagons ahead of them, trusting the show as a whole to set the path. The wagons where lanterns burned in the windows were still silent, raising the question of whether the light signaled wakefulness or merely superstition. The power of superstition in the circus could not be overlooked by any measure. It was a powerful thing, and some said it was what kept the axles turning without breaking, even when they rode over hard prairie. Say your prayers proper, make your offerings when you can, and the world will pass you by.

At the back of the train—not quite the end, which was

reserved for the wagons containing the dancing bear, the aging lion, the strange, terrible creatures of the oddities wagon, and the human attractions of the freak show—a small wagon bounced along, pulled by a pair of mules. One wore a straw hat. It was the sort of foolish affection adored by children everywhere, and the mule bore up with stoic silence, plodding ever onward. Like so many of the teams in the circus train, the pair had been tied to the wagon ahead of them.

Unlike so many of the wagons around them, the occupants of this one were awake. Sadly so: Annie Pearl, mistress of the freak show, feeder of lions and bears and whatever else she was asked to care after, sat restless and awake beside her daughter's narrow bunk, mouth pursed tight in worry.

"You'll feel better if you take your medicine," she said, in the cajoling, hopeful tone that has belonged to mothers since the very dawn of humanity. "Come along, now, Delly-my-dear. Be a good girl, and let me soothe your throat."

Adeline shook her head. The wagon lights struck stubborn glints off her dark doe eyes. Annie sighed. Seven years old and the girl was still stubborn as a post, and twice as difficult to budge.

"I know you don't like the taste of it, but there's nothing to be done for that," Annie said. "When we come to the next town, I'll see if I can't set enough aside to buy you some cherry syrup. Won't that be fine?"

Adeline eyed her mistrustfully. She knew her mother well enough to know that an offer of that sort always came with strings attached.

"But you have to take your medicine now."

Adeline frowned and shook her head fiercely, raising her right hand in the sign that meant 'no.'

This time, Annie's sigh was heavier. "Delly, you won't sleep until you take your medicine. Until you sleep, I won't sleep. If I don't sleep tonight, I won't be able to handle the bears in the morning. Do you want your poor old mother to be eaten by bears?"

Adeline giggled soundlessly at the thought before signing, 'Bears would get sick on you.'

"Yes, probably, and then where would you be? Another circus orphan, and you can't even sing for your supper. Really, you're much better off simply keeping me alive, which means letting me give you your medicine so we can both get some sleep tonight."

Adeline rolled her eyes. Recognizing the first signs of a pending concession, Annie sat back and waited.

Life with a child who could not speak came with challenges and compromises she could never have expected back when she'd been a pregnant wife with a belly full of potential and a head full of dreams. Had someone asked her then what she hoped, she would have answered without hesitation, "A boy, perfect in every possible way, smart as his father," and she would have been lying through her teeth. Boys belonged to their fathers. That was simply the way the world worked. If the midwife who yanked her firstborn out from between her legs had shouted, "You have a son!" her involvement in her own child's life would have as good as ended then and there, with her still bloody from the waist down. Her role would have been to cook and clean and look on indulgently as nannies and tutors saw to the young master's every need, guiding him gradually farther and farther away from his mother.

He would have been his father's son, and while she knew it was wrong to love one child more than another, she loved Adeline so much more than the heir she'd never given to the man she'd married.

What mother demanded perfection of her children? She couldn't even manage perfection in *herself,* and she'd had all the best tutors, all the right opportunities. Even without the damage to her vocal cords that had rendered her perpetually silent, Adeline wouldn't have had any of those things: she was growing up in creaky circus wagons and under the shadow of the big tent, not in damasked parlors and lacy gowns. No one had ever rapped her knuckles for failing to sit like a little lady. Most of the cakes she'd eaten in her life had been sweetened with honey, not with sugar, and she didn't know how to properly drink her tea, and she was utterly flawless, no matter what anyone else said.

No matter what her father had said.

It was easier now that Adeline could write when she had something complicated to say. She had some sign, learned from a Blackfoot man who'd traveled with the circus for a time. His Christian name had been Andrew, and his Blackfoot name had been a closely guarded secret, making most of the circus suspect that he was wanted for some crime or other.

(Annie rather assumed he had other reasons for his secrecy. She'd seen the roustabouts find excuses to mock names they found in the slightest bit foreign without mercy, and there was an awful tendency to assume Indian names were foreign, even though all this land had belonged to them ages before the white men came in to spoil things. She figured no one would set himself up to be tormented when he had another choice, and Andrew had been a proud man—most sharpshooters were. If he chose to hide his name so it couldn't be used against him by people who didn't understand pride, she had sympathy for that. She'd made similar choices, in her time.)

The sign was useful, and wasn't it lovely to watch Adeline talking with her hands? They danced and fluttered like little birds, and sometimes Annie thought she was about the luckiest of mothers, because when her daughter sang, she could see it with her eyes and hear it in her heart, where it would echo on forever.

But then there were nights like this, where she couldn't help thinking the argument would go faster if she could just *talk* to the girl, and not have to work around a gulf of silence. "Well?" she asked. "Are you going to be kind to your poor old mother and let me have a moment's peace?"

Adeline looked thoughtful. Then, with a small smile, she nodded.

"*Thank* you, Delly-my-love, dearest Delly in the world wide. Why, there are no finer Dellys in England or in France." She produced the green glass bottle from the pocket of her skirt, removing the cork with a practiced twist, and held it out toward Adeline. "Your spoon, please."

Adeline wrinkled her nose. The smell wafting from the open bottle was camphor and bitter herb, not dampened in the slightest by the honey Annie had mixed into the concoction. There were other ingredients in there, hidden under the surface layer of medicinal sharpness, things to soothe the mind and relax the body. Adeline couldn't sleep without it. They both knew that. It didn't make the taking of the stuff any more pleasant.

"*Please*," repeated Annie, with more urgency.

Adeline sighed—one of the few audible sounds she was capable of making—and produced a wrought iron spoon from under her pillow. It was a heavy thing, surprisingly delicate, made for her by one of the wainwrights from an old railroad tie. He'd said it would keep bad luck at bay. Adeline wasn't sure that was true. It delivered her nightly medicine, after all, and that was about the worst luck she could imagine.

Only about. She knew what bad luck looked like, the shape of its face and the color of its eyes, and her nightly medicine had nothing on true disaster.

"Best of children, sweetest of girls," Annie cooed, and poured thick, greenish syrup into the bowl of the spoon, stopping at the notch that indicated a proper dose. "Now down it goes, and off you go to dreamland, my dearest, my darling girl. Come tomorrow, we'll have a new show to set, and you'll be dangling from the rigging like a sailor at sea."

She put the cork back in the bottle, watching patiently until Adeline stuck the spoon between her lips and swallowed every drop, grimacing as she did. When Delly pulled the spoon out of her mouth and held it up for her mother's inspection, it was perfectly clean once more.

Annie nodded approvingly. "Good girl," she said. "Sleep well." She leaned in and pressed a kiss to her daughter's forehead before standing and beginning to tidy the wagon. It was a small, unnecessary task—the wagon was as close to spotless as it could be at all times, for the sake of Adeline's throat and her own sensibilities, which were still, at times, too finely honed for her current circumstances—but it kept her in the room without making it seem like she was hovering.

When she had finished dusting all four of their plates and wiping an imagined spill off the narrow counter that served as their kitchen, she looked back to the bed where her daughter slept. Adeline's eyes were closed, her chest rising and falling in a steady motion. Annie smiled in exhaustion and relief. At last.

The wagon had two doors, one at the front and one at the rear, although the door at the front was really more of a glorified hatch, intended for use only if she needed to lunge out and grab control of a runaway horse. She opened it, letting the night air in, and hung a lantern on the hook at the front. Any roustabout who looked that way would see the light and know its meaning: "unmanned wagon, driver out." If the wheels started to drift or the horses tried to balk, someone would be there to pull things back on track.

Roping the wagons together for night travel came with

risks—if something happened to one of the leaders, the whole circus could be compromised—but it was essential if they wanted to maintain the illusion of privacy between them. Not every wagon could be equipped with a driver capable of staying up all night, and even if they could have been, not everyone was happy to share their living space. Life at the circus meant having someone in your back pocket at all times. Any scraps of solitude that could be stolen were important.

And no one wanted to share a wagon with Annie and Adeline. Delly was too quiet for the younger women, the dancers and the aerialists and the made-up fortune tellers who really sold the chance to glance at their powdered bosoms through the magnifying lens of a crystal ball. She could come up on them like a ghost, like the accident that had stolen her voice had taken her footsteps with it, and scare them right out of their youth. She made the older women sad. They remembered their own children as laughing, idealized sprites, creatures that had been too good to stay, and knowing that she would never give her own mother that pleasure broke their hearts. As for the unattached men, well . . .

Even if Annie had been so determined not to be a burden as to allow one of them to share her wagon, Mr. Blackstone would never have been willing to stand for it. He was a gentleman at heart, which was a dangerous thing to be in a place like this one.

Annie took her cloak from its hook by the back door, slung it around her shoulders, and stepped outside.

There was an art to dismounting from a moving wagon. The steps could be extended only when the train had stopped; otherwise, there was a chance the friction from the ground could rip them right off their hinges, damaging the wood and requiring surprisingly extensive repairs. Annie waited on the lip that served as the wagon's "porch" until she could feel the rocking of the road in her knees—only a few seconds, a dramatic contrast to her first years with the Blackstone Circus—and then stepped off, as fearless as a high diver plunging into her pool.

Her toes hit the ground first, followed by her heels, which made impact at the moment her knees bent. To an observer, it looked like a very short curtsey. Then she was upright again, heading briskly for the next wagon in the train.

This one was larger than the wagon Annie shared with Adeline, fancier, covered in gingerbread curlycue nonsense that had to be polished for at least an hour before a show—but when it was polished nice and proper, how it shone in the sun! Half the take for an afternoon could be determined by how brightly the trim was shining that day. The sides were painted with larger-than-life advertisements for the wagon's contents, telling anyone who chanced to look their way that they could see! The Terrifying Swamp Beast! They could thrill! To the Ferocious Man-Eating Fish! They could even, if they liked, gaze in awe! At the Fearsome Tiger, Master of the East!

The freak show wagons rode behind this one, and many was the night Annie had spent among them, massaging sore muscles, tending to sprained backs, and most difficult of all, salving wounded feelings, which were slower to heal than wounded bodies. Thankfully, tonight, all the wagons rode dark and quiet, with their windows shuttered and lanterns hung to signal that everyone aboard was already off to dreamland. Her nursing duties were done for the night. Now was the time for her to do the rest of her duty.

Annie walked around to the back of the wagon that held their traveling caravan of oddities, unhooked the door, and hoisted herself up with a practiced hand, vanishing into the musk-scented darkness.

Chapter 2

The wagon of oddities was never lit when there wasn't a person present. It would have been a waste of good wax, and a fire hazard, and besides, some of Annie's "pets" didn't much care for light. They could stand it—anything that couldn't handle a little candlelight wasn't going to display too well in the daytime—but they preferred the comfortable security of the dark that they'd been born to. Rustling and hissing filled the wagon as she lit the lantern next to the door, chasing some of the shadows back into the corners where they belonged.

"Now, now," she chided, in the tone she'd used for Adeline when the girl was younger. "There's no need to make such a fuss. I'm just here to make sure that all of you are secure. Once I know you're fresh and fine, I'll leave you alone until morning." Adeline would be deep in dreamland by then, far from the concerns of the flesh, and Annie would be able to slip into her own bunk, surrendering the weight of the day to blissful unconsciousness.

The sun would rise far too soon for her liking, and another day would begin. Best to get her duties over with quickly.

It wasn't as if the wagon of oddities was a good place to linger. There was no one with the show more familiar with it than she, not even Mr. Blackstone, who was technically the owner of the wagon and everything that it contained. He disliked the wagon, disliked the way the shadows seemed to weigh down the corners until they had become something more concrete than simple darkness, something lingering and terrible. He disliked the smell of it, animal and rank and oddly unnatural, for all that the bulk of it came from the bodies of the creatures kept there. They would never have chosen to cohabitate in the wild; would have torn each other to pieces if given the opportunity, filling their bellies with the flesh of the things that were currently their neighbors. A zoo like this, a smell like this, could never have existed in the natural world.

The fish came first. Two great tanks of them, kept on opposite sides of the wagon, to prevent opportunistic attempts at predation. The larger tank was iron-banded, with a padlock holding the lid in place. That didn't mean Annie—or anyone with sense—trusted its occupants not to find a way to gnaw through the chain.

They were small creatures, at most five inches in length, with red bodies that always looked as if they had been dipped in blood that had then somehow failed to wash off in the water. Their mouths bristled with the jagged points of their teeth. When Annie had assisted Karina, the circus taxidermist, in preparing a few of the smaller specimens for outside display, she had been horrified to discover that those teeth didn't fit neatly together the way a human's did, or even slide seamlessly into holes in the creatures' jaws, like a crocodile's. No, they jutted out at all angles, making it impossible for the fish to feed without biting themselves, which no doubt only enraged them further.

The man who'd sold them to her called them "nibblers." It was a coy name for creatures that really should have been called something more akin to "devourers." She supposed it was a statement on the world they lived in that the names more befitting the toothy terrors had to be reserved for things even larger and more horrific.

The nibblers tracked her with their eyes and with tiny adjustments of their terrible bodies as she walked to the front of the wagon. There was never any doubt as to whether they were paying attention: when something warm and fleshy was nearby, the nibblers were nothing *but* attention. They were the most attentive creatures in the world.

"You're next," she said reproachfully. "And don't gnash your teeth at me, you dreadful things. You can't bite through glass." Of that, she was reasonably sure. Had they been equipped to chew through glass, she would have long since been bones, even if she was the last meal they would ever have. Nibblers, thankfully, could not breathe air any more than any other fish. Had they been amphibious, she was quite sure they would have eaten the entire circus long since, and died gasping but content.

The other tank was filled by the single hulking form of an albino river catfish. The big cat' shifted in the water as Annie approached, whiskers quivering, watching her with oddly soulful eyes. Sometimes she thought the catfish was really more of an aquatic puppy, a dog that had somehow been forced into the wrong body.

"Good evening, Oscar," she said gravely, picking up the jar that contained his food. The circus orphans gathered nightcrawlers for him every morning and evening, digging up the fat, slick worms and wiping them mostly clean before dropping them in pilfered dishes at the back of the oddities wagon. Annie didn't mind the worms themselves, but if she didn't consolidate them into the jar, they had a nasty tendency to slither into all corners of the place, dying and drying up like leathery threads.

(Townies were oddly horrified when they stumbled across the dead, dried-out worms—oddly because they were in the wagon to see terrible things, all the horrors and wonders of the unclaimed West. After beholding a feasting nibbler or a loop of bloodwire wrapping itself tight around the body of a captive squirrel, why should a worm hold any mystery? But somehow that little mundane reminder of the natural world was more than the sensibilities of some paying customers could handle, leading to Mr. Blackstone ordering her to keep the worms under control. Really. Annie had been a townie for most of her life before running away to join the circus, and yet sometimes she felt as if she would never understand them.)

The cat' stirred in the water, beginning to rise from his place in the thin band of muck along the bottom. They couldn't give the poor old boy as much mud as he wanted; it kicked up too much mess, blocking him from view, and quite countering the point of having a catfish of his size and coloration. If people couldn't see him, they wouldn't *pay* to see him, and if they didn't pay to see him, he'd wind up on the grill before the silt had settled.

"Yes, yes, I see you," said Annie. She tapped the surface of the water three times with her index finger. Oscar accelerated, rising to the top of the tank in a glorious sweep of open fins and creamy flesh. If she closed her eyes, she could almost hear the gasps and awed exclamations of the townies, many of whom had never seen a proper cat', as far as they were from the mysterious Mississippi. Even the most squeamish among them were often willing to pay a penny for the privilege of feeding him a live, wriggling worm—the same worms that would send them fleeing when dead and dried up on the floor.

Deftly, she extricated a nightcrawler from the jar and dangled it over the surface. Oscar stuck his mouth out of the water and slurped the worm daintily from her fingers, making it disappear.

"Good boy," she said, and repeated the trick three

more times before dropping a handful of worms into the tank for him to chase down and devour. He found them all with remarkable speed, given his poor eyesight and small catfish brain. Then, after nosing about in the silt for one last morsel, he settled back down, apparently content.

Oscar always amazed people with his "tricks." Most folks figured fish couldn't be trained, and maybe they couldn't—he was never going to go fetching any sticks or jumping through any hoops. But fish could *learn,* and Oscar knew that humans meant food and safety. Had known, in fact, since he was just a tiny thing, lurking around the edges of the pond, coming out to eat only when human fishermen were there to frighten away the bigger fish, who would have seen his unusual coloration as a sign of weakness. Albinos were easy targets in the wild, which made them even rarer than they would otherwise have been.

Annie turned to look at the nibblers. They were still watching her. "I hate you," she informed them.

Fish couldn't talk. That would have been *silly.* Sailors who claimed to have heard fish speaking were clearly delusional from too much time spent at sea. But caring for the nibblers had convinced her of one thing: fish could hate. Fish could hate very, very well.

Carefully, Annie pulled on the welder's gloves that hung next to the tank and unlocked the padlock on the first hatch. The nibblers became more active. She opened the cold box next, withdrawing a skinned goat shank. There were some in the circus who grumbled about how well the fish were fed, given how often roustabouts and handworkers went to bed with empty stomachs. Mr. Blackstone's method of dealing with the complainers was to bring them to watch at feeding time.

"That," he would say, as the nibblers stripped their supper to the bone in seconds, "is what they're like when they've been fed recently. Can you imagine if we ever let them get *hungry*?"

That was usually enough to silence the complaints for a few weeks, until hunger overwhelmed common sense once more. What he didn't seem to realize—and Annie couldn't make him understand—was that the nibblers were *always* hungry. Give them a steak and they would want a cow; give them a cow and they would want the whole damn herd. Whatever cruel God had seen fit to fill America's rivers with such horrors had not seen fit to also give them the capacity to be satiated.

"If you leap, I will leave you," she said, hoping, as she often did, that the fish would somehow learn to understand; that they would see the logic in muzzling their hunger for human flesh long enough to let her feed them the dead, cold things that they deserved. She knew her hope was pointless. That didn't stop it from kindling in her breast every time she had to perform this least-favored of chores.

The nibblers shifted in the tank, eyes always following her, jaws beginning to gnash. Little lines of blood colored the water around them, exciting the swarm more. She couldn't imagine what it must be like to encounter a school of them in the wild, where she had heard they could number in the hundreds. Imagine! It was a wonder anything survived within a hundred miles of the rivers. They should have been long abandoned, surrendered to the hunger that never died.

Two deadbolts secured the metal plate directly above the water. Annie hooked the end of a sharp metal chain through the goat, wrapping the chain twice around her hand, and pulled the deadbolts free. Speed was of the essence now. Saying a silent prayer to whatever gods might be watching, she yanked the plate back and dropped the meat into the water, taking a hasty step back.

Luck was with her: one more night when she would

not die in the course of keeping herself employed and keeping her daughter alive. Only a few of the nibblers jetted toward the surface, and they withdrew without leaping once they realized that she was out of range. The rest of the school had already closed around the shank, and the few who had been willing to attempt going after her were forced to fight their way through the thrashing bodies in order to get their terrible teeth on the prize. The goat shank vanished, first beneath the press of bodies, and then behind a veil of bubbles as the wildly eating nibblers churned the water into an impenetrable veil.

The carnage lasted only a few seconds before the nibblers were swimming back to the glass, fixing their terrible eyes on her once more. The shank bone, freed from its fleshy confines, drifted lazily down to the bottom of the tank to join the graveyard forming there.

Annie kept a wary eye on the nibblers as she pulled the chain and hook free. Occasionally, the dreadful things would attempt to hitch a ride with the assemblage, forcing her to get the tongs. She couldn't let them die, much as she might have liked to. Whatever nibblers required to breed, it wasn't present in the tank; if they all died off, she'd be left without an attraction, and the children *adored* the nibblers. Many of the adults, as well. When the show was truly short on funds, Mr. Blackstone would occasionally ask a few of the rougher men from the crew to host "private shows" for locals, wherein they fed live rabbits, kicking and screaming, into the tanks.

Annie was never present for that. Nothing could have muzzled the screams of the poor rabbits.

Quickly, she used a fireplace poker to shove the plate back into place before locking the nibbler tank, checking twice to be sure that everything was secure.

The rest of the wagon's horrors—oddities, oddities; they must always be called by the proper name, even when she was only speaking to her own heart, lest she slip and use the wrong name in the presence of a paying customer—were easier to care for. Some of them only required feeding every few weeks, like the various serpents, the great spiders, and the bloodwire, which was still wrapped tight and content around its latest opossum. Unlike the nibblers, it had no trouble growing; someone needed to take the shears to it again soon, or else it was going to overgrow its tank.

Finally, she walked to the very back of the wagon and unlocked the kennel that waited there. Its occupant made a discontented grumbling sound, like a train engine trying and failing to fire.

"Hush now," said Annie, dropping to her hands and knees and crawling, quite indecorously, into the dark.

Vast yellow eyes opened a few inches above her head, reflecting the light from the lanterns in ghost-flicker luminescence. It would have been unnerving, had it not been so familiar. Annie held her hand out toward the eyes. A moment later, a tongue the size of a lady's handkerchief rasped across her palm in rough greeting.

"Yes, hello," said Annie, crawling farther inside, until she bumped against the lynx's side. She turned over then, rolling onto her back and resting her head on the great cat's back, reaching up with both hands to scratch under her chin. The purring intensified. "Oh, you silly mush. You silly, silly mush. Did you think you'd been forgotten?"

Lacking words, the lynx simply purred on. Annie closed her eyes, letting the sound comfort her.

When she had fled her life to come to the circus—which had not, to be quite honest, been her original intent; her only target had been "away," which was a terrible goal for a woman who knew nothing of the wilds, running for her life with an infant strapped to her chest—she had been able to take very little. Her jewelry, most of which had long since been sold or melted down to ease them through the lean times; her mother's silver brush set, which she had since allowed to grow dark with tarnish, in the hopes of discouraging thieves; her daughter. Even her name had been left behind, buried and now virtually forgotten, to make her trail harder to follow.

But tucked into her valise she had carried a lynx cub, one last gift from the man who had been her husband, who had thought she needed "protection," although it was never quite clear from what, if not from him. She had refused hunting hounds and mastiffs, calling them poorly suited to the heat and empty spaces of Deseret, where rain was a rumor and green spaces were a lie. Besides, dogs were messy, nasty creatures, and she had not cared for animals then, in any sense of the word; had not enjoyed their company, nor known the tricks of keeping them alive. When pressed, she had allowed that cats were not so bad, and a week later, a box had been left in her parlor, hissing and growling at anyone who attempted to get close.

The cat's name, according to the man who delivered it, was Tranquility; she was a lynx, which was apparent to anyone with eyes. Less apparent was the fact that she had been prepared to live with humans, bred in a private zoo, presumably to be hunted; her adult teeth had been blunted, to make her less dangerous to the people around her. She still had her claws, of course. Removing them would have removed her integrity as a protector.

"No one will even think about troubling you with a watchdog like this on your property," the man had said jovially. Then: "Your husband must love you very much."

"I suppose that's true," she had said, and began making preparations to run.

When the time had come to actually go through with it, she hadn't been able to bring herself to leave Tranquility behind. Without the lynx, she might not have realized the depths of her husband's hubris, or how unwilling he was to listen to her. More, while Tranquility would not have been the only living thing she left behind, she would have been the most vulnerable. It wasn't the big cat's *fault* that she'd been an unwanted gift. It wouldn't have been fair.

In a way, Tranquility had saved them twice. Annie had run as far and as fast as she could, and just as the money was running out, she had stumbled across the Blackstone Family Circus and Traveling Wonder Show. The thought of joining the circus would never have occurred to her were it not for the people who had seen her with the baby on her hip and the half-grown lynx slung across her shoulders, and assumed that she was circus folk already.

"Does the cat do tricks?" The question had come from the roustabout at the gate—Danny, she'd learn later, raised under the big tent, circus orphan–turned–gawky lookout–turned worker. Unskilled, like the bulk of the bodies that made up the circus, but when had that ever stopped anyone from having a place in their own home? As long as Blackstone rode the American territories, and the territories of the nearby associated lands, Danny, and the people like him, would have a place to call their own.

(But not Deseret. Even before Annie had come to the show, they had never played for Deseret. That, more than anything, had eventually convinced her that it was safe to stay—that she would never open the doors to the oddities and find herself looking into the one pair of eyes she hoped never to see again.)

"The cat does not do tricks," she had replied. Tranquility had been panting against her throat, small, sharp breaths that tickled her skin and reminded her of the silent child on her hip, who was so much less equipped to make her needs known. "But the cat could use some water and a shady place to rest, and my daughter is hungry. I can do mending. I can clean. Whatever's needed, if it buys us rest and a bottle of milk."

Danny had looked at her with the blank incomprehension of someone who had never been required to think in his life: someone who, if shown a wheel, would gladly put his shoulder to it and push for all that he was worth, but who would never have been able to locate the wheel on his own.

"I don't know that I'm allowed to hire, ma'am," he'd said.

Annie's first reaction had been despair. This was it, then: this was the end of the road. She had run until she'd found herself with no road remaining, and now even the people who would supposedly welcome anyone—the circus folk her own long-ago nannies had told her stories about, who stole naughty children, whisking them off so that they were never heard from again—wouldn't have her.

"I see," she'd said dully. "Thank you for your time."

"You're *sure* the cat doesn't do tricks?"

Tranquility could take down a rabbit in full flight from the predator at its heels, and would share, most nights, surrendering half the meat to Annie and Adeline. Tranquility could growl like something three times her size, scaring off predators, whether animal or man. Most of the rougher sorts found in towns and in well-lit places did not, it seemed, want to tangle with a lynx, half-grown or not.

(Annie had not been fool enough to linger outside of cities—not yet. As the money ran out and her clothing became more and more disreputable, she had become resigned to the fact that one day she would have no choice. On that day, she would place Adeline in a church pew and pray that God had some mercy left for the West, where little girls with stolen voices deserved as much of a future as any other child; where her daughter ought to have a few good days, before everything fell apart, as it inevitably would.)

Tranquility could keep her warm at night, could purr the pain in her shoulders away, could be a companion where she would otherwise have none save for Adeline, who was too young and too silent to understand what was happening around her.

"No," she'd said, weary to the bone. "The cat does no tricks."

"We'll have to fix that," had said a voice behind her, and she had turned, and beheld Nathanial Blackstone for the first time.

Any man whose name was painted in giant gilt letters on the side of a wagon train should have been larger than life, six feet if he were an inch, with shoulders like an oak door and a face like a monument. He should have dominated any space that he inhabited, a myth walking. Nathanial Blackstone . . . didn't.

Oh, he was tall; taller even than her own father, who had regularly hit his head on doorways and tree branches that no one else would have worried about. But he was also gaunt, a skeleton of a man with his skin drawn taut across his bones. He was one of the darkest men she'd ever seen, with skin so brown that it made the whites of his eyes seem to glow like Tranquility's did by firelight, seeing everything, even the things that should by rights have gone unseen. There was not a single hair on the top of his head. As if to balance that fact, a bold handlebar mustache graced his upper lip, waxed and curled into a parody of itself, the sort of mustache that would be remembered after everything else about its bearer had long since been forgotten.

"Sir," Annie had said, unsure what else to do. Her manners, like everything else about her, had been worn thin by the road.

"My name is Nathanial," he had replied. "We always have need of someone to do the mending, especially if you're clever with a needle and thread; we always have need of someone the children will listen to, if you think you might be able to enforce some discipline over them. Everything else can be worked through in time, if you feel like the circus might be the place for you."

"Truly, sir, I don't know whether there's a place for me in this world," she had replied. "But it's worth trying, and if there's a bed in it for us, I'm happy to do whatever you propose."

"Good," Nathanial had said, and put a hand on her arm, and steered her to his wagon.

Now, years and miles and hundreds of shows from there, Annie was the keeper of the freak show and the guardian of the oddities. She still did mending, when necessary, but that hadn't been her primary job in years. The circus orphans had to find their makeshift mothers in other wagons; all her motherhood was taken up by Adeline, who was delicate and delightful, and needed her.

The cat still, despite the efforts of some of the best trainers the show had to offer, did not do tricks. But she purred. Oh, how she purred.

Her head resting lightly on the flank of a deadly predator, surrounded by monsters, Annie Pearl closed her eyes and slept.

Chapter 3

A hand gripped Annie's ankle and tugged. It wasn't strong enough to drag her out of the cage, but any motion in the oddities wagon was cause for concern. Her eyes snapped open and she sat upright, banging her head on the top of the cage. She made a wordless sound of pain and dismay. Behind her, Tranquility grumbled, the low, deep muttering of a discontented predator.

The wagon wasn't moving anymore. Annie squinted through watering eyes, trying to see what had grabbed her. Nothing was biting at her flesh or attempting to devour her alive, which meant that it was probably human; other than Oscar, Tranquility, and a few of the nameless snakes, there was nothing else in the wagon that would be so kind.

Her vision cleared. She realized that she could see surprisingly well: sunlight was oozing in around the edges of the closed windows, driving most of the wagon's occupants deeper into the shadows of their enclosures. Very few of the things in the wagon of oddities cared for direct sunlight—especially Oscar, whose pale flesh could burn just like a human's.

Adeline was crouching in front of the cage, her fingers still wrapped tight around her mother's ankle, watching her unblinkingly. Annie let out a sigh of relief.

"Hello, my Delly," she said. "I'm so sorry. I must have fallen asleep while I was checking on Tranquility." After so many nights spent running with the lynx asleep at her head and the baby asleep at her breast, the purr of the lynx was a soothing thing. She didn't succumb to its lure as often as she once had, but still, there were times when the promise of peace was more than she could ignore.

'I woke up and you were gone,' signed Delly, a reproachful expression on her face.

"I know, and I am truly sorry." Annie reached behind herself to give Tranquility a final reassuring pat before pulling her ankle free of Adeline's grasp and rolling onto her hands and knees. She crawled out into the open, her back protesting the motion. She was not a young woman anymore, to spend her nights sleeping on the floor of a cage without paying for it in the morning.

Adeline was not appeased. She waited until her mother was facing her again before signing, 'I thought you were eaten.'

"Tranquility would never let that happen."

Adeline fixed her mother with a disbelieving stare. If most of the things in the collection of oddities wanted to eat Annie, a simple lynx wouldn't be able to stop them. Even if Tranquility's loyalty were strong enough to make her join a fight, she couldn't possibly win. They would both be devoured.

Annie sighed. "Again, my love, I am sorry, and I didn't mean to leave you alone. We've stopped. Are we laying camp, or has Mr. Blackstone found us a stopping point?"

'Camp,' signed Adeline, and followed the word with, 'Hungry.'

"Yes, my dearest. Come along." Annie stood, turning to close and lock Tranquility's cage behind herself. The lynx had already gone back to sleep, and didn't so much as twitch an ear.

Looking down at herself, Annie wrinkled her nose. Keeping oneself clean on the road was a trial, made more difficult by their current unpredictable circumstances. They had run off their usual seasonal route a week prior, and although they had stopped several times for an afternoon of opening the exhibit wagons, they had yet to set up for a full show. Without a full show, there was no cause to set up either the big tent or the boneyard, and without the boneyard—their shared campsite and temporary home during a show—there was no bathing tent. It was enough to make a woman think of clawing her own skin off in the hopes of removing the filth along with her flesh.

"May I change my dress before we go for food?" she asked. Giving Adeline a frank look, she said, "We should do the same for you, lest we encounter townies who decide I beat you every night, and twice in the morning."

Adeline giggled soundlessly, making a fist and miming punching herself in the jaw. Then she nodded.

"My thanks," Annie said gravely. She offered her hand. After a moment's contemplation, Adeline took it, and the two of them walked together out of the oddities wagon.

It would have been impossible for someone who saw them together to mistake the fact that they were mother and daughter. Adeline's hair was the color of corn silk, while Annie's was the darker, more mature color of corn. Both had naturally pale complexions, which tanned quickly in the sun, and eyes like chips of meltless winter ice. They shared a chin, and a nose, and a tendency to furrow their brows when frustrated, as if they could glare the world into submission, or at least into becoming comprehensible.

Adeline was shorter, of course, being only seven years old; her hair was longer and very rarely styled, although she would generally consent to having it brushed. Both of them walked quietly and stood straight-backed and proud, even when there seemed little to be proud of. There was always survival. Survival, under the right circumstances, was enough.

The wagon train was stopped at the side of a road that

seemed barely worthy of the name: it was a trail, worn into the earth by wheels and hooves and feet, but never planned, nor tended by anyone who cared for its condition. They had moved onto the grass more out of courtesy than necessity; it seemed unlikely that anyone else would come riding through this particular stretch of desolation anytime soon.

There were trees, but not many; their scrubby branches would provide little shelter if it happened to rain again. Annie gave the sky a wary look as they stepped down from the oddities wagon. The earth was soft, skirting the line between dirt and mud with an expert hand. One more good rainstorm would be enough to see them stopped for days. The earth out here took water easily. It gave it back slow.

There were no houses in sight—not so much as a shack. Whatever they'd stopped for, it wasn't to put on a show. Most of the wagons had their windows open, which only drew attention to the lack of a crowd. They would *never* have risked townies seeing into their private places outside the boneyard. The fact that they were willing when they didn't have the proper protections up only proved there'd be no entertainment for the masses. Not here, not today.

"Morning, Miss Annie," said one of her freaks—a name she didn't much care for, but which they bore as a badge of honor. She supposed the word was all in where you were standing while you looked at it. For her, a woman of decent breeding brought low by circumstance, being called a freak would have been an insult. For Edgar, born with hair on almost every inch of his body, so that he appeared in shorts for the amazement of the masses under the name "Arizona Werewolf," well. "Freak" was a word that meant a place to sleep, and full bellies for himself, his wife, and all three of his children. (The youngest of them looked set to take after her fa-

ther, and had been born with a fine coat of downy fur
covering her entire body. She was only three years old,
and Mr. Blackstone had a firm policy of not displaying
living children too young to understand what was going
on. Dead children were another matter, and the show had
its share of "abomination" babies in jars, infants born
too flawed to have ever lived past the cradle. Dead children were simply residents of a graveyard with a view.
Live children had rights.)

"Good morning, Edgar," said Annie, trying to pretend
she wasn't wearing the previous day's clothing, that she
didn't have straw and animal fur in her hair. Adeline continued tugging on her hand, urging her onward. Annie
grimaced apologetically. "I would stop to chat, but . . ."

"Say no more, ma'am," said Edgar, an understanding
smile on his furry face.

Annie smiled back, as much out of relief at the conversation's end as anything else, and allowed herself to
be hauled onward, back to the safety of her own wagon.

The lantern had burned out during the night. Annie felt
a pang of guilt as she looked at it. Once Adeline was actually asleep, it was virtually impossible to wake her. If
there had been a fire . . .

If there had been a fire, she would have burned to
death while her mother was sleeping soundly in her caravan of monsters. Annie would have woken to find herself alone in the world, and she didn't think she would
survive that. She had been many things in her life. She
had never, as yet, been alone.

"You are a mess, my poppet," she said, pointing at the
chest of drawers that contained Adeline's wardrobe. "I
want to see you in clean clothes, and washing your hands
and face, before I have my corset off. Hop to it!"

Adeline did not hop. She did give her mother a put-
upon look before heading to the chest, presumably to
follow directions. Annie turned her back to give her a

little privacy. The child had been to the manor born, as had Annie herself; she should have had entire rooms for nothing but the changing of her clothes, and here she was, sharing a cramped wagon with her mother, forced to expose her body whether she wanted to or not.

At least it was only Annie who seemed to understand the difficulties of their situation. Adeline didn't remember where she came from and had no trouble with the cramped quarters or the lack of privacy. She didn't even seem to understand that she should care.

Quickly, Annie stripped down and unlaced her corset, dropping it on the floor and taking several deep breaths as she allowed her waist to expand to its natural dimensions. Some of the men who traveled with the show asked the women why they bothered with corsetry when there wasn't a show. It was difficult to make them understand that when all your clothing was cut to fit over something, it could be hard to go without. Besides, a good corset was also good armor, and there were plenty of things to fear at the circus. Kicking horses, swinging doors, even the occasional fistfight between roustabouts—they could all be made less dangerous by the right corsetry.

Annie grabbed a clean corset and tied herself up with quick, sharp jerks, drawing the laces tight enough to allow her skirt to fit, while leaving them loose enough that she didn't need to get a hook. They were stopped, for now; she didn't need to worry about presentability, just modesty. She pulled on a patched shirt and an ankle-length red skirt that had started life as part of one of the smaller tents. She wasn't the only one at the show wearing clothes made of that material. It could practically have been a uniform if only it hadn't been remade into so many different shapes and types of thing.

"Are you ready, Delly?" she asked, turning, and barely managing not to jump when she discovered that Adeline was standing directly behind her, having crossed the wagon on silent feet while her mother wasn't looking. She pressed a hand to her heart, trying to calm it. She had long since learned that there was no point in scolding Adeline for sneaking up on her; the child couldn't help it. Some of the clowns even found it endearing, calling her a natural and beseeching her to don greasepaint and enter the ring.

(Those requests earned silent giggles from Adeline and shakes of the head from Annie, who knew better than anyone how important it was that her face never appear on a poster, even interpreted by an artist's hand and concealed beneath a harlequin's slap.)

Adeline was wearing a simple patched sundress with a shawl wrapped tight around her shoulders to ward away the end of summer chill. The hem covered her feet, making it difficult to tell whether she was wearing shoes. Annie decided not to ask. Adeline was a delicate child, but her constitution was good enough to handle a little mud, and it was best not to push too hard when there was no show to distract her.

"Very well," said Annie. "To breakfast, then."

Adeline smiled and took her mother's hand, and the pair of them walked out into the morning air once more.

The Blackstone Circus was a small train, as such shows went: they had more wagons than was strictly required for transport of their equipment, but that was due to the number of families they had traveling with them. It had the benefit of making the circus seem larger than it was. Larger shows should have been a more tempting target for robbers, being more likely to have full coffers and healthy supply wagons, but somehow, the larger the circus, the more apt it was that raiders and the like would simply pass it by. Mr. Blackstone liked to say that it was a form of civic duty, the bad seeds of the badlands sparing the people who could take their minds off their petty woes for a few precious hours. Annie had a great deal of respect for Mr. Blackstone, but rather thought that he was talking out his nethers when he said that sort of thing.

Large circuses had powerful patrons. Powerful patrons didn't like their toys being damaged by other people. Large circuses were thus substantially more likely to have dedicated security, gunslingers and the like who looked like ordinary roustabouts until they had reason to draw. A small show was less likely to have anything worth taking, but it was also more likely to be vulnerable. The extra family wagons were a form of camouflage, like a garter snake slapping its tail against rocks in an effort to sound like a rattler. They were trying to look more dangerous than they were.

There was no room along the road to set up the mess tent. That wasn't enough to stop the chuck wagon from surging into action the moment they'd stopped. Annie and Adeline wove their way between parked wagons, following the smell of fatty bacon and honey-touched oatmeal, until they emerged into the clear band of space between the rest of the train and their temporary commissary.

They weren't the first to come looking for breakfast, by a long shot. People sat on the porches of nearby wagons or on the ground; a few enterprising souls had even spread out picnic blankets. A group of circus orphans was clustered near the mess tent proper, eating their oatmeal as fast as they could, presumably in hopes of a second helping before the breakfast period ended. Adeline looked hopefully up at her mother.

"Of course," said Annie, and let go of her hand. "Only please, attempt to eat like a lady, instead of like a wild thing found by the side of the road."

Adeline wrinkled her nose and ran off to join her friends, kicking her skirts high enough in the process for Annie to see that the girl's feet were, indeed, bare. She sighed. Autumn would come soon enough, with its thick socks and thrice-mended shoes. Best to let the girl have her fun now, while there was still fun to be had.

"Miss Pearl. Just who I was hoping to see this fine morning." Nathanial stepped up next to her. He was nowhere near as quiet as Adeline, who could sneak up on Tranquility on some mornings, but he was quiet enough to startle two times out of three. "Did you sleep well? I was under the impression that you preferred your bed."

"Does everyone know I spent the night in the oddities wagon, or are you simply reminding me that the ringmaster sees all, knows all, and has an opinion on all?"

"A few of the roustabouts saw you enter but didn't see you leave. They came to me with their concerns when we stopped." Nathanial smiled, the corners of his mustache flexing upward like the whiskers of a satisfied cat. "They did not, it seems, feel equipped to enter your chamber of horrors if it had already devoured you."

"Seems they have a sense of self-preservation, then," said Annie. "I fell asleep in Tranquility's kennel."

"You could take her into your wagon."

Annie shook her head. "There's no room for her, and she can be unpredictable where Delly is concerned." Sometimes the big cat was Adeline's fiercest protector. Other times, she would mutter and growl, eyeing the child like she thought that Delly might be a threat to her mistress. The loyalty of a lynx was not like the loyalty of a dog: it was not unshakable and inbred. It was a wild thing, as she was a wild thing, and Annie had lived through too many tragedies to go seeking another.

"Besides," she added. "She has the loudest roar of anything short of those mangy tigers in the big tent. If there were actually a threat to the wagon, she would be able to notify me no matter where in the train I happened to be. That's a powerful thing to have, given the other things she rides with."

"All are fed and secure?"

"Yes, although I'll need another dozen rats soon for the snakes, and more worms for Oscar. He's getting bigger. Larger things need more food."

"Yes," agreed Nathanial, eyes on the chuck wagon. There were so many children clustered there that it seemed like a magic trick. How had they wound up with so many children?

In the usual ways. There were families traveling with the show; there were apprentices to be considered; there were the circus orphans, who could have been turned away, but who had nowhere else to go. If they were old enough to work, or came with a sibling who was old enough to work, he let them stay. That was how he had always run his show, and that was how he always would. It was a small thing, when set against the casual cruelty of an entire world. It was less than the world deserved.

Nathanial Blackstone had never been a slave. His parents had been freed before the accord that ended slavery across the continent: he had grown up being told over and over that it was the cut of his character, more than the color of his skin, that would determine his future. And that was all well and good, but when the white families around them had relatives back in the rich and settled East who were happy to keep sending money and care packages and everything else under the sun while his family and the families like them had to face the West without any support but what they gave each other, well. It was difficult not to see that as a lasting ripple from the great stone of slavery, still spreading outward, not yet reaching whatever wall would make it stop.

People liked to claim that once you pulled the knife out of someone's back, everything was fine, but anyone who'd ever been stabbed knew that just wasn't so. Knives made wounds. There was bleeding and infection to deal with long before the process of healing could properly begin, and even after the healing happened, there would always be scars. He'd bought his circus from a family that didn't want it anymore, back when it had been three crumbling wagons, a rickety tent, and a handful of freaks who barely deserved the name—Wilma the Bearded Lady, with her spirit gum and her peach fuzz cheeks; Peter the Human Lobster, who should really have been called "Peter Who Never Learned Not to Grab Knives by the Blade," and all their ilk—and he'd never looked back. He had painted and patched and bought more wagons, more attractions, expanded his tiny traveling empire until it almost seemed worthy of the name.

His mother, God rest her soul, had never been able to understand why her eldest son wouldn't want to put down roots; would choose to be a tumbleweed rolling across the West instead of a safely rooted sycamore growing in fertile soil. What she didn't understand and he had never been able to explain to her was that sometimes being a tumbleweed was the key to staying alive. As long as he didn't set down roots, he could move on whenever there was danger.

But he *had* set down roots. Every wagon in the circus train, every person who depended on him for their daily bread, they were his roots. It was his responsibility to make sure they didn't wither and die.

"Is something wrong?"

Annie's voice snapped him out of his contemplation. He sighed, turning toward her and attempting to force a realistic smile—or at least a believable one. "What would make you think that, o pearl beyond price?"

"You're never quiet for this long," she replied, crossing her arms. "What is it?"

Annie was a good woman, with a solid head on her shoulders. There had been times when he'd considered courting her in earnest. Adeline didn't bother him the

way she did some of the men with the circus: she was a
good girl, and her silence wasn't her fault. There just
never seemed to be *time*. Running a circus was a constant
commitment. Even when he was alone in his wagon, he
was looking at routes, calculating supplies, and figuring
out what needed to happen next. There was no such
thing as a truly free moment. Not for him.

"Our next two shows have canceled," he admitted in
a soft voice, not intended to carry. "They sent their apologies, and one of them paid the cancellation fee—which
was mighty nice of them, under the circumstances—but
the harvests haven't been as good as they'd been hoping
when they booked with us, and they simply can't afford
to have us disrupting the town for a week. Not with autumn coming and the last of the stores needing to be
brought in."

"But the children—" she began, and stopped when she
saw him shaking his head. "The children will be working, too."

"Yes," he said. "Farm children generally need to."

"How can anyone farm out here?"

"How can anyone *not*?" He spread his arms, indicating the rolling plains around them. "There's no supply
train here, no one coming to make sure the pantry is
stocked and the larder is full. It's hunt and farm and hope
and fail, and pray that failure won't be enough to see you
in the ground."

There was a hard edge to his voice that made Annie
want to step away from him, fearing the sound. "What
does this mean for us?" she asked instead.

He sighed. "It means we press on. We have to find at
least one more show before the end of the season, or
we're not going to make it through the winter."

Winter was when the circus stopped, at least until the
roads thawed. Winter was when they rented rooms from
suspicious townies, or slept six to a wagon and hoped

that their bodies would be enough to keep the air from freezing. It was when they stabled the animals and repaired the tents and pretended, for a time, to be comfortable under a fixed roof, surrounded by strangers who grew more familiar by the day. They lost a few people every winter, when the lure of town life was too much for them to resist. They gained a few people, too, riding out in the spring with formerly respectable merchants and seamstresses clinging to their bunks, eyes full of stars and bones full of wonder.

"Do we have a destination?"

Nathanial hesitated.

That was never a good sign. When Nathanial hesitated, it was because he knew that whatever he was going to say was not going to be well received.

"Nathanial," she said.

He sighed. "Oregon," he said. "There's a town there. The Clearing. They have a reputation for being kind to outsiders; I know a puppet show that passed through there last summer, and they made five times their normal fees, in addition to gifts from the locals."

"So why are you wary?"

"Because anything that sounds too good to be true almost certainly is." He looked moodily at the crowd around the chuck wagon. "I just don't see where we have a choice."

Chapter 4

Circus folk were contentious by nature: they would argue with almost anything, from their portion at supper to the orientation of the big tent's entrance. It was no surprise that there had been several objections to Mr. Blackstone's plan to take them into Oregon for their last show of the winter.

It had been more of a surprise when several of the roustabouts and smaller acts chose to stay behind rather than throwing their lot in with the circus.

"Bad things happen in Oregon," said Adrianne, a knife-thrower, before she packed her bags and slipped off down the road.

"Last circus I was with said that they'd tried to go to The Clearing, and there were no roads, and there was no route on the map, and everyone they'd asked about it told them no one lived there," said Vlad, a roustabout, before he put his hat on and walked away.

"People there have superstitions I can't be having with," said Edgar, his wife's hand clutched firmly in his, their children arrayed behind them like the spokes on a wheel. "If you make it back this way, we'll be happy to have our wagon back, Miss Pearl, but I'm not risking my children for a few extra potatoes in the pot."

"But where will you go?"

Edgar shrugged. "Last town we passed through was nice enough to us, and they didn't stare as much as some. Daisy's lacework is good enough to pay for a room, and if I had to stay inside until winter, I've done more for less. Be careful out there, will you? Oregon's too close to California for my liking, and *much* too close to the sea."

"You be careful, too, Edgar," she said. On an impulse, she leaned in and kissed his furry forehead. When she pulled back, she thought that he might be blushing beneath his lush brown coat.

Adeline stepped up to take her hand, and the two of them watched in silence as the dog-faced man and his family started down the road, carrying as many of their worldly goods on their backs as they could manage. They'd been forced to leave so much behind. There was no guarantee that any of the things they'd abandoned would still be there when the show came back this way. Annie could try to defend their wagon's place in the freak show, but there were always bodies looking for a bunk, especially with the winter coming on, and once people moved into a space, it was hard to keep them out of the closets and the drawers.

"Damn," breathed Annie. Adeline's hand tightened on hers. She looked down into the wide, shocked eyes of her daughter, and grimaced. "I'm sorry, my dearest. I just worry about what they're going to do with themselves, all alone like that. Circus folk look out for their own. They're still ours. They'll be ours until the day we die."

Adeline pulled her hand out of her mother's so she could sign, 'Bad words aren't right.'

"You know, when you say things like that, I question the wisdom of letting Andrew teach you how to sign. Lecturing me! Well I never." Annie crouched and began tickling her daughter, fingers seeking out the most sensitive spots with an ease born from years of practice. Adeline giggled soundlessly, twisting and squirming, but never quite making an effort to get away.

A throat was cleared behind them. Annie stopped tickling as they both turned to find Mr. Blackstone standing on the path, his hands folded behind his back, watching the picture they presented.

"Are all your people aware of our planned route?" he asked. There was a formality in his voice that made it clear he was speaking in his capacity as head of the show and not as her sometime friend, or Adeline's honorary uncle. So much about the circus was contextual. Sometimes Annie wondered how they could keep it all straight.

But they did. They had to. The show must go on. "They are," she said, straightening. Adeline fell into place at her side, standing close enough that she was half-veiled by her mother's skirts. "Edgar and his family are returning to our most recent stop. The snake-dancers are willing to perform but worry about the chill in Oregon; they're asking for extra firewood to keep their serpents warm."

"And you?" he asked. "Will you be returning to our last town, or asking for favors?"

Something was gnawing at him. Annie straightened farther, tilting her chin up until her eyes were locked on his own, and said, "We are far closer to certain territories than I care to be. Anything that carries us farther is a lovely idea as far as I'm concerned. I hear Oregon is splendid in the fall. Now will you stop questioning me like I'm something you just found under a rock and tell me what troubles you?"

Nathanial hesitated. Then he crouched down, dipping one of his long-fingered, clever hands into the pocket of his waistcoat and coming up with a piece of polished quartz. It looked more like bone than stone. He offered it gravely to Adeline.

"Miss Cynthia dropped this on the path this morning. I believe it's one of her lucky stones. Would you do me the immense favor of returning it to her? She'll be so pleased to see it again that I expect she'll have a reward for the one who returns it."

Adeline took the stone, casting a hopeful glance up at her mother. Miss Cynthia had a reputation for hiding sugar candy in her wagon, enough that she had, on several occasions, attracted ants. It took an impressive amount of sugar to catch the attention of ants while in a moving wagon, but Miss Cynthia had managed it.

"Yes, go ahead," said Annie. "Come straight back to the oddities wagon when you're done. I'll let you help me feed Tranquility." The little girl was endlessly fascinated by the big cat. Annie still found it best not to leave them alone together.

Adeline nodded agreement and took off running, bare feet flashing under the hem of her skirt. Even at a dead sprint, she made no sound.

Annie sighed fondly. "I'm going to have to strap her down and nail shoes to her feet like a mule, I swear. I have never known a child so fond of running barefoot through the world."

"I have never known a child like Adeline," said Nathanial, straightening up again. He folded his hands behind his back, looking gravely at Annie. "Walk with me, Miss Pearl?"

"Of course." She fell into step beside him, letting him set the pace as they began walking back toward the wagon of oddities. Her orbit during the day never took her far from her charges, whether human or animal. When not speaking with her freaks, she could always be found near the oddities, which needed more intense monitoring to ensure that they didn't attempt an escape. The fish were calm enough, and it was cold outside, rendering the snakes dormant and torpid, but those were not the only things her wagon contained.

Sometimes Nathanial wondered whether she realized how dangerous her collection had become, and whether she would care if it were pointed out to her. The oddities fed her daughter and kept a roof over her head, and while they might kill her one day, they hadn't killed her yet. The future was ever and always another country.

"Miss Pearl, our planned route is a dangerous one," he said, after they had traveled a few yards from the residential wagons. "While everything I told you before was true, and you know I would never endanger the show without good cause—"

"There is no reward without risk," she said, sounding almost serene about it. "That is something I have been hearing from the men in my life for as long as I can remember. The Clearing sounds like a paradise. Small and isolated, which will make them desperate for entertainments, while still open enough to outsiders that they pay well when strangers come to town. So why isn't it spoken of in glowing terms on every route from here to Hampshire? The answer can only be that something is wrong with this magical wonderland."

"Not with the town itself, exactly," said Nathanial. "There have been . . . disappearances, let us say, among the shows that have gone there. Most return unscathed, and speak of generosity and compassion."

"But some do not."

"No," he admitted. "Some do not."

"How many, would you say, come back complaining of whispers in the dark?"

"One in four, at most. The majority profit well and leave secure in their futures."

"And how many have told you stories of this haven?"

Nathanial was silent.

"Ah," said Annie. "Enough that you worry for our safety, that we might be that one in four. I must ask you this, then: If our chances of disaster are one in four, should we undertake the trip to Oregon, what are our chances of disaster if we stay exactly where we are?"

"Much higher." He gave her a sidelong look. "Our

stores are not yet depleted, but the summer was hard for everyone. We added six to our number, and none of them as yet old enough to earn their keep. They take more than they can give."

"We could always give them back."

"How? Even if we wanted to track down their people—if we had the time, and the resources, and the bodies to spare—there's every chance in the world that their people were the ones who boosted them onto our wagons. When the harvest is thin and you have an extra mouth to feed, there are worse things to do than send it away with the circus. Unless the circus is starving." Nathanial scowled. "I said once that I would never leave a child to go hungry if I had a choice in the matter. Well, it's still my name on the side of the wagons, and the choice is still in my hands. We keep our family going. If that means a few risks . . ."

"Every one of us knew, when we chose to follow you, that there would be risks," said Annie. "We take risks every night, just by climbing into our wagons. The world is dangerous and wild. Those who want safety for the winter have already gone, and the show endures."

"So you're not angry that there was more danger than I warned you of?"

Annie actually laughed. "Really, Mr. Blackstone, do you think yourself the first man who felt it was his decision whether or not I risked myself? You are not even the fifth. You may belong to the first ten—I would have to think about it, and I prefer not to. Why should I treat you as anything special?"

"Because I would treat you as something special, if you allowed me to do so." The admission hung between them, shimmering and simple.

Annie stopped.

Nathanial continued a few feet more before turning to face her. "If you tell me that you're uncomfortable with this journey—if you are—I'll move Heaven and Earth to keep you here. I'll rent you a room in the nearest town. I'll tend the oddities myself through the winter, and when the thaw comes, you'll find us riding triumphant over the hill to take you home."

"'Home' is a funny word, don't you think?" asked Annie. She started walking again, more slowly now, like she had to consider each step before she made it. "It implies belonging; it implies a connection. There's a thing about home that you don't seem to have considered."

"What's that?"

"If you run away from it, it isn't home anymore. Even if you come back later, something will have been changed, and changed forever." She shook her head. "I don't run. Not from my homes."

"You ran from—"

"I know what I ran from." Her voice was the crack of a whip, the closing of a door; it was a fortress of a voice, firm and implacable. "Believe me, I know better than you will ever, *ever* know what I ran from. You weren't there. No one who had been, be they man, woman, or child, could blame me for running away. But when I ran, what I ran from was no longer home. If it ever truly was. The past is a broken mirror, and all it reflects are regrets."

Nathanial sighed. "My apologies. I misspoke."

"You did."

"I only wished to protect you."

"And I appreciate that impulse, believe me. Protecting Adeline has been my life's work, and I am still learning how to best accomplish it."

"You might protect her better by staying behind."

Annie's lips twisted in the parody of a smile. "Oh, lovely work, Mr. Blackstone. Turn my own argument against me. Very nicely done. But what you haven't considered is that this is the only home she has ever known, and she spends the majority of her time with your circus orphans. If I attempted to remove her to the town, she would run from me, even as I once ran; she would run for the promise of home. I have all faith in her ability to make it back to our wagon before I even knew that she was gone. I have less faith in my ability to catch up with the train before the first frost comes and I am shut out by the weather. Protecting my daughter means staying with her. It means knowing which battles I can win. This is not one of them."

"Which means my battle is not winnable either, if I fight to make you stay behind."

Annie's smile was brief. "There, you see? You can be taught."

"The Clearing—"

"Sounds like a perfectly lovely place for a final show of the season. I've always liked Oregon. Such a verdant country. Sometimes America astounds me with its diversity of climes."

The wagon of oddities came into view ahead of them, the painted filigree gleaming in the morning light. As was almost always the case, the area around the wagon was clear. Even the bravest of the roustabouts had cause to fear the collection of monsters Annie had accumulated.

(Some few had quit the show entirely after a trip through Annie's wagon. Human freaks, sword-swallowers, and weary tigers imported from the Far East were all normal, workaday things for the circus-oriented mind. Bloodwire and wasps the length of a man's forearm were something else altogether. Those men went on to spread dire warnings of the Blackstone Circus and its convoy of monsters, expecting that they could stop the show. Instead, they had enhanced its profile immeasurably, until even scouts from other shows had been known to buy tickets to walk through the oddities and admire them in all their terrible glory.)

"If you'll excuse me a moment," Annie said, and moved

away from Nathanial, climbing the wagon steps and slipping inside. She left the door open behind her. He waited on the ground nonetheless. There had been only a few injuries stemming from Annie's collection of monsters, and all of them had come about because of someone failing to listen when she told them how to keep themselves safe.

It was difficult to imagine, but when Annie had wandered into his life with a dirty baby on her hip and a half-grown lynx slung around her neck like a fashionable lady's shawl, the wagon of oddities had been a few dead things in jars of formaldehyde and two tired rattlesnakes in a cracked fish tank. Most folk didn't care to pay to see a rattlesnake; not when they could see one for free just by flipping over a few rocks out in the yard. They had been talking about emptying the wagon and turning it into something more productive, like storage or a rolling costume rack.

But then Annie had come along with her lynx, which wasn't going to be able to share a bunk with its humans for long. Even if Annie didn't seem to realize how large the cat was going to be when it finished growing, Nathanial knew, and more, knew that avoiding tragedy would require a cage and a separate place to sleep. He had suggested she move Tranquility into the wagon of oddities, and when she had objected to the seeming special treatment—if only she had known how much special treatment he had been prepared to extend her, even then—he had asked if she would tend the wagon as a whole.

He had offered her a task. He had offered her legitimacy. He had expected her to tire of feeding the aging rattlesnakes before the end of the season, and that after that, the wagon would have become nothing more than a rolling home for the lynx.

By the end of that first season, she had purchased Os-

car from a fisherman, installing the great white catfish—
officially "the River's Ghost"—in the front of the wagon
to attract townies. They might not have cared about the
rattlesnakes, but the wise-faced, fast-moving fish had
been something else altogether. Less than a month later,
another fisherman had rolled up, saying cagily that he'd
heard "the miss" liked unusual river things, and would
she look at his bucket?

The bucket had been full of listless, half-dead red
fish that perked right up after being fed an entire opossum. The nibblers were even more popular than Oscar,
drawing crowds from two towns over to gape at the
oddities in open-mouthed awe. If he had wanted to nip
this rolling house of horrors in the bud, that would have
been the time, before it had gained the mass or notoriety
to become an essential part of the show. But he hadn't.
The money was nice. The added cachet it brought to the
human freaks was nicer. "Freak" was just a way of saying "somebody who isn't like the folks around them,"
and they deserved the same respect and fair treatment
as the rest of the show. The oddities were officially a
part of the freak show. The more money they made for
the show as a whole, the better the other workers treated
the freaks. It was social economics, and it worked in
everyone's favor.

Annie emerged from the wagon and back into the present, Tranquility padding at her heels. The vast cat had a
joint of some unnamed meat clasped in her jaws; she descended the wagon steps and flopped onto her side in
the mud, gnawing at the bone with teeth the length of a
grown man's thumb.

Nathanial liked to talk about how safe they were from
robbers and the like when they rolled through bad country. Publicly, he attributed that to fellow-feeling and not
wanting to damage one of the few sources of pure joy
left in the West. Privately, he thought it had rather more

to do with Annie's habit of letting Tranquility sun herself when they were stopped. No man with half a brain in his head would attack a show that thought a lynx was a lapdog. There was simply no way of knowing what horrors they had locked away.

"Adeline should be here in a few minutes," said Annie, sitting down primly at the top of the wagon stairs. "Are you quite done playing the doom crow, or would you like to say a few more dire things about our coming show?"

"Only that I worry for your safety."

Annie sighed heavily. "Leaving me here would do nothing to enhance my safety, I assure you. As long as we keep moving, I am safe. Settle me this close to Deseret, even for a season, and there is every chance that someone would carry back a tale of the lovely widow with the silent daughter."

"Why don't they do that anyway?"

"I suppose because no one who knew me before you did would believe that I would lower myself so far as to live beneath a moving roof, by lantern light." She looked toward Tranquility—not out of fondness, as he had once assumed, but out of a sort of pensive melancholy. It was like the lynx represented her lost home, which could be looked upon but never reached for. "I've changed my name. My child is older, and she was young enough when we ran that it was unclear whether she was quiet or speechless. I have taken all precautions not to bring danger down upon this show. But leave me alone, without the glitter and mirrors to distract, and I'll be lost."

Annie looked back to Nathanial, smiling sadly. "If you try to save me, you sacrifice me—and I warn you, I will not go quietly. There are worse things in the world than a few dire rumors about dark things in the wood. I'll accompany you to Clearing."

"The Clearing," Nathanial corrected.

Annie raised an eyebrow. "Come again?"

"The name of the town—The Clearing. Like 'New York,' I suppose. Why they would choose to put 'the' in their name, I have no idea, but there it is, and being respectful guests means we should admit to it."

"The Clearing, then. I'll accompany you. We'll put on the finest show they've ever seen. We'll bleed their coffers dry and spend the winter living high on their coins. Come spring, we'll be back out on the road, older and wiser and with another stop on our itinerary. You'll see. I have faith in your ability to lead us into and out of even the darkest places."

Nathanial's smile was a pale thing. "Why do you have such faith in me? I rarely do."

"Because you saved me once, and as no one else has ever felt the need to do such a thing, I must regard you evermore as a prince among men and hence worth believing in." Annie leaned over and clucked her tongue. Tranquility dropped the joint of meat and rose, pacing over to sit next to her mistress's knee. Annie busied herself with scratching behind the lynx's ears, looking up at Nathanial as she did. "We'll be fine, Nathanial. You worry too much."

Nathanial Blackstone, who sometimes felt that he didn't worry nearly enough, looked away and said nothing at all. Under the circumstances, it didn't feel as if there was anything to say.

A cold wind blew past them. Summer was coming to an end, and they had far to go before the freeze.

Chapter 5

The trip from Idaho to Oregon took slightly more than a week. The maps said they should have been able to make it in five days, but the maps didn't have to contend with fussy children, hungry animals, or broken wagon axles—two in the first three days, requiring the wainwrights to work late into the night if they wanted to be able to roll out come morning.

Eight days. Eight days of rolling down increasingly narrow roads, with everything familiar fading behind them and a whole new world of trials looming up ahead. The unknown was everywhere in the West. Sometimes Annie thought that, and not the cardinal direction, was truly the definition of their world. They didn't live in the West; they didn't struggle to win or at least survive the West; they didn't wander the West, children of another continent looking for acceptance on this one, which had every reason to reject them. No. They did all those things, but they did them in the Unknown, which was far more fleeting and even less forgiving. Every map, every trail, every helpful recollection eroded the Unknown a little more, made it a little less powerful.

It was difficult to look at the rocky, broken trail between them and their destination and not see it as the Unknown pushing back against those who would destroy it.

The wagons had been rolling single file since morning, moving slowly and cautiously down the trail. According to the wainwrights, they only had supplies to repair one more broken axle; anything more than that and they'd have to start leaving wagons behind. No one wanted that. The weather was getting cooler the closer they came to their destination, and there was no question of whether a wagon would survive the winter fully exposed to the elements. It wouldn't. Even the most lucrative of stays in The Clearing wouldn't be enough to replace a wagon and resupply the show. So they rolled slow, and they rolled cautious, and they tried not to think about how close they were to disaster.

Annie sat on the running board of her wagon, the reins clutched firmly in her hands, her eyes fixed on the road ahead. She did not, she had found, care for the closeness of the evergreens which held sway here: they pressed too close on the path, and their branches, which seemed singularly like the arms of some terrible, furred creature, reached out overhead, lacing together to block out the sun. Oregon was a territory trapped in eternal twilight, thanks to those damned trees. If there were ever a fire great enough to consume them all as kindling, she rather thought the survivors would die of fright when they saw the unfettered sun for the first time.

Adeline rode next to her, listless, slumped over until her head rested against her mother's side, just below her ribcage. It was an awkward position, but Annie had no objections; it made it easier for her to check her daughter's temperature, which she did regularly, laying the back of her hand against Adeline's forehead and counting to eight.

The child was running warm. The child had been running warm all morning, and no amount of medicine seemed to be helping. Sometimes Adeline simply wilted, like a flower, falling into long declines that ended just as abruptly.

(They coincided, almost always, with departures from

the land around Deseret, as if some small part of the girl still remembered where she had come from and was longing to go back. Annie had done her best to raise Adeline to be wild, and free, and unsuited for the life she had been born to, but that did not stop her from wondering what would happen if she ever confirmed, truly and for certain, that the girl's health was somehow tied to Deseret. Would she take her back, to live as a captive? Or would she smother her with a pillow where she slept, to end her suffering without forcing her into a cage?)

"We should be there soon," she said, forcing a note of amiable joviality into her voice. "What do you think a town called 'The Clearing' will be like? I'll tell you this much for free: I'm hoping it's not meant to be ironic, like that roustabout we had last season who went by 'Tiny' when he was near to seven foot tall. I am well tired of trees."

Adeline, as always, said nothing. Annie glanced at her sidelong. The child's hands were still, silent; if not for her open eyes, it would have been reasonable to think that she had gone to sleep.

"I'm hoping for a nice field to set up in, or better yet, a prairie. Do they have prairies in Oregon, do you think? They certainly do not want for pine trees, or for mountains. I've seen more mountains in these last few days than in all the years before them. Arizona's mountains are friendlier. They seem to want you to come closer and have a good look at them, while these mountains . . . it's as if God tried to build a wall to keep people out, and when He failed, He dropped rocks everywhere in a fit of pique."

Adeline shifted positions slightly, slanting a suspicious glance up at her mother. Annie attempted an amiable smile.

"It's not blasphemy if I don't say that He *did* it, and if

I'm not taking His name in vain. I'm simply saying what it looks like. Do you care for these mountains?"

Adeline shook her head slowly in negation.

"Why not?"

There was a long pause as Adeline thought. Then she sat up, showing more animation than she had demonstrated yet that day, and signed, 'Bad rocks.'

"They have bad rocks? How can rocks be bad?"

Adeline shrugged. She did not know how rocks could be bad; she simply knew that these rocks somehow were, and that was enough for her.

Annie opened her mouth to ask another question but paused as someone shouted from farther up the wagon train. The message continued traveling back, until it formed words: "Stop ahead!"

"Stop ahead!" she shouted, passing the message back for the wagons behind her, and the moment passed: the trail was sloping downward ahead of them, and there was no more attention to spare for things like asking Adeline what she meant by "bad rocks." They could return to the subject later, if necessary.

Then the trees receded, and the land opened up, and everything except their destination was washed clean out of her head.

Had Annie been asked to describe her idea of what a town out of a fairy tale looked like, her description might have sounded much like The Clearing. It was built in a natural depression, almost a bowl scooped out of the surrounding land, where there were no trees, for all that they clustered in close on all sides, making the openness of the settlement all the more striking. The woods lurked only feet from every threshold, but the streets were wide and open, the earth that formed them tamped down until they were practically paved.

The construction style was similar to what she'd seen

in Montana and Idaho, all low roofs and slanted angles, to prevent the buildup of either rain or snow. The outer ring of the town seemed to be entirely homes, small, compact, and built to survive the weather. There was a band of empty space between them and what she had to view as the center of town—maybe eight buildings, only one of which had a second story, all of which were built of a strange, reddish wood that she assumed grew locally. Maybe those towering evergreens had a purpose to them beyond looming over innocent travelers and frightening them out of their wits.

The wagon train was beginning to wind its way around the outside of the bowl, following a road that had been cut into the curvature of the land. She could see the wisdom in that, even as she questioned the practicality of it all: turning the road into a spiral meant that anyone who came or went would have twice as far to travel before they could be said to be either coming or going. A shorter road would have been steeper. It would also have been faster, and in the long run, easier on the draft animals.

But this was not her town, and these were not her traditions, and she was going to comport herself as a guest in their home. More than a guest—a hired laborer, who had no more right to criticize the way they chose to run their lives than she had to pluck the moon from the sky and give it to her daughter as a plaything.

What a spectacle they must have made for the people of The Clearing! What a marvelous sight! While she might fault their winding spiral of a road for practicality, no one could question the innate showmanship of a town that would choose to make its only available means of passage such a brilliant display of any visitor! They wound down into the town, with Mr. Blackstone's glorious rainbow of a wagon in the lead, and all the others following, no two quite alike. They were a kaleidoscope, a rainbow, a gilded lily of potential pleasures, and while they might well disappoint—someone was always disappointed when the circus came to town—no one would be able to say that they hadn't put their best foot forward.

Clowns and contortionists began to appear on the roofs of their wagons, already painted and prettied up for the show. They struck strange poses and did silly dances, and generally worked as hard as they could to attract attention without falling off the roof of the moving wagons. Annie knew that, behind her, the lion-tamer would be opening the side of his wagon, exposing his worn-out old cats to the open air. Tranquility would have been a more impressive sight, if not for the fact that showing her would have required exposing all the oddities, and that was something that required a coin or two.

Adeline sat up straight, practically vibrating as she looked around with wide eyes. She pointed.

Annie followed the line of her finger to a pair of little girls in sunbonnets—sunbonnets? Why? It wasn't like they'd ever seen the sun—kicking a hide ball between them, and smiled.

"You can play with the town children, if they'll play with you," she said.

Adeline ducked her head.

There were always other children around for Adeline to play with. It was one of the virtues of traveling with the circus and its endless supply of orphans. But they formed bonds between themselves, and Adeline's silence did not always endear her. She often preferred to play with townie children, who would see her as a novelty and not have time to tire of her closed lips before the show moved on again.

Annie's own mother had often told her that women were meant to be seen and not heard. She wondered what her mother would have made of her perpetually silent granddaughter, who was so good at fading into the background that she was sometimes neither seen *nor* heard. She rather suspected the old woman would have liked her. She had enjoyed being a mother. She had never been fond of the parts that required her to interact with children.

Maybe if she had been, Annie would have been more prepared for her own attempts at motherhood. She sadly doubted it. All children were unique, and while she had been blessed with a sylph of a girl, silent and sickly, that didn't make her either easier or more difficult to raise than others of her kind. She was simply Adeline. To make her into anything else would have been to grant her too much credit and not enough grace.

People were beginning to emerge from their homes and places of business as they spotted the circus train wending its way down the spiraling road. Some of them pointed. Others removed their hats, holding them against the back of their necks as if that were some universal sign of awe. Annie raised a hand and waved, as grandly as she could. Beside her, Adeline mimicked the motion.

"Look lovely, my dearest; there's only one chance to make a first impression." So far, her impression of The Clearing was a favorable one. There was plenty of space outside the town proper for them to set up, and she could see several wells, which meant there would be no short-age of water. If the people were half so friendly as they were supposed to be, the show would do well, and be more than halfway to the town where they'd be camped until spring before the winter came on in earnest.

It took the better part of an hour for the entire train to wend its way down into The Clearing. They rolled into the open stretch of land behind the town—presumably intended for some future expansion and hence wisely set aside—before rolling to a halt, the show wagons toward the front, the personal wagons tucked, as much as pos-sible, in the rear.

They would all have to be moved, of course, arranged and rearranged until the right configuration could be achieved, the one that left them with space for the tents and easy access to the entertainment wagons and privacy for the boneyard. But that would all come later. For now, they had work to do.

"Best face forward," Annie said softly, and slid down from the running board, walking at an unhurried pace toward the front of the cluster of wagons.

Mr. Blackstone was already there when she arrived. Of course Mr. Blackstone was already there. Sometimes she thought the man knew how to ride the wind when it stood a chance of depositing him in front of a crowd. Several of the performers were there as well, lounging in the grass as if they did everything in greasepaint and sequins, and didn't spend the majority of their time looking exactly like everyone else.

Annie stepped up next to Mr. Blackstone. She had no official authority within the show: she could speak for herself, for Adeline, and for her oddities, both human and otherwise, but she could no more commit the circus to a course of action than she could turn back the hands of time. That didn't matter. She looked respectable. There was a mannerly set to her shoulders that she would never, no matter how long she lived, be able to fully shake. By standing her next to Mr. Blackstone, the show sent the message that they were good, honest people, not rapscallions looking for families to destroy and women to abduct.

(Annie had never encountered a single person who had actually been stolen by a circus, although she knew more than her share who had chosen to run away. Still, she was sure that her estranged husband, if he had known of her eventual fate, would have sworn to the heavens that she'd been stolen, rather than allowing her the freedom of choosing to flee. Black Jack Davy, indeed.)

"That is a *fascinating* road," she said quietly.

"One good flood and they're a fish tank," agreed Mr. Blackstone, equally quiet. "We'll be out of here before the storms come, and they can all turn to mermaids without us."

"Really? You're so sure of when the storms come to Oregon that you feel you can make me that promise?"

Nathanial was saved from needing to answer by the appearance of a round-bellied man in a bowler hat and waistcoat. He looked as if he had just been transplanted in from Boston or Philadelphia or some other fine, cultured town, full of business and luxury. Even his shoes had been shined, so bright that they seemed to be struggling to make up for the lack of sunlight. Annie blinked. Beside and behind her, she heard the faint exhalation of air that served Adeline as laughter.

"My," said Nathanial.

The man came closer. When he was near enough to speak without shouting, he hooked his thumbs into his belt, stopped, and said, "Why, hello, friends, and welcome to The Clearing." The way he pronounced the town's name left no question that both words were capitalized. "Might I ask the nature of your business here?"

Annie had to fight not to turn and look at the side of the nearest wagon, where BLACKSTONE FAMILY CIRCUS AND TRAVELING WONDER SHOW was painted in large gilt letters.

Nathanial smiled, bowed, and said, "My name is Nathanial Blackstone, and this is my circus, sir, the finest assemblage of human talent, natural oddity, and practiced skill to be seen this side of the Mississippi River. We heard that you were a township in dire need of a show and thought that we would come in answer to your prayers."

"A little late in the season, aren't you?" asked the man. "I'm Mayor Young, and while I'm delighted to see you—a little joy is always wanting around these parts—I'd be lying if I didn't say I thought you should turn and go back the way you came. The roads will be impassable soon enough, and you don't want to overwinter here."

"It seems a nice enough town to spend some time in, and it's scarce September," said Nathanial. "I promise we can offer you a few nights of entertainment and still be on our way well before the ice comes."

"You're not from around here, son," said the Mayor— not unkindly. That was the interesting thing, Annie thought. He was warning them off, but there was no harshness to it. It was more like he was fulfilling an elected duty than anything else.

"That's true, sir, but I am well traveled, and I have never seen the snow fall before October." Nathanial's smile was like the unseen sun, almost too bright to look upon. Even the cadence of his words was changing, falling into the easy showman's pitch that he used when dealing with townies. "I've heard such wonderful things about your town. Why, almost unbelievable things until we got here and saw it with our own eyes. Best of all, I heard that you welcome a traveling show, from time to time."

"The trees are deep and entertainment is often wanting this far from the big cities," said the mayor.

Annie, who couldn't think of the last town she'd seen that she would call a "big city," said nothing.

"So allow us to stay and delight you," said Nathanial, wheedling a little as he took a half-step forward, closer to the mayor. The differing height between the two men was almost startling. It was difficult to look at the two of them and recognize them as members of the same species. "We are a fully self-contained show. We have our own tents, our own wagons; we'll need no lodging in your town and will disrupt no daily routines. But oh, in the evenings! We have entertainments galore, and all for your town."

The mayor looked at him with a gleam in his eye, and Annie realized with slow dismay that they, the show people, had been played by this seemingly harmless little man. He'd known exactly what he was doing when he told them to leave.

"You're here because the season is ending and your coffers aren't as full as you'd like them to be, aren't you?" he said, in a tone that was suddenly much sweeter and substantially less sincere. The trap, such as it was, was swinging closed. "It's always nice when a show comes to town already understanding the situation."

"Sir?" said Nathanial, with unfeigned bemusement.

"We're happy to have you. We're *delighted* to have you, especially now that you've given me your word not to disrupt our lives. Some of our widows can be a mite delicate, and they don't care for strangers in the streets." The mayor turned to look frankly at Annie. "If you've need for things in town, this lovely lady can serve as your ambassador. She looks respectable enough."

"Charmed," Annie said frostily, visions of shopping lists dancing in her head. She was going to wear out her shoes running back and forth between the boneyard and the town once they started getting paid for their performances: there wasn't a single wagon in the train that didn't need *something* for its supplies. If the rest of them were banned from The Clearing proper for being "disreputable," or whatever fancy word the mayor would use to paint them all, then she was going to have a lot of running to do.

"Sir—" began Nathanial.

"You may set your show here, outside the town's borders; we're always happy to have visitors. I can pay you fifty dollars for the week. That's less the land use fee, of course."

"Of course," said Nathanial.

"Welcome to The Clearing," said the mayor, with another sunny smile. It died quickly, blowing out like a candle. "Be sure you're out of here before the snow comes down, or you'll be wintering with us. I doubt you'd enjoy the process. And keep your children out of the wood. Even the people who live here can get lost in there. You'd be sorry to lose them."

He turned on his heel and walked away before either Nathanial or Annie could respond. Annie wasn't sure what she would have had to say to him.

"What a strange little man," she murmured, once she was sure he was too far away to hear her. "You've brought us to a lovely paradise, Mr. Blackstone. Truly, I don't know how I could have questioned you for even a second."

"Fifty dollars is nothing to sneer at," he said. "That should pay for supplies enough to repair anything that's broken and buy the basics for the chuck wagon. Anything after that is extra and can go toward wintering over."

"And there *will* be extra," admitted Annie. She sighed a little. It would almost have been better if the mayor had ordered them to get out, had treated them as invaders instead of as semiwelcome guests. The thought of spending even a day in the shadow of these trees was . . .

It was unsettling. Something about the way their branches caught and gathered the shadows beneath them didn't sit well with her.

"I'll tell the roustabouts to start setting the tents," said Nathanial. "Tell anyone you see that they're not to go into town without permission, and that we'll open on the morrow."

"Do we have the supplies for dinner?"

"Most of them," said Nathanial. "I'll send a few men into the wood to bring back a deer, and then we'll have the rest of it. Chin up, Annie. Things are turning around for us, you'll see."

He turned and trotted off into the maze of wagons, waving to someone unseen. Annie watched him go, unable to stop the feeling of discontent that was spreading through her, like a drop of wine diffusing into water. She looked back toward the town and barely suppressed the urge to jump.

There were people watching her from what looked like every window and doorway in sight. Women held their brooms tightly, frozen in the act of sweeping the porch; men rested hands on their hats, standing on the sidewalks or in the doorways of their homes. There was something oddly intimate about their eyes crawling over her, like they were judging her and finding her wanting in the same instant.

She was Annie Pearl, keeper of the oddities, and she was not theirs to judge. Straightening her spine, she offered them a bright showman's smile and curtseyed before turning to follow Nathanial's route into the wagon train. It was time to begin establishing the boneyard. For tonight—for a little while—this was going to be their home, and it needed to be treated accordingly.

artin had been with the circus, one way or another, since he was six years old and his ma—God rest her soul—took sick with some sort of infection of the lungs. It ate her up over the course of one winter, taking her from hale and healthy and brighter than all the stars in the sky to a withered parody of his mother. His little sister, Bessie, she'd been young enough that she'd been sent off to stay with relatives, for fear that the sick would come into her lungs and take her, too. He supposed no one had worried after him, or maybe it was just that he'd loved his ma so much that no one had been willing to take the two of them away from each other, not when it was so clear that the world was already taking her away.

But then she'd gone to the ground, and his pa hadn't been able to stand the sight of him, like it was somehow his fault that sickness had eaten his mother from the inside out, reducing her to fragility an inch at a time. He supposed his pa hadn't been able to stand the sight of Bessie, either, which was why his little sister had never come home from wherever it was she'd been sent. The relatives who'd been willing to have a healthy little girl young enough to be a blank slate, ready to be overlain with their ideals and values, well. They hadn't wanted a little boy who woke up crying every night, reaching for the mother who was never coming home.

Martin supposed he couldn't blame them. He'd been too young to blame them then, and after that he'd been too hungry and afraid to blame them, and now that he was a grown man of eighteen, he was too weary of the world to blame them. Things were hard enough without taking on someone else's children just because their parents'd had the bad luck to go and die.

His pa had kept him for the better part of the spring after his ma died. Had fed him, and clothed him, and let him sleep near enough to the fire that he hadn't frozen. And then the circus had come to town, and oh! Hadn't that first night been grand? Sometimes he thought he could live to be as old as anything and still not forget that first night, when his father had pressed three whole pennies into his hand and set him in front of the wagons with their many mysteries, telling him to enjoy himself. Telling him that he'd earned it.

If his father had been gone by the time he turned around, well, that was just the way life went, wasn't it? Sometimes parents vanished, and the children they left behind had to find the way to live with the loss. Martin had wandered through the circus until he was too tired to stand anymore, and then he'd curled up on a bale of hay and slept through the night with the sound of the calliope ringing in his ears, like a promise the world was finally intent on keeping.

That had been the Smithson Family Circus, a small show owned and operated by a pair of third-generation circus folk. He'd never known their real names, or whether he was supposed to call them sir or ma'am, but they'd kept him when they found him, putting him to work luring townie kids closer to the wonders in their wagons. Three years he'd ridden the roads with Smithson, and when they sold him as a working boy to a show heading east, he hadn't been surprised or disappointed in the slightest. This was how the world worked. People gave you away, and you went, because fighting never helped anyway.

After Smithson had come a short stint with a show that had no name, where the wagons groaned at night with the chewing of the termites slowly eating their way through the walls, and the so-called "tiger" had been a big mountain cougar painted orange and black every morning by whoever didn't run fast enough. Only two years there, and at eleven he'd been sold again, this time to Blackstone, who'd said he needed boys with clever hands.

Martin couldn't have said what he'd been expecting from his latest home, but it hadn't been what he'd received: a bed of his own in a wagon with four other boys and one older roustabout who kept an eye on them. Bowls of oatmeal and thick stew and slabs of bread that might have been thick with hulls and half-milled grain, but was still *his,* needing to be shared with no one. He supposed he would have been loyal forever on the basis of bread alone.

Now here he was, a man, and he was stepping out afternoons with Sophia the seamstress's apprentice, who had eyes as brown as polished oak and cheeks pocked with the ghosts of old illness, which meant she didn't judge him for his own shortcomings. They liked each other well enough, and he supposed they'd marry one day, set up in a wagon of their own and keep traveling with the circus, which was, by now, the only life either of them could ever imagine living. Him, a man! And he owed it all to Mr. Blackstone, who hadn't looked at him and called him damaged goods or worthless, or any of the other things he'd heard so often since his ma died. He would have done anything for Mr. Blackstone, anything at all to prove that he deserved the chance he'd been given.

As he looked at the unbroken green line of the forest

looming up in front of him, he thought, for the first time, that maybe the past didn't purely pay for the future: that maybe he ought to put more value on his life than just "a man was kind to me." Sophia would be heartbroken if he died, and possibly out of her position if he died before marrying her, depending on whether her monthlies had just been fooling with them when she skipped the last couple.

The trees seemed to loom taller than they were, and given that they were already tall enough to brush the sky, that was a terrifying thought. They were a wall, all green branches and woody trunks as far as the eye could see, and the reason for the town's name made sudden, terrible sense. If you found something as unique as a clear patch in these trees, you'd want to commemorate it. Of course they'd called their place The Clearing. It was probably the first such anyone had seen in weeks.

The people who'd come to colonize this land must have been mad, or desperate, or both. The forest cast a great shadow over everything, like the hand of some ever-reaching creature, hungry for the world. The smell of it lingered thick in his nostrils, all resin and sap and a strange, virulent greenness that had no relation to the green fields outside the house where he'd been born, or the various greens that the circus had rolled through with him clinging to the wagons and breathing it all in. Those had been good greens, *honest* greens, growing greens that wanted to nurture a body as part of their own growing. This green . . .

He'd seen trees that had grown down into graves before, only to be knocked over by a storm. When they fell, their roots came up all tangled in bones, wearing dead men like bracelets on their woody arms. This green felt like that, like a whole forest made of trees that dreamt of decorating themselves with the dead. This green was *hungry.* It was hungry, and it was impossible to shake the feeling that it knew he was there.

It would have felt like stupid superstition if it hadn't felt so strong, so true. The trees saw him. The trees saw the rifle in his hands, and they knew what he intended, and they did not approve.

But Mr. Blackstone's instructions had been clear. "We need to eat tonight, and we won't be able to go into town for provisions until they get used to the idea of us," he'd said. "I want you to go out into the woods and bring us back a deer. Two, if you're shooting lucky. That'll put meat in the pot and bones aside for the animals, and it'll see us to the end of this lean time."

It was a simple enough thing to ask of him. Martin wasn't the best hunter they had—that was little Emily-Ann, and she was striking off into her own patch of wood, along with two of the other roustabouts, which should have meant enough bullets to put meat in every pot tonight—but he was dependable, and he'd done this sort of thing before. He knew, even if Mr. Blackstone wasn't saying, that the hunt was doubly important because Miss Pearl's oddities hadn't been fed in a few days. They were never safe things to have. Some folk with the show thought they should all be put out to die, before they got loose and did what came naturally. But they were profitable, and they were safe enough, as long as they were well-fed.

The show needed that deer for so many reasons. They needed him to bring it back to them. They needed him to be a man.

Martin did not want to go into those woods.

His rifle was heavy in his hands, so heavy that he wasn't sure he could stand it. If he looked back and down into the bowl of the clearing, he would see the town, and he would see the shape of the circus, even now rearranging itself into show and boneyard, settling in. The circus was never as alive as when it put down temporary roots and opened its bright doors to the world. The circus—his home—was looking to him to feed them, fill their bellies and fix their future. He had to go.

Clutching his rifle close against his chest, trying to ignore the weight of it, Martin walked forward, into the trees. Fallen twigs and dried-up pine needles crackled under his feet. Stealth was not his friend here. He swallowed and kept walking, trying to hold on to the thought that he was not the only person walking through these trees. Even if the other three from the show had gone in different directions, he still wasn't alone. Being alone in these trees, well . . .

He didn't think he would have been able to bear it, and that was the honest truth. He would have gone back to his wagon and locked himself in until Mr. Blackstone found someone else to send into the woods, because although he wanted to save the show, he wanted to save his soul just as much. If he didn't have that, he didn't have anything at all.

It took only a few steps before the sunlight dropped away entirely, leaving him feeling like the world had been replaced by trees. He looked over his shoulder and saw only more trees, cutting off the light, blocking any sight of open ground. He swallowed hard. Walking in a straight line was the only way he was going to get out of here; he could see that now. If he turned at all, if he lost his way at all, he was going to be walking these woods until he died.

He wondered whether the roots would wrap gently around his bones, cradling them close and keeping them from the cold. He was direly afraid that he was going to find out.

Something hooted in the distance. Something rustled in the nearby brush. Martin fought back the instinct to turn and flee, forcing himself to keep walking until he found a fallen tree that could provide some small measure of cover. Then he crouched down and waited, rifle in hand, for something to come along. Hunting was as much about patience as it was about skill. The person who could hold still for the longest was the one who would bring home the bacon.

The forest seemed to settle around him, growing colder and darker. It was like it had just been waiting for him to stop moving. Martin sank into his crouch, trying to clear his mind of anything beyond the task at hand. He needed to take a deer. He needed to feed the show. He needed to feed Sophia, especially if there was a chance she was with child. He wouldn't be a father like his father had been. No child of his would ever go to bed hungry, or wondering where their next meal was going to come from. No child of his would ever be alone.

He sank deeper into pleasant dreams of a future where he would have a wife and a wagon and a child of his own, supporting them off the circus while the circus supported them all the way across the West. Son or daughter, it didn't matter, as long as the child was healthy and hale, and never had to want for anything.

He didn't notice when something passed behind him on ghost-soft feet, making no sound on the needle-covered ground. It was almost close enough to touch at one point, so close that he wrinkled his nose at the distant smell of wet, rank fur. Finally, he looked behind himself.

There was nothing there.

When he faced front again, a deer was standing between two trees. It was a young buck, fat and perfect, save for a white splotch on one flank that looked almost like a handprint burned into the fur. Martin didn't waste time asking himself what could cause such discoloration; he raised his gun and fired, the sound echoing through the trees. The deer leapt, one great, convulsive motion, before collapsing to the ground.

Martin stood, carefully walking toward his kill. Sometimes death could be a ruse. If the buck sprang back to life, he didn't want to be close enough to find himself gored by the curving rack of its antlers. It didn't move. He reached it, nudging it with the barrel of his rifle, and still it did not move.

Life with the circus was many things, but it was never easy, and it did not encourage softness. Martin was a short, relatively slight man, stunted in some ways by the privations of his childhood. He had no trouble at all in hoisting the buck over his shoulders, letting the weight of it settle on his spine before he turned and made his way back the way he had come, trusting his own footsteps to lead him true.

Some of the places where he had kicked leaves and needles aside seemed oddly scuffed, like something else had been over that track, obscuring it in the process. Martin thought nothing of it. There were deer in these woods, and for all he knew there were larger things as well, wolves and bears and the like. They'd be a danger in the spring, when they had cubs to protect, and in the depths of winter, when hunger motivated them to try for prey they would normally have left alone. For the moment, they lived close to a human settlement. They knew about guns and fire and all the other tools mankind used to keep the wilds at bay. For all that he had gone into their place to take what he wanted, he wasn't worried. The trees frightened him more than the possible threat of predators.

He would have been wiser to look to the sides, to search the trees for eyes, for signs that he was being watched by nameless forces looking to do him harm. He would have been wiser to be afraid. But he was not a wise man, never had been, and when he saw the trees thin to let the light through up ahead, all he felt was relief. He walked faster, the buck a welcome burden, and stepped back into the light of the fading day.

The Clearing was a picture postcard view before him, perfectly framed by the bowl of their depression. Smaller trails had been cut into the lip of the basin, presumably for use by local hunters; it was one of those that had allowed him access to the wood without needing to walk all the way around. He slid down the trail on the sides of his feet, kicking up a small rain of dirt and pebbles. The town came even more clearly into view, and with it came the circus, now well into the process of setting itself up.

The wagons had been separated into two distinct camps. The smaller, less gaudy vehicles—the ones where people lived, rather than displaying their wares and talents—were pulled to the back, veiled from easy view by the long shapes of the supply wagons and by helpful sheets of shielding canvas and oilcloth. Once the tents were up, most townies wouldn't even realize that something was being hidden from them. Misdirection was the watchword.

The tents were being assembled, spread out over what would be their footprints. They were placed behind the show wagons, creating a layer cake of attractions. Annie Pearl's oddities were positioned near the tents, along with her freaks; it wouldn't do to force good, honest people to look at them if they didn't want to. It was like watching a nest of ants going about their business. Martin paused on the road, smiling. His people were going to be all right. They would survive this winter the way they always did, and come out the other side ready for a new year of good things and good shows and new chances to see the world.

He slid down the second cutout trail, and a third after that, hitting the ground outside town and starting toward the show. He stopped as three townie men seemed to materialize out of nowhere, stepping between him and the ring of wagons.

"What've you got there, boy?" asked one of them.

Martin frowned. "I'm not your boy," he said. "I have to get back to the circus. Excuse me, please." There: that was polite enough. No way Mr. Blackstone could say he'd been picking fights with the townies. He'd left that habit behind him when he'd started stepping out with Sophia, who needed him intact and capable of taking care of her, not spitting teeth and resting in the hospital wagon.

"Looks to me like you've been hunting," said another of the men.

"Sure seems to be a deer he's carrying," said the third.

Martin looked around the circle of men, frowning. "Mr. Blackstone spoke to your mayor before he told me to go find dinner," he said. "If you have a problem, take it up with him." He didn't know for sure that Mr. Blackstone had gotten permission for him to hunt, but that was another matter. He hadn't been told to be discreet about what he was doing, or anything that would have made him pick a less direct route back to the show. As far as he could see, the deer in these woods were anyone's for the taking.

"We don't care for strangers hunting in our woods," said the first man.

Martin's frown deepened. "I can't see how anybody could say they owned those woods," he said. "They didn't feel owned to me. They felt wild." Wild, and angry about the intrusion past their borders.

"There's an easy way to settle this," said the third man. He was suddenly smiling. Martin didn't think there was any way that could be a good thing. "Since you clearly know your way around a rifle, how about you just give us that buck as payment for hunting in our woods, and you go get yourself another one? We promise to let you pass."

"No, thank you," said Martin doggedly. "I promised Mr. Blackstone I'd come back with a deer, and that's what I'm going to do. I've got to help with setup. How about you go and get your own deer, if it's that simple?"

"Boy, I don't think you understand how much trouble you're making for yourself," said the first man. All three of them took a step forward, shrinking the circle around Martin.

He swallowed hard. Was a deer really worth the beating he was about to receive? At the end of it, he'd have wounds to tend and no deer, and worse, they could find themselves run out of town for fighting. Townies were always eager to believe that their people had been innocent lambs assaulted by some wandering wolf, rather than admitting that sometimes the wolves were inside the gate. If he stood his ground, he could endanger the entire circus.

Something white flickered behind the men. Martin raised his eyes, squinting. The shape resolved into Adeline. She lifted a finger to her lips, making a wholly unnecessary shushing motion. No one with the show had ever heard that girl make a sound.

But if she was shushing *him* . . . "I'm sorry, fellows, but this buck belongs to the circus, and it's not mine to give away," he said.

From off to the side, blessedly welcome as the first of May, a voice boomed, "What is the meaning of this?"

All three townie men backpedaled away from him, creating space where there had been none. Martin turned. A short, fussy-looking man in a waistcoat was boiling up on them, with the reassuringly lanky shape of Mr. Blackstone following behind him. The lengths of their legs were so different that where the shorter man was all but running, Mr. Blackstone seemed to be out for a leisurely stroll.

"Mayor," said one of the men. Martin wasn't sure which one. He'd lost track as soon as they'd all moved, and none of them had any real distinguishing marks—they were just men, like the kind he'd seen at towns all across the West.

"This man," the mayor indicated Martin, "is a guest in our midst. Is this how we show hospitality in The Clearing? Through aggression and grift?"

"No, sir," said all three men in ragged chorus.

"What makes us better than animals? Well?" The mayor planted his hands on his hips. "Would any of you care to wager a guess?"

"Manners and restraint," said one of the three, eyes downcast.

"That's right. These folks have come here to entertain us, and that's what they're going to do. We're not going to taunt them for being strangers. Strangers breathe new life into a settlement. Now say you're sorry, all three of you."

The men muttered apologies to Martin. Only one of them looked resentful. The other two seemed practically cowed, like they couldn't believe themselves doing what they'd done.

"Come, Martin," said Mr. Blackstone, stepping fluidly around the cluster of men. "What an excellent deer you've taken for us. Let's get back to camp and see what wonders we can make from this." More softly, he said, "Walk, and don't look back."

Martin knew well how to follow orders from his master. He bobbed his head and obligingly began to walk. Adeline fell into step on his other side, and the three of them proceeded toward the colorful edge of the circus.

When they were almost there, Martin asked, "What just happened?"

"Emily-Ann got roughed up and lost two of the four rabbits she'd been able to get before we were able to intervene," said Mr. Blackstone. "It seems the people in this town don't care for strangers as much as they claim."

Then they reached the circus, and safety swallowed them once again.

Chapter 7

Step right up! Ladies and gentlemen, our display is not for the faint of heart, but for the price of one copper penny—one single coin!—you can see the wonders of the modern world spread out before your eyes. Have you heard the stories of the American West? Well, ladies and gentlemen, I assure you that they pale before the reality. No refunds in case of fainting or fleeing in terror! Test your bravery, stretch your mind, one copper penny—"

The barker's cry went on and on as the crowd gathered outside the wagon of oddities. Inside, Annie moved quickly between exhibits, checking that each of them was ready for the public.

Only the nibblers had been fed. They became aggressive when hungry—more aggressive than they already were—and could potentially rush the wall of their tank. Annie didn't believe they could break the glass. That didn't mean she was going to press her luck in front of townies, especially townies who might well come back for another look at her wagon's many wonders. The nice thing about a crowd was the way it rushed itself along. On a slow day, a person might pay their penny and spend an hour slowly exploring the oddities, seeing them each in detail, getting their fill. They'd have no cause to come back. On a busy day, everyone was rushed through by the person behind them, and some folks would come back three, four, even half a dozen times before they felt as if they'd seen everything there was to see. It was a blessing for her coffers, and for the circus as a whole.

(The wagon of oddities and the freak show were not the only revenue-generating exhibits. The contortionist, the dancing girls, the mentalist, and the magicians all made their share of profit, and it all rolled back into the circus proper, one way or another. But the oddities made the most money for the least investment and, more, were unique enough to make a lasting impression on the people who saw them. Someone who had seen the oddities in one town was likely to come and see them again in the next, if only to reassure themselves that yes, those things existed. Yes, those things were real.)

The barker was winding his pitch to a close. Annie looked across the wagon to Adeline, who stood motionless next to the exit, her hand on the latch.

"Go," she said. "I'll see you later tonight."

Adeline nodded and opened the door, vanishing into the afternoon air. Annie smoothed her hands along the front of her dress, removing the wrinkles, and walked to the entrance, picking up her coin pot before opening the door.

The crowd outside was not the largest she had ever seen, but it was still large enough to be striking. Annie smiled as mysteriously as she could, trying to play the benefactress of beasts, and held out her pot.

"A penny buys you passage," she said. "Who walks this way first?"

"I do," said a barrel-chested young man, earning himself cheers and applause from his fellows. He swaggered forward, dropping a penny into the pot. Annie stepped aside, letting him enter.

Which will it be? she wondered. *The nibblers? The snakes? The spiders—*

He froze only a foot or so past her. Unable to resist,

she glanced over her shoulder to see what had trans-fixed him.

Many of the cages in the wagon of oddities had been repurposed from other things. The tallest enclosure had once been used for a parrot owned by one of the sleight-of-hand operators, a great gold-and-red thing imported from some exotic land. It had spoken with a voice like a man, and had been halfway to being an oddity itself, be-fore it had sickened and died for reasons unknown. Par-rots were not suited to the harsh realities of the West. But the cage was good wrought iron, and once the bird had no longer needed it, Annie had claimed it, knowing it would be occupied again in short order.

Its new occupant was a mockery of the human form, two feet high and made entirely of green leaves, like corn husks twisted together by an unkind hand. Its head was a leering pumpkin with deep-set eyes that burned like coals. It grasped the bars of its cage with two-fingered corn husk "hands," tugging itself up against the metal. Those burning eyes were fixed on the townie man, and its mouth was working silently, shaping unheard obscen-ities.

"The man who sold it to me called it a 'corn stalker,'" said Annie. "They walk the fields in Oklahoma and Ne-braska, looking for a place to lay their roots. Don't go too close, good sir. It might well seek to plant its roots in you."

It was impossible to keep those outside the wagon from hearing her words. They surged forward, eager to pay their pennies and see what had frightened one of the bravest men in town. Annie took as many as she could before beckoning the barker forward to handle the rest and retreating into the wagon to answer questions and keep an eye on the patrons.

She was explaining bloodwire to a wide-eyed little girl when there was a snarl from the back of the wagon.

Quick as a blink, she whirled and shoved her way back there to find two little boys standing outside Tranquility's cage. One of them had a stick guiltily held behind his back.

"Hey!" he protested, as Annie snatched it away.

"Am I to assume that you were prodding at this poor cat?" she demanded, waving the stick in front of him like a switch. His eyes tracked it, waiting for it to descend. "She never did a thing to you. Why should you want to hurt her?"

"It was just lying there," said the boy. "I just wanted it to do something."

"You never sleep? Does your mother come into the room at night and jab you with a stick to see what you'll do?" Annie waved the stick again.

Tranquility had risen at the sound of her mistress's voice, turning in her cage and pressing her face against the bars. Seeing the stick in Annie's hand, she quite reasonably assumed that it was intended for her to play with, and stuck one vast paw between the bars, wrapping it gently around Annie's calf and pulling her closer to the cage. She made a rumbling noise, not quite a growl and not quite a purr, expressing her interest.

The boys, who were not accustomed to being this close to large cats, yelled in dismay and stumbled backward, flinging their arms around each other in their terror.

Annie bent and gave the stick to Tranquility, who promptly bit it in half. The two boys fled the wagon. Annie smiled. Sometimes the easiest solutions were the pointiest ones.

She moved through the wagon, answering questions about the oddities, asking people not to touch things they didn't understand, and nudging small children away from the snake tanks. All the serpents were housed behind thick glass; not even the largest of them had the necessary strength to break free. But snakes were not the cleverest of creatures. When they felt threatened they would strike, and she had watched rattlesnakes break their teeth against their enclosures often enough to feel protective of even these slithering members of her entourage. They had their own quiet beauty, as long as one steered clear of their fangs. They deserved the same respect that was afforded to everything else.

A man stood transfixed in front of the tank of terrantulas, staring at the skull-shaped markings on their abdomens. Annie stepped up next to him and said mildly, "These specimens were collected in New Mexico by a man who had seen them devour an entire wagon train. I started with a dozen of them, only to discover that when unfed, they will fall upon their siblings. These five are all that remain. If you return tonight, there will be a private show for adults only, where you may watch them eat."

Privately, Annie couldn't imagine *wanting* to watch the terrantulas eat. They swarmed over their prey, first pumping it full of caustic venom, then dissolving it with their powerful digestive juices. The spiders were too aggressive to allow her to clean their tank, but it didn't matter much; by the time they finished eating, only bones remained, and those were so damaged by their acidic juices that they quickly broke down and dissolved, adding to the white "sand" that lined the enclosure. A very small hole, no bigger than the tip of a bullet, was drilled into one corner of the glass; by uncorking it, she could bleed off the "sand" whenever necessary, leaving a trail of bone dust scattered across the continent, while her chamber of horrors remained blessedly intact.

So many of the oddities required that kind of careful compromise. Feeding them, keeping them healthy and whole . . . sometimes it felt like a form of blasphemy. These weren't things that deserved to roam the earth. They needed to be buried somewhere they would never be found, never be brought back into the light. Keeping them alive was *wrong*.

But living monsters brought in more coins than dead ones did, and who was she to judge? There were people who would call Tranquility a monster, with her sharp claws and taste for raw meat. There were people who would call Adeline a monster, citing her silence as proof of some deeper defect. There were even people who would call Annie a monster, for no honest woman would have fled her husband as she had done. Monstrosity was in the eye of the beholder, and while the oddities would have gladly devoured this entire town, given half the chance, they were never *going* to have that chance. They were captive. They were contained.

The man transfixed by the terrantulas turned to look at her, almost desperately. "They have skulls on their backs," he said. "You paint them there?"

Please, said his tone. *Please, tell me you painted them there; please, tell me this is some kind of a hoax that I just don't understand. I won't be angry. I won't even ask for my money back. Just lie to me, and all will be forgiven.*

"You couldn't pay me enough to paint on the backs of these spiders," she said. "They're vicious things, and they don't forgive people who interfere with them. No, this is as Nature made them, and whatever her reasons, I'm sure that they were good ones. It's best not to look too long, sir. People have been known to start seeing the faces of their beloved dead in those skulls, and the nightmares that follow are nothing I would wish on my worst enemy." It was a lie, of course, but a believable one, under the circumstances. She didn't like to eject people from the wagon—those who'd been thrown out were less likely to pay for the opportunity to come back again—and yet she had been operating it for long enough to recognize the signs of a breakdown.

Men always thought their wives were fainting flowers,

and true, more women than men had fainted within the confines of the wagon of oddities, but when it came to true confusion and dismay, nothing could top the anger of a man who had seen his own mortality reflected in a captive monster's eyes. Women danced with death every time they loved their men, knowing that a bad pregnancy could take them from the world in an instant. Men . . . they hunted and they fought and they did their manly things, and yes, those things were dangerous, often by their own choice. That was the key word: *choice*. A man could choose whether to draw his gun or stay safe at home. A woman faced her greatest dangers in the place where she lived.

After watching a child choke on their own breath when the fevers came, few women found much to fear in monsters like Annie's. All the oddities in the world couldn't hold a candle to the dangers of the home.

"Ah," said the man in a faint voice, and turned away.

He would be back. Annie knew enough about human nature to be absolutely sure of that. The ones who were the most distressed by some member or other of her menagerie were always the ones who came back when the lights were down, like they could face their fears and thus conquer them forever.

She could have told them a thing or two about facing fears. About the power that fear could have, no matter how many times it was stared down. But fear—seemingly safe, seemingly contained—was much of what kept the pennies dropping into the pot, and so she said nothing. Food on the table was more important than honesty.

The rest of the afternoon passed quickly. Show days always did. Once word got out about the contents of her wagon, the crowds were steady. She saw the same faces three and four times as they came back with friends, now content to play the role of the world-wise explorer, parroting back the same things she'd said to them on their first trip through. She hid her smiles as she hovered nearby, tidying things, straightening shelves, always listening, always making sure that the things that were being said were close enough to true that they wouldn't turn dangerous.

(And there *were* dangerous rumors that could be spread about her creatures; there were always dangerous rumors. One town had somehow gotten it into their heads that eating the flesh of a nibbler would cure disease, as if the vicious, bony little fish were a secret panacea placed in the rivers of America for the brave and the desperate. She hadn't caught on quickly enough. That stop had cost her three nibblers, and cost a boy with an ailing father his left hand, and the circus had been forced to leave so quickly that for a while there had been a question whether or not they would be able to keep all the wagons. Now she listened like a hawk, and when words like those were spoken, haltingly, for the first time, she was there to ensure that there would not be a second.)

The ebb and flow of the crowd told her what was happening outside. When the men vanished and the women came through like bright birds, the dancing girls were performing—and the women without the men were something to see! In the company of husbands, brothers, or suitors they were timid things, swooning behind their hands, clinging to the arms of their menfolk like they could no longer stand on their own. When they walked through in the company of other women, they were bold as anything, staring into the tanks with an intensity that would no doubt have frightened their menfolk.

"I kill bigger things than this in the privy at least once a week," sniffed one of them, looking at a pit wasp with disdain.

"I think I've eaten these," said another, looking at the corn stalker.

Annie hid her smile behind her hand and said nothing. She was privileged, as the somehow sexless keeper of the wagon, to see people as they were when not observed. It had taught her more about the true nature of humanity than she ever would have thought to see, back when she'd been a cosseted society wife. As lessons went, there were worse to take to heart.

For reasons of propriety and not being accused of wrongdoing, children were allowed only when in the company of a parent. Despite this, a surprising number of parents left their children in the wagon when they moved on, and sunset found her chasing the last trio of boys out, shooing them off to find their mothers.

The sky was the color of slowly drying blood, and the moon hung suspended in the middle of it all, like a clot of curdled milk. Annie paused at the back door, looking up and frowning to herself. That moon . . .

Some moons were kind and some moons were cruel, and superstitious as it might be, she couldn't stop herself thinking about them in those terms. This moon, though. This moon was cold, like it was standing in impartial judgment over everything it saw. It made her miss the vast, cream-colored desert moons, which might be harsh but at least seemed to somehow care what happened to the people who lived and loved and died beneath their all-seeing eyes.

All moons were faces of the same moon. She knew enough about the sky to know that. And yet it was difficult not to look at *this* moon and shiver, for she felt as if she'd never seen it before.

The show was winding to a pause around her. It would spin back up as the night grew later, when the men returned for more ribald entertainments, and the women returned for closer looks at things that would have been scandalous by daylight, and everyone returned to see the oddities eat. In the meantime, the circus could take a breath, and eat.

Annie closed the back door, turning the bolt before heading to the front. The barker currently on duty was Martin, the boy who'd gone to the woods to bring them back a deer for the previous night's supper. He was leaning against the wheel, trying not to look like boredom was crushing the life from his body.

"I'm going to close up for an hour, check on Delly and get myself something to eat," she said. "If you'd like to get something for yourself—"

"I'll see you in an hour," said Martin, already straightening and starting to leg it away into the twilight.

Annie smiled to herself. Everyone with the show knew that Martin was stepping out with Sophia, and that the two would probably be married in the spring, assuming a baby didn't force their hands before then. They were a charming pair, and she wished them well. Everyone did, so far as she was aware. There were jealousies and petty betrayals within the show—they were all only human, after all—but love was love, and it was a pleasure to see.

Carefully, she stepped out onto the wagon steps, closing and locking the door behind her. The oddities were weapons, in their own ways, and they were to be treated as such when the circus was stopped: unless she or Adeline were present, the doors were never to be left unlocked. Many of the things she cared for would die if they were released; the nibblers would choke on the air, the corn stalker would freeze in these unfriendly climes. But others would survive, at least long enough to take the slow and the foolish with them to Hell. An unlocked door on a wagon such as this was an invitation to an early grave.

The moon was cold and so was the evening, feeling more like early winter than early fall. Annie drew her shawl tight around her shoulders as she walked toward the boneyard. Roustabouts and barkers waved in her direction and she nodded back, not stopping or slowing. She hadn't seen her daughter since the show had opened. She was consumed with a sudden strong need to gather Adeline in her arms and cover her face with kisses until she squirmed and tried to break free. Motherhood was a long trek from the coast of childhood to the territory of independence, and while she had traveled some of that distance, she was in no hurry to finish the journey.

The door to their shared wagon was open. The lights were out inside. Annie paused, frowning. Adeline rarely chose to go to sleep early, and when she did, she almost never remembered to extinguish the lights before taking her medicine.

"Delly?" she called, trying to tell herself that the sudden dread circling her heart was only foolishness, brought on by too many hours in the company of her oddities.

Nothing moved inside the wagon.

Annie climbed the steps and peered inside, searching the pooled shadows for a flash of pale hair, or the shape of a little girl curled beneath a coverlet. No such signs presented themselves. Adeline was not there.

Well. That didn't necessarily mean anything was *wrong*. Adeline was as strong-willed and stubborn as her mother, and on show days, she would sometimes run from tent to tent for hours at a time, peeking at things she wasn't meant to see for years yet, taking advantage of the fact that few of the barkers ever wanted to chase the gentle, silent girl away. Barring that, she might be in the mess tent, or playing with the circus orphans out behind the boneyard. There were so many options. There was no cause for concern.

Adeline was not in the mess tent. Half the circus orphans were, and when she asked them if they'd seen her daughter they shook their heads and answered with shy "no"s, their eyes still mainly on their meals. Most of them were wary around parents, as if they had been treated so poorly by their own that they could not trust anyone else's.

Adeline was not out back. Nor was she in the other show wagons, nor peeking at the dancing girls. Adeline was gone.

Half an hour later, when she had exhausted every option, and a few more beside, Annie felt that there was every cause for concern in the world. She stumbled toward the big tent, heart hammering against her ribs, trying to keep her face composed. Showing distress in front of townies simply wasn't done. It muddied things and could cut into profits. And while she remembered all those things, it was difficult to find it in herself to care.

Mr. Blackstone would be in the tent. He would be able to tell her that she was being silly, that Adeline's father had not managed to somehow track them down and snatch her away while Annie was distracted. He would be able to *fix* this.

The boys who had been in the wagon earlier, prodding Tranquility with sticks, had joined another group of boys and were near the show tent, snickering and kicking something back and forth on the ground in front of them. Annie slowed, eyes widening. Then she charged toward the boys, catching their leader by the ear and yanking.

"Ow!" he howled. "Let me go!"

"Where did you get that?" she demanded, pointing at the object on the ground. It was a hide ball, battered and patched many times, until it was difficult to tell its original color. She gave his ear a vicious twist. "*Where?*"

"From a little dummy who wanted to play with us," said one of the other boys, his mouth running ahead of his brains. His eyes went wide when she turned on him, his friend's ear still clamped between her fingers. "I mean, there was . . . this girl, she said that we could . . ."

"Where is she?" demanded Annie.

"We said she could have her ball back if she went in

the woods and brought back a pinecone we could kick around!" simpered the third boy. "Please, miss, we didn't mean any harm!"

Annie gave the lead boy's ear one more hard tweak, causing him to wail, before letting him go and snatching the ball up off the ground. "All of you, get out of my sight," she hissed.

"I'm telling!" shouted the first boy, clapping a hand over his injured ear. "I'm telling!"

"Please," she said. "I look forward to telling your parents what you did to *my daughter.*"

The boys, who remembered her as the mistress of monsters, exchanged a glance and fled. Annie watched them go, helpless. Then she turned her eyes toward the trees.

Adeline was out there somewhere.

She needed to bring her home.

Chapter 8

Everything was darkness in the trees. The light from Annie's lantern cast a pale circle around her, not seeming to penetrate more than a few feet in any direction. If she held it as far from her body as possible, she could almost see through the trees ahead—but if she did that, the darkness closed in around her, enveloping her like a blanket, thick enough to carry a terrifying illusion of weight.

Annie had never been afraid of the dark. Even when she'd lived in Deseret, the plaything of a man who cared little for her needs or desires, the dark had been a friend. In the dark, she could scowl or weep, and no one would see her. Becoming the mistress of oddities had done nothing to change how comfortable she was in shadows. They thrived best in perennial twilight. They *needed* the dark, and it was on her to give them whatever they needed to stay alive. But here, now . . .

Darkness was not supposed to have weight. Darkness was not supposed to be cottony thick and smothering, like walking through cobwebs suspended from the sky. Darkness was supposed to be feathery and soft, like the air that it was comprised of. It was absolutely not, under any circumstances, supposed to *push*.

This darkness pushed. This darkness was doing everything in its power to eject her from the forest, to shove her back into the open—and beyond. It was difficult not to feel as if this darkness would happily push her off the bluff, leaving her to tumble end over end into the bowl where The Clearing waited, surrounded by its protective shell of ordinary night. Somehow, they had carved themselves an exception from this profound dark. In this moment, walking through the trees, she envied them as she had rarely envied anything in her life.

"Adeline," she called. "Adeline, it's your mother. Come to my voice, darling. You're not in any trouble. Only come to me, and we'll go home."

There was no response. Despair washed over her, as hot and harsh as it had been on the day when she had realized that her husband had stolen Adeline's voice with a slip of his scalpel. The child had been born howling as lustily as any babe in Deseret, and now she made no sound, ever, not even when her life was in danger. If Adeline needed her mother—if she had stepped in a rabbit hole or trapped her leg under a branch or, sweet Lord forbid, fallen into a hole—she would have no way of making her dilemma known.

All Annie could do was walk through the wood, desperately looking for her daughter, and pray that her steps would happen to parallel Adeline's own.

Something glimmered on the forest floor, pale as bone. Annie stopped and bent to brush the pine needles away, revealing a smooth white stone. She picked it up, thoughts of Hansel and Gretel flashing through her mind. Adeline knew the story; she had read it to the girl herself, on the long nights when the circus was in motion from one place to another. If Delly had gone into the wood, she might have marked her way, to be sure that she could go out again.

(And Delly had gone to the wood: of that much she was absolutely sure. The girl was absolutely fearless. She had to be, to survive in a world where strangers waited around every corner, ready to make fun of her for things she had no control over. If those boys had promised her acceptance in exchange for a pinecone—and no doubt tempered their promises with mockery, implying that Delly wasn't brave enough or strong enough to survive in their woods—then there was no question. She had gone. She wasn't visiting friends in another wagon or watching a show from some hidden corner that Annie had failed to find. She was in the wood. Once Annie had accepted that, everything else had followed.)

Carefully, Annie set the stone down again. If it was a coincidence, meaning nothing, there was no reason to burden herself. If it was a sign of Adeline leaving a trail for herself, then it could serve as a trail for Annie as well. She could follow the stones out of the darkness, once she had found her little girl.

There was no question of her leaving the wood without her daughter. That was not going to happen. It was *not*. Protecting Adeline had always and ever been her only purpose.

"Adeline, darling, it's your mother," she called, and pressed on into the devouring dark.

Annie and forests were never going to be friends. She was a daughter of Deseret, born to the salt lakes and the high desert. She had been planted in sandy soil, and she had blossomed there, believing herself in the right environment. Some poor souls wilted in the unrelenting heat and the salty desert winds, which stripped the moisture from their skin and left their hair limp and lifeless. Not Annie. She had been a beautiful child, salt-scoured into pearlescent perfection. The heat had set her curls, rather than stealing them away, and the wind had soothed her skin, keeping it free of blemishes. She was still lovely away from the desert, but in the desert, she had been divine.

That was what had attracted the majority of her suitors. Not her beauty—beautiful women were a dime a dozen in the cities and the houses of the wealthy, where the latest tonics were available for the purchase—

but the clear connection between that beauty and the world around her. Like the lizards in the rocks or the hawks in the sky, she thrived in the desert. Her children would, of necessity, be equipped to do the same.

Maybe that would have been true had she married a different sort of man. A man who was more willing to sit back and let nature take its course. A man who would never dream of subjecting his pregnant wife to the terrors of his brilliant, broken mind. She had been unwise in her choice of suitors, and everything else had spun from that.

But it had given her Adeline, and it had given her the circus, and if leaving the high desert behind had stolen a certain degree of the luster from her skin or a certain volume of curl from her hair, that was a small and easy price to pay. Annie had never worked to become a beauty. It had simply happened, like dawn, or winter. When something unearned went away, there was no point in mourning it.

The trees pressed in on all sides, their spindly branches snatching at her shawl and hair. The light from her lantern was enough that she had yet to walk face-first into one of them, but it was hard to believe that trees could grow so close together without killing each other. Surely their roots were tangled together, choking one another off. The entire forest had to be on the verge of death at all times. Annie swallowed hard, forcing down her fear, and walked on.

Adeline was not like dawn, or winter, or the desert wind. *Adeline* was not something that had simply happened, unavoidable and unearned. Adeline was hers, and she had fought for every minute of every day that they had spent together. Out of everything she had accomplished in her life, Adeline was the thing that she was proudest of, because Adeline had nothing to do with her being beautiful, or well-bred, or mannered. Adeline was about blood and sweat and effort. Adeline was mistakes and triumphs and fumbling her way through motherhood one day at a time. She was perfect. She was irreplaceable.

She was going to come home.

"Delly!" called Annie, and paused as the light from her lantern found another small white stone. They were too regular to be accidental; someone was leaving her a trail to follow. Whether it was her daughter or something else in these trees didn't matter right now. They would see her out again when she needed it, and that was enough. She began to walk faster.

When the trees dropped away and she found herself walking into the open, it was enough of a shock to her system that she stopped dead, one foot already raised. She was trembling. The air still felt heavy, but now it felt empty as well, like some essential, intrinsic element of its character had been stripped away, replaced with nothingness.

At the center of the clearing, at the absolute limit of her lantern's reach, something gleamed white. It was too large to be one of the little stones: it was the size of a fallen deer, or of a little girl with white-blonde hair.

"Delly?" whispered Annie, throat suddenly dry, tongue feeling too large for her mouth. Even forming that most familiar of words was a trial.

If that is her, if she's hurt, she needs me, Annie thought, and forced her foot to continue its forward motion, carrying the rest of her with it. That single small motion was enough to break the spell on her. She was walking again, and then she was running, casting caution to the wind as she raced toward the center of the clearing.

Stones turned under her feet, trying to trip her. She somehow turned her fall into more forward momentum, never quite losing her balance, racing onward until she dropped to her knees a few feet away from the white shape, breath rasping in her throat, and struggled to stop herself from screaming.

The white was bone, the cathedral curve of a rib cage stripped almost entirely clean of meat. Beneath that, blending into the dark ground, was only blood, and the glistening colors of flesh and offal, like the painted walls of a circus tent, promising wonders within. They were not wonders she had any desire to see. She pressed a hand against her mouth, keeping the growing whine in her throat contained. It would do her no good. It would do her no good, and so she would not let it out.

The body was not Adeline's.

It was human: of that, there was no question. The shape had been undeniable even from the trees, even shrouded in shadow. It was a young man, lithe of limb and gold of hair, his neck bent hard to the side and his open eyes staring up at the stars with no comprehension, like a discarded ventriloquist's dummy. The hand that was closer to her was open, spilling a fan of polished white stones out onto the ground. It was his trail that she had been following, and not Adeline's at all.

Somehow, that discovery was almost worse than the discovery of the body itself. He wasn't circus folk: she didn't recognize anything about him. A town boy, then, or a hunter from some other nearby settlement—were there other nearby settlements?—who had been caught out in the wood after the sun went down and had failed to realize the danger that he was in.

His belly appeared to have been opened by one swipe of some vast clawed paw, so large that it made Tranquility's saucer feet look dainty. Another swipe had removed his throat, while some internal pressure had cracked his chest. She had watched Tranquility bring down deer, on the rare occasions when the circus had camped far enough from civilization that it had been safe to let her lynx run free. The big cat liked to shove her head up under the ribcage, shattering the sternum from within. That appeared to have happened here. Annie couldn't imagine how large the creature that killed him would have needed to be to do that to a human chest, which was broader and tougher than a deer's.

A bear, then, or a catamount. Something vast and terrible and streaked in human gore that stalked these woods even now, feasting where it would, taking what it wanted. Annie looked quickly around, feeling the full force of her exposure. The things that hunted by night had better eyesight than she did. They could be watching her, concealed by the trees, aware of her presence in a way that she would never be aware of theirs.

She scrambled to her feet, pine needles sticking to her hands and the fabric of her skirt. Adeline was out there somewhere, with this predator, this unseen danger. She had to find her daughter.

This boy was dead. She had to tell the town. They were all in danger, and she was no closer to finding her little girl than she had been when she left the circus. She shouldn't have run off without raising a search party to help her; she saw that now. She should have brought every able-bodied adult the circus had, and however many they could recruit from the town. It was those boys who had sent her daughter into the woods. It was only right that their parents should help her bring Adeline home.

Haltingly, she made her way back toward the trees. She wanted to be back with her people, surrounded by light and hope and the knowledge that she was not the only woman left in the world, more than she had wanted almost anything in her life. The word "almost" was what betrayed her. She wanted nothing if she had to have it without her daughter.

The white stones had been a false trail, lain down by

a man who had already died for the crime of trespassing in these trees. Very well. It would still lead her back to the beginning, and then she could begin again, finding *Adeline's* trail, letting Adeline be the one to lead her through the dark. She held her lantern close as she made her way through the trees, watching for the gleam of white stones against the dark ground.

From time to time she paused and listened to the world around her, closing her eyes and narrowing her reality to nothing but sound. If the thing that had killed that boy was following her, it moved like a whisper through the wood, so sure-footed and silent that not even the crackle of pine needles gave it away. Nothing natural was that silent. Even most of her oddities made more noise than that. She would open her eyes and continue, confident that she was not being stalked; not yet.

(What of her oddities? If she died out here, devoured by some unseen beast, who would take care of the oddities? They needed special care and handling. They needed to be treated with cautious respect. They were not worth her life, or the life of her daughter, but she feared for what would happen if she died here.)

The white stones were more frequent than she had believed them to be; many had been dropped in a way that left them half-covered with loam, difficult to see from the direction she had been coming. She walked faster, confidence growing . . .

And stopped. Three white stones had been dropped in almost the same place, forming a triangle. One was close to her. The other two formed the start of two new paths. One would, presumably, take her back to the forest's edge and the edge of the bowl that contained The Clearing. The other would lead her into some unknown part of the wood. Her breath caught.

"Ah," she sighed, soft and sad and virtually silent. She had no desire to attract the attention of the beast; speech was a human luxury, unnecessary here. But it still made her feel a little better to voice her dismay.

While Annie had no intention of going home until she had found her daughter, there was a difference between descending into The Clearing long enough to rouse a search party and abandoning her search altogether. She had been hoping to have the opportunity to do the former, to gather the roustabouts and sharpshooters they paid to accompany the show and turn her solitary hunt into something more likely to be successful. Mr. Blackstone would not mind her making off with half of his men. Under the circumstances, he might well decide to join her.

Only now, she had no way of knowing whether the direction she chose would lead her home, or take her deeper into danger. There were no good choices left. There was only the darkness, and the promise of the beast in the trees, all claws and teeth and hunger.

"I believe," she said, to herself, voice barely above a whisper, "that I felt myself bending to the right as I ran, which would make the leftmost stone the correct choice. But if I am second-guessing my route, the rightmost stone may be the one to follow. I would greatly appreciate it, world, if you would send me some sort of a sign as to which way I should go. My Delly is only a little girl, and she needs her mother now as much as she ever has."

The world did not send her a sign. The world was rarely so accommodating.

Annie sighed and started forward again, stepping toward the leftmost stone. Another gleamed in the dark beyond it; she kept walking. It felt better to be moving than to be standing still. Even if she were heading in the exact wrong direction, at least she was doing something.

The foolishness of searching the entire forest by herself was undeniable. Oregon was a wooded territory. It would take humanity hundreds of years to clear the land, even if they were to make a concerted effort to try—based on the inhabitants of The Clearing, the people drawn to this green and shadowed land had no interest in making it open to more habitation.

If she had been in control of the state, if its future had been hers to determine, she would have ordered her men into the forest to thin and clear all this wood away long ago. Force the woodland back from the town, if only a little; give them room to breathe. People needed room to *breathe*. They weren't meant to live all penned-in like livestock, unable to safely roam.

These woods were too thick, too dense, too untouched by the hands and cutting tools of mankind. They needed to be cut back and put into their place; they needed to be tamed. Annie had walked in woods before, with none of her current misgivings. It wasn't just her daughter's absence—that colored everything, but she was spending so much energy on suppressing the urge to panic that she could view the trees with a certain amount of detachment. It was the closeness of it all, the intolerable darkness clinging to her skin and filling her nostrils. She couldn't breathe.

Adeline must have been so scared, out there alone in the dark. She was just a little girl. She was fearless under normal circumstances, but she had never been so far from her mother's sight before. When something distressed her, or when her lungs began to burn and she needed her medicine, she would run back to her mother's side, and what was wrong with that? She was still so young. She was still so small. She would always be fragile, thanks to the circumstances of her birth. It was only reasonable that she should need her mother, almost as much as her mother needed her.

The white stones were more closely spaced than Annie remembered, and the ground around them seemed to be virtually undisturbed, as if no one had walked there in quite some time. Perhaps she had taken the wrong turn after all. She hesitated, preparing to backtrack.

Something howled behind her. It was the long, drawn-out wail of a hunting coyote, but too deep and low to have come from any coyote's throat. A wolf, then, vast and terrible and somewhere behind her. Following the trail of stones back to the fork was not an option.

Annie began to walk faster, still taking care to set her feet down as lightly as possible, in case there was some chance—however slight—that she would be able to slip away without being heard. She couldn't leave until she found her daughter. But she was not designed to move silently through these trees, or to avoid predation. She could not climb. She could not fly.

The snarl came from only a few feet behind her, low and deep and angry. It was a sound filled with teeth, and hearing it reminded Annie of the one thing she *could* do.

She could run.

Her old companions in Deseret would have been astonished if they could see her now, running through the dark Oregon woods as fleetly as any roe deer or road-runner. She felt as if her feet barely touched the ground, bearing her onward with all the speed and strength they had earned during her years with the circus. She was a physical creature now, made for the road, tempered by the hard labors of all the many days between her and her origins, and when she set herself to run, she *ran*.

The sound of snarling continued to pursue her, never growing any closer. Either she was matched in speed to the beast, or—more likely—it was toying with her, allowing her to exhaust herself before it pounced. Her lantern swung wildly as she fled, making the shadows dance and spin around the trunks of the nearby trees, lending a mad levity to the scene. How could this be anything but a dream, when nothing about it remained constant between one second and the next? How could this have real consequences, when it was so clearly not really happening?

But the smell of blood and rank animal piss wafted from behind her, shed from the skin of the creature at her heels. Even if this were a dream, it was not a gentle one— and if it was not a dream, then there was a very good chance that it would kill her if she slowed, or stumbled, or showed any other sign of weakness. She could not die and save her daughter. The two things were antithetical.

Annie ran. She ran as she had never run before, leaning forward to reduce the drag from the world around her, following the jittering light of her lantern as she struggled to avoid the trees. Their branches snatched at her hair and clothing, almost like hands trying to slow her down. Still she ran. Running was all that she had left. As long as that beast followed at her heels, running was the only thing that stood any chance of saving her and, by extension, saving Adeline, who would need her mother.

The *thing* behind her snarled, louder and closer than ever. Annie, who had been flagging, put on a fresh burst of speed, running as hard as she could.

The trees ended.

One moment, she was running through the close-packed dark. The next, she was breaking into open air, into more ordinary darkness, beneath a sky so spangled with stars that it seemed, for a moment, to verge on blinding. She realized what came after the end of the trees and skidded to a halt, digging the sides of her feet into the earth. She stumbled. She did not fall.

Small clods of dirt, kicked loose by her arrival, rolled down the bowl that contained The Clearing to fall, with a pattering sound, to the track below.

Panting, Annie looked back. She thought she saw a shape at the wood's edge, but only for a moment; then whatever it was pulled back and was gone, if it had ever been there in the first place. She turned to face the town, and froze.

The circus was burning.

Interlude the First

Welcome, wanderers in spirit and in science, seeking answers beyond those offered by the ways of ordinary men. Welcome to the famed City of Wonders, Salt Lake, and to the glorious independent state of Deseret, where none who walk with Christ in their heart and with good intention in their hands will be turned aside. Come in peace, go in peace. Or better yet, stay. Stay and serve the great machines, bringing progress and plenty to the world beyond Deseret's enlightened borders.

Come.

From a distance, the city of Salt Lake—often referred to as "the City o' Gloom," and none who have walked there would ever question the origins of the name—was a great gray smudge, as though the thumbprint of some uncaring God had been pressed into the landscape, blurring the desert's natural beauties away. The closer a visitor drew, the more visible the city walls and spires would become, until the smog had become an accepted part of the landscape, virtually unnoticeable. It was a slow dive into deep pollution, and taken one step at a time, there would be no shock to the system.

(But when that same dive was repeated in reverse, oh! The shock of clean air, the pain of breathing all the way down to the bottom of the lungs! Common indeed were travelers who left Deseret and hacked and coughed until they had expelled what seemed like a bucket of tar from their chests, leaving them light and aching and unwilling ever to return. So many of them *would* return, sadly. Deseret was its own kingdom, and what wonders it contained, it did not yield easily to those who refused its hospitality.)

Up close, the bones of the city were visible, still as strong and lovely as they had been upon their original construction. There were wonders to be found in Salt Lake, beautiful walls and elegant architectural curves. It could have grown up from the surrounding desert, perfect in its symmetry, if not for the gray smog that hung over everything, staining stone and fogging windows. The people who hurried through the streets wore masks over their mouths and noses, trying to protect themselves from the sting of pollution for just a little longer. Those who had been felled by black lung or by other, darker diseases could not work in the factories, could not do their part for the ascension of Deseret.

It was easy for a traveler to think that this was all that Salt Lake had to offer: these narrow, stained, beautiful streets filled with weary, strained, unbeautiful people, whose lives were being consumed one day at a time by the factories. Indeed, for the uninvited or the faithless, this might as well have been all that there was of the city. They would never be allowed past the walls, into the beautiful gardens or the elegant homes of the faithful. They would never see how sweet life could be in Salt Lake City, where elegance and humility went hand in hand.

But for those lucky few, ah! They could make their way through those dirty streets to the walls that separated the homes of the common folk from the elegant neighborhoods set aside for the children of Joseph Smith, for whom Salt Lake would always be a Holy City, greater even than distant, lost Jerusalem. They could walk through the gilded gates and find themselves walking down streets of polished marble, where everything was scrubbed and perfect, seemingly untouched by the smog that hung only a few blocks away. Women strolled along the boulevards, modestly dressed but with their own benchmarks of beauty on display: clear skin, lovely hair, eyes unclouded by pollution.

Their children were similarly healthy and hale, and walked beside their mothers like well-mannered shadows, already learning their place in the world. The boys walked faster than the girls, who trailed a foot or so behind, well schooled at even the youngest age in the ways of obedience and humility. Their clothing was fine, machine-stitched and hand-finished, tailored to present them as the little ladies and gentlemen that they were becoming.

Even these houses, close to the border of the secular part of Salt Lake—unkindly referred to as "Junkyard" by many of those who didn't have to live there, and wearily called the same by those who had no other choice—were often regarded as small and shabby, too near the pollution to be truly worth coveting. The streets wound their way deeper into the Holy City, and then out again, heading for the border, where the homes of the truly wealthy and truly elite sat on their own large plots of land, surrounded by slices of captive desert where no rattlers swam and no unwanted dangers lurked.

Toward the very edge of the city, barely contained within Salt Lake's boundaries, sat a home large enough to be considered an estate. Three stories high, with wide, carefully landscaped gardens surrounding it. They were desert gardens, cactus and blooming succulents and hardy brush plants, but they were no less beautiful for their dryness. If anything, the fact that they were equipped to thrive in this climate, without demanding expensive watering systems or excessive labor, only made them more beautiful. They were things that could *thrive*.

The front door was mahogany, imported from wetter climes, inlaid with swirls of abalone shell, until standing in front of them was like beholding the world's largest perfect pearl, so close to untouched that they might as well have been constructed by the very hand of God. A cunning bell system had been installed, allowing visitors and tradesmen to summon a butler with the press of a button. It was a small technological wonder, hinting at the amazements that were to come, if only access to the house were granted by its owner.

Dr. Michael Murphy did not grant that access easily, or often. Had not done so, in fact, since the death of his wife some seven years before. Grace Murphy had been the finest woman any of his servants had ever known, and her sudden passing had cast a pall over the entire household. Childbirth was always a dangerous time for a woman, but she had seemed to bounce back easily from the ordeal, and had even been seen walking in the halls in good spirits before she had taken to her bed and faded away.

(Few admitted it aloud, but childbirth in Salt Lake—in all of Deseret—had become more dangerous still since Dr. Hellstromme had come, with his marvelous machines, and made them over into the technological capital of the West. Something about the air, perhaps, damaged the already weak constitutions of nursing mothers, rendering them prey to every infection and disease that came along. The number of orphans and widowers in Salt Lake grew by the season, and no one said anything, because there was nothing that was safe to say.)

After Grace's passing, Dr. Murphy had closed the windows and locked the doors, retreating more and more often into the safety of his lab, which was tucked down below the house, where it would not attract the curious eyes of his servants. Many of them had expected to be dismissed when the parties ended and the dinners were no more, but as their letters of dismissal had never come, they had continued to work.

The question of remarriage had been raised by the Elders, by concerned friends, even by the other scientists who toiled for the great future of their country. Somehow, none of it had ever come to anything. Dr. Murphy was a man in mourning, and he saw no reason to change that, now or ever.

A man in a tattered cloak and old leather hat slipped through the front gates and started up the walkway toward the house. He was a brown stain on the beige and bone landscape, long, lanky, and entirely out of place here, in a land that was not, could never have been his own. He walked with the easy stride of a gunslinger or a hired man, completely comfortable in his own skin. His eyes traced the gardens around him, marking the position of cactus spine and rattlesnake den—for here, in the desert, even the seemingly safe was never anything of the kind.

He reached the door. He rang the bell. He waited.

Footsteps heralded the approach of a member of the household. The stranger stood a little taller. The door was opened, revealing a woman in a demure dress, her hair covered by a plain white bonnet. She stopped, eyes widening for a moment before she composed herself.

"We do not require any landscaping services," she said. "Good day, sir."

"Wait." The man's voice was rough, the grate of rocks against one another, the sound of sand on stone. He did not reach for the door to stop it from closing. He didn't need to. His gaze was enough to freeze her where she stood. "I'm here on official business. I need to see Dr. Murphy, if you'd be good enough to fetch him for me."

"Dr. Murphy is not receiving visitors."

"He'll receive me." The man hooked his thumbs through his belt loops, looking at her with the steadied unconcern of a hunting coyote. "Tell him I've got an answer to his pearl problem. He's been waiting a long time. I don't suppose he'll be happy if I tell him that you made him wait even longer than he had to."

The woman's eyes widened again, and this time, they stayed that way. "Please, sir," she said, taking a step back and beckoning him inside. "Come with me."

The stranger stepped over the threshold, knocking dust off his boots and onto her nice clean floor. The woman said nothing, merely waited for him to be inside before she closed the door and beckoned for him to follow her deeper into the house.

"Nice place you've got here," said the man, staring shamelessly at the fine silver, the priceless artwork, and the other marks of Dr. Murphy's hard-won wealth. "One man needs all this?"

"Dr. Murphy is a philanthropist and an upstanding member of the church," the woman said stiffly. "His charity and generosity are without peer."

"If you say so," said the stranger. Then: "I thought you Mormons believed in the same man having as many wives as he wanted. Why's your master still looking for the one he lost? Shouldn't he just get a fresher plot to plough and," he made an obscene sucking sound, "give up on the old baggage?"

The woman's cheeks flushed a brilliant red. "I'll thank you not to speak of Miss Grace in such terms," she said. "That's the last help you'll have from me. Use that sort of vulgar language to refer to the mistress in Dr. Murphy's hearing, and your next of kin will be the ones receiving an unwanted visit."

They might, she thought cruelly, have been better off in that circumstance. This man was worn thin and hard by the desert and the road. His skin was leather, pocked with old sores; his teeth were too straight and white to be his own. He was a scavenger, stealing everything he had from the world around him. If he died here, Dr. Murphy would feel compelled to pay compensation to whatever family he might have, and she had absolutely no doubt that this man was worth far more dead than he would ever be alive.

"Understood, ma'am," said the man, eyes twinkling with unholy mirth. "I can't help notice your own rush to defend the lady. You don't believe this nonsense about her being dead, do you? Why, a smart woman like you. You must have figured it all out long ago."

"That is none of your concern," she snapped, before catching herself and buttoning her lips. This man, this dreadful desert-clad man, was trying to tempt her into a place of blasphemy. He wanted her to speak against her master, her household, and her Lord, all in a single sentence. She had seen the body of Grace Murphy with her own eyes, laid out pale and perfect and finally free from the trials of mortal flesh. To claim Grace were anything but dead and gone, why, it was to play at a second resurrection, which would not be granted to any living soul left on this world now that the Messiah had come and gone.

It was not right. It was not suitable. This man had no place outside Junkyard—no. He had no place in Deseret. His kind could not be saved. They could only be pitied, and allowed to go about their vile business until Kingdom Come, and the faithful were lifted into a better world, leaving the filth of this place behind them.

He chuckled. Even his laughter sounded dirty, like it was smearing on her skin, leaving her somehow tainted. "I always forget how mannerly you Deseret girls are," he said. "While you're home, anyway. I've known a few of your castoffs in my day, and I promise you, they're as rude as any other lady the night has ever known."

The woman said nothing, but walked a little faster, relief flooding through her as she saw the arched door to Dr. Murphy's lab come into view. As a senior member of his household, she not only had her own key, but had his express permission to disturb him while he was working—unless, that was, he had told her that his day's efforts involved volatile chemicals or, more rarely and dangerously, a visit from Dr. Hellstromme. He had given neither warning today, only mumbled vague pleasantries before making his retreat.

She unlocked the door. Opening it turned on a small blue light on the wall, where she couldn't help but see it; a visual reminder of the course she was setting for herself. A matching light would come on after five seconds in the master's lab, notifying him of her approach. The pause was to give her time to change her mind and withdraw—and quite honestly, she often did exactly that, deciding that whatever problem had caught her attention wasn't worth troubling Dr. Murphy, who was a brilliant, sensitive man and didn't deserve to be burdened down with the petty business of running a household.

Slowly, she began the descent toward Dr. Murphy's lab. The man from the desert followed, so close behind her that she could smell his stinking breath, rich with the scents of spoiled meat and the Devil's whiskey. She resisted the urge to wrinkle her nose. Showing him that she was disturbed would only reward his vile behavior. A man like that, in a place like this, why, he must be looking to shock. That was the only reason the unfaithful ever came to the Holy City. They wanted to shock, to startle, and to tempt good men and women away from the path of righteousness.

She would not be tempted, either in word or in deed. She was stronger than they.

The stairs ended at a doorway, matched to the one in the hall upstairs. She knocked three times before unlocking it, stepping through before the man could shoulder past her. Dr. Murphy's privacy was being violated. He deserved to know the reason.

"You have a visitor, Doctor," she said, voice frosty. "May he enter?"

The lab was a vast, cavernous space cut into the bedrock beneath the house. The walls were smooth stone, sanded and polished until they shone, and the floor was made of the same stuff. Inflammable, virtually indestructible, and gray as the smog that hung over Junkyard, creating the odd illusion that the entire lab had been sliced out of the sky above the factories and somehow transported to this underground location. Equipment she couldn't name and didn't care to understand lined the walls and filled the center of the room, creating a labyrinth in steel and flashing lights and unnervingly thick leather straps. Standing tubes tall enough to contain an adult human were set up along the far wall, shrouded in white sheets. She had never seen beneath their coverings. Something about the shape of them . . .

No one who worked in Dr. Murphy's household knew the exact nature of the work he did beneath it. None of them wanted to. Knowledge would carry a responsibility they did not desire.

The doctor himself was bent over something small and mechanical on one of the slabs. He looked up, eyes magnified to three times their natural size by the loupe clipped to his glasses. He blinked, the simple gesture turned huge and horrifying by the magnification.

"Helen?" He flipped the loupe up, revealing his wire-framed glasses, reducing his eyes to their normal size. His gaze went to the man behind her, a frown tugging at his lips as he saw the man from the desert. "Is something wrong?"

"No, Doctor," said Helen. She finally stepped to the side, letting the man step forward. "This man says he has information for you."

"Does he?" Dr. Murphy straightened, eyes still on the man. "Information about what?"

"I'm no fisherman," said the stranger. "Still, even the most landlocked of men might find themselves with their hands on a bushel of oysters. They might find a pearl or two."

Dr. Murphy went perfectly, utterly still.

He was not a physically imposing man: someone passing him on the street could have been forgiven for thinking that he was nothing of consequence, just one more accountant laboring in the great factories, keeping the numbers in line. His hands were long and slender, a piano-player's hands, and his shoulders were narrow, the shoulders of a man who had never done a lick of physical labor in his life. He was thin, thanks to a general disinterest in the pleasures of the flesh, but there was still a softness to him, beneath his fine linen and cotton clothing, marking him as no real challenge. His hair was brown, like the hills outside, and his eyes were blue, the color of the sky that hung above the Holy City, visible only to the faithful.

"Helen," he said finally. "You may leave us. Pack a traveler's lunch for our friend. I am sure he'll need it, when he goes."

"Sir—"

"Charity begins at home," said Dr. Murphy. This time, there was steel in his tone, a hard core of unquestioning strength that put a lie to his outward appearance. "You may leave us."

"Yes, sir." She bobbed a quick curtsey and was gone, running back up the stairs as fast as her legs could carry her.

Dr. Murphy turned his eyes on the stranger. He started toward him, removing his thick leather gloves as he walked, every motion seeming like a threat in the process of being made. "Sir, I am afraid you have me at a disadvantage," he said. "Oysters do not keep well in desert countries."

"Perhaps not, but it's well known that you've been looking for your pearl for a long while now," said the man. "I heard there was a reward associated with the little miss."

"Yes," said Dr. Murphy. "A reward. Go on."

"Word was your wife didn't die. She left you. Ran off in the night with your daughter. A pity. No man should have his good will used like that. You left her with enough freedom to feel she was a valuable pet instead of a captive, and what did she do? Grabbed what meant the most to you and ran." The stranger shook his head. "It's no wonder you'd want her back. If anything, it's only a wonder you haven't torn this country apart looking for her."

"Appearances must be maintained," said Dr. Murphy, sounding stunned. "Have you seen her? Have you seen my Grace?"

"She calls herself 'Annie' now. Annie Pearl." The stranger's expression sharpened, like a hunting hound scenting the kill. "There's the matter of my reward to be discussed before we go any further. You understand, being a businessman and all."

"You shall have every penny you desire upon this Earth," said Dr. Murphy fervently. "Only tell me, where is my Grace? Is our daughter with her?"

"You mean the silent girl? She's there. Ghostly little thing. Walks like she doesn't know what sound is for, and the way she looks at a man . . ." The stranger shook his head. "But she's alive, if not hale. I hear the girl has something wrong with her. In her lungs. She's sickly. That's one more crime you can lay at your wife's feet."

"No, it's not," said Dr. Murphy. He dropped his gloves on the nearest table. "Pearl was always unwell. It was . . . a consequence of her birth. For Grace to have kept her alive for so long is nothing short of a miracle."

"The girl goes by 'Adeline' now."

"Does she? A pretty name. My wife's choice for her, if

I recall correctly." His tone made it clear that he recalled correctly: that he had never been wrong about such a thing in his life. "Where did you see them?"

"My reward—"

"Will be paid in full once I have my answers. Do you think me a man who fails to pay his debts? If you do, perhaps you should take your leave of me now."

The stranger's eyes narrowed. "I have information."

"Yes, and thank God for that. But what one man may uncover, another may find as well. Now that I know they're out there to be found, and not bones in a hidden grave, I'll find them. Sooner or later, I'll find them. Speak and be rewarded, or hold your tongue and leave."

There was a long pause as the stranger weighed Dr. Murphy's words. Something about the smaller man was unnerving, unsettling in a way he couldn't quite put his fingers on. Finally, he said, "You drive a hard bargain."

"Yes."

"They're with a traveling show. The Blackstone Family Circus. Not that there's any family to it, just a man named Nate Blackstone with delusions of grandeur and reputability."

"A circus? I see." Dr. Murphy cocked his head to the side. "Where is it now?"

"I left them in Idaho. Too many freaks in one place for a God-fearing man like me. But I heard they were heading into Oregon, for a town called The Clearing. They should be there now. My payment?"

"Yes. Mustn't allow a debt to go unpaid." Dr. Murphy's long-fingered hand moved, swift as a swooping hawk, and the stranger's throat opened like a canyon, spilling a ruby waterfall of blood down the front of his filthy shirt.

The stranger made a choking sound, grabbing for his throat like he thought he could somehow stuff the blood back inside. It was too late. It had been too late the moment he had rung the bell at the front door. Some traps were all the more dangerous because they were so easy to walk into.

Dr. Murphy dropped his scalpel and walked to the wall, where he pressed a button. There was a crackling sound. "Helen," he said, into the speaker. "I need you, and three men large enough to assist me in dressing and disposing of a body. Please send message to Dr. Hellstromme, informing him that I will be needing some time away from my duties."

"Very good, sir," said Helen's voice, as clear as day. "What shall I do with the lunch you asked me to prepare?"

"Have it sent to Junkyard, to be given to some needy soul. Charity begins at home."

"Yes, sir," said Helen. The intercom clicked off.

Dr. Murphy turned back to his lab, looking at the body on his floor with distaste. There was so much *work* to be done, and it was well past time that he began.

Chapter 9

Annie slid down the side of the bowl that contained the town, nearly toppling end over end in her hurry to reach the settlement and the distant flames that engulfed the bright oilcloth tents of her home. As she got closer, two things became clear: that the boneyard was essentially untouched, far enough back from the fire as to have been spared, and that the damage was almost entirely confined to the attractions around the rim of the show. The tents must have gone up like candles, primed to the slightest touch of flame, but the wagons, the games of skill and chance, those were still largely intact.

Her feet found the flat ground of the bowl's bottom. She stumbled, once, from the sheer change in her situation. Then she broke into a run, heading as fast as she could for the show. People were running in the opposite direction, townies fleeing from the fire. Annie hated them. She was not a woman much inclined to hatred, but in that moment, she hated them all the way down to the bottom of her soul. She would have thrown every damn one of them to the oddities, and let the godforsaken creatures of the American West decide their fates. She did not think any of those fates would be kind.

The closer she drew to the circus, the more of her own people she saw. They were everywhere, racing around with buckets of water and of dirt, throwing them on the flames. Annie ran past them all, heading for the wagon of oddities. The question of Adeline still loomed large in her mind, but it was no longer the only dilemma she faced. The oddities. The freaks. Tranquility. They were all her responsibility, as much as Adeline was, and she had left them alone. She had turned her back on them.

The smell of ash and charred oilcloth hung heavy in the air, an accusing perfume. Annie ran faster still, until she rounded the tent where the dancing girls shimmied and swayed on better nights, and beheld the dreaded spectacle of the wagon of oddities, burning.

It was not engulfed in flame: the fire was confined to the roof, where it crackled to itself as it consumed the mossy shingles. Annie grabbed the bucket of water she kept next to the wheel for the use of thirsty dogs and horses, swinging it as hard as she could toward the fire. The wave landed with a loud splash, and the fire died back, not going out, but dying down enough that she felt safe running for the door and yanking it open.

Inside, cacophony. The animals that *could* make a sound were, roaring and hissing and rattling around inside their cages, anxious to be free. Tranquility's snarls were anything but tranquil, shattering the air in loud trills, like the revving of a chainsaw. Annie rushed across the wagon and opened the latch on Tranquility's cage, allowing the lynx to rush out.

She did not look back as she ran down the length of the wagon and leapt through the open door. Annie could only hope that she wouldn't go too far. The townsfolk were understandably upset by their current circumstances. Adding a panicked lynx to the scene might be a step too far and result in bloodshed.

Backtracking to Oscar's tank, Annie scooped out a healthy bucket of water. The great white catfish watched her warily from his place on the bottom, whiskers twitching.

"I would free you if I could," she said, and ran back outside, adding her second bucket's contents to the first.

It took four trips, and four buckets of stolen water, before the flames were out. Oscar's tank was more than half-empty, leaving the great cat' pressed against the bottom, half-hidden in the silt. Annie dropped the bucket and sank to rest her hands on her knees, struggling to breathe. It felt as if all the wind had been sucked out of her, extinguished along with the flames.

All over the circus, similar scenes were playing out. She could see a good few of them, people beating out fires with sheets of canvas or with their bare hands. Circus orphans swarmed from place to place, straining under the weight of the buckets they carried. She saw no townies moving through the chaos. They had their own problems, presumably, and no sympathy to spare for strangers.

But there had been no flames that she could see in the town proper. All the damage was to the circus.

"Annie!"

The voice was Mr. Blackstone's. She straightened up, wincing as her strained shoulders expressed their displeasure, and turned. The normally dapper ringmaster was running toward her, smudges of ash and char on his formerly immaculate shirtfront. He looked like a man on the verge of absolute collapse.

He ran until he reached her. Then he seized her, drawing her into an embrace before she had a chance to protest.

"I was so afraid that you'd been taken!" he exclaimed, his voice right up against her ear, closer than any man's voice had been in years. "Annie, Annie, where have you *been*?"

"Adeline," she replied, and pulled away, moving so that she could see his face. "Some of the children from the town tricked her into going into the woods to fetch them a pinecone, of all things. I went to bring her back again. I got . . . I was turned around in the trees. The darkness there is . . . it's very dark, in the trees. When I stumbled out, the circus was in flames. What happened? Has anyone been hurt?"

"You weren't here." He sounded almost amazed, like he couldn't believe his own luck. "You missed the whole thing."

Annie opened her mouth, ready to tell him about the dead body, about the sound of snarls in the wood. Then she stopped, and frowned, and looked at him. Really *looked* at him, not just at the idea of him, the phantom friend who haunted her memories.

Mr. Blackstone's skin wasn't merely covered with ash; it was ashen, like all the blood had been removed from the flesh behind it, turning him into an empty tent waiting for the show to begin. The wax on his mustache had trapped a remarkable amount of char, turning that great black display piece gray as old charcoal. A ring of red showed all around the whites of his eyes, a sign of strain and terror. It was like he had forgotten how to blink.

"Nathanial," she said, touching his hand. He started, although whether from the contact or the rare use of his given name, she couldn't possibly have said. "What happened? I'm sorry I wasn't here. I can't stay. I have to find Delly. But what *happened*?"

"Things." The word, which should have seemed vague, was so laden with meaning and with dread that Annie had to fight against the urge to take a step backward, away from the man who spoke it.

Nathanial's hand suddenly moved, grabbing hers and holding it so tight that it hurt a little. Annie went very still. She had promised herself, after leaving Deseret, that no man would ever hurt her again. The only thing that kept her from slapping his face and running was the fact that when Michael had hurt her, he had done it to remind her that she was his property. He had done it on purpose. Nathanial didn't even know that he was causing her pain. He was a man on the verge of falling off the world, and he was holding on for dear life.

"Things from the woods," he said. His voice shook. "They came . . . they came out of the trees. I was in the tent. I didn't *see* until they had already descended into the bowl." Because this wasn't a valley, not really; it was too shallow. It was a killing ground.

Why hadn't they seen that before? They should have looked upon The Clearing and seen it for the honey trap that it was. Not a natural valley. Anything herded into it wouldn't be able to get out. They would be trapped. They would be lost.

Annie shook her head, chasing the thought away. It was the delusional raving of the panicked mind, of a mother with a missing child, standing in the body of her burning home. She needed to be rational now. For Adeline's sake, and for her own.

"What sort of things?" she asked.

Nathanial shook his head. "I didn't see them," he said. "There was a great tearing sound, and a smashing, and when I made it out of the tent—through the panicking bodies of the townies, who were already fleeing toward their houses—they were already gone. As were at least seven of our people."

Annie gasped. "Who . . . ?"

"Sophia, the seamstress's girl. Piotr and Patrick, from the knife-throwing act. Three of the roustabouts. And one of the newer orphans, the towheaded boy from the last town." His lips drew downward, ashy mustache bristling. "His parents told him to run away with the circus for his own safety, for a full belly and a trade. How can we ever go back there now, with him missing in this god-forsaken land?"

"Things in the woods," she said faintly, her brain finally

catching up to the situation. She let go of Nathanial's hand, taking a step backward. "Adeline is still out there. I have to find her. She must be so afraid—"

"Half a dozen of the wagons have been damaged, and that was before the fire," said Nathanial. "We couldn't leave here if we wanted to. We're trapped until the wainwrights can repair them. There's no shortage of lumber, but . . ."

"Why are you standing here with me?" Annie buried her hands in the skirt of her dress, hiding them from view. She didn't want him to see her ball them into fists. She had nothing to hit, but oh, the urge to swing was strong. "The circus is in flames. Your people need you."

"The flames are under control. The townies have been evacuated back to their safe streets; the creatures from the woods are gone. I thought you were gone as well." He allowed himself the sliver of a smile. It barely reached his eyes and did nothing to lessen the strain in his face. "I am allowed a moment's rest and relief before I lurch into the next crisis."

"Nathanial . . ." She paused. "Never mind. I can't stay here. I only came because I saw the fire."

There was a shout off to the left. Both of them turned, tensing, only to relax as Tranquility came pacing out of the shadows. The big cat's head was down, and her short tail was lashing side to side with a force that would have been terrifying from one of her wild cousins. She continued forward until she reached Annie's side and buried her face in her mistress's skirts, pressing it against her leg.

"Shhh, Tranquility, shhh," said Annie, bending slightly to scratch the lynx behind the ears. "You're a good girl. You did well, coming back to find me."

"And without a train of angry townies calling her the monster that brought this down upon them," said Nathanial. "If anything is the miracle here, it's that. Annie,

I'm not comfortable with you walking alone into the woods. You should stay here, at least until morning. Go when the sun is in the sky, when you can see where you're going."

"I'll do no such thing," she said. "Adeline is out there. She *needs* me."

"I need you."

"I am her *mother*, sir," said Annie, her voice like the cracking of a whip. "She has no one in this world if she does not have me, and I do her no good by standing here and continuing to argue my case with you, who has no authority over my actions."

"I run this circus."

"Then leave us behind when you go. Leave us to make our own way in the world. Find someone else to tend the oddities, if that's what you require. But I *will* find my daughter. I will bring her safely home, even if home is no longer ours to claim."

Nathanial seemed to wilt. He was still one of the tallest men she had ever known, even with his shoulders slumped and his spine stooped, but he lacked the authority that he had always commanded. He was just a man, tired and charred and frightened.

"Will you at least take someone with you?"

"Not you, sir," she said calmly. He flinched. She continued, "The circus needs you as Adeline needs me. If you would wish to come with us, under better circumstances, that's something we can discuss later."

"That's something we've needed to discuss for a while," he said.

"Maybe so. But I will not take you into the woods now."

"I'll go," said a voice.

Annie and Nathanial both turned, Annie stumbling slightly as the motion brought her into contact with Tranquility's head, still buried against her leg in a bid for comfort. Martin was walking up on them. His shirt was torn, the edges of the slash red with blood. His hair was wild. His eyes were wilder, filled with the shadows of silent screams.

"I will go with you," he said. "Those . . . *things,* whatever they are, took my Sophia."

"Martin, you're hurt," said Annie.

He shook his head. "It doesn't matter. She screamed. I was beating out the fire on a roustabout wagon, and she . . . she screamed, and I didn't get to her in time. I never asked for her hand. We'd talked about it, a little, but I hadn't asked. If she dies . . ." His voice broke. "If she dies out there, she dies a spoiled woman, and it's my fault."

"Women are never spoilt," said Annie firmly. "We can get dirty at times, but that's our choice as much as the choice of the men around us. We are not pots of cream, to go bad simply because our lids have been removed. Of course you may accompany me to the wood. We'll go now."

Tranquility made a deep chuffing noise in her throat. Annie sighed and smoothed the lynx's ears.

"Tranquility will come as well," she said.

"Please," said Nathanial. He stepped toward her, grabbing her shoulders this time, making it impossible for her to pull away without physically shaking him off. "Be safe. Come home."

"Not without my daughter," Annie said gently. She didn't move, waiting until he lowered his hands and stepped back before she smiled and touched his cheek. There was nothing of joy in her expression. It was the smile of a woman who knew the sky was falling and was willing to stand in the open and let it rain down on her head if that was what the world required. "But I *will* come back to you, if the world allows."

She turned then, retrieving her lantern from the ground

before walking toward the trail that would take her back to the edge of the bowl. Tranquility paced by her side, and Martin hurried to catch up. She gave him a sidelong look. He had a rifle in one hand, leaning against his shoulder with the muzzle turned toward the sky. His face was a grim mask under his concealing layer of ash. He looked like a man marching off to war, unsure whether he would return, unable to care for his own safety. It was of the least importance in this moment.

The sound of shouts still rang from the circus behind them, lacking the urgency of the earlier screaming, but pained all the same. Annie couldn't help wondering how they must look in that moment, turning their backs on the people who should have been a part of their family. The circus needed them, and they were walking away.

I must find my daughter, she thought, and she did not look back.

When they reached the sloping footpath up to the road, Annie took the lead, scrambling up the hillside despite the rocks that turned under her feet, threatening to dump her back to the bottom. Tranquility was close behind her, at least in the beginning. After only a few feet, the big cat struck out on her own, walking effortlessly up the side of the bowl. She was a desert creature, as unsuited to these woods as her mistress, but the desert was a land of buttes and towering stone as much as it was sand. Nature had equipped her well to survive in that environment.

"Your cat's leaving," said Martin, watching Tranquility scramble out of sight over the lip of the bowl.

"She won't go far," said Annie with a confidence she didn't feel but couldn't stop herself from projecting. So much in her life was pretense. Always had been. "She knows she's to stay close to me, unless she wants a scolding."

"Don't know if I could scold something with that many teeth, ma'am."

"You get used to it."

They trudged on in silence for a few feet more before Martin said, "I heard you tell Mr. Blackstone that you were going to look for little Delly. Is she really missing, ma'am?"

"Yes," she said. "Some of the local boys convinced her to go into the woods and she hasn't returned. I'm worried for her. So I'm going to bring her home." She didn't mention the body, or the sounds in the trees, or the way the darkness had seemed to hold its breath and follow her, dogging her footsteps like a living thing. He would see many of those things soon enough, and nothing she said was going to make him change his mind and go back. He needed to find Sophia as much as she needed to find Adeline. People with something to die for were surprisingly difficult to dissuade.

Tranquility's head appeared over the edge of the bowl, her ears flat and her lips drawn back in an expression of curiosity that many would have taken for a snarl. Annie forced a smile.

"It's all right, pet," she said soothingly. "We're slow and plodding things, humans are, but we're coming for you. It's all right."

"How much does she understand you?" asked Martin.

"Are you wondering whether she'll attack you?"

"The thought had crossed my mind," he said reluctantly.

"If you harm her, or me, or Adeline, she'll have your throat out so quickly that you won't have time to suffer," said Annie.

From the look on Martin's face, he didn't find this very reassuring.

She grabbed a dangling root, using it to pull herself the rest of the way up the side of the bowl. Tranquility backed up as her mistress stepped onto solid ground and straightened, dusting her hand against her skirt. She turned to offer that same hand to Martin, pulling him the last few feet.

"There," she said, letting him go. "Come. They're waiting for us."

They turned toward the trees, and stopped.

The darkness had not receded any with the passage of time or with the flames from below: if anything, it had deepened, pooling between the trees like thick syrup, black and deadly, imbued somehow with a terrible independence of purpose and thought. It was impossible to look upon that darkness and not feel as though they were being somehow watched.

Martin took a step backward. Tranquility flattened her ears and growled deep in her throat, giving the lie to her name. Annie reached down and rested a hand between the lynx's shoulders, trying to lend her some comfort. Tranquility stopped growling but did not relax. If anything, she tensed further under her mistress's hand, like she was suddenly aware of the fact that she had something to protect.

"This isn't right," muttered Martin.

"From your lips to God's ears," said Annie. She turned to look at the man. His face was a pale shadow in the flickering light from her lantern. "Did you see the thing that hurt you?"

"Yes, ma'am," he said. "It was like nothing I'd ever seen before, not even in your house of horrors—begging your pardon, ma'am, I don't mean to speak ill of what you've made. It's just there's some things under your roof could make a good man fear the Devil."

"They make each other fear the Devil, too," said Annie. "What was it?"

"I thought a bear, at first. It was big enough to be a bear, big enough to be the King of All Bears, if it wanted to be. But it was too fast, and too hairy, and I ain't never heard of a bear that had teeth like those. It was like . . ." He didn't shudder. Instead, he did the opposite, freezing from tip to toe, until he didn't even appear to be breathing.

Finally, he said, "Those fish you have. The red ones, with all the teeth. It was like the thing wasn't the King of Bears. It was the King of Fish. Fish that shouldn't be. When it opened its mouth, it wasn't anything but teeth. It wasn't even the idea of anything aside from teeth. Just teeth, and teeth, and teeth, forever."

"Your shirt?" asked Annie gently. They needed to be moving: every word he said only made her more certain that Adeline was in terrible danger. But moving in ignorance was even worse than standing still. If he was talking, she was going to let him, until there was nothing left for him to say. She needed to *know*.

"Claws." He looked down at his torn and bloodied shirt like he was seeing it for the first time. Perhaps he was: it was sometimes easy to overlook small injuries in the face of great disasters. "They had claws, too. They just . . . the claws seemed to matter less, because the claws belonged. You see something big and shaggy and terrible, of course it's got claws. Of course it has a way to rend the world. It's the teeth that shouldn't be. Nothing needs that many teeth. Not in the natural world."

"I see." Something with that many teeth would use them whenever possible: would be an appetite walking, equipped by some ungodly hand to devour the world.

Annie was well acquainted with the ways of ungodly hands. It had been her treatment at her husband's hands—so pious and so profane at the same time—that had led her to care so well for her oddities, which were at least natural, if terrible. They had been born, not made. Whatever this thing in the woods was, this paragon of teeth and hunger, it was natural. It was just a larger oddity, and however terrible she found it, she was well acquainted with its kind.

"If it has not devoured her already, she is waiting for us somewhere in these trees," she said. "If she has been devoured, you owe it to her to avenge her."

Martin paled. "How can you . . ."

"Because the same things are true of my daughter. She is lost. Somewhere in this wood, she is lost. It is down to me to find her and bring her home. Living or dead, I will bring her home." She looked steadily at Martin. "Are you prepared to walk with me?"

He took a deep, shaking breath before he said, "I wouldn't have come this far if I weren't, ma'am."

"Excellent," she said. "We proceed."

Hand still resting on Tranquility's back, she started forward, into the syrupy darkness clinging to the trees. Martin followed, half a step behind, his gun resting against his shoulder, ready to fire.

The night opened its terrible jaws and swallowed them whole, leaving no sign that either of them had ever been there at all.

Chapter 10

The woods had seemed to skirt the limits of what darkness could be before. Now Annie knew that for the lie it was: the woods had been dark, yes, but they had been nowhere near as dark as they could become. Even with her lantern raised, they couldn't see more than a foot ahead of themselves. Both of them had walked into the rough trunks of the clustering trees, stubbing toes and bruising noses. Sap trickled down her cheek, thick and viscous, like clinging mucus.

Tranquility was growling again. She had been growling almost constantly since they had passed the tree line. Her back was tense under Annie's hand, all hard muscle and bristling fur. Annie dug her fingers in, clinging as hard as she dared to the big cat. Let Tranquility be the strength her shaking legs and trembling fingers lacked. Together, let them bring her daughter home.

"Find her," she whispered, knowing that the cat's ears were sharp enough to pick up the words. "Follow her scent, and find her."

Tranquility made a chuffing noise and continued to walk deeper into the wood. Annie followed, leaning on the lynx, trusting her to know the way. She could feel Martin's presence behind her, a comforting shadow. He was following her light, and she was following her cat, and together they were going to bring their people home. They were going to do it. Any other outcome was not to be considered.

"Ma'am?" Martin's voice was shaking, querulous; the poor boy was terrified. And he *was* a boy—she had to remember that. Maybe when this night was over he would be a man, but the world had never given him that opportunity before.

Much as I was a girl when Michael took my hand and promised me the streets of Heaven, she thought, not without a certain wry bitterness. Aloud, she said, "Yes, Martin?"

"Do you . . . do you know where we're going? There's a lot of wood here, and there doesn't seem to be a trail."

"Tranquility knows where to go."

"Begging your pardon, but would she even think to look for my Sophia? Or is she just looking for your Delly? Because I got to bring my lady home. I promised her, when we started stepping out, that she'd never need to worry about me leaving her alone."

Annie strongly doubted that his promises had taken into account creatures from out of the deep wood—or perhaps they had. She didn't really know what young people got up to when they were courting, or what people got up to when they were courting at all. She had been less "pursued" and more outright sold by her father, who had recognized the future in Dr. Michael Murphy and wanted it for his eldest daughter. Courtship was a poor woman's game.

(She was not foolish enough to think that poverty was a desirable state, and especially not for a woman, who was vulnerable enough without adding such trials to her condition. But there was no denying that poor women were more frequently allowed to choose their suitors, marrying based on their own preferences, rather than the preferences of their families. She couldn't envy that. Her own experience was too alien to it, and besides, her marriage had brought her Adeline, who was worth every trial in the world. But she could admire it, safely, from a distance.)

"If the creatures that took your Sophia also took my Adeline, we're being led to the same place," she said. "If not . . . there is no question that they'll have left a blood trail, whether Sophia is hurt or no. They'll break skin without meaning to. I am sorry to say it, but it must be taken as an undeniable truth."

"Yes, ma'am," said Martin, voice gone sullen with dread.

"Tranquility can't pass up a blood trail. She's a wild animal, for all that I adore her, and she'll bend us toward the beasts, if only to follow the scent of supper."

There was a long pause, during which the only sounds were their feet crunching on the pine needles underfoot. Finally, Martin said, "I'm sorry I asked."

"I have that effect on people."

"Ma'am . . ."

If you're so sorry you asked, stop asking *things,* she thought sharply. "Yes, Martin?"

"Do you think they're alive?"

Annie was silent. Her shoulder struck a tree, sending a bright bolt of pain through her arm. It was almost welcome. It centered her in her skin, giving her something to focus on apart from the darkness that clawed at their skins, trying to pull them deeper into the wood. They were already going deeper. Why should they not be allowed to proceed there at their own pace?

Finally, she asked, "Sophia. Do you love her?"

"Yes, ma'am. With all my heart. I'm going to make an honest woman of her, soon's I have the money for a wagon of our own. Maybe sooner, if she—" He stopped.

Annie imagined she could hear the boy blushing, bright enough that she should have been able to see it even through the treacly dark. He should have been a lambent beacon, glowing through the trees, leading their lost ones finally, blessedly home.

"Is there to be a baby?" she asked delicately.

"I don't know, ma'am. I think there might be."

"If there's to be a baby, she won't care about having a wagon of her own. She'll care about giving that baby a name, one she can take to town with her when she goes to do the shopping. It's a small thing, having a name for your child, but it opens doors that she won't want closed."

"Yes, ma'am."

"You needn't sound so embarrassed. I know how babies are created. I have a daughter of my own, after all."

"Yes, ma'am."

"You love her. In all this world, she's the one you've chosen—and you're the one she's chosen in reply. If you were to stand before God Almighty on Judgment Day, and Him ask who your family was, you would cleave to her."

"Yes, ma'am."

"Then you must believe she's alive, even as I must believe that Adeline is alive. Love is a powerful thing. It's a form of faith. We haven't anything in this black and blasted land but love, which lifts us up and tears us down, and keeps us breathing even when we'd rather let it cease. If she is still alive, she'll need you to love her, and if you love her, you'll believe she lives right up until the moment you can no longer sustain the dream."

Martin was quiet for what felt like an eternity but couldn't have been more than a stretch of seconds. Finally, he said, "Thank you, ma'am."

"Think nothing of it. You're helping me find my daughter; a few words of pale encouragement are genuinely the least that I can do."

The darkness pressing down around them was getting deeper with every step they took, until the faint rasping of the tree branches against one another started to sound like the breathing of some unseen beast, until Annie's flesh crawled with the feeling of eyes upon her skin. Her own breathing quickened, matching the tempo of her heart, which was too tender to be sensible, and was speeding up in answer to the presumed threats around it. She tightened her fingers in Tranquility's fur. The great cat's growl changed timbres for a moment, warning Annie that she was hurting her companion, and she relaxed her grip before Tranquility could decide to shake her off. She thought that if she lost this last anchor to her life back at the circus, she might go mad.

No, she scolded herself silently, *you won't. You do not get such easy exits.* No well-lit sanitariums and well-trained, efficient nurses for her! Those were the things that had tempted Grace Murphy, once upon a lifetime ago, when she had risen from her birthing bed and beheld her husband's plans for their offspring. She had flirted with madness then, considering it as she might have considered a new bonnet or a trip to the dressmaker. It was a perfectly respectable state for someone with her standing in society, enough so that she suspected many of her peers viewed it as a vacation, or a vocation, both of which were often denied to them otherwise.

(She had seen true madness since then, people plagued by voices, or racked with anxiety to such an extent that they could not leave their beds come morning. They were playing at nothing. This was neither vacation nor vocation to them: this was reality, as undeniable as dawn, as brutal as nightfall. They got on with their lives because they had no other choice, and were they to be locked away by "concerned" relations, the sanitariums they'd be consigned to would bear no resemblance to the airy palaces of Salt Lake. She did not mean to belittle them when she thought of the form of madness she'd been raised to fear; she simply lacked the words to call it anything else.)

The branches continued to rustle, the illusion that something was breathing in the trees nearby becoming more difficult to ignore. Annie stopped walking. Martin, unable to see, stumbled into her before stopping in turn.

"Ma'am?" he asked.

"Shhh," she replied. She lowered her lantern, making its light even more difficult to follow. She closed her eyes, shutting out the deep dark of the woods for the softer, tamer dark within.

Annie breathed, willing her heart to stop its pounding, willing her blood to move through her veins as it was meant to, and not to clump and creep under the influence of her terror. She kept her fingers laced through Tranquility's fur, feeling the vibrations through the big cat's skin as she continued to growl. That was important. Feeling the sound let her filter it out, removing it from her picture of the wood.

The susurration of the branches didn't fade with her slow silencing of her own body. If anything, it got louder, until—

Her eyes snapped open, beholding only the dark ahead of her. "*Run,*" she hissed, and raised her lantern, and leapt forward, trusting Tranquility to keep pace with her as she fled. Martin was no fool, and more, he had been with the circus more than long enough to be in the habit of following orders; she heard his footsteps behind her, fast and heavy and so reassuringly *human* that she felt her own love for him swell. It was a maternal love, closer kin to what she felt for Adeline than to what she felt for any other human, and she decided that if they survived this night, she would do whatever was in her power to help him get his marriage wagon. The boy deserved to start his own life, indebted to no man, with Sophia by his side.

Then, behind them, came the sound of another pair of feet; the feet of a man tall enough to be the envy of every circus in the West, or of a beast large enough to be called the King of Bears. Annie ran harder, not worrying about where she was going, worrying only about whether her light was bright enough to show her the trees before she slammed into them. Martin was depending on her. Tranquility was depending on her. *Adeline* was depending on her, and that alone was enough to put fire in her feet, urging her onward despite the growing weariness in her bones. Let her body give out on her. She would find a way to keep running.

The light from her lantern seemed to be reaching farther than it had only seconds before. Annie's eyes widened. "We're coming to a clearing!" she said, not bothering to shout; Martin was too close to need that. She ran harder, and so did he, and they hit the edge of the trees at full speed, bursting out into the open.

It was hard to slow down when moving at such a speed. They stumbled to a stop halfway across the clearing, panting as they turned to face the trees. Martin swung his rifle down, getting it into position to fire. They did not discuss their next move; they didn't need to. Both of them were worn out, too winded to run any farther, and if there was an advantage to be had, they would have it only in the open. Once they went back into the trees— once they crossed the clearing—any advantage would belong to the thing that had been pursuing them.

Tranquility paced forward, putting herself between her mistress and the trees. She crouched low, paws spread so that her claws dug into the earth, lips drawn back to expose her blunted teeth in a snarl. The men who had doctored her for human companionship had thought that sanding the edges off her incisors would be sufficient to render her harmless. They had either never seen an adult lynx, or didn't understand the atavistic terror most people would feel upon seeing a large predator.

Something moved at the tree line, too distant and

shrouded in that all-consuming darkness to be clearly seen. Whatever it was, it was clearly larger than a man, larger than a bear; its outline was a shaggy slice of distortion between the branches, giving the impression of menace without leaving any details behind. It was terrible. It was deadly. Annie's guts twisted, seeming to become a solid mass of frozen fear.

Tranquility's snarl rose in volume and timbre, becoming a scream.

Annie realized what she was going to do a heartbeat before she did it. "Tranquility, *no*!" she shouted, lunging forward, grabbing for the scruff of the lynx's neck.

It was too late. Tranquility ran, almost too fast for the eye to follow, her paws digging divots in the ground as she raced across the clearing toward the hulking shadow of the thing in the trees. She leapt when she reached the tree line, her body impacting with the shadow. She roared. It—whatever it was—howled, the sound chilling and cruel, not meant for human ears.

A hand grabbed Annie's elbow. She whirled. Martin was there, staring at her, wild-eyed.

"She's bought us time," he hissed. "We have to *go*." Then he ran, towing Annie with him, leaving her no time to argue or fight.

She stumbled at first, body heavy, inwardly screaming. Then she got her feet under herself and lifted her lantern, falling into step behind him. The thing behind them was still howling. Tranquility was still snarling. She might win. She might be stronger, or faster, or just plain angrier than her opponent. She would find them, if she won. She would—

There was a yelp from the trees, more canine than feline, the sound of an animal that had been grievously wounded. The howling stopped. So did the snarling. It was impossible to know, in that moment, which of them had won.

Annie was direly afraid that she knew anyway, and she mourned in her heart for a present that she had never requested, a gift that had saved her life and her soul a dozen times over.

"Oh, you mush," she whispered. "You silly, silly mush."

The woods on the other side of the clearing loomed, and they dove into them, continuing to run. The darkness seemed less profound here, less aggressive; it was the natural darkness that could be found in any body of trees or closed room, and not the all-consuming darkness of the trees between them and the circus. The rasping of the branches against one another was just that, with no secrets or hidden predators. They ran for another twenty yards or so, far enough that they felt safe to stop, panting.

Annie dropped to her knees, feeling the pine needles bite into her skin, and set her lantern carefully to the side before burying her face in her hands. Tranquility would have caught up to them by now if she had been the winner. She would have come to demand treats and fussing-over, to be told that she was a good mush, and a silly mush, and a mush deserving of all the good things that the world had to offer.

"Ma'am, we can't stay here." The voice was Martin's, heavy with anxious concern. "We don't know whether that thing is following us."

"You must give me a moment," she said through her fingers. They smelled of warm fur and musk, the way Tranquility had always smelled. If only she had held a little tighter, trained her a little more harshly to the ways of obedience . . .

Then Annie would be dead, her and Martin both. She had no doubt of that. Tranquility had saved them, and if she had sacrificed her own life in the process, well. It was an easy thing, to be a lynx, to have people to protect. For Tranquility, there had been no question of what was the right thing to do. The right thing was whatever left her mistress standing.

"I have to stand." Annie lowered her hands, the enormity of the big cat's sacrifice sinking in. Tranquility could just have easily have turned and run, choosing freedom over the human who had kept her captive for most of her life. Instead, she had given everything to save the woman who loved her.

For Tranquility's sake, Annie had to stand.

She staggered back to her feet. To his credit, Martin did not offer to help her; he stood a few feet away, rifle in his hands, watching, scanning the trees for danger. The fact that she was a woman did not sway him from his duty. He was giving her as much space as he could, under the circumstances, and if it was not enough, well. When had the world ever been willing to give enough?

"We must be going the right way," she said. "If that . . . thing was following us, it means we're on the right track." Her heart was a dead thing, hanging heavy in her chest, unyielding. Tranquility had been her friend. More, Tranquility had been the last living thing who'd known her—truly known her—in Deseret. Adeline had been a baby when they had fled from her father and his terrible intentions. To Adeline, "Deseret" was just a word on a map, the name of a place so inconsequential that they never bothered going there at all, choosing to stay instead in kinder climes and on fairer roads.

As if anything in the West had ever been *kind.* If humanity knew kindness, they had left it somewhere else. Somewhere more forgiving.

Martin nodded. "Seems right," he said. His eyes were still on the trees behind them, searching for some sign that they were going to have to fight again.

This wasn't over. Of that, they were both quite sure. The only question now was how long their window of escape was going to last. Annie did not think that it could possibly last for long enough.

"Come," she said, touching Martin's arm. "We have to go."

He nodded—he had only, she realized dimly, been waiting for her—and turned to follow her deeper into the trees. They still couldn't see. The branches still blotted out the moon and stars, casting them into an endless shadow that deepened with each step they took away from the clearing. Still, Annie's lantern made it possible for them to walk without slamming into a tree, and the farther they went from whatever it was that had been following them, the better.

Annie's free hand itched, fingers clutching reflexively at the air, only to relax when Tranquility was not there to bear her up. Sorrow had yet to find her; her eyes were dry, and while her heart still felt hard and dead, it didn't ache. That would come later, once Adeline was home, when she had the time to think about what she had paid for this night, this search, this unwanted adventure.

"Ma'am?" Martin's voice was soft.

Annie stopped, turning to face him. "Yes?"

"Look." He was a dim outline in the gloom. Annie held her lantern out toward him, bringing some of the detail back into his silhouette. He was pointing at something on the ground.

She leaned forward. The light found a scrap of white fabric tied tight around a tree root, the stained ends fluttering in the soft breeze that blew across the forest floor. Annie gasped, moving quickly to kneel and rub the fabric between her fingers.

"Delly," she whispered. The fabric was rough, but there was no mistaking it: this was a scrap ripped from the hem of Adeline's gown, tied to mark her way.

"This is the way she went," said Martin. "Ma'am, she's been here. Maybe my Sophia's been here, too."

His desire to conflate their missing loved ones would put Adeline in the path of some terrible beast, something large enough to destroy a circus and carry multiple people away. Annie didn't say anything. She was still willing to hope that Adeline's disappearance was unrelated to the attacks on the show, but she was smart enough to know that she needed Martin, and his rifle, if she wanted to survive wandering through the woods—and more, much as she wanted to believe that she was wrong, she was becoming more and more convinced that he was right. It was too much of a coincidence, all these things going wrong on the same night.

Mr. Blackstone had spoken of disappearances in The Clearing. He had called them "rare" and said he doubted such things could be a concern for them. Annie suddenly wished that she had thought to ask him what all those disappearances had had in common. Had they all happened at night? Or after a child had gone missing in the woods?

Or after the mayor had warned them that the season was coming to an end, and that the roads would freeze over soon? Something was terribly wrong in this little town, with its surrounding bands of wilderness and shadow. Something here didn't *want* them, or wanted them for reasons other than the strength of their hearts and the effort of their hands.

Martin and Annie continued moving carefully through the trees, through the shadows that only clung, and did not struggle to impede. They found two more strips of white fabric tied to tree roots, down low, where a child would have had no trouble placing them.

There was no sign of Sophia, or of the other missing members of the circus. But there were footprints pressed into the soft ground, fully twice the length of Martin's not inconsiderable feet, and deep enough to make it plain that whoever had made them had been of substantial size. Martin said nothing when he saw those prints, only set his jaw and ground his teeth, continuing to walk deeper into the wood. Annie resisted the urge to tell him pretty lies. It would do neither of them any good to candy-coat what was coming.

If you died here tonight, my Delly, at least you died free, with the stars in your hair and the wind in your throat, she thought, and there was no comfort in the words. There was no comfort left in the world if her Adeline was gone.

They continued to walk, stepping on a normal stretch of ground. Martin gave a shout, half scream and half yelp, like he had thought better of it and tried to swallow the sound before it could be fully formed. Annie whipped around. A trap had closed on his foot, holding him fast.

The sound of a rifle hammer being cocked came from the trees in front of them.

Chapter 11

Martin, can you get your foot free?" Annie's voice was tight as a drum, vibrating with the low pulse of fear and sudden adrenaline, which rushed through her veins like flame up a fuse.

"No, ma'am," he said.

"Give me your gun."

There was a pause before he thrust the rifle toward her, stock first, the lantern light gleaming dully off the metal. She took it with a murmured "thank you" that never quite reached the stage of becoming actual words, bracing it against her midriff as she turned toward the sound from the trees up ahead. She couldn't figure out how to aim and hold her lantern at the same time, and so she gave it up as a bad job; she simply let the barrel swing where it would, trusting that there was nothing there that couldn't be improved by a bullet to the gut.

"Who's there?" she called. "Show yourself!"

No reply.

"I know you're not one of those . . . those *things*. They didn't carry weapons. Now come out!"

"If you know 'bout the things in the trees, miss, you know why I ain't in no real hurry to do that," replied a voice. It was low and gravelly, the sort of voice that didn't seem to get much use: a voice reserved for psalms on Sunday and the occasional coarse language after a toe had been stubbed or a fishhook had snagged in a finger.

Oddly, hearing that voice made Annie feel better. Her father had had that sort of voice, may God rest his soul. He had never met a word he didn't think was better off unspoken, and when he'd finally died, they'd all spent days trying to remember the last thing he'd said, so that it could grace his tombstone.

(In the end, the marble had borne his date of birth, his date of death, his name, and the word "father." Anything else would have seemed too much for a man who had defined himself through silence.)

"I must insist," she said, her own voice shaking only slightly. The rifle betrayed her nervousness. The barrel continued to swing, not quite wildly, but enough that shooting straight was an unachievable dream: she'd be lucky not to shoot herself, or Martin, in the process.

"Who are you?"

"Ma'am, I'm bleeding." Martin's voice was urgent. It took Annie a moment to realize why. Pain was bad, yes, and pain that caused bleeding was worse; it spoke to an underlying injury that could take a person out of the workforce for weeks. Martin was a circus roustabout. He'd endured worse.

But not in the woods, crawling with monsters that could, in all likelihood, pick the scent of blood out of the air and use it to track down their prey. Blood at the circus upset the oddities, sending some of them into a frenzy of hunger. That was the worst it did. Blood here, now . . .

"Did you lay this trap, sir?" she demanded of the voice from the wood. "Come release my companion at once. We are fleeing from a terrible thing, and I would rather he not be caught because you were unwilling to share a wood larger than the territory of Montana."

There was a mirthless chuckle from the trees. "Miss, I promise you, if you knew what was in these woods, you wouldn't want to share them, either. I put that trap down. I needed to be safe. How well do you know the man?"

"Ma'am," said Martin urgently.

"Well enough to know that he does not deserve the pain you're causing him," said Annie coldly. "Well enough that if you didn't have a gun, I would be helping him right now."

"You can't see me to know where to aim," said the man in the woods.

"And you can see us quite well, thanks to my lantern," said Annie. "Believe me, we're well aware of the disadvantages of our situation."

There was a crackling noise. Annie tensed, fighting to drop neither lantern nor gun. One made them a target; the other was their only ready form of defense. Without them, all would be lost. Martin was silent beside her. He must have been in excruciating pain. Somehow, he was swallowing it all down, waiting for her cue.

If we survive this, I will be a better friend to you, she thought. She would be a friend to him at all, when she never had been before. She would welcome him to her wagon for hot tea and honey at the end of a long day's ride; she would teach him to care for the oddities, preparing him for a trade with another circus, or even with their own once she had retired. Monsters were a young woman's game. One day her reflexes would fail her, and she would be short a hand and need someone else to feed the fish.

"Lift your lantern a little higher, miss; let me see you." The voice from the trees was closer now.

Swallowing pride and fear and a hundred other terrible emotions, Annie raised her lantern, bathing herself and Martin in its light. They must have seemed like something from another world, here in this wood where the trees swallowed everything but shadows. No matter how high she hoisted her lantern, she couldn't see more than a few feet ahead. Whoever was approaching them, he remained a cipher. Friend, foe, or something altogether else, it didn't matter. They'd never see him until he wanted to be seen.

"Has either of you been injured, apart from by my trap?" asked the stranger.

"No," said Annie. Her voice was ice and needles, unforgiving. She had long since stopped allowing men to make of her a showpiece. Her tolerance for such behavior had died in Deseret.

"It caught me across the leg, sir," said Martin.

The stranger paused. "But you can keep walking? You're not incapacitated?"

"Not as yet," said Martin. He left off the "sir" this time. Annie wondered if the stranger understood how thin the ice beneath him was becoming. No one's patience was eternal.

"All right." There was another crackle, and a man stepped into the light.

Annie's first impression was of ruin. His face was a wasteland of wrinkles and old scars, carved so deep into his left cheek and the left side of his forehead that he might as well have been a mountain, subject to the destructions of the weather. Somehow, whatever had made those scars had missed his eye, leaving it to peer through the desolation. Both his eyes were bright blue and sharp as razors, raking along her body and Martin's in almost the same glance. There was nothing inappropriate about the stranger's gaze: he was assessing, looking for signs that they might have lied to him.

His hair was a mass of white, spiky and thin: the hair of an old man, untended and ungroomed. He was thin, his clothing adding bulk to his spidery frame. The rifle in his hands was well over double the size of the one in hers. If this had come down to bullets, she would have lost before it had even begun.

He held up a small rust-speckled key, like something to be used in winding a child's toy. "I'm going to release your friend," he said, eyes on Annie. "Means I might hurt him a bit. Don't go blowing my head off while I'm doing you a favor."

"I will struggle to keep my feminine weakness in check," she said, voice tight.

The stranger chuckled bleakly as he knelt and reached for the trap on Martin's leg. "There's no room for feminine weakness in Oregon," he said. "Any woman who made it this far would have left any such fripperies in a more civilized land."

The tiny key in his hand went into an equally tiny slot in the side of the trap that had captured Martin's leg. There was a tinny click, and the trap came open. Martin immediately withdrew his foot, staggering back a step before he stopped to look down at the damage and hiss. Blood had soaked the leg of his pants, darkening it until it almost matched the shadows around him.

The stranger remained kneeling for a few seconds, resetting his trap and covering it with a layer of leaves, until not even the tips of the teeth showed through. Then he stood, brushed his hands against his trousers, and recovered his rifle from the tree he had leaned it up against. He moved quickly, fluidly, but with no visible sense of urgency; he knew these woods.

I have finally found a man made for Oregon, thought Annie, and said nothing.

"The two of you, follow me," he said. "I don't want you to, but I'll not have your deaths on my conscience tonight. Not before the first snowfall."

"I'm looking for my daughter," said Annie.

"I'm looking for my sweetheart," said Martin.

The stranger gave them a look full of sorrow and strange reluctance. Then he shook his head. "You won't find either of them if you go leaving a blood trail through the woods. You need to have that cleaned and wrapped. Follow me, or don't, but if you choose to go your own way, be aware that it's on your own heads." He turned and started to walk away.

Annie and Martin exchanged a silent look. Martin nodded, very slightly. Annie handed the rifle back to him and offered her arm. After a pause, he took it, leaning against her as he limped by her side.

The stranger walked quickly—almost too quickly, at times, for the injured Martin to keep pace. He stepped between trees and into patches of absolute blackness with the calm confidence of a man who knew his surroundings so well that he no longer needed to see them to know that he was going the right way. Annie did her best to keep up with him, lending more and more of her support to Martin, jollying him along to keep the stranger from slipping out of the watery light cast by their lantern.

They had gone some unknown and unknowable distance when the man stopped, looking back over his shoulder at them, and said, "The ground slopes down here. Not as bad as it does going into town, but bad enough that you should be aware."

"Thank you," said Annie, startled into courtesy.

The stranger's smile was fleeting. "A man knows his land," he said, and stepped into the next rank of trees.

The ground did slope a few feet farther on, trending gently down for five or six steps before abruptly sheering off, becoming a steep slide. Martin moaned and clutched at Annie's arm, struggling to keep his balance. She bore up under the pressure, refusing to let her discomfort show. If he let go, if he fell, she would never be able to get him back to his feet.

"We're almost there, Martin," she whispered, as close to his ear as she dared. "Buck up. Sophia needs you."

He shot her a grateful look, barely visible in the pale light of the lantern.

The ground leveled out again, so suddenly that Annie

stumbled. This time it was Martin who caught her and held her up, keeping her from falling. He offered her a smile, wan as it was, and said, "Careful, ma'am."

"Call me Annie," she said.

The trees had ended when the ground leveled: they were standing in another of those odd bowls, shallower and smaller than the one that contained The Clearing, but open all the same. The stars were cold diamonds in the sky above. The stranger was ahead of them, moving toward the black, ramshackle shape of a small house.

Annie looked at Martin again. This time, their smile was shared, the fragile bond of comrades in arms who had survived some terrible trial.

Not that the trials were over. The night was young yet, as such things went, and their loved ones were still missing. She offered her arm again. He took it, stepping closer than propriety would normally have allowed. There was nothing improper about his closeness, not here, not now; without her, he would have fallen. They were truly companions in arms, and no more.

Almost as if he had heard her thoughts, Martin murmured, "I suppose Sophia'd have some pretty pointy questions if she could see us right now."

"Mr. Blackstone might have some of the same." She started walking, tugging Martin with her toward the house.

There was an awkward pause before he asked, "Ma'am—Miss Annie—are you and the master . . . ?"

"No. But I think we'd both like to be. We've just been waiting for Delly to be old enough to have an opinion, and to understand what's being asked of her. She is always my first concern, and always will be. You'll see, when you have children of your own. They eclipse everything else, even your love for their other parent. They are the world. Mr. Blackstone is . . . well, the moon, I suppose. I love him dearly, and I believe he loves me." It was surprisingly easy to be honest under these cold, distant stars. The rest of the world was so far away that its rules didn't matter anymore. "Still, Delly must agree before I would consider remarriage."

There was also the matter of her first husband to be considered. Dr. Murphy was not, so far as she was aware, actually dead; he was still in distant Deseret, doing his work. If she had left alone, he would no doubt be married to some fresh new daughter of the faithful and utterly repudiating his runaway bride by now. But Adeline's existence changed all that. He was many things. A terrible husband; a terrible man. Terrible husbands and terrible men often thought of themselves as born fathers.

They had reached the house. Annie frowned to see that the porch was separated from the ground by four steep steps.

"Here," she said, moving Martin's grip to the rail. "I will go ahead and pull you up."

"There's no need," he protested. "Go in. I'll be there as soon as I can."

"No one else gets left behind tonight, Martin. Certainly not you." She moved to the first step, offering him her free hand. The lantern dangling in the other cast pale light over his face, illuminating his discomfort. He wanted her to run, to save herself; that much was perfectly clear.

When she did not run, he slid his hand into hers, leaning heavily, bracing himself as she tugged him, one step at a time, up onto the porch. He was panting and shaking by the time they finished the climb, his wounded leg trembling so viciously that it seemed it must fold beneath him and drop him into the dirt at any moment. Annie offered him a warm, encouraging smile and turned to the closed cabin door. Her smile faded into a frown. Why had the stranger left them outside?

She knocked. The door opened. Light spilled out, thick and bright and almost painful after the darkness of the woods. She blinked and squinted, tears springing to her eyes. The stranger stood so as to fill the entire doorway, keeping them from seeing anything beyond his shadow, and the light.

"You made it," he said, sounding surprised. Then, with a note of grudging respect, he added, "Best come in," and stepped to the side, revealing a small room.

Annie stepped inside, a limping Martin leaning heavily on her shoulder.

Inside, the cabin was a sturdy testament to the man who'd constructed it: thick pine walls, the cracks between the planks plastered with clay until they presented an absolutely solid surface; a floor and ceiling to match. The fireplace was made of rounded stones glued together with more clay, and the chimney wound upward for several feet before melding into tin, the transition occurring almost seamlessly. What furniture there was—a chair, a table, a bed—all appeared to have been made from the same wood as the cabin.

There were windows, but they were covered by thick oilcloth, trapping every scrap of light inside. Annie helped Martin to the room's single chair before turning to see the stranger lowering a canvas sheet over the closed door, blocking the cracks in the doorframe. No light would be able to escape there, either.

"Why?" she asked.

The man turned. His expression was bleak. It was easier to see him now, and she revised her estimate of his age upward: he might be as much as seventy, yet still somehow scrabbling in this forest for a living, or at least to stay alive. It was almost inconceivable, and yet there he was, still breathing, proving the truth of his existence with every movement.

"Light attracts them," he said. "It's a little miracle that you made it as far as you did with that lantern of yours. You wouldn't have, if they hadn't eaten recently. You

should feel damned lucky, and you should curse your-
selves for the fools you are."

"We don't know what 'they' are," protested Annie.

Martin didn't say anything. He made a small, pained
noise, and Annie turned to see him trying to peel the cuff
of his trousers away from the wound in his ankle. She
looked back to the stranger.

"Do you have water and a wet rag?" she asked. "I need
to clean Martin's wound before it can become infected."

"There's worse things than infection in these woods,"
the stranger said grimly. He walked across the cabin to a
shelf and began taking down objects, tucking them under his arm. "You shouldn't have come here. That was
your first mistake."

"To the wood?" asked Annie.

"To The Clearing," said the stranger. He walked
back to her, dropping a small pot of salve, a bundle of
rags, and a clean stick on the table next to Martin's
chair. "You'd have done better to steer clear of Oregon
entirely. This isn't a safe place to be when the winter's
coming on."

"It's mid-autumn," said Annie stiffly. She knelt next to
Martin, slapping his hands away from the cuff of his
trousers. He withdrew with a silent gratitude that she recognized all too well from her attempts to tend to Adeline's various small wounds and bruises. There was
something comforting about knowing that the mending
was in someone else's hands. "If this is when the winter
comes on here, you should all move to kinder climes."

"There are no kinder climes. There are only different
forms of cruelty."

Privately, Annie agreed. Aloud, she said, "The water, if
you please. I need to flush these wounds. Why are you
setting such vicious traps in the middle of the wood?"

"Why does anyone set traps? There are things in the
trees I'd rather not have roaming free, either because

they're a meal for me or because they would make a meal *of* me, given the chance. I check my traps in the morning, when the sun is in the sky and I have the best chance of safety. Sometimes they feed me for the day. Other times they tell me that they've kept me safe."

"How does a trap tell you anything?"

"Sometimes a trap contains a foot," he said brusquely, walking back to her and depositing a bowl of water on the table nearest to her hand. "You shouldn't have come here. There's no good to be found in these trees, and the ill that waits for travelers is so great as to render all benefit moot."

Annie looked at him for a moment, aghast. Then, with a shake of her head, she turned her attention to Martin's leg.

The trap had bitten into his flesh just above the ankle, breaking the skin in a nasty circle all the way around his leg. The deepest of the punctures appeared to be well over an inch, and wide enough for her to slip her finger inside, had she desired to do so. She lifted down the bowl of water, wetted the cloth, and began gingerly dabbing each of the punctures, washing away blood and dirt. It was an action complicated by the fact that wiping the wounds agitated them, causing them to begin bleeding anew.

Martin hissed but did not object. He had been with the circus long enough to have seen wounds go septic when they were not cleaned immediately, crippling or even killing those unfortunate enough to have been injured. A little discomfort now would be justified if it resulted in his continued survival.

"How often do you clean your traps, sir?" Annie asked. "The light was poor in the woods. I was unable to tell whether I would be fighting rust, in addition to everything else."

"Weekly," he said. "They're oiled and sharpened. The

damage will be greater than if the tines had been blunted, but there should be no rust."

"Cold comfort," said Annie, and returned to her work. She could feel the stranger watching her, his eyes cold on the back of her neck. Belatedly, it occurred to her that she should have offered her name, and Martin's, and inquired after his. Her manners had suffered greatly since going into the woods. And why shouldn't they? Everything else had suffered greatly since she had gone into the woods. Her manners were simply one more consequence of her choices.

Martin closed his eyes as she cleaned the wounds and salved them liberally with the stuff from the small pot, which was viscous and smelled of tallow and boneset. Finally, she tied a length of cloth around his ankle and stood, drying her hands on her skirt.

"You won't be walking on that for a day or so, I'm afraid," she said, with genuine regret in her voice. "The wounds will need time to scab over, and exerting yourself too much will cause them to begin bleeding again. That raises your risk of infection. I'd rather have you stay put and keep your leg, if it's all the same to you."

"It's not all the same to Sophia," he said, looking at her solemnly. "I'm sorry, Miss Annie, but I can't let you go looking for my girl by yourself, and you need someone with you in those woods, now that your cat's gone."

Annie considered arguing, or pointing out that she had gone into the woods by herself once already, and come out alive. She did neither. More and more, it was becoming clear that her survival thus far had been a matter of chance and circumstance, rather than any particular skill. There were monsters in those trees. Anyone who walked there alone would be in danger.

"Neither of you is going out there before sunrise," the stranger said gruffly. "It's not safe."

Annie and Martin turned to look at him, once more

united in their disbelief. It was Annie who found her voice first.

"I beg your pardon, sir, but who are you to forbid either of us anything?" she asked. "You have been kind enough to allow us a place to treat the wounds which *you* dealt, with your careless trapping, and for that, we thank you. You are not my husband, or Martin's father, or any other form of authority that we should obey. You are a man. You do not control these woods."

To her surprise, the man chuckled darkly. "No man controls these woods. That's the trouble, miss: no man has *ever* controlled these woods. The things that walk here are beyond man's control and have no interest in our petty laws or manners. You should run."

"Run?" asked Annie. "Run where? The trees close in on all sides. If it's the woods I need to fear, my fate is sealed."

"Run until Oregon is only a memory," said the stranger grimly. "It's not the woods you should fear. It's the things that walk in their shade. For those things are hungry beyond all measure, and they can never, never be satisfied."

Chapter 12

"My name is Hal, and until some fifteen years ago, I lived in The Clearing," said the stranger. There was no second chair in his tiny cabin; instead, he moved to stand by the fire, gesturing for Annie to be seated on the bed.

It seemed improper, sitting on a strange man's bed, but she was tired from the passage through the wood, and she knew Martin would not judge her. She sat gingerly on the edge of the pine-stuffed mattress, the smell of the woods puffing up and surrounding her. Even here, the trees made their presence known.

"My family and I had come to settle in Oregon looking for a new life—a better life, if there's such a thing to be found in this world, where it seems like God is looking to kick a man in the teeth as soon as look at him. We had started our married lives in Montana, where a fever had claimed our two elder children, leaving us haunted by ghosts we could never truly repudiate, for fear that they would leave us. My wife begged me to find us something else, something better, or at least something different enough as to make the world seem new again. Brighter. Our Poppy was still little more than a babe in arms. She deserved something more than to grow up in the graveyard." Hal chuckled mirthlessly. "If only I had guessed at the future. I would have told my wife that our daughter was lucky to have a home with history, and raised her in the shadow of her older brothers' graves, and seen her to her wedding day."

"I'm sorry for your loss, sir," said Annie.

"Everyone's lost someone here," said Hal. "We traveled weeks, going from caravan to caravan, wagon train to wagon train, buying, begging, and bartering our way from group to group, until we heard tell of an expedition heading into Oregon. Everything was green there, they said; no more desert wastes, no more rattlesnakes or pit wasps, no more taste of ghost rock in the air. Everything grew. They spoke of a bright and verdant land, and we were so enthralled by their stories that we never stopped to ask ourselves how such a paradise could exist in this world. We spent our last few dollars buying ourselves a place in that train, and we rode with them out of the desert, into the green glory of the West."

Annie said nothing. Neither did Martin. They were listening now, caught up in the story of a man and his family. There was no question of a happy ending. Even had the stranger been bright of eye and sunny of disposition, no one whose family was living happily in town would be tucking himself away in a cabin in the woods. It did not fit with the world as either of them understood it. There was no way it could be so.

"The Clearing was a new town then, smaller than it is even now—but not as small as it should have been, to accommodate the number of us who came in on that wagon train. That should have been the first clue that something was wrong. Too many houses sat empty, waiting to receive us. For each of them there was a story, something sad and believable. We heard tales of sickness, of accidents in the wood, of natural death from old age or in childbirth. Even then, we might have questioned them more, but Poppy had fallen in love with our new home the moment she saw it. To be a father, to see my child so overjoyed with the prospect of her new life in a new place . . . it warmed my heart. It stopped my senses. I told my wife that we were finally home, and she dutifully agreed with me. To this day, I don't know whether she shared my initial misgivings. I never asked her. Time ran out before I could."

Silence fell in the cabin, broken only by the distant crackle of the fire. Hal took a deep breath.

"I won't lie to you: I won't tell you that it was a nightmare. We had good years in The Clearing. That's part of how this place gets you. If it were cruel from the get-go, there'd be no one for it to betray. People understand cruelty in the West. We know how to endure. We're a nation of people who know how to endure. Oregon doesn't want you to be able to endure. It's kind before it's cruel, so that you'll never see the cruelty coming."

He paused for a moment, looking pensively at nothing. He didn't even seem to realize that they were still there. The story had become its own reward, something he could only cleanse through the telling of it.

"Three years we lived there. I hunted and did repairs for others in town. I've always been good with my hands. My wife mended clothing and did the laundry for those few with money to spare, who were too good to wash their own dainties. She had a way with a needle that couldn't be bought for all the money in the world. I still wear some of the clothes she made for me, and they're as good as the day that they were finished. Our Poppy grew up fast and strong, blooming like the flower that she was, and I thought, this is good. This is what a man is meant to do. He's meant to find fertile ground and plant his roots deep, so that he can feed his family from the land. It was always about hunger. We hungered for a better life. We hungered for a future. We thought that we had managed to find those things. We thought that we were going to bloom in Oregon. We thought the promise of the golden West was finally ours to claim."

Hal's scowl was sudden. "We had never been so wrong. I failed my family by bringing them here. You've done the same to yours. If you know what's good for you, you'll leave this place come morning and never let yourself see what's become of your loved ones. You can still walk away."

"No." Martin stood, or tried to—as soon as he put his full weight on his injured leg he hissed and collapsed back into the seat. He glared at Hal. "We're not walking anywhere."

"You're certainly not," said Annie. She stood and walked to stand behind Martin, resting her hands on his shoulders. To an outsider, it would have looked like a comforting gesture, friends drawing strength from each other. In reality, she was holding him down. He lacked the strength or the leverage to push her off.

Eyes on Hal, Annie asked, "What are you dancing around telling us, sir? There's a secret here, one big enough to swallow us all whole. You need to tell us the truth."

"Funny that you should say 'swallow,'" said Hal. "Maybe you have half of it sorted out already, and simply don't want to admit what's going on. That happens, sometimes. We don't want to see what's right in front of our eyes. It's too terrible. It can't be allowed in a rational world. So we don't let it."

"Sir, if you don't stop speaking rubbish and start speaking reality, I'm going to slap you across the face," said Annie. "My daughter is out there. I have little time to waste on nonsense."

"But you're not moving toward the door," said Hal. "You know something is wrong with the woods. You want to be brave. You want to save your child. Those are admirable things. And somehow, you can't find it in yourself to move alone. You know that if you do, you won't save her. You won't even save yourself."

Annie hesitated before grimacing, a pained, poignant expression. She said nothing.

"Have either of you heard of the wendigo?" Hal paused, giving them time to respond. When neither of them did, he shook his head and said, "I thought not. There are two kinds of legend in this world. The ones we share, and the ones we hoard, keeping them close to our hearts. Not because they're good things, no—we share the cities made of gold and the fountains of eternal youth, we tell everyone we meet about the good green land over yonder, even when we'd be better off keeping it all for ourselves. And the little bad things we brag about, like they make us stronger somehow. We talk about bears and biting fish and how dangerous it is to live where we live, and we pretend that makes us strong. We pretend that makes us *better*."

His eyes were far away. "The second type of legend, that's what we conceal. We don't want anyone to know, because if they knew what it cost us to live where we do, to do what we do, they might think less of us. They might think, 'If those fools had the sense God gave the little green apples, they never would have stayed.' They might think we brought this on ourselves. And, God help us, they might not have the opportunity to suffer the way we did. We *want* other people to suffer like we did. No matter how often we say we'd rather save the world that pain, that's not true of the human heart. Misery loves company. Misery *revels* in company. Misery needs company to tell us that it's not our fault."

"Sir . . ." Annie began, and stopped. This was a man lost in his own private reverie, sinking deeper with every word he spoke. If she shook him loose, he might need to start over from the beginning. That would save them no time. That might lose enough to condemn them.

"The wendigo is hunger. The wendigo is cold. The wendigo is the starving winter given physical form and forced into the world to torment those of us who have not yet succumbed. I don't know where it came from—but perhaps there is a reason that this is such a good, green land, yet so empty. Even the natives did not settle here before The Clearing was established, and even the settlers have never come to question why the town survives when it loses half its population every other winter. It's like we're all blind until it's too late, and then, once our eyes are opened, we can no longer look away. The wendigo cannot be satiated. It will eat, and eat, and eat until everything is gone except for the wendigo itself—and when that happens, the wendigo will begin to devour its own heart, one bite at a time."

"I am well equipped for monsters, sir," said Annie. "I have served them and been served by them. Saying that there are monsters in these woods is not enough to turn my course aside."

"These monsters used to be men."

Annie stopped. So did Martin, both of them staring at Hal. The fire crackled. The wind whistled outside. All else was silence.

Hal nodded, apparently satisfied. "You begin to understand," he said. "I don't know if it's a curse or a punishment laid down by the land itself, and I don't suppose it matters; the end is the same, and I'm not one to go fight with God to make things other than they are. Maybe if I'd been a younger man when all of this had happened . . . but if it were possible to wrestle something like this back into the ground, I'd like to think someone would have done it before me. Some things are too terrible to let stand. Whatever the cause of them, if there were a cure, it would have been provided eons ago, because no one deserves this."

He stopped then, staring silently into the fire for several seconds. Annie tightened her hands on Martin's shoulders. She wanted to scream at the old man to get on with it, to finish his story and free her back into the night . . . but she also wanted him to keep talking, to keep metering out his story a drop at a time, and spare her the freedom to leave. Because the darkness was like treacle syrup, catching and clinging, and something was out there, something so terrible that it could punch through her mother's love and straight down into the raw red heart of her, where her own instinct for self-preservation still lingered, coiled and ready to strike. She didn't want to go back out there, not even for Adeline, and knowing that was almost enough to kill her.

"We've all heard the stories," Hal said finally. "A farm that got snowed in, the provisions exhausted, the roads blocked off. Someone goes out to chop wood and doesn't make it back alive, and the family finds themselves with a terrible choice in their laps. Eat the dead and make it to spring, or save their immortal souls and starve. It's funny. We forget that we're all made of meat. We want to make it like our bodies are somehow sacred, when they're just meat after we go to meet our maker. In the stories, some traveler finds the farm after the thaw, and they're all dead inside, half with their mouths stuffed full of Uncle Edgar, who would have wanted to save them. That's what we forget. We *want* to save them. If some god or devil had come to me and told me that by giving my body to my wife and daughter, they could have seen the end of the winter, I would have given it gladly. I would have been *happy* to die for the sake of their survival. Any real man would be."

"I'd die for my Sophia," said Martin.

Hal flinched a little, like he had forgotten anyone else

was there. Annie had a sudden image of him telling this story over and over again to the empty cabin, trying to exorcise his demons by talking about them.

"Winter came on hard," he said. "Worst we'd seen since we'd come to Oregon. We were hungry. Not just hungry—starving. I didn't know what hunger was until that winter. The children chewed on pine needles, drank the sap like it was mother's milk. People licked the ice off windowpanes to still the gnawing in their stomachs. My wife brewed old napkins in the kettle to make soup, and we drank every drop, not caring how old it was, or how bad it tasted. We needed to make it to spring. If we could make it to spring . . .

"Then people started dying. A body can only go so long without putting real food into itself. When the napkins and the needles ran out, well. There were a few suicides. The mayor's brother hanged himself in the stable—didn't scare the horses, though. We'd already eaten the horses. Tasted like failure. Tasted like survival. And surviving was all we were about. My Poppy, she was a skeleton draped in skin, eyes big as saucers, folding in on herself, fading away. Broke my heart every time I saw her. It was like she was eating herself from the inside out, and when she ran out of meat, she was going to begin on the bones. I couldn't stand it anymore. I couldn't watch her die. So I took my gun, and I kissed my wife, and I said I'd be back soon with food. I promised her salvation. She believed me."

Hal fell silent again. Annie shivered. The air in the cabin felt colder somehow, like he was pulling all the heat out of it with his words.

"I climbed out of the bowl. I went into the woods. The darkness there seemed solid, almost. It pooled around the trees. It *grabbed* at me. You know what it was like. There's no need to look so surprised. The darkness was like that tonight. Sometimes, when it sees something it wants, it does its best to keep them. I was a fool. Not even a young fool like your friend." Hal nodded toward Martin. "That might have forgiven some of my mistakes. I was just a fool, and as I walked through those trees, I sealed my family's fate. I fell, you see. I found this clearing when I stepped wrong and tumbled down into the trees. I didn't break my ankle, but I sprained it badly enough that I couldn't walk on it. I thought I was a dead man. Then my eyes caught a cave on the other side of the clearing. I crawled all the way, through the snow. There had been bears living there once. Lucky me, they were already gone, victims of the winter that was killing my family, but there were signs of their presence left behind, roots and nuts and other scraps from whatever constitutes a bear's larder. It wasn't enough to make me fat again. It was enough to keep body and soul together while I shivered in the back of their den for three days, waiting for the snow outside to stop, waiting for my ankle to heal enough to hold me.

"After three days, the sun rose on a clear sky. I crawled out of the den. I found my rifle in the snow. I used it as a crutch to walk myself back to The Clearing. I had a pocket full of acorns, and while I walked, I saw a rabbit run. I shot it down. It was like the winter was rewarding me for surviving the worst it could throw my way. My family would live. Not well, perhaps, but who needs living well? Living at all is blessing enough. Spring would come, and we would rebuild. Perhaps we'd go back to Montana, live under that big sky, far from the clinging dark between the trees. We'd have *choices*."

Hal's face twisted, crumpling inward on itself, becoming a mask of sorrows. "But when I got back to The Clearing, it was to find an empty house, with the door shattered outward on its hinges, like something had burst from the inside. It was to find blood on the porch steps, and no sign of my wife or daughter. They were gone, both of them, along with half the town. I thought a monster had come and carried them away."

"Wendigo," said Annie softly.

"Yes, and no." Hal turned to look at her. "It was the wendigo that had them from me: of that there is and can be no question. It was the wendigo that took them to the woods and will never give them back again."

"They killed them?" asked Martin.

Hal laughed. It was a bitter sound, as bleak as the wind that howled outside. "No. That would have been too kind. The wendigo has no form until we give it form; the wendigo has no teeth until we give it teeth. The wendigo has only hunger. It enters the hearts of men when the cold wind blows out of the mountains, and it festers there like a black seed, until we do the unthinkable and eat the flesh of our own kind. Then it bursts forth. It *changes* them. It changed my Poppy, and my sweet Marie. It made them into monsters."

"What?" The question was Annie's, but that didn't matter: it could have come from either one of them.

Hal looked at her levelly. "They were starving. I had left them, promising to return with food, and then I hadn't returned. Can they be blamed for thinking that I'd died in the woods—or worse, that I'd deserted them? That's what haunts me more than anything else. Did they do what they did believing that I'd left them behind, striking out for some better life? As if there could ever have been a better life without them."

"What did they do?" asked Martin.

"They ate human flesh, boy," said Hal. The statement seemed oddly hollow, after the way he'd talked around the point for so long: it was like he had found himself backed into a corner, unable to shy away from it anymore. "They joined in with the others, and they ate our unburied dead. My little girl with a man's arm in her hands, her teeth gone black with blood . . ." He stopped and shuddered. "They did what was forbidden, and the woods claimed their own."

Annie stared at him. "Surely not."

"You're a desert girl, aren't you? You come from someplace high and hot."

"Deseret," she admitted.

"Lots of ways to die in Deseret," said Hal. "More ways than a body really needs, if you ask me. Poison and exposure and falling and things that come up from beneath and gulp you down. It's the sort of place it's good to be *from* but not so great to *be*."

"I don't disagree," she said stiffly. "There are many reasons I left that land behind me."

"Deserts aren't kind, but they're honest about their dangers. A good, green place like this, it hides what's rotten and wrong about it. It *creeps*. It put that hunger in my girls, and when the hunger bloomed, it *took* them."

"I'm sorry," said Martin. "I don't . . . I mean, I'm not trying to . . . the way you talk about them, it's like you don't think they're dead."

"Because I know they're not," said Hal. "I've seen them. Many times. Eight feet tall, with mouths full of teeth and hands made of claws. They're huge and hulking and hairy as any beast of the field, but they're my girls. A man always knows what's his. The wendigo took them. They *are* the wendigo now, and they're never going to be human again, because they can't take back what they did, even if they had it left in their hearts to want to. But I know my Poppy's eyes, and I know the shape of my Marie's shoulders. They walk as monsters. They still walk. I still mourn them."

"Can they be returned to human form?" asked Annie. "Perhaps a cleansing, or—"

"They ate human flesh," said Hal. "They sank their teeth into the body of a man like you or I. They filled their stomachs. They satiated their human hunger and exchanged it for something that burned a thousand times brighter. There's no undoing what's been done. Maybe God could save them, but if there's anything I've learned in these last fifteen years, it's that God doesn't give a damn about Oregon. He has turned His eyes away from us and left us to our own devices."

"Then why are you still here?" asked Annie.

"Because my girls still walk these woods, awash in their own terrible hunger, and because I was the one who failed them," said Hal. "If I had been a better father—a better husband—I might have been able to save them before the ice sank its teeth into their bones. I won't fail them a second time. I'm going to find the way to kill them, and I'm going to free them from the cold torment that their lives have become."

Annie stood. "My daughter has not yet been lost," she said. "The winter isn't here yet; her belly is full. The fate that took your family has yet to steal mine, or Martin's. Our loved ones are still out there to be saved. You say you're sorry. You say you feel you failed them. Do something about it. Help us bring our people home. Will you help us?"

Hal looked at her, expression bleak. The wind howled outside. Finally, he looked back toward the fire, and he sighed.

"All right," he said. "If you insist on going out there, I'll go with you. But I won't give you false hope. They are likely already gone."

"If they are, that's on us," said Annie. "We'll save them all the same."

Hal nodded, and said nothing, and the wind howled on.

Chapter 13

Martin couldn't walk.

It wasn't that he didn't want to: the spirit was more than willing, but the flesh, as has so often been the trouble with man, was weak. He could stand for short periods, as long as he braced himself against the table or had something to lean upon, but taking even so much as a step meant dealing with excruciating pain and the risk of bleeding. Hal watched from the far side of the cabin as Annie eased Martin back into his chair for the third time.

"He can't come with us," he said. "You *know* he can't come with us. The smell of his wounds will attract the wendigo before we've made it back to the trees."

"It didn't attract the wendigo before, and it's not as if he injured himself," she snapped. "You were the one setting mantraps in the damned woods, like they're your own private hunting ground. Did you even consider that you could catch an innocent?"

"A man has a right to defend himself," said Hal.

"Sir—Miss Annie—please, stop," said Martin. They turned to look at him. The young roustabout was leaning back in his chair, face pale from the attempt to walk. He shook his head. "He's right, ma'am. I can't walk yet. Maybe come morning, when the scabs have set, but for right now? Maybe if I were being chased, I could run. Anything short of that, I'd just be slowing you down. Sophia doesn't deserve that. Your Adeline doesn't deserve that. I'll stay here and keep the fire going. That much I can do."

"I hate the thought of leaving you alone," Annie said reluctantly. "Are you sure . . . ?"

"Yes, ma'am." Martin nodded firmly. "Getting me back to the circus, well. That's up one hill, and through a forest filled with monsters and such, and then down another hill to something that might well still be burning. Staying here seems the better choice for everyone, don't you think?"

"You are a brave boy," said Annie. Impulsively, she leaned in and kissed his forehead, leaving him scarlet cheeked and staring when she straightened up again. "We'll find your Sophia, and we'll bring her back to you."

"Don't make promises you can't keep, girl," Hal said brusquely. "Are you ready?"

No, thought Annie, who suspected that she might never be ready to go back out into that night, where the darkness crept and crawled like a living thing. She retrieved her lantern from the table and turned to face the woodsman, who was standing by the door, impatience sketched into every line of him.

"I was waiting for you," she said.

He snorted, faint amusement in his eyes—he knew that she was lying—and opened the door. Darkness seemed to flood into the cabin, going against the normal laws of light and shadow; it beat back the glow of Annie's lantern and even the brighter, fiercer shine of the fire, pooling on the floor in great puddles of gray. Hal stepped out.

After one glance back at Martin, Annie followed.

The stars gleamed overhead, cold and cruel and immutable. They had seen worse nights than this, and worse days; they had seen everything that Oregon had to offer, and while they might not judge, they also did not forgive.

The moon was less understanding. It seemed to leer

down on them, its light less a beacon and more a signal
flare to whatever might be hunting through the trees,
looking for manflesh to devour. Hal scowled at the moon
before turning his attention on Annie's lantern.

"The light's going to attract all manner of damned
thing," he said.

"I can't see without it," she replied.

"I'm not asking you to. It took me years to learn to
navigate these trees without a light to hand. If not for the
fact that I can still fill my belly on rabbit and roots, I'd
think I was half a wendigo myself." His smile was bitter,
wry, the twisted mouth of a man who had nothing left
to serve as refuge from his life. "I just want you to be
warned. You walk these woods lit up like that, you're
going to lure a lot more than moths to come and pay attention to your passage."

"That's a risk I'll have to take."

"That's a risk I'm glad you're taking." Hal descended
the narrow porch steps, leaving Annie with no choice but
to follow him if she wanted to know where the traps
were. He navigated the clearing like a dancer, stepping
over one patch of ground, treading with absolute confidence upon the next.

Annie frowned as she did her best to emulate him. "I'm
afraid I miss your meaning, sir."

"If you attract the wendigo, there's a chance you'll attract my Poppy or my Marie," he said, pausing at the
edge of the trees, giving her time to catch up with him.
"Fifteen years I've been seeking to lure them close enough
to let me grant them peace. Fifteen years they've been
avoiding me. I don't know whether wendigo remember
who they were before the hunger took them. They might
be nothing more than beasts who used to be good, honest men and women, led astray by winter. But I think . . ."

He hesitated, long enough for Annie to wonder
whether the seemingly limitless well of words that had

opened when he'd found her and Martin wandering in his woods had finally run out. She'd met his like before, men who had resigned themselves to silence while making no pledges to that effect. They could talk the stars out of the sky, once they realized that someone in the world was willing to listen. Dangerous men, every one of them. It took something to shock a tongue to silence without a vow of same to keep it lying fallow.

Finally, he said, "I think they know. What they are; what's become of them; what they've lost. I think they know, and that they mourn, in their own cold ways, because anything that has understanding of itself has understanding of right and wrong. They damned themselves in an instant. They can never be redeemed in this world. I think they avoid me because they are ashamed. True evil can't exist without knowing what it is to be ashamed."

Annie said nothing. There seemed to be nothing she could say. Instead, she followed the old man into the woods and waited for the wendigo.

The darkness here was the more familiar sort, the kind of shadow she had grown up with and was long accustomed to. If it still clung a bit more closely than was the norm, well, she had almost come to expect that in her short time in Oregon. This was not a state that yielded easily to the light.

Hal moved through the woods like he had been born to them, slipping easily through the space between trees, seemingly confident that she could keep up, despite her ignorance of the terrain. The silence fell into an easy rhythm, him leading, her following, neither one of them speaking, for fear that any intentional noise might bring the night down on their heads. The lantern was dim enough that Annie gave serious thought to throwing it aside, letting it light some other path. The wendigo might go after the light and leave her alone, if they thought that she was just another deer.

Another deer . . . "There was a man before," she said abruptly, and flinched away from the sound of her own voice, which seemed to expand into a shout in the confined space beneath the trees.

Hal stopped walking. His shoulders tensed. He did not turn. "What man?" he asked.

"It was another clearing, like the one Martin and I were in when we met you. Not the same one." She couldn't imagine that it had been the same one. Even as dark as it was, there was no way she could have missed the poor man's body if she'd come so close to it a second time.

(The alternative—that it *had* been the same clearing, but that the wendigo had come and carted him away while she'd been making her return trip to the circus—was not worth consideration. If they manipulated these woods so easily, first setting and then concealing the site of a slaughter, then there was no point in continuing their quest. Humanity had already lost the day, and would soon lose the night as well.)

"Go on," said Hal.

"There was a dead man lying in the open, with his . . . his chest cracked open like an eggshell. I didn't know him, either from the circus I travel with or from the town."

"And have you been in town long enough to know every soul who lives there?"

Annie didn't answer.

"I thought not. Let me tell you something about life in The Clearing, miss, something I wish had been said to me when I was young and innocent and still believed that Oregon was capable of kindness: it's never fair." Hal started walking again, forcing Annie to follow or be left behind. "The mayor's not a wendigo—hard to run a settlement when you're seven feet tall and made of starvation—but he might as well be. He's a tick, feeding on the blood of those around him."

"I don't understand."

"No? The first year in a new land, it's understandable that there might not be enough. No one's had time to learn the land. Crops won't grow right. Nothing seems to go the way it did back in Montana, or Maine, or whatever territory you're from. Livestock is still struggling to get established. It's reasonable, expected even, that you'll lose half your people in your first winter. It's almost suspect when you don't."

Annie, who had grown up hearing the stories of the settlement of Salt Lake, and the bodies her paradise had been built atop, said nothing.

"First few years, it's still understandable. A new settlement is an uneasy thing. You're always teetering on the edge of 'enough.' Is there enough grain to see you through the winter? Is there enough space to keep your people from going stir-crazy and tearing each other to pieces during the first big freeze? Is there, God help you, enough open land behind the church to bury the bodies properly, before the starving start to have the sort of thoughts that led to our current situation? It's so damned *delicate* when it's all new like that. It's delicate, and it's difficult, and it falls apart if you give it half a chance."

"A circus is very similar," said Annie.

Hal snorted. "A circus moves. That's part of what makes it a circus. If you keep losing people, it's because you never get the chance to know the land. You're always at the mercy of the towns around you, and half of *them* will be new, or teetering, or already falling. A settlement should find its feet at some point. It should learn to be dependable. But The Clearing never has."

"Never?"

Hal stepped over a protruding root, motioning for her to do the same, and shook his head. "Never. The mayor, he says every year that this year will be the year that things turn around, and to his credit, sometimes he keeps his word—they've had good years down there. Good harvests. Times when things went the way they were expected to. Marriages and babies and all the other things that come with being a healthy place."

"But?"

"But they don't outweigh the bad years, and they don't outbalance the accidents. The healthy hunters who should be able to bring in enough to see them through the winter, who somehow wander into the wrong patch of wood and wind up split stem to stern. The blighted fields, the spoiled provisions. And you know who thrives throughout it all?"

"The mayor," guessed Annie.

"And his family. They thrive while everything around them withers. They're not wendigo. Doesn't mean they don't have something of the wendigo's hunger in them, or that they wouldn't eat your heart if they thought they could get away with it and still maintain their pretty faces." Hal spat off to the side, like he was warding himself against the evil eye. "Bastards. Every damn one of them."

Annie shivered, looking around. The trees closed in on all sides of them, and she realized, with some dismay, that she had no idea where they were. They could have been walking back toward town, or heading in a circle, or any number of other terrible things. She was alone in the woods with a strange, armed man, in the middle of the night, and she had a dreadful suspicion that if she were to scream, only the wendigo—assuming the wendigo were real and not the ravings of a madman—would be close enough to hear.

"Where are we going?" she asked gingerly.

"I suspected you wouldn't believe me forever," said Hal. "I know how I sound. I know how little proof I offered you. A man living on his own in the middle of nowhere, well. There can be reasons for that, and not many of them are likely to be good ones. So I brought you here to show you, once and for all, that I'm no liar. Come."

He motioned her forward. Lacking any other options, Annie followed.

The trees thinned around them. The trees had been thinning for some time, she realized; it was only the darkness that made them seem so uniform and unrelenting. Carefully, they picked their way out of the wood and into a stretch of clear land. The curdled moon glared down, hateful as ever.

Hal continued to walk. Annie continued to follow. When he stopped, so did she, and raised her lantern to behold another bowl like the one that contained The Clearing, or his cabin. Such bowls seemed to be a feature of the local landscape, like the sandstone hills of Deseret.

Her light was not enough to drop more than a few feet below the lip of the bowl. Hal bent, picking up a dry branch. He held it out to the lantern, motioning for her to open the glass. She did, and he slipped the end of the branch inside. It must have been in the open for quite some time; the pitch caught fire with a crackle, filling the air with the smell of smoke and burning pine. It was pleasant after the living, hostile scent of the woods.

"Look," said Hal, and hurled the branch, end over end, across the bowl. It flew in a long arc, burning as it went, until it fell like a star, illuminating everything around it.

The township it revealed might have been the one she'd walked away from, had anything lived there, or had there been a circus camped at the edge of the bowl. But there was nothing, only buildings sliding into decay and open ground grown choked with weeds. Annie gasped.

"A ghost town?" she whispered.

Hal nodded, expression grim. "They called it 'The Clearing' once, before the mayor misjudged how many people they could afford to lose in a single winter. According to the town records, the official maps of the area, this place never existed. Come with me."

He offered her his hand. After a moment's frozen hesitation, Annie took it.

Hal knew the route into the ghost town as well as he had known his way through the woods. He walked confidently, never hesitating or looking back, and Annie felt compelled to follow him the same way, setting her feet where his had been only a second before, letting him lead her down, down, down into the darkness. The shadows here were the ordinary kind, but steeped with a strange melancholy, like they understood the sacrifices that had been made in their name. She shivered, suddenly wishing that she had brought a second coat with her when she ran from the circus. Nathanial's, perhaps.

Oh, Nathanial, will I ever see you again? she thought, and rather suspected that the answer would be a short and simple "no." It hurt to contemplate. Not as much as it hurt to think that she might never find her daughter, but that was what made it a safe question to ask in the silence behind her eyes. Mr. Blackstone—Nathanial—however much she might love him, and however much she suspected she might have been able to allow herself to love him, had she been given time and the opportunity to do so, was expendable in the end. Her mother's heart could afford to let him go. She could never do the same for Adeline.

Delly was everything she had. No one who was not a parent could understand how deep that little girl's roots had sunk into her heart. If she lost her, there would be no more Annie. There would be nothing but a husk that walked like a woman. She might as well follow her captive corn stalker out into the fields and let it plant a scarecrow in her heart.

Annie shuddered, trying to clear away the unpleasant

thoughts. When she lifted her head, she found Hal looking at her sympathetically.

"It's easy to haunt yourself in this place," he said. "Don't need no ghosts when you're standing inside one. Remember that whatever you left up above is still there, waiting for you to come and find it. Nothing you think you see here is true."

"If this isn't true, why did you bring me here?"

"Because it's close enough to show you the things you'll need to understand," said Hal. "Come with me." As before, he walked, and as before, she followed him. She had followed this far. At this point, it truly felt as if there was nothing else that she could do.

The ghost town looked so similar to the living town of The Clearing that every step closer to its outlying buildings made a scream rise higher in Annie's throat, choking her. How had they been able to conceal this? How had the survivors of whatever tragedy had come here been able to turn their backs and walk away, as if abandoning an entire settlement was *nothing*?

She had seen ghost towns before. Some were sad things, dandelion fluff buildings and broken streets, starved to death by a change of fortune, drying slowly in the desert heat. They were a litany of dead wells and terrible illnesses, and even the circus orphans wouldn't loot their rickety old structures for fear of waking the ghosts that haunted them. Others were terrifying in subtle ways, their walls riddled with bullets, their wells reeking with bodies that had never been laid to rest. Towns could die in an instant or over the course of years. Much like a person, she supposed. There were a million ways to die, if you weren't careful.

This town, though . . .

This town hadn't died of natural causes, or even been murdered. This town had been *sacrificed,* its throat slit by its own people in the name of placating some unspeakable and unspoken divinity. Walking through its streets was like stepping onto unholy ground. Her skin shivered until it felt as if it would fly off her body entirely, slithering away and becoming its own creature. The shadows were too dark. They were thin as normal shadows, but Annie half-thought that was only so they could creep up on a body without being seen until it was too late.

Glass still glittered in some of the windows of the houses around them. Not much—maybe every other pane—but still enough to tell her that they had left quickly, not taking any more than they could carry, and had never returned. Glass was precious. Here in the West, glass was a sign of comfort and civilization, a marker of wealth that few could afford to obtain, much less afford to leave behind. Glass meant having *enough,* not just to survive, but to put on airs again. Putting on airs was important. Having a Sunday dress, or a pot of white sugar, or a glass window, it meant that there was *enough*.

And these people had walked away, and they had left their glass windows behind.

"What happened here?" she asked. She didn't mean to whisper, but she did so all the same, the darkness seeming to swallow her voice, until there was almost nothing left of it. Even the darkness here was hungry.

Hungry: yes. That was it. The woods, the shadows, even that damned curdled moon, they were all *hungry* in a way that she hadn't been able to put her finger on until she'd heard her voice gulped down by the quiet. They wanted something she couldn't give them, because if she started to give, they would take, and they wouldn't stop taking until there was nothing left of her. This was a place with no concept of *enough*. Glass meant nothing here. The idea it defined was impossible.

"The stores ran out." Hal walked beside her. He looked . . . resigned, like the hungry shadows had devoured so much of him that they had no power over what remained. He was a shadow himself, of the man he'd been before. "The mayor said that someone must have been stealing, that there had been enough when the winter started, and if we were running out in mid-January, it had to be because someone had decided that their family deserved to live in comfort while everyone else suffered. That was bullshit, pardon my French, ma'am, and everyone knew it. No one in the town was comfortable except for the mayor himself, him and his damned family."

Annie, who had seen a great deal of bullshit lying by the side of the road during her time with the circus—and had, yes, seen her share of damnation as well—said nothing. Hal needed little prompting to start his stories. She was already coming to understand that it was best if she just let him go. She would learn what she needed to know, and that knowledge would lead her to Adeline.

If she's still alive, whispered the voice of the hungry shadows all around her, and she shuddered, and was silent.

"Their boy was fat," said Hal in a reflective tone, like he couldn't believe the words. "Did I tell you that already? Cutest little thing you ever saw, not three years old and fat as a Christmas goose. He didn't bruise when he fell down, just skinned up his palms and bounced right back to his feet. My Poppy, you could count her ribs through her dress, and she had every scrap that we could give her, and there's the mayor, pointing fingers, saying that *someone* in town was stealing from the rest of us, *someone* in town was acting against the greater good. It wasn't the boy's fault. Children should be fat. That's what gets them through the winter. But every time I saw him running, laughing, all bundled up in good furs and with his belly like a promise of seeing the spring, I near wanted to split his skull. I'd always known envy. A man can't live in a hard world and not know envy once in a while, however much he might wish otherwise. I'd never known what it was to covet before."

The buildings around them were changing as they walked, growing green with moss and speckled with the leering, poisonous caps of toadstools. Annie saw colors she would have sworn Nature didn't understand, and she shivered again.

"Where are you taking me?" she asked. Surely not to see the mayor's son: she'd seen him already, back in The Clearing, a strapping boy almost Martin's age. He'd outgrown his boyish fatness and found a stout, well-fed handsomeness in his adulthood.

"The same place a man always takes a woman," said Hal. His smile was a white slash in the night. "I'm taking you to church."

Interlude the Second

Helen looked up sharply at the sound of a closing door. It was a whisper, a murmur, barely standing out against the rest of the household noise, but it made the skin on her breasts and belly tighten all the same, pulling her upright, into the polished, perfect posture that Dr. Murphy expected from all the servants in his employ. It was an honor to work in the home of such a great man. It was a privilege to serve his every want and whim. It was for the sake of her family, who benefited from her position, and from the status of having a daughter embedded in the household of one of Hellstromme's best men. Why, without her holding her position, they would all have been destitute years ago, what with Papa's debts—shameful things that they were—and Mama's poor choices of associate.

There were those who lived in Junkyard and said that everyone who walked the gilded streets of the Holy City proper lived charmed lives, that if they had just been fortunate enough to have been born into the life of the Saved and not been sinners from the start, they would never have wanted for anything. Helen supposed that was true enough, in its way. The troubles that she had lain out before her were nothing compared to starvation and damnation and the illnesses that seemed to plague those who lived in the shadow of the smokestacks. She was blessed with good fortune and she was blessed in the eyes of the Lord, and those were two very different things that went by the same name, as so many things in this world did. She could not complain about her lot in life. It would have been shameful to do so.

But sometimes, she wished that it were not so difficult to be saved.

Dr. Murphy was a great man. A refined man, delicate and mannerly. He considered himself refined in all ways, among them the art of moving quietly through his own home, that he might hear the smooth tick and turn of the clocks on the walls, or the hum of the fine steam-powered devices he built in his spare time and set as curiosities on shelves and bureaus. Helen agreed heartily whenever he asked if he had startled her, but the truth was, that small lie was one she had decided God would forgive her. It was rude to scream in the presence of the man who paid her, and so when she heard him approach the kitchen doorway, she continued chopping potatoes for the soup, giving no sign that she knew he was there.

"Helen," said Dr. Murphy. There was a coiled smugness in his pronunciation of her name, an almost shameful pride. He was *proud* of himself for sneaking up on her like a common thief.

If what he wanted was a performance, she would grant it to him, if only for the sake of keeping the peace. She squeaked and jumped, dropping the knife she had been using. It clattered harmlessly on the cutting board. Had she been genuinely surprised, she might have cut herself, or dropped the knife on the floor, where she would have risked scratching the wood. Dr. Murphy couldn't stand to have his house in disrepair. She would have been on her hands and knees for days, sanding out the scratch as penance for her disrespect.

No. Lying was the right choice here. Lying allowed her to do as her employer wished, without causing extra work for herself, extra work that would take her away from the essential need to serve him.

"Sir!" She pressed a hand to her chest, as if to slow her beating heart. "I'm sorry, sir. I didn't hear you."

"Is her lunch prepared?" He nodded toward the counter, where a small plate waited, already prepared with slices of cheese, and apple, and cold boiled chicken. No salt or spices, alas. Only good, plain, easily digested fare. The poor lamb. Some days she could have only oatmeal, or cold boiled potatoes, and those were the worst of all.

"I was going to take it up in a few minutes, sir," said Helen. "I was finishing slicing her apples."

"I'll take it to her."

"Sir?" Helen caught herself before she could ask anything else. If he wanted her to understand, he would explain.

Working in the house of a great man like Dr. Murphy had seemed like such an honor when the job was offered to her, and maybe it was; maybe she was a sinner, harboring thoughts like the ones she sometimes had. All men were sinners, that was what the Elders said, and women were weaker than men—why, look at what Miss Grace had done, and she the most pampered and privileged woman in all the world! It was only natural that Helen might find herself harboring thoughts that were less than good, less than gracious, less than worthy of her station. Yes. Only natural.

"I will be taking her lunch to her today," said Dr. Murphy. His tone was patient, but there was a glitter in his eye that warned her of thin ice beneath her feet: she was trying his nerves. "Your services will not be required."

"Yes, sir," said Helen, and bobbed a quick curtsey. She might harbor improper thoughts, but no one would ever accuse her of being a fool. She knew when to fall into line. "Shall I finish the apples?"

"You might as well; we need to tempt her," he said. "When I took her measures this morning, she was listless. I doubt she'll have much of an appetite."

Helen had her own opinions about that as well. It was impossible not to, really, and she didn't feel bad about them. Still, she kept her peace, only nodding and saying, "Yes, sir."

"Thank you, Helen," he said. "Whatever would we do without you?" His tone was still patient, still perfectly appropriate, and yet it was impossible not to hear the warning that lurked behind it. Her place in this household, as an unmarried woman who had neither aspirations toward nor the possibility of becoming the master's wife, was a low one. She forgot that at her peril.

"I really don't know, sir," she lied. He would do as he had always done: he would forget her name inside the week. He would open his doors to another daughter of a middling-well-off family, one who needed a job that was neither beneath her nor too good for her, and someone else would slice the apples, and if she were lucky, she would be sent home.

If she were unlucky . . .

She was not the first to hold her position, only the longest-lasting. Dr. Murphy was a great man. Discontinuity upset him, distracted from his work. She kept her job in part because he did not wish the fuss and bother of replacing her, and in part because she was clever enough to know that she could be replaced. From what the other members of the household had said, those who were dismissed were rarely seen again in the Holy City, although their families were well compensated for their loss. It wasn't that the doctor was a *bad* man, no, not in the least. It was simply that he had important work to protect, and it wouldn't do to have loose-tongued former employees spilling his secrets to anyone who flattered their egos.

"The apples, Helen," he said, and there was a gentleness in his tone that spoke to an understanding of her thoughts—what the thoughts of any woman in her position would have been, really.

"Right away, sir," she said, and turned back to the cutting board, already reaching for the knife.

Apples were often hard to come by in Deseret. The soil didn't offer them up easily, and the amount of water it could take to tend a single tree—not even to bring it to fruit—was more than even the richest and most holy of citizens could easily afford. They had to be imported at great expense from the heathen territories to the East, where people who knew nothing of godliness toiled in orchards that sounded something like Eden in their greatness and their greenness. Helen hadn't even tasted an apple before she'd come to Dr. Murphy's service. When she'd been a girl, her parents had said that there was no need to bring a symbol of temptation into their home, and that had been good enough to explain their lack.

(It still was, if she were being perfectly honest. Why would anyone want to cultivate a taste for a fruit that symbolized the weakness of woman and the uncleanliness of man? Better to eat prickly pears and good blackberries, and leave the apples to the indolent and the Easterners, who knew no struggle, and no redemption.)

The knife sliced through the crisp white flesh with ease, sending up a sweet, acidic perfume. Helen arrayed the last of the apple slices on the plate before picking up the tray and turning to offer it to Dr. Murphy.

He was standing right behind her. This time, her gasp was not feigned, and her flinch was almost enough to knock the tray out of her hands. Dr. Murphy smiled as he took it from her.

"Thank you, Helen," he said. "I will not need you for the rest of the afternoon. If you have any personal business, this would be a good time to attend to it."

"Yes, sir," she said, and bobbed a curtsey. He was already walking away by the time she straightened. Perhaps that was for the best. She sagged against the counter, heart pounding, and waited for the fear to pass her by.

Dr. Murphy didn't look back. He walked out of the kitchen and toward the stairs, head held high, the picture of a man who had never been afraid of anything in his life—or perhaps the picture of a man who had been so afraid, for so long, that he no longer knew how to show it. Fear was weakness in his world, as sure as it was in the world outside the Holy City, and sometimes the only solution was to freeze it out.

The carpet was soft beneath his feet, plush and yielding. Sometimes he wished it were socially acceptable to have hardwood floors, like the ones he'd grown up with, the ones he still insisted on in the kitchen and the washrooms. They were easier to clean, and they didn't feel so much like walking on cobwebs. He'd stepped in a terrantula's burrow when he was a boy, putting his foot clean through the crust of earth that covered it and into the spongy mass within. The beast that had spun the web had been gone or dead, but that hadn't stopped the terror in the moments when he'd been trapped, before his older brother had doubled back and yanked him free. Carpet was too much like that long-gone burrow, and he hated it.

(Sadly, he worked for Hellstromme, and a certain amount of "keeping up appearances" was required, even if his doors rarely opened to anyone outside of his household. The master wanted people to believe that all his scientists were good, moral, upstanding men of virtue. Why that meant carpet was less than clear, but Michael had never been a man to argue with those he chose to follow.)

The stairs were carpeted as well, but more thinly, in a runner rug patterned with roses. It had been Grace's choice. She'd fallen in love with the design the moment she'd seen it, declaring it a garden for the eyes, and when she'd told him that she had to have it, well, he'd done his duty as a husband and obliged her, hadn't he? Everything she'd told him she wanted, she'd had, as soon as she'd proven herself deserving. He had never left her wanting. But she had left him, running out the door like a frightened hare as soon as she realized that their life together would be more than dinner parties and dresses. He had needed more from a wife than a pretty ornament for his parlor, and Grace had balked.

The door at the top of the stairs was locked. Helen had a key, as did Josiah, his doorman. Michael would have been more comfortable if only he had been able to open that door, but he understood the necessity of equipping his household. If there were an emergency—if, God forbid, the house caught fire or something happened to him while he was away—someone would need to be able to get into the second floor and tend to what waited there. He could be a careful jailer. He could not be an absolute one.

A twist of his key and the lock was open, the door swinging wide to reveal a meticulously clean hallway. The carpet that dominated downstairs was here as well, but covered in a sheet of pressed canvas, giving it almost the consistency of honest wood. It was necessary, to keep the dust down. The curtains that blocked the windows were equally necessary. Some of his medicines reacted poorly to light and needed to be kept in a cool, dry place. Coolness had been the greatest challenge: Deseret was a desert territory, and the sun held dominion over all. Half of his time over these last eight years had been spent in devising more and more clever mechanisms for steam-powered cooling engines. He had them down to the size of a gold bar, tiny and cunning and capable of keeping the house no warmer than a spring afternoon. The trick was proper calibration of the balance of ghost rock and mercury at the engine's heart, measuring it out in specks no bigger than a grain of sand. The sun held no more dominion here.

The door at the end of the hall was open, barely more than a crack. Michael stood a little straighter, put a smile onto his face, and proceeded toward it, stopping just outside.

"My, my, my," he said. "It looks as if Helen has failed to do her job once more, leaving this door open. I shall have to let her go."

There: a sound, distant and faint, but distinct all the same. The enraged squeal of a child hearing her misdeeds blamed on someone else.

"Oh, my," he said. "Was it not Helen? Was it, perhaps—you?" He thrust the door grandly open on the last word, revealing the room beyond.

It was a confection of lace and silk and gauzy netting, all of it white, all of it cleaned daily by Helen, who rotated the draperies according to a set schedule, removing anything that looked even slightly dusty, or dingy, or otherwise imperfect. It was less vanity than it was necessity: there was no way to keep the room truly sterile, not exposed to the rest of the house as it was. All the doctors he'd consulted had told him the same thing, saying that infection came from allowing too much mess near someone who was already ill. He might not be able to stop the infections entirely, but he could create an environment in which they would not thrive.

The bed was larger than a child's bed would normally have needed to be, for it was her entire world. The mattress had seen countless tea parties and slow, meandering adventures for her plush toys, which were, like the draperies, replaced on a regular basis. In the middle of it all lay a little girl, dwarfed by the size of the bed around her, and by her own frail frame, which looked utterly breakable, like the slightest touch would shatter her forever. Pillows propped her up, holding her just shy of a seated position, so that she could watch the door or, on good days, the window, where the curtains were opened only on Michael's word.

They were closed now. Electric light filled the room, pale and more forgiving than sunlight. He could almost pretend that there was color in her cheeks, which seemed pale as milk even when compared to the white-blonde of her hair. Her eyes, a brown so dark that they could look black to the casual glance, were holes drilled into her face, gazing at him out of eternity.

"Hello, Papa," she said, after a pause to catch her breath. "Where's Miss Peg?"

"Helen and I thought that it might be best for me to bring your lunch today, pet," said Michael, walking across the room and settling on the bed next to her. She shifted a hairsbreadth closer, enough that he could feel the heat coming off of her perpetually feverish frame. She was never cold. That, too, had influenced his design for the cooling machines. With her body set on consuming itself to stoke its own inner fires, it only made sense to keep the house as cool as possible. It might bring her more toward balance.

"What is it?" She sat up a little, straining to see.

"Apples, and cheese, and chicken."

"Will you eat with me?" She turned hopeful eyes toward his face, lips drawn into a practiced pout.

Michael's heart seemed to swell and shrink at the same time. Fatherhood was nothing like what he had expected it to be. Nothing, it seemed, had been, not since the day he had taken a wife. "There's not enough for both of us, poppet," he said. "I will sit with you while you eat, and we can talk about your day. Will that suffice?"

She frowned, but only a little: the true victory had already been won. "Do you *promise* not to go away until I finish?" she asked.

"Only if you promise to eat every scrap and crumb on this plate," he said.

"What if I'm not hungry?"

"Then I must conclude that my presence dampens your appetite and remove myself as the cause of the problem." He made as if to stand.

Her hand shot out with surprising speed, grasping his elbow. He stopped immediately. She could be swift—remarkably so, given how thin her limbs were, how devoid of muscle—but she was not strong, and she was so much more delicate than she seemed. If he hurt her unintentionally, he would never forgive himself.

"No, Papa, I'll eat," she said, eyes wide and pleading.

"All right," he replied, and settled back on the bed, reaching over to smooth her hair with one hand. She smiled at him. He smiled back. "Hello, my Annabelle."

"Hello, Papa," she replied. She let go of his arm and reached for the tray, making little grasping motions with her hands.

Michael picked it up and placed it gently across her thighs, propping it so that most of its weight was supported by its wooden legs, which had soft felt on their bottoms, to keep them from bruising her. She bruised so easily these days. More easily all the time, it sometimes seemed, no matter what he did to try to make things better for her.

"Is this all right?" he asked.

She shifted slightly. "I'm well, Papa."

"Good." He stroked her hair before leaning back to watch her eat.

Annabelle moved with that same eerie quickness when she grasped her food, consuming it in small, neat bites that she scarce seemed to chew before swallowing. She had little sense of taste, thanks to some of the treatments she had received; all food was simply sustenance to her, intended to fuel her broken, breaking body. Still, there were things to be learned in what she chose. She had never been distracted by tastes or preferences, and selected her meals purely on the basis of the signals she received from her stomach. Today, she began with the chicken, moved on to the cheese, and finally, almost grudgingly, began to eat her apples.

"Don't you like them, pet?" he asked.

"They taste like medicine," she said.

Given how numb her tongue was, that meant that she disliked the tingle of the acid in the fruit. Interesting. "Can you eat them anyway?" he asked. "For me? I would very much appreciate it."

Annabelle nodded and continued dutifully eating her apples.

Michael watched her, stomach twisting, already regretting what he would have to do. She was such a delicate child, had always *been* a delicate child. She deserved so much better than the life she'd had so far. She deserved green fields and blue horizons, she deserved to run and play and be as free as the children of the families around them, the ones he sometimes saw kicking a ball in the street or flying kites on the butte. Annabelle had done nothing *wrong*, nothing that should have seen God confining her to this cottony prison of a room, to her fragile cocoon of a body.

He had done wrong, oh, yes; he had been a sinner in the days before he'd settled down and taken a wife, pledging to be true to her and to the teachings of the Church, to do what he could to serve state and Science at the same time. Dr. Hellstromme was a great man. Being chosen as one of his protégés was an honor almost beyond dreaming of, so impossible that Michael had scarcely dared to hope for it before it had been given to him. That, alone, should have been enough for him. He had had a beautiful wife and the patronage of a great man.

But no. He had wanted more. He had wanted children, and when Grace had failed to provide them in the natural manner of things, he had turned to the one mistress who had never done him ill or let him down, the constant that had defined his entire adult life: to Science, glorious and shining and profane. He wondered, sometimes, how the Church could justify its co-existence with Science and all Her wonders, for She was so clearly a divinity in Her own right, something that each and every man who prayed at Her beakers and burners set before the grace of God Almighty. Even Dr. Hellstromme was a part of the sacrilege, for what could he possibly be apart from the high priest of their chosen, pagan goddess?

Science, and Dr. Hellstromme, had guided his hand, had helped him mix the medicines and measure the treatments that would enable Grace to do her wifely duty and provide him with an heir. She had been willing, at first, afraid of being put aside or joined by a sister-wife if she remained too long barren. No one would have questioned him for either one, and indeed, taking a second bride would have been in many ways easier. But he had always liked to run a tidy household, and the men he knew with more than one wife seemed to be forever embroiled in this petty dispute or that marital quarrel. He and Grace had long since worked out their peace, and he saw no reason to unsettle that, not when children would already change the delicate balance in their own way. Children always did. Grace was the woman he loved. Grace was the woman he had wanted to be the mother of his children.

Grace was the one who had, at his request, consumed the tinctures and suffered through the procedures, until he knew what it was to feel like God Himself, creator of all life. He had watched his wife's belly swell, and he had been so proud that he had felt as if his head would burst. Even Dr. Hellstromme had been proud of him, singling him out for praise, holding him up as an example for the rest of the scientists in Hellstromme's employ. Dr. Michael Murphy was going places.

Then the babies had been born, two of them, so entangled that it was impossible to tell where one ended and the other began.

Then he had realized the price of his hubris, as Grace had screamed and the battle for his daughters had begun.

Idly, absently, he reached out and stroked Annabelle's hair again, thinking of his other daughter, his lovely Pearl, who was still alive, and strong, and healthy, and *hale*. Who would save her sister, and in saving Annabelle, save him.

"We are going on an adventure, my poppet," he said, and there was nothing in his eyes but hope.

Chapter 14

The church stood at the edge of town, surrounded by a fence that shouldn't have been necessary in a place like this, where no one would even dream of desecrating holy ground. Only when they drew closer—close enough for the lantern's watery light to chase back the shadows—did she realize what the fence was for: it was there to define the graveyard.

Annie gasped, her free hand going involuntarily to her mouth, trapping the sound inside. There were so many headstones standing in shaky, uneven rows. Many of them were cracked; all of them were coated in thick layers of stringy moss. Without them, there would have been nothing to mark the placement of the dead. There were no graves. There were only holes in the earth, deep pits from which unspeakable things had been dragged.

"You're probably trying to tell yourself that they moved the dead when they left this place behind," said Hal. His voice was gruff. "It would be the Christian thing to do, taking the dead with you. Don't let yourself believe that lie. They didn't move a damn thing. The wendigo did this."

"Why . . ." Annie stopped herself, slow horror twisting and untwisting in the pit of her stomach. Why would the wendigo desecrate the graves?

Because they were hungry and the graves contained bodies, and to the wendigo, the bodies of the dead were more meat for the bellies of the beasts.

Slowly, almost as in a dream, Annie walked closer to the church. The gate had been broken off its hinges; the shattered remnants shifted with the breeze, making a soft creaking sound. She stepped through, onto what should have been holy ground, and felt no holiness there. Only cold, and the ever-impending threat of the winter yet to come. She walked to the edge of the first grave.

From this close, it was impossible to ignore the roughness of the edges, or the claw marks gouged into the dirt around the hole. Some great beast had dug this pit, delving ever downward to find the terrible meat concealed within. She had never really thought of humans in terms of meat before. Oh, she knew that man was made of flesh, and that there were plenty of creatures in the West who would be happy to devour the unwary—coyotes and buzzards, catamounts and nibblers. It was never safe to walk in the world. But she had considered places like this to be sacrosanct, so well defended that there was no need to be afraid.

"Families, transformed by the fruits of their own hunger, returned here to unearth their dead," said Hal from behind her. "Mothers who had laid their children to rest not two winters prior scrabbled through the earth and clawed open their coffins, taking their babes back into their bodies."

"Why are you showing me this?" whispered Annie.

"Because you didn't believe me when I just told you about it. You thought me a mad old man, rambling about what he'd lost. A warning is only as good as the one who gives it."

The grave smelled of wet fur and sour earth, instead of good, clean dirt. It was not the fact that someone had been buried here that had tainted the ground. It was the fact that the someone had been removed, ripped away from what should have been eternal peace.

"They just . . . what?" Annie shook her head. "I don't

understand how this is possible. I don't understand how any of this is possible."

Hal grasped her elbow, steering her gently away from the grave. "Come with me," he said. "There's more for you to see."

Half sick with worry and with fear, Annie did not resist. She simply turned and allowed herself to be led down the narrow, hard-packed path to the church.

It was a simple structure, befitting a settlement of this size, but there was room around it for expansion, space that had been carefully carved out with lines of brick to keep the graveyard from creeping in too close. The people who raised this church had expected to stay, to keep worshipping and beating back the woods one tree at a time, until they had a good, clear land to call their own. Like the gate, the doors had been broken. Unlike the gate, they had been shattered on their hinges, rendering the steps treacherous with splinters and with the moss that fed on the decaying wood. Hal walked through it without hesitation, leaving Annie to pick her way through the mess, trying to keep herself firmly at his heels. She knew better than to let herself be left alone without her guide in this blasted place.

The pews were still in place, for the most part. A few had been knocked askew or broken, but the rest stood in their tidy rows, as if they were waiting for the return of a congregation that had long since gone on to greener pastures.

(The thought made her shudder. Oregon was nothing if not green, and all green things needed to feed. How many of the missing were fertilizing the trees or filling the bellies of the wendigo, not making new lives for themselves somewhere far away, under a kinder sky?)

They walked toward the front of the church. Seen up close, the pews were less intact than they had seemed, ripe with rot and swelling with the fleshy bodies of toadstools, blue-capped and slick-looking. Some of them seemed almost to glow in the dimness, lit from within by their own terrible poisons. Hal followed her gaze.

"I don't know what those are," he said. "They seem to sprout when stores are low, or just before a blizzard."

"Are they poisonous?"

Hal's laughter was a sharp, short bark. "You'd be dead before you had the chance to swallow. I've seen men risk it anyway, when they were hungry enough, when it was that or join the wendigo. They shit themselves to death, writhing like there was a noose around their necks. The flies wouldn't even eat the bodies. The wendigo still would, though. Nothing kills them once the winter takes them. Nothing natural, anyway."

"Wait." Annie stopped walking, frowning at Hal. He stopped as well, turning to face her, the ruined church framing him like some terrible pagan god of the winter and the woods. "How many people here *know* about these things?"

"Most of them." He shook his head. "You think anyone can live in a forest full of monsters and *not* know that the woods are watching them? There's not a man or woman who's lived in The Clearing for more than two spans of seasons who doesn't know about the wendigo, and what they are to us. Some of the children may still be innocent. My Poppy was. My Marie was as well. They didn't know what would happen to them when they filled their bellies. The mayor, now . . . he knows. He's always been *very* careful."

"Why do they stay?"

"Because some of them are like me, with friends and loved ones running in the deep woods, eating the world alive. Some of them are like the mayor. He's powerful here. He's in *control* here. You take him out of these woods, and what is he? Just an aging little man whose settlement failed—and if he tried to tell people why, well, he'd be lucky to avoid the nuthouse. There are men in this world who hunger for power the way a wendigo hungers for flesh. He's one of them. He'll never give up what he has."

Annie said nothing, but thought of Michael, whose hunger had been so great that it had consumed almost everything it touched. She had escaped, and she'd moved Adeline well beyond his grasp, but it had cost her more than she had ever thought she'd be called upon to pay. It had cost her a daughter. It had cost her name. It had very nearly cost her life.

Hal nodded. "You've met that kind of man before. No one walks away from that sort of thing without scars, even if they don't all show to the eye. He'll never leave The Clearing."

"He left it once," said Annie.

"No. He left the shed skin of his town behind, and he built something better. The new town is bigger than this one ever was, stronger, more prepared to weather the winter. They're learning to live with the land. Give them a hundred years and they'll be the sort of nightmare that travelers warn each other about. Not the wendigo. The townsfolk."

"Not a town of cannibals, but a town making sacrifices to cannibals for the sake of their own survival," said Annie. The slow horror was back, twisting in her stomach until it felt like she had swallowed a worm, some dreadful thing that would eventually burst out of her in a shower of blood and bile. "We were told . . . we were told that The Clearing was a good place for a traveling show. That they paid well." That wasn't all that they'd been told, but it had been so loud, and so tempting, that the rest had been surprisingly easy to ignore.

"They do, for the shows that come and go during the summer. How the children love a circus! But if you could count the traveling shows scattered across the continent,

I think you'd find that a surprising number of them have gone missing right after coming here."

"I know," interrupted Annie. "I talked—"

Hal continued as if she hadn't spoken. "There were always reasons. The world is *full* of reasons for the things it does to us. There were blizzards, or roads had been washed out, or there were highwaymen in the area. I think you'd find that those reasons didn't matter. That many of those people were gone, and that the ones who remain . . . well, the ones who remain aren't anything that could be called human anymore."

Annie didn't say anything. She was starting to wonder whether Hal's silence had been broken forever: whether he needed to talk, and talk, and talk until all the words he'd been hoarding had been spent, leaving him empty again, ready for another decade alone in the woods. She lifted her lantern, eyes fixed once more on the altar, and walked forward.

The claw marks were scored deep into the wood of the narrow steps leading up to the spot where the priest had once stood, making his speeches, delivering his sermons, trying to lead the people of his flock toward a brighter tomorrow. The churches of the heathen West were not much like the churches of the Holy City where she'd grown up, and she didn't have much time or use for religion anyway, but it was still hard to look upon the desecration. This was meant to be a place of God. This sort of thing had no business here.

She stepped onto the dais. The podium was cracked straight through, as if struck a mighty blow by some unseen hand. She took another step, and stopped dead, all the blood in her body seeming to suddenly freeze, until she felt like a wendigo herself, cold from one end to the other, unable to even understand what was before her eyes.

They had left the body of the priest behind when they

fled this place—or perhaps he had refused to leave his church, planting his feet on holy ground and declaring that this was as far as he could go; this was where the line must be drawn. Whatever the truth, the end result had been the same.

There was no flesh left on his bones. Even without the wendigo, time would have taken it from him, for the skeleton had clearly been here for quite some time, exposed enough to the elements—that damned broken door—to have become weathered and yellowed. There were bite marks on some of the bones, but not as many as she might have expected, given Hal's description of the beasts.

The floor creaked behind her before Hal said, "Father Hines believed that there was still good in the beasts. He claimed to be able to minister to them. He said that he could go out into the woods and read to them from the Good Book, and that they responded—not as men did, not anymore, and yet, clearly enough that he continued in his efforts. When the choice was made to move The Clearing to its new home, he refused. He said the wendigo wouldn't know where to find him. He wouldn't go."

"Did they kill him?"

"I don't know."

Annie turned. Hal looked at her gravely.

"I think they were toying with him. They had plenty of food—the woods were rich with deer, and even with the hard freeze, the people in the town had survived until spring. There was always someone else to slaughter. Perhaps the wendigo kept him as a pet. Or perhaps some among them still believed that they could find absolution if they only listened closely to the homilies and hymns, if they only believed that the Lord their God was still watching over the lost members of his flock, the sheep that had been transformed to wolves."

The image of monsters trying to sing "Bringing in the

Sheaves" or "This Little Light of Mine" was ridiculous enough to be faintly comic, even under these grim and unforgiving circumstances. Annie swallowed her laughter. It sat sourly in her stomach, joining the fear already prisoned there. She was going to burst soon, from an excess of foul humors.

"They ate him in the end, of course, whether they killed him or no," said Hal. "But they left the body here. I suppose they thought it was funny."

It was interesting, how he moved between humanizing the wendigo and dismissing them as nothing more than monsters, terrible beasts powered solely by their hunger. Annie said nothing. She knew that sort of emotional turmoil all too well. There had been times when Michael had been the best of men, and the best of husbands. He had bought her beautiful things, expensive things, some of which she had barely expressed an interest in before they had been gracing her home. He had been a surprisingly gentle lover, coaxing her through the things he wanted like the scientist he was, like sex was an experiment that could be brought to a successful and reproducible conclusion. He had been a *good* man.

He had also been a nightmare, jabbing needles into her spine and drawing out the golden fluid that pooled there, as clear as amber, as rare as diamonds. His temper had been legendary, and she supposed that it would only have grown worse since she'd left him; some days, she'd felt as if he'd married her as much to have someplace to direct his aggressions as for the appearance of propriety that she provided. He had been a monster who walked like a man and a man who walked like a monster, and to this day, she couldn't have said which face had been the true one.

"Are they going to come back here?"

"No. There's nothing left for them in this town. They ate its heart, and it died." Hal sighed. "There have been times when I thought about leaving my cabin for one of the houses here. Some of them have held up surprisingly well, and I could pretend that I still had people around me to care about. That's why I can't do it. I'd break my heart every day, when I woke up and I was alone. And how would Poppy know how to find me? A girl needs her father."

His girl seemed more likely to eat her father than to need him. Annie shoved the thought away. "My girl doesn't need her father; she needs me," she said gently. "You brought me here to make me understand. I still don't. I need to find Adeline. She's out here somewhere. Please. We need to find her."

"I also brought you here to show you the graves," said Hal. "The wendigo *do* have a sense of humor, or maybe just a sense of putting things where they belong, and they always make a mockery of laying the children to rest. If they'd already taken your daughter and devoured the soft parts of her, we would have found her body in the yard."

Annie stopped dead, staring at Hal with wide, wounded eyes. He had brought her here, knowing full well that her daughter's body might be waiting for her. If that had been the case, if Adeline had been in that churchyard . . .

Something inside her would have broken forever. She had fled the Devil once, when she ran away from Deseret. She did not have it in her to flee the Devil a second time.

"You monster," she whispered.

"I never claimed to be anything else," he replied. "I am not a wendigo. That's the best that can be said for me. But take heart. If she is not here, they have not killed her."

That didn't mean she had survived. The wendigo were not the only monsters in these woods, nor were they the only things that could lead a scared young girl to her death. "We haven't checked all the graves," said Annie, and hated herself.

Hal, however, looked almost pleased. "No, we haven't," he said. "Come."

They walked out of the church in silence. This time, Annie took the lead, pulling as far ahead of Hal as she dared. She didn't want to lose him, didn't want to be stranded alone in this terrible place, but neither did she want to look at him. He could have told her. He could have *warned* her. It would have been so easy to say "the monsters bring their kills to this churchyard, be aware of what you may see." Or he could have told her to wait at the fence, calling her to join him only when he knew what she was going to find. There were so *many* things he could have done. He had chosen the sharpest, coldest of them.

He might not be a wendigo himself, but there was no question that he was already of their kind.

Annie and Hal moved through the graveyard like ghosts, peering into the open graves. Some of them contained bones, piles of them heaped in the bottoms of the holes, thrown together like there was no importance in what they had been in life. Annie shivered at the sight of a half-shattered skull, holes driven through the cranium like nails through a board. There was no question that they were tooth marks, and it terrified her to think that her little girl was out there somewhere with the monsters that had made those markings.

Other graves held scraps of cloth, faded remnants of older victims, ones so long gone that the smaller scavengers of the forest had carried away even their bones. There would be crows' nests tucked in the high trees, built of teeth and hair and rib bones, like ghoulish testimonies to the cruelty of the Oregon woods.

They had traveled more than halfway around the exterior of the church when they came to the first occupied grave.

The boy it contained—and he *was* a boy, barely old

enough for his whiskers to have started coming in, still years and miles away from his manhood—had been ripped open, his chest cracked and his belly sliced. One of his arms was missing, gnawed away, leaving only a bloody stump behind. The wendigo that killed him and dumped his body in the abandoned graveyard had been thoughtful enough to leave his face virtually untouched; Annie recognized him, her stomach twisting tighter and tighter, until it was wound so completely that she could no longer swallow.

"His name was Thomas," she said, voice hollow and distant, even to her own ears. "He ran away with the circus five years ago, with his family's permission, on his thirteenth birthday. He wanted to be a wainwright one day. He was apprenticed to the best of them. The last time my wagon broke an axle, he was the one who fixed it."

She could still see him, bark-brown hair shining in the sun, eyes cast shyly downward when she came out to ask whether he wanted a drink of water. Everyone knew that he didn't like to talk to women, be they his own age or older, for fear that they would expect him to carry his end of the conversation. He'd been possessed of a stutter since he was a child, severe enough that he'd learned some of the signs Adeline used, just to avoid the need for speaking. But he'd been a sweet boy, and smart as a whip, and he'd been carrying on a quiet affair with one of the boys who worked the trapeze.

What would Alonzo do now that Thomas was gone? Who would teach him to spell with his hands, or help him string the ropes for the big tent between shows?

No one died alone. Every death took a thousand potential lifetimes away, and consigned them to an unmarked, unsung grave.

"He was with the circus," said Annie, and those five

words were everything she had left to offer, and they were nothing at all; they could never have been enough. "We can't leave him here."

"We don't have a choice," said Hal. "The wendigo store their kills here, but there's still meat on those bones. They'll be back for it, when they get tired of hunting."

"You mean when they get hungry again."

"I don't know what it's going to take to get this through your head, girl: the wendigo are *always* hungry. They could eat the moon and be looking at the sun a second later, wondering what it would taste like. But they're smart enough to know that sometimes they have to turn their back on a meal in the hand if they want to catch two more in the bush. So they store what they haven't finished, and they go for more, and more, and more."

Annie shuddered, straightening. "We have to hurry," she said. "Adeline is out there somewhere."

Hal said nothing.

They checked the rest of the graves before moving on; they were empty, each and every one. Wherever Adeline was, she was not here—not yet. Both of them knew that the girl's time was short if she remained in the woods alone.

Annie still holding her lantern, Hal still holding his rifle, they walked out of the ghost town and back to the trail that would lead them out of the bowl. They climbed without looking back, Annie in the lead, Hal ready to steady her if she started to fall.

When they reached the top, they did look back, both of them. The shadows had already swept in, swallowing the town, until it seemed like they were looking into nothing but darkness, as deep and unfathomable as the sea.

"Will this place ever be laid to rest?" Annie asked.

"Someone may come along one day and burn it all to the ground," said Hal. "Fire cleanses. Until that day . . .

I don't know that the people who died here will ever know peace. Come. We have to hurry."

Annie nodded and followed him back into the woods.

Something rustled at the edge of the trees, something white-furred and terrible. Then it was gone, disappearing like it had never been there at all.

Chapter 15

Of all the things he had ever disliked—and there had been plenty of 'em, from his parents to Sophia's cornbread, which was made with more love and enthusiasm than skill or flavor—Martin thought that sitting alone in a tiny cabin in the middle of a forest filled with monsters was probably going to be top of the list for the rest of his life. That was almost pleasant, really. Nothing that happened to him after this was ever going to be quite as bad, short of whatever actually killed him. Even then, dying would probably be quick and easy and over with before he had time to really hate it. This, though . . .

He couldn't say how long he'd been sitting there alone. It felt like hours. It probably hadn't been. It had been long enough that he was just about sure the others were gone, climbing out of the bowl and heading off to find Adeline and Sophia. He surely hoped Annie would remember that it wasn't just her daughter she was hunting for, that his lover and maybe his own child were also lost out there. He hoped Annie would bring Sophia home.

(The deep, dark, terrible part of him that had been truly listening when Hal spoke knew how vanishingly small the chances of that were, and how much smaller they were getting with every second that passed. Adeline had run off on her own. The wendigo might not even have her. She could just be lost, or down a hole, or trapped in one of Hal's twice-damned bear traps, unable to call for help, what with her poor broken throat. But Sophia . . . he'd seen her carried away by something out of a nightmare, something his mind still refused to let him remember clearly, and if she was still alive, it was a miracle, and if she was dead, he could only hope that it had happened quickly. There was a third option now, according to Hal, a thing that wasn't life and wasn't death, and he prayed to God he never looked at a nightmare and saw Sophia's eyes looking back.)

An owl hooted outside, soft and low, the sound carrying through the heavy walls. If the owls were coming back, that meant there wasn't anything in the clearing, didn't it? No monsters, no wendigo, just the forest and the night. Just Sophia out there somewhere, waiting for him to come and save her.

Cautiously, he tried to stand again. The scabs had begun to set over the wounds made by Hal's bear trap, and no fresh blood ran down his leg. There was still pain, enough to make him hiss a long breath out between his teeth, but it was a bearable sort of agony. The trap's teeth hadn't bitten deep enough to hit bone or sever muscle. He'd gotten off lightly, if such a thing could be said about this sort of injury. There were bear traps that could take a man's leg clean off, designed for grizzly and worse. This one . . .

If Hal were really hunting wendigo, wouldn't he have set bigger traps? This one wouldn't have done much more than slow a brown bear down and make it angry, and the things that had attacked the circus had been well bigger than a brown bear. One of *those* would have just pulled the trap off like it was nothing.

Maybe there were bears in these woods. Maybe there were other things for a man to be afraid of. Other things that would come with claws and teeth and hunger to devour a man living on his own, with no one to help him hold the dark at bay. Maybe it only made sense to set

traps of different shapes and sizes, and Martin was bor-
rowing trouble for nothing.

But Hal had been eager as all get-out to share his story,
hadn't he? At first he'd seemed like some sort of hermit,
as ready to shoot them as look at them, and then he'd gotten a good look at Annie and he'd started sharing. He'd
told them more than they'd asked at every turn. He'd told
them how his story wasn't so far off from theirs. He'd . . .
he'd . . . Martin struggled to find the right word. He'd
empathized, that was it. Hal had found all the reasons
that their stories were the same, and he'd spread them
out on the table like he was playing follow-the-lady with
the townies.

Martin didn't run any of the rigged card games himself. His hands were fast enough, and his tongue was slick
enough, but he thought it was cheating, a bit, to take
wide-eyed townies just looking for a bit of fun and use
their own innocence against them, taking their money
again and again just because they didn't realize they were
playing against a professional. Keep their eyes on the
cards and their ears full of patter, and they'd never realize that this was a game they had no possible chance of
winning.

Had Hal been playing follow-the-lady with them? Had
he been painting the sort of picture he knew couldn't be
resisted by a frightened mother—a woman with no gun,
with no reason to know how to defend herself, whose
protector had been conveniently injured?

Martin stood again, testing his ankle. It held him up.
The bindings were tight: he might already smell of blood,
but he wouldn't be leaving a trail behind himself as he
walked. That would have to do. Suddenly, he wasn't so
comfortable with the idea that Annie was out there, alone
with Hal. Monsters didn't always come with claws and
teeth and such. Sometimes they came with friendly faces,
helping hands outstretched to grab and yank and shove.

"I'm coming, ma'am," he said, and cast around the cabin, looking for something he could burn. There: a barrel next to the stove, filled with premade pine torches. Hal must have used them when he was hunting, or when he was trying to attract the wendigo. Martin pulled one out, studied the pitch-coated tip for a moment, and walked back to the fire, still testing his ankle.

There was no question now of whether he was going outside. He needed to. Once he'd started thinking about Hal, about *why* he had told them all those things about the wendigo, he hadn't been able to stop thinking about it. Annie needed him. Sophia needed him. By extension, Adeline needed him, too, because what was going to happen to that little girl if something happened to her mother? Nothing good, that was what.

He thrust the end of the torch into the fire. The pitch caught with a crackling whoosh. It wouldn't burn forever, but it would burn long enough to get him across the clearing, and after that, he'd be in the forest, where there was no end to things that he could potentially burn. Torch in one hand, rifle in the other, he walked to the door. It wasn't locked. It opened easily.

Outside, the night seemed to have returned to a normal degree of darkness. The trees were spikes set against the starry sky, and the moon cast enough light that he figured he could see the ground well enough to avoid any traps, at least for a little while. If he got his leg caught again—or worse, if he got his *other* leg caught, his *good* leg—he'd probably die in the trap, unable to free himself before the smell of blood attracted something from out of the trees. That was a risk he was going to have to take. Turning his back on his troubles wasn't going to make them go away.

Martin took a shaky breath, filling his lungs with the taste of pine and loam, and started across the clearing toward the trees. He thought he was going in the right direction. It was hard to know for sure: the curdled moonlight wasn't bright enough to show him whether there were footprints to follow, and he didn't dare lean down. Getting his torch too close to the layer of dead pine needles that covered the ground would end with him setting the whole damned clearing on fire, and while that might provide a bit more light, it would be a lot more likely to provide him with an unmarked grave.

He realized, maybe for the first time, that he didn't want to die out here. He wanted to save Sophia, and he wanted to find Annie before Hal could do something terrible to her, but he didn't want to die out here. Not in the woods. Not in Oregon. Martin had always considered himself something of a man without a country, a citizen of the circus rather than a citizen of America, or Deseret, or wherever else might have wanted to claim him; every place was his home, which meant that no place was his home. Where he lived, where he died, where his children were born, none of that mattered as long as the wagons kept rolling and the road kept on welcoming him back for more.

Only now he knew one thing about his citizenship: wherever it was rooted, it wasn't here. This place was not for him, and he was not for it, and assuming he survived, he couldn't think that Oregon would be sad to see him go.

Shuffling his feet in the needles as he walked, he kicked the chains attached to two more traps, but not the traps themselves. He briefly considered tracking them down and using fallen branches to trigger them, rendering them useless until they were reset. He decided it would be a waste of time. Hal might be what he claimed to be or he might be a villain: either way, he didn't deserve the effort it would take to dismantle everything he'd made.

(And if he was a good man—if he was talking too much out of the pure relief of having someone to talk *to*—it wouldn't be kind to leave him defenseless and thinking himself protected. There were some things that would be a march too far, if only because they would put Martin on the level of the man he feared Hal to be.)

Climbing the hillside was a lot harder than he remembered, probably because he was injured and alone, instead of hale and matching his steps to Annie's. He tried to picture her beside him—or better, Sophia—and metered his stride accordingly, accounting for the phantom woman. It got a little easier after that. His ankle complained less, and the slope seemed less extreme. Soon he was standing at the top of the rise.

He looked back once, frowning down on the clearing where Hal's cabin stood and fighting the urge to throw his torch behind him. Let the place burn. Let all of Oregon burn.

It was an uncharitable thought. He stopped cold, still frowning, but now frowning at himself. Thoughts like that weren't normal for him. He'd lived his whole life by the charity of others. Hal might be good and might be bad, but if he hadn't been willing to ruin Hal's traps, why would he be willing to destroy his home? It didn't make sense.

"This place gets in your head," he muttered, and turned back toward the wood. The space between the trees was black and cold. He couldn't shake the feeling that the trees had been waiting for him somehow, aware that he would come back to them if they just waited long enough.

Oregon was a cold place. He couldn't imagine that anything growing here would be anything else. Shuddering, he started forward.

It was a little easier going with the torch than it had been with the lantern. The fire cast a brighter, more aggressive light, beating the shadows back enough for him to see where he was putting his feet. He still shuffled, wary of more traps. The last thing he wanted was to be caught here.

The ground remained placid under his feet. Nothing snapped closed on him; nothing tore his flesh or attacked. Martin continued walking, until the trees dropped away and he was stepping into a clearing.

It was hard to say whether this was the clearing he and Annie had fled across when the monster had followed them through the trees. If it was, there was a chance that he would find Tranquility's body somewhere on the other side, broken and bloody, the only monument to the brave beast that had saved their lives. He didn't think he wanted to. Annie would take no peace from the confirmation that her pet and companion had died to save them. It was better to let her hope that maybe Tranquility had survived and gone back to the wild, choosing a life lived in the growing green, far away from the concerns of humanity.

Martin, never a very religious man, crossed himself before setting out across the clearing. It might not be enough to keep the monsters away, but then again, it might help. Anything that might help was worth trying, here, in this cruel green world.

He had gone no more than halfway when something growled from the trees ahead of him.

It was a low, dangerous sound, and it sent a bolt of ice racing down his spine, freezing him on the spot. His torch still burned bright, and he realized with some dismay that he didn't know what to do. He couldn't fire his rifle without putting the torch down. If he put the torch down, he might set the entire damn forest on fire, and himself still solidly in the middle of it all, with no clear hope of escaping. What was the point in getting off a shot if he burned immediately after? He wouldn't save himself that way. He would only consign himself to an even more terrible demise. Better teeth and claws than fire.

Something else growled, this time off to the side. One by one, more voices chimed in, until he knew that he was surrounded. Dropping the torch and raising his rifle wouldn't save him even long enough for the fire to have him: fell one of the growling beasts and the rest would converge, ripping him to pieces even before he could turn to run.

"Might as well come out," he called. "No point in playing with me."

I'm sorry, Sophia, he thought. *I'm sorry I didn't save you. I'm sorry I won't get to marry you. I'm sorry I won't get to see the baby. I'm sorry about just about everything.* Never had a man gone to the grave more filled with cold regret for all the things he'd never had a chance to change.

The growling grew closer. It was definitely coming from all sides now, and from at least ten different throats, a choir of terrors singing to him out of the darkened woods. Martin tensed, his hands clenching tighter around torch and rifle. This was it. This was where he died.

Wolves padded out of the woods. No, not wolves: he had seen wolves before, and these weren't them. Wolves were like big, wild-looking dogs. They were thick in the shoulders and long in the jaw, and they weren't something that should be taken lightly—wolves were the monsters in half the fairy tales he knew for a reason, no question about that—but they were still close kin to the beasts that slept by the fire and farted without raising their heads. Wolves were to dogs as men were to apes. There was kinship there. These things . . .

They had the shape of wolves, roughly, with canine jaws and broad foreheads over amber eyes. They had tails like wolves and ears like wolves, currently swiveled back and pressed flat against their skulls, giving them the appearance of snakes preparing to strike. And he was sure that white wolves existed somewhere in the world, adapted to hunt in snowy climates. He just couldn't imagine an entire pack of white wolves, especially not here, where they stood out against the trees like paper cutouts.

(Maybe that was why the shadows were so deep here. They had an agreement with these things that weren't wolves, and they worked twice as hard as shadows should to keep them hidden, tying up the whole world in a fight that wouldn't have existed if the wolves had just been sensibly brindle, gray, and brown, like they were everywhere else.)

They were too *big* to be wolves. The largest wolf he'd ever seen had been maybe half the size of one of these things, each of which looked to be as large as or larger than a full-grown man. There was something wrong with their paws. They almost looked like knuckled-under hands, nails curled against their palms, fingers bearing the bulk of their weight. Apes had hands like those. Wolves didn't. Wolves walked on honest paws, and they were barely removed from being dogs, and they weren't these things.

"What *are* you?" he breathed, too terrified to move— too terrified even to piss, although he thought that might change soon, given the weight in his bladder and the way it pressed against his trousers. The thought that one of them might get a face full of urine when it tried to take him down was soothing, but not enough to make him feel any better about his own impending demise.

The wolf-things stopped. One of them sniffed the air, ears swiveling forward again, so that they were pointed straight at him. The others looked to it as if they were waiting for guidance. Martin held himself very still, not wanting to do anything that might disrupt this inexplicable stay of execution. They were going to kill him one way or another. There was nothing wrong with wanting to put it off for as long as he possibly could.

The lead wolf-thing sniffed the air again before barking. The sound was short, sharp, and again, somehow *wrong,* like it was more the idea of what a wolf should sound like than the real thing. The others took a step backward.

Martin decided he didn't care how wrong the one in control was, it was still going to be his favorite.

The lead wolf-thing turned and trotted away. Some of the others followed it. The rest resumed advancing toward Martin, closing the gap between him and them, until they were only a few feet away—close enough to leap, close enough to bring him down like a deer if that was what they wanted to do. Even with their numbers cut in half, there were still too many of them for him to shoot before his throat was on the ground, and so he stood very still, waiting to see what would happen next.

One of them walked forward, nudging the back of his knees with its nose. Even that soft impact was enough to knock him forward by a half-step, nearly losing his balance. The wolf-thing whined.

Martin looked back. They were watching him, and while he didn't see anything he could read as friendliness in their pumpkin-colored eyes, he didn't see malice, either. They watched him coldly, as wild things so often would, but they didn't look as if they were preparing to make a meal of him.

"What do you want?" he asked.

The wolf-thing nudged him again, harder this time. The message was clear: *go.* They wanted him walking, and with them outnumbering him the way that they did, he couldn't see a clear or easy way out of it.

"Should've stayed in the cabin," he said, and turned, looking toward the edge of the wood, where the white bodies of the wolf-things that had gone ahead stood out against the dark trees like burning brands. They wanted him to follow. If he hadn't been sure of that before, he was sure of it now: nothing waited like that unless it wanted a person to follow.

They might just want to kill him somewhere more convenient for them, some den or dark hollow where they wouldn't have to fight the wendigo for his body. But in this green new land, where starvation could make monsters out of men in every sense of the word, who was to say that the cold hadn't found a way to make men out of monsters?

"I'm going," Martin said, and began to walk.

The wolf-things stayed close at his heels, nudging him with their muzzles or growling when he didn't move fast enough. He didn't look back, not wanting to see the teeth that their drawn-back lips revealed. He was a smart man. He knew full well that any one of the beasts could kill him in an instant if that was what they wanted to do. That didn't mean he wanted to be reminded of how precarious his position was.

They walked back into the trees, the wolf-things herding him, keeping him from the need to search for traps on the needle-strewn ground. Even if they knew what the traps were, they wouldn't be going too close to them with their prey, and he was already close enough to helpless that they didn't need to incapacitate him; if there'd been any chance for him to run, it had come and gone while they were in that clearing. Better or worse, he was in this until the end.

It was easier to walk through the woods now that someone else was setting the direction; with the wolf-things guiding him, Martin could let his mind wander, drifting back to the good days with Sophia, the days after they had passed the early, uncomfortable parts of their courtship and settled into long afternoons lounging in fields behind the circus, their duties done for the day, with nothing left for them to worry about but each other. He remembered all the times he'd made Sophia laugh, all the times she'd smiled at him, run her fingers through his hair, held his hand. He'd never felt particularly handsome before he'd had her, but the way she could look at a man—hoo, the way she could look at a man had made him feel like the handsomest man in the world.

He would have called himself a boy before her, said that he was barely more than a stripling, not ready to claim a man's duties or estate. Sophia had made him want to be a man, for her, and for the family they were going to make between them.

If all that was over, if Oregon had been the end of every good dream and the birth of a thousand bad ones, at least the good times had been there. At least he'd had her. For a little while, he'd had her, and she'd had him, and life had seemed so good. So much better than he'd ever hoped it would be.

The trees dropped away as they emerged into another clearing. His torch was burning down, but it was still bright enough to show him the mountain looming up in front of them, all granite crags and green moss. A cave had been worn into the face of it. More of the white wolf-things were gathered there, some lounging, others standing sentry. In the midst of them was something that was not a wolf-thing, although it was just as pale, just as impossible—

Martin dropped his torch. It landed on damp mud, narrowly missing a pile of pine needles, and burned nothing.

The pale-haired little girl in the dirty white dress rose from where she had been sitting among the wolf-things and ran to him. She stopped a few feet away, her bare toes digging into the earth, a bright smile on her face. She looked utterly relaxed, at peace with the world and with her place in it.

"Hello, Adeline," said Martin.

Chapter 16

The woods were dense and deep, enough so that Annie realized, shortly after leaving the ghost town, that she had no idea where they were. They could as easily have been walking in circles as bending back toward the woods where Adeline had disappeared; she had no way of knowing, and without some small landmark that she could point to, she wasn't sure how to even phrase the question. If she angered Hal while she was alone with him in the woods . . .

No. She refused to think like that. She was done letting the fear of men run her life—had *been* done since the day she had grabbed her living daughter and run from Deseret.

"Where are we?" she demanded, and her voice rang strong and clear and unafraid.

Hal looked back, seeming unimpressed by her courage. "The woods," he said. "Around here, you're either in the woods or you're not."

"But are we *lost* in the woods? I need to find my daughter."

"No one knows these woods better than I do."

"That doesn't actually answer my question." Annie raised her lantern, thrusting it forward, until the light danced across his grizzled features, chasing the shadows away. "Where are we, right now, and what are you doing to lead me to my child?"

"Get that damned light out of my face," said Hal,

pushing her hand aside. He glowered at her, eyes almost obscured by the shadows that came rushing back as soon as the lantern wasn't shining directly on him. "You think you're lost with me? You can't imagine how lost you would be without me. You have no idea. These woods go for miles and miles. You could walk forever and never find your way out."

"And yet I found you, which seems as likely as the proverbial needle in the haystack, when you say things like that," said Annie. "Perhaps the woods go on forever, but the woods directly around The Clearing? Those seem to be a bit more crowded. This is where the people are, which means this is where the wendigo are. Either my daughter is alone or she's with the wendigo, and either way, she can't have gone far. I need to find her. You need to help me find her. You *promised* to help me find her."

Hal's glower faded, replaced by a look of satisfaction. "I did, and I will. It's good that you have some fight in you. Meek and mild doesn't serve you very well, here in the woods."

"So you know where we are?"

"I do." He raised one hand and pointed off into the trees. "The wendigo don't get along with one another most of the time, but they all den in the same mountain."

"I saw two mountains when we were on the road."

"The other belongs to the wolflings," said Hal. At Annie's blank expression, he shook his head and said, "Dark, dire creatures, like wolves but larger and smarter, with a human's hands and cunning fingers. They would devour us all, if not for the wendigo."

"The wendigo . . . protect you?"

"The wendigo frighten them, and since the wendigo are usually found closer to town, they keep the wolflings at bay. Don't let this make the wendigo sound like they have our best interests at heart—they don't. They just have enough humanity left to play at being farmers, and tend their flocks. We're all they eat, given half a choice. If they ate the whole town in a night, there'd be no more man-flesh here for years, maybe even decades. They don't want that. The wolflings don't care about being farmers. The wolflings are just as happy to eat deer, or rabbits, or true wolves, and they'd fill their bellies once and then forget we'd ever been here. I've heard tell of the two beasts forming alliances in other places, where the meat is more plentiful, but here there's not enough for them to share. They have to fight, for the sake of their own appetites."

"So one set of monsters protects you from the other," said Annie, in a low, hushed tone. "We'll need to check both mountains."

"No, we won't," said Hal. "If your girl bent toward the wolfling mountain, she's gone. They'll have made a meal of her before she even knew that she was in danger. The wendigo at least may have kept her alive."

"To fatten her up?" Like some dreadful witch out of a fairy story. It was difficult not to think of gingerbread houses and all the horrors that could be contained therein, safely tucked away behind baked walls and spun-sugar windows.

Hal snorted. "To lure you in. The wendigo were us. They may not have a parent's love in their frozen hearts, but they know a parent will follow a missing child. Why devour the babe when they could have the mother first? You'll have a great deal more meat on your bones."

"My little girl is sickly," said Annie. "She's never been able to gain weight."

"Then the wendigo will definitely delay eating her until they've attracted anyone who might come to her cries."

Adeline could cry as much as she liked: she would never make a sound. Telling Hal that seemed unwise. What if her daughter's silence meant the wendigo saw her as useless and consumed her immediately? Worse, what if it didn't, but Hal assumed it would? She could be abandoning Adeline to her fate, solely because she had made the mistake of telling her native guide that her daughter couldn't scream.

"So we're going to their mountain."

Hal nodded tightly.

"What's to stop the wendigo from eating us?"

"Nothing," he said, and chuckled darkly. "They'll have us both if given half the chance. They can see in the dark. They can smell us from a mile away. These are their woods, and not ours in the slightest. Still sure you want to go?"

"It's my daughter," said Annie. "I never had a choice."

Hal nodded, and the two resumed their passage through the woods.

Annie had long since set aside the frills and ornate fabrics of her youth: her clothes were simple, as close to form-fitting as was appropriate for a woman of her age and position, with a skirt that fell straight down toward her ankles and a blouse tailored to fit snugly over her corset. Even so, the trees grabbed at her clothes and hair, tugging her back, trying to keep her. The smell of pine sap flowed over everything, until it seemed like it was conspiring with the shadows that tangled at their feet, trying its best to enclose and preserve her, like a bug caught in amber. There were so many ways to freeze in Oregon, and so very few ways to thaw.

Hal didn't seem to notice how much trouble she was having. He moved through the shadows without pause or hesitation, slipping between the trees and never looking back. Annie had to push herself to keep up with him. The same trees that had allowed him to pass unhindered reached out with spindly branches and snatched at her, until she was half-ready to believe that they possessed some independent intelligence, some innate ability to know that she didn't belong.

The tallow in her lantern was running low; she estimated that she had two hours, three at the absolute most, before it would gutter and go out, casting the both of them into darkness. Hal wouldn't mind, but she? She wouldn't be able to see her hand in front of her face. If he decided to run off and leave her, there wouldn't be anything she could do to stop him.

Adeline was the most important thing. She would risk anything, lose anything, if it meant getting Adeline back. But if they didn't hurry, there was every chance that she would join her daughter in being utterly lost in the woods.

"We're almost there," said Hal, voice low.

Annie startled, staring at the back of his head. "Am I so predictable?" she asked.

"In these woods, everyone is predictable. In these woods, we're all animals, and animals are always easy to read. Now come."

He began walking faster. Annie hurried to keep up.

The trees began to change around them, becoming no less dense but becoming thinner, somehow, like their roots had been starved of nutrients when they were young, stunting their growth, making it impossible for them to reach their full potential. The branches grabbing at her hair and clothing grew sharper, crueler, and less laden-down with needles. Annie breathed in and realized that even the smell of pine was fading, replaced by the thicker, more terrible smell of wood decaying while it was still alive. The trees here were dying. They were already dead. They just didn't realize it yet.

Hal turned to face her, raising one finger to his lips in an exaggerated request for silence. Annie nodded understanding, and he began to walk again, leading her through the dead and dying trees.

It was a shock when the wood ended. It did not taper off: it simply stopped, as abrupt as if it had been harvested by some unseen forester. Except that not even stumps remained. The ground was churned-up, ripped and torn, unstable. Annie stopped in the shelter of the final line of trees, gaping.

The mountain did not rise out of the earth: it erupted. It ripped its way free. It was granite, solid, ancient, and yet somehow still seemed to be on the verge of moving, straining for even greater heights. The curdled moon hung overhead, casting its terrible light on the mountain-side, making it possible to see much of the way to the top . . . and nothing grew there. Not moss, not brush, not the stubby, clinging trees that she had seen on so many other mountains, finding thin patches of windswept soil to sink their roots into. Other mountains were composite organisms, living through the smaller things that lived upon them. This mountain . . .

This mountain lived as a ghost town lived, or a mine shaft that had collapsed and claimed the lives of a dozen miners. There were places, terrible, tormented places, that pulsed with their own vital energy, unspeakable and cruel. This mountain was not a nursery for wildflowers or a place for hawks to build their nests, but it lived all the same. It lived, and it looked upon its domain, and it hungered for the things it found there.

"My God," whispered Annie.

"Your god has no place here, and neither does anyone else's," said Hal. "Unless there's a god of the wendigo— and if there is, I hope never to be wicked enough to see its face."

At the base of the mountain was a cave, gaping like a vast and starving maw. Annie looked at it and knew two things with absolute certainty: that she did not ever, in her life, want to go into that cave, and that if she failed to go into that cave, she would never know whether the wendigo had her daughter.

The memory of Nathanial offering to leave her and Adeline behind, to set them up with some cozy townie apartment until the winter passed, haunted her. She could have accepted. He would have thought no less of her, and she would have her daughter in her arms even now, holding her tightly, unaware of how close she had come to total disaster.

But I chose the circus, she thought, and looked to Hal, waiting for him to tell her what to do.

"The wendigo den inside the mountain," he said. "It's a honeycomb of horrors in there, but unlike the bees, they have no queen. There's nothing can stop them when their hunger's up, and when they decide it's time to feed. We go in there, there's all likelihood that they'll rip us apart. So we're not going in."

"But my daughter—"

"Do you hear her crying? Those caves, they're like a pair of cupped hands. They make sounds bigger. They bounce them out into the world. That's how they bait the hook. If your girl were in there, she'd be crying her heart out, and we'd hear her."

"Adeline cannot speak."

Hal went still.

"When I say she cannot speak, I don't mean that she is silent but can still scream, or cry. I've met silent children who could do both those things, whose mouths simply lacked the capacity to form words as we understand them." One of those children had been a boy who sang like a bird, trilling and chirping until every bird that could hear him came down from the sky to meet the child who called their names. The other had been a girl whose mouth refused to follow her directions but whose hands had been infinitely clever, stitching seams so fine that they seemed nonexistent.

Silence was not a sentence. It was simply another state of being.

Hal was stone-faced, unmoving. Annie pressed on.

"When she is hurt, she weeps, but there is no sound.

When she takes ill, she sneezes, still without sound. The only sound I've ever heard her make is a cough, and that isn't her; that's the air, speaking for itself as it escapes."

(A lie, but one she had told so many times over the years that it sounded like truth now to her own ears. Adeline had been born screaming, like any babe. It was her father's hand that had stolen her voice away from her, forever. But she hadn't been Adeline then, any more than a newly sprouted seed could be called a rose. She had been the potential for Adeline, and when Annie had taken the steps necessary to plant her in fertile soil, she had bloomed.)

"They could have her, and she could never tell me, because I can't *hear* her. She speaks with her hands and her heart, not with her lips. Those were never where her voice lived anyway. Please. You have to help me find my daughter. You *have* to."

"I think you'll find that I *have* to do nothing. You asked me to bring you here. I brought you. I told you before we arrived that your daughter would be used as bait—didn't you think that they might kill her once they realized she couldn't cry? That they might not have any use for a child who couldn't attract its parents?"

"She's just a little girl—"

"And my Poppy was just a little girl, but the wendigo took her all the same!"

Annie was quiet for a moment, simply looking at him. Poppy had been taken by the wendigo, yes, but not in the same manner Adeline had. Poppy had tasted the flesh of her own kind and gone to the wendigo as one of their own.

She was opening her mouth to say so when Hal's hand clamped down on her shoulder, fingers digging in tight.

"Lower your light and be silent," he hissed. "They come."

The trees were thin and scrubby, but still packed tightly

enough that Annie was able to move her lantern half-behind her own body and half-behind the nearest trunk, blocking out the majority of the light. Hal stepped partially in front of her, blocking the rest. Anyone coming up from behind them would have seen it— wouldn't have been able to miss it, given how dark the woods were, how scant the light was—but from the mountain, they were cast entirely into darkness.

Silence reigned. Then, like a whisper, like a sigh, something rustled from the mountain. The bell-like shape of the wendigo cave was working against its owners: they might be silent as an owl's wings in the forest, in the world, but the killing field they had designed for their own use was inanimate and hence disloyal. It didn't care what it amplified; it didn't care that it amplified at all. And so it caught the sound of their movement and threw it out into the world, where it settled like a warning, like a prayer.

The first of the wendigo emerged.

Annie did not gasp. She was, briefly, terribly grateful to Michael, who had trained the habit of gasping out of her, first with his words, and later with his open palm, slapping her into submission, into the quiet, perfect doll he wanted her to be. She swallowed her terror and dismay, adding it to the turmoil already stewing in her belly. She would be pregnant again by the end of this night, she half-thought, growing gravid with the terrible offspring of Oregon.

She had been the mother to a monster's child once before. Adeline was none the worse for wear from her heritage. If a sibling was the cost of getting her back, Annie was sure her Delly would be an excellent older sister.

The wendigo were taller than a man, shaggy, like something bred of man and bear, but worse than either. Their mouths were a forest of teeth; their noses were all but nonexistent. It gave them a skull-like appearance, like they were the spirits of the dead tangled in a forest of roots and cobwebs. Their fur might have been white, had it been clean; as it was, they were a dozen shades of gray and brown and red. One, which had apparently gotten wet after its last meal, was a surprisingly appealing shade of petal-pink, like the blood had been partially but not completely rinsed away.

Hal's fingers clamped down tighter on Annie's shoulder as two wendigo emerged, closer together than most of the others. One was of a size with the rest. The other . . .

It was difficult to call something taller than an adult man "short," but everything was a matter of scale. Compared to the rest of the wendigo, the second was short, almost dainty. A child monster.

Poppy.

Annie glanced to Hal. Tears were standing in the old forester's eyes, which were fixed on that diminutive monster. He watched her all the way to the edge of the clearing, where she followed the rest of the wendigo into the trees and disappeared.

His eyes flicked to Annie. He gave a little shake of his head, indicating that she shouldn't ask. She didn't. She already knew what his answer would be, and in that moment, the greatest cruelty she could have committed would have been forcing him to say it out loud.

"Come," he whispered instead, voice barely louder than a sigh, and started across the open ground toward the cave. Annie followed on his heels, hurrying to keep up, not looking back. The wendigo and the woods were one. If anything was coming from behind them, they were already dead.

The land between the wood's edge and the mountain was blasted and dead, the soft loam of the forest giving way to hard-packed dirt that could never have nurtured so much as a weed. There was no life. There was no cover.

Whatever approached the wendigo did so in the open, with neither shade nor shelter to protect them.

The mouth of the cave loomed like the maw of a great beast, ready to swallow them down and consume them whole. Hal stopped a few feet from the entrance, putting one arm out to signal for Annie to do the same.

"Once inside, any sound will echo back out onto the woods," he said. "If the wendigo are close, they *will* hear, and they *will* return. Be as silent as you claim your child is. Do you understand me?"

Annie nodded. "Yes."

"Good. May God have mercy on both our souls." He started forward once more, leaving Annie with little choice but to follow him.

She raised her lantern high as they stepped past the edge of the cave, into the deeper dark contained within.

It was immediately clear that the wendigo had gone, all of them, for the shadows inside the cave they called home—if such things could ever truly be said to have a home—were only shadows, thin and natural and no more clinging than shadows had ever been. The thick darkness of the woods was absent here. Annie felt sick as she realized how pervasive the presence of the wendigo was. They had been with her in the trees all night, thickening the shadows, filling the air with dread, and she had pressed on, because there had been no other choice.

The stone was worn so smooth that Annie's feet found little purchase. She walked slowly, setting her feet down with exaggerated care, to stop herself from making any sound. That was another thing: the cave was silent. Soundless. Nothing breathed; nothing stirred. Her heart gave a lurch as she realized what that must mean.

Then they stepped around the bend in the cave, and Hal reached back to press a hand over her mouth, gently stopping the scream he must have felt building there. Annie's eyes bulged under the sudden pressure of her horror and dismay.

The wendigo had eaten well this night. The central chamber of the mountain—for it must have been the center; it was so large, and the entrances to other tunnels gaped from every wall like dead black eyes—was awash in blood, fresh and red, drying and brown. Annie's eyes skipped over it, refusing to fix on any detail, unable to stop *seeing*.

There: a severed leg, muscle gleaming wetly red, skin still intact from the ankle down, covering the meat in creamy brown.

There: a ribcage, cracked open, so devoid of flesh that she couldn't say whether it had belonged to a man or a woman.

There: a woman's head, long, golden hair matted with blood, eyes open and staring at nothingness forevermore.

There were at least ten dead among the carnage, all of them rent and sundered from themselves, until the feasting hall became a mass grave, an abattoir of blood and bone and viscera. The people had become puzzles in their dying, the pieces that remained so jumbled together that they could never be separated or reassembled properly.

There was no white gown—or perhaps there had been, and it was so soaked through with blood that it was no longer white. But Annie's eyes searched the killing floor, tracing limb and bone and viscera, and found no child-sized limbs, no trace of white-blonde hair or gauzy gown. She let out a shuddering breath, struggling to keep it as quiet as possible, no longer able to quite care. Adeline wasn't here.

"Hello?"

Annie and Hal both stiffened, turning to each other before turning toward the sound. The voice had come from one of the tunnels on the other side of the chamber. It was female, weak with fear and shaking with exhaustion. The thought of someone being held captive here, being kept *alive* through the feast that must have destroyed the rest of the taken . . .

It was horrifying.

The voice spoke again. "Hello, please? I can see your light. I know you're not the things that took me. They don't need light." The speaker had a faint Spanish accent, as if English was not her first language. "Please, help me, before they come back."

Annie started forward. Hal grabbed her arm, pulling her to an abrupt halt. She turned to look at him, and he shook his head in a firm "no."

Annie's eyes narrowed. Not for the first time, she wished that everyone spoke Adeline's language, which was silent and subtle and needed no ears; had Adeline been here, she could have told her daughter what to do without attracting the attention of the wendigo. She jerked her arm free, shaking her head in reply. No. No, she would not walk away from someone in need—someone whose accent marked her as from elsewhere, and hence almost certainly a part of the circus.

If I walk away from Sophia, Martin will never forgive me, she thought. That, alone, was enough to move her feet forward, stepping between the pools of blood, moving onward, into the dark.

Chapter 17

The shadows were deeper in the tunnel, with its narrow walls and low ceiling. The chamber had diluted them somehow, making them easier to bear. Here, even though they lacked the viscosity they had possessed in the wood, they clung and clutched, seeming to blank out the world. Annie pressed on, until her light illuminated the dirty, huge-eyed face of Sophia.

The girl's eyes widened even farther, until it seemed they must fall out of her skull, no longer anchored by the shape of her skin. "Miss Pearl!" she exclaimed. "Oh, I knew someone would come for me!"

Annie shook her head exaggeratedly and pressed a finger to her lips, trying to signal the girl into silence.

"It hurts, it hurts," moaned Sophia, either missing or ignoring the cue. "Please, can't you do something?"

Annie shushed her again, fighting the urge to look over her shoulder. If the wendigo were returning, it was already too late to run. This time, at least, Sophia seemed to take her meaning; the girl quieted, settling down against the wall.

The wendigo lacked the patience or humanity for ropes or cages: they had trapped Sophia by wedging her foot between two stones. Both were large—too large for Annie to shift on her own. She stepped closer, leaning toward Sophia until her lantern illuminated every bruise and scrape on the terrified girl's face. She pressed her lips against the filthy tangle of Sophia's hair, praying that she was close enough to speak without the sound being carried by the cave.

"I have a friend waiting in the chamber," she said. "I need to get him, so he can help me move these stones. You must be utterly silent. Make no noise, or the beasts may return. Do you understand? Nod if you understand."

Sophia nodded haltingly, tears cutting new trails through the mess on her face. She didn't make a sound.

Annie nodded back, trying to convey her approval, as she straightened and walked back to the chamber. The light from her lantern hit a waiting figure, and for one terrible moment her heart seemed to stop at the sight of him. Then his features became clear: it was Hal, not one of the wendigo. She beckoned him forward.

He shook his head in fierce negation.

She beckoned again, more pleadingly this time. Without his help, she would never be able to move the stone from Sophia's leg; she could stay with the girl until the wendigo returned, she could sacrifice both of them so that Sophia wouldn't need to die alone, but she could never *save* her.

Hal was too far away, too shrouded in shadows, for her to see his expression. But his shoulders slumped and he started forward, stepping over broken body parts until he joined her at the mouth of the tunnel.

"Thank you," she mouthed, and turned to lead him to Sophia.

When the light struck Sophia's face again, the girl looked from Annie to Hal, something like hope blooming in her eyes. She indicated her trapped foot. Hal, scowling, went to kneel in front of her, beginning to work at the rocks. They scraped against each other as he moved them, sending up little grinding noises.

Annie glanced nervously over her shoulder, looking for signs of movement. There were none. She looked back to Hal and Sophia, holding up her lantern to light their efforts—

And froze as the shadows, which had previously been beaten back by the light from her lantern, stubbornly refused to yield. They were thickening, strengthening, growing as solid as any flesh. The wendigo were coming back.

Hal, working at Sophia's leg, didn't appear to have noticed. Either the shadows were gelling slowly, like pudding setting, or he had been in these woods for so long that he no longer noticed such little dangers. As for Sophia, she was frozen in her fear, unable to register anything but her own dilemma.

Until her eyes widened, fixing on some point behind Annie, and she screamed.

It was a high, ringing sound, amplified by the shape of the tunnel until it became something akin to a weapon. Annie whirled, raising and swinging her lantern like a club, and smashed it against the face of the wendigo that had come up behind her, claws extended, ready for the kill. It howled, and that sound, too, was amplified by the shape of the tunnel.

"Hal!" shouted Annie, as she swung the lantern again. There was no further need for silence: they had been discovered. "Get her free!"

This close, the wendigo smelled rank, like something dead that had been rotting in the sun for days on end. It opened its mouth and snarled, lunging for her. In the tight space of the tunnel, there was nowhere for her to go— but there was no way for the wendigo to press the advantage of its size, either. One massive paw caught her in the shoulder, slamming her against the wall, claws biting deep into the muscle of her arm. Annie cried out, as much in rage as in pain. The wendigo opened its mouth wider, lashing forward to rip out her throat.

She shoved the lantern into its jaws.

The wendigo, already mid-motion, bit down before it realized what it was doing. There was a shattering sound, and Annie had time to see the startled look on the wendigo's face before the last of the tallow drained from the lantern's reservoir and down the creature's throat. The wendigo slumped forward, driving its claws deeper into her shoulder before it fell, the weight of its body pulling them free. The light went out. Darkness slammed down upon them.

Annie stumbled a few feet to the side, shocked, clamping a hand over her bleeding shoulder. "Hal?" she said, voice a querulous gasp.

He was silent for several seconds—long enough that she began to think the wendigo had not returned alone, that he was dead, and Sophia as well, leaving her alone.

Finally, Hal said, "Tallow."

"What?"

There was a loud clatter as the rock finally yielded to his efforts, and moved. A moment later, Annie heard the distinctive sound of flint scraping against stone, and a spark lit up the darkness. Hal held up a small torch, no longer than her forearm, slim enough that it would burn down quickly. He must have had it inside his coat the entire time, allowing her to light the way.

Sophia was clutching her leg, knee drawn up against her chest. As Annie watched, Hal offered her his hand and gently coaxed Sophia to her feet, allowing the injured girl to lean against him. Sophia's head barely came up to the level of his shoulder. It was difficult not to look at them and see him as he must have been with his own daughter.

"It kills them," said Hal. "Pour tallow down a wendigo's throat and they die. I don't know why. To be honest, I've never given a damn. It happens."

"Then I . . ."

"You killed it." Hal looked at the wendigo, fallen so

as to almost block the tunnel, and the sorrow in his face was deep and cold. "You killed her."

Annie didn't say another word. She stepped over the wendigo's arm, with its long and curving claws, and moved to stand on Sophia's other side, offering the woman her free hand. Sophia took it.

Together, the three of them left the tunnel where Poppy's body lay, so long removed from the little girl who had hungered in the endless wintertime, now finally at rest. They crossed the cavern of carnal terrors, stepping around puddles of blood and the bodies of those who had been taken. Sophia closed her eyes for that part of the journey, relying on Annie and Hal to hold her up, to keep her from falling. She was limping, but not so badly that she couldn't walk. She would make it.

No other wendigo came to confront them on their way out of the mountain. Poppy, who had been the last to leave, had been the only one close enough to hear the noises they had made. Had she still been a human child, she might have brought her mother when she went to investigate an unexpected sound. But even the thin memories of her human life hadn't been enough to override a wendigo's hunger. If she went alone, she could fill her belly alone. So she had come back by herself, and had filled her belly with tallow, and now her dreadful jaws were finally closed.

Annie stole glances at Hal as they walked, trying to read the expression on his grizzled face. If he was angry, he wasn't showing it. He stared straight ahead, stoic as ever, and never once looked back at the narrow hole that would be his daughter's final resting place.

The air outside was almost painfully fresh. Annie breathed in, trying to let it chase away the terrors of the mountain. Sophia leaned a little harder on her arm.

"We need to keep moving," whispered Hal. "The wendigo will come back, and they'll be angry when they see what we've done."

"They won't fear us? We killed one of their own."

"They won't care about that. It's the stolen meal that will enrage them. We need to get back to my cabin."

The cabin, where Sophia could rest: where Martin was waiting, terrified that she was already lost. It was the best solution, and more, it would put walls between them and the wood.

It would put walls between them and Adeline.

"We can't stay there," said Annie.

Hal scowled at her. "I don't know where else your daughter could be."

"Adeline?" Sophia looked between the two of them. "Adeline is missing?"

"Yes," said Annie. "Was she . . ."

"No." Sophia shook her head. "She was never there. I would have seen her."

Annie found that she could suddenly breathe again. She pulled in a great gasp of air, letting it re-inflate her lungs, trying to feel her way back to solid footing. Adeline hadn't been taken by the wendigo. Adeline might still be alive. Out there somewhere alone and frightened, but alive. That was more than she had been daring to hope for.

They moved through the woods as quietly and quickly as they could, Hal holding up his makeshift torch to light their way, Annie offering Sophia a steadying hand whenever necessary. The shadows thinned, making it easier to breathe, making it clear that the wendigo were elsewhere, maybe harvesting the settlement for more prey, maybe doing whatever it was that monsters did when not filling their bellies. It seemed an unwise topic of conversation.

"Not far now," said Hal. "We'll help you down the hill."

"Martin is there," said Annie.

Sophia straightened, eyes going wide with sudden hope. "Martin? *My* Martin? He lives?"

"He does, and he's been searching for you," said Annie. "He'll be the happiest man alive when he sees you well."

"I never thought to see him again," said Sophia. Her tone was wondering. "I thought this was where our stories ended."

"Oregon has ended a great many things, but not that," said Hal.

They continued on in silence, Sophia now attempting to urge them on, walking as quickly as her injured foot would allow. Annie began to hope that they might make it.

Something moved in the trees ahead of them.

Hal stopped instantly, motioning for the others to do the same. Annie halted, putting an arm around Sophia, keeping her from running, and a white wolf melted out of the woods, pacing toward them.

It was vast, as wolves went, as large as the well-fed dogs of the traders in Montana and the Badlands. It walked with its head low and its ears flat, and Annie fancied she could feel its growl all the way down to the soles of her feet, vibrating up from the earth, pulling her downward.

"Wolfling," spat Hal. "Stay back." He dropped his torch to the ground, where it sputtered and struggled to catch among the damp needles, and raised his rifle.

Four more wolflings melted out of the wood, forming a loose semicircle in front of them. They did nothing, only stood there. That was enough. They menaced with their very presence, presenting a terrifying wall of teeth and fur and incipient swiftness.

Something rustled behind them. Annie knew without

turning that it was the rest of the pack, hemming them in as neatly as taking a breath.

"What are they?" whispered Sophia.

"Wolflings," said Hal again. "Not real wolves. Cousins. Or the damned souls of real wolves, condemned to walk these woods for their sins."

One of the wolflings barked, sharp and cold. The others flattened their ears and growled.

"They seem to understand you," said Annie. It was a struggle to keep her voice level. It seemed worth the effort. The last thing she wanted to do was trigger some sort of an attack. "Perhaps stop insulting them."

Something nudged the back of her legs. This time she did turn. Three wolflings stood there, one for each of them.

"You may be considering shooting your way out of this," said Annie, still keeping her voice as calm as she possibly could. "Consider, however, the alternative: don't. They aren't attacking us. They appear to be herding us. Perhaps we should go with them."

"They're beasts," hissed Hal.

"Yes, and we've just killed a wendigo. We're beasts in our own right, if looked at the right way." The wolfling nudged her legs again. Annie gritted her teeth. "I want to live to see my daughter again, sir. Let's do as the giant wolves wish."

"I'm scared," whispered Sophia.

"We're all scared, dear," said Annie. "It's just a matter of being more angry than afraid. Once you can accomplish that, anything is possible."

The wolfling nudged her again. She started walking. Sophia moved with her. Hal did not. Annie glanced back, once, to see two more wolflings moving toward him. She turned her eyes resolutely forward after that. It was simple math. There were too many wolflings for him to shoot them all: even if he tried, he would miss one, or two, or more, and that would be enough to put all three of them into the ground. Going along with the creatures might seem more dangerous than fighting them, but it would keep them alive for longer, and as long as they were alive, there was a chance.

Hal hurried up next to her. Annie glanced at him.

"I see they convinced you," she said.

He scowled, and said nothing at all.

Walking through the forest in the company of great white wolves was oddly soothing. Yes, the creatures were potentially dangerous, and yes, they could all die at any moment, but while the wolflings were there, nothing else was going to make its presence known. Even the shadows were behaving themselves, acting more like ordinary shadows, cast by ordinary trees, than the thick, fear-fueled things they had been since the circus arrived in Oregon. It was almost a relief. Yes, she was being herded through the woods by wolves larger than any she had ever seen, but at least if they decided to have her heart, she would die breathing easy and at peace with the world.

But what of Adeline?

The thought was chilling. She stumbled, earning a growl from the wolfling behind her. She hadn't thought of her little girl since fleeing the wendigo mountain. It had only been a handful of minutes—surely no more than ten, fifteen at the very most—and yet it still felt like a betrayal, like she had done something she should never have been able to do. She had forgotten, if only for a moment, that she was a mother. She had been thinking of herself as an independent creature.

Of all the wicked things she had encountered in the wood, forgetting her child somehow seemed the wickedest of them all.

Sophia's footing was unsteady, her leg weakened by the time she had spent with it crushed between the stones.

The bones seemed to be unbroken, but still, she limped and staggered and required constant assistance to keep her from falling. Annie tried to focus on Sophia, and not on the fact that she was being herded by creatures that were almost but not quite wolves, or the thought that she had forgotten her daughter, even for an instant. Even for a *second*.

"They're going to eat us alive," said Hal.

"Why haven't they done it, then?"

"Probably didn't want to spill blood that close to the wendigo. Wendigo and wolflings, they don't hunt together. They don't share their kills." Hal shook his head. "What one takes, the other cannot have. Both are smart enough to covet."

"That means they're smart enough to sin, and whatever's smart enough to sin can be redeemed," said Annie sharply. "Let them have their moments of redemption, and for God's sake, stop encouraging them to eat us."

"Don't need no encouragement," Hal muttered darkly. But he quieted after that, and that was all Annie could have asked.

They walked for what seemed like miles, crossing several small clearings, before the woods dropped away and another mountain rose out of the ground. This one, unlike the mountain of the wendigo, was alive: its slopes were covered in growing green, in briars and brush and scrubby pine trees. More wolflings lounged on low rocks and around the mouth of a cave. Smaller ones—adolescents and cubs, from the size of them.

"My God," breathed Hal. "There's a whole damned pack of the things."

Annie said nothing. Her heart felt as if it had stopped in her chest, becoming a small, dead thing trapped between the straining billows of her lungs. Her throat was dry and tight, not allowing her to breathe in.

There, on one of the bushes near the mouth of the cave,

was a strip of gauzy white fabric, clearly torn from Adeline's gown.

"Ma'am?" Sophia looked at her in alarm. "Ma'am, are you all right?"

Annie's knees buckled. The wolflings were still trying to nudge her onward, Sophia still needed her to stand, and none of that mattered, none of that was real, because Adeline was dead. These were the monsters that had stolen her daughter away, and Annie had let her be taken, while she had chased wendigo and whispers through the wood, turning her back on the little girl who needed her. She had failed. She had finally, after years of running, years of struggling for just one more day of peace and freedom, failed.

The ground was hard, studded with tiny stones that bit into her skin when she folded into a kneeling position, hitting her knees so hard that it brought tears to her eyes. That was almost a relief. She *should* be crying. It was a failure of biology and motherhood that she wasn't. Something was wrong with her. The treatments Michael had given her, all those years ago, had changed her as surely as they had changed her children, and she had been a fool to think—

Something moved at the mouth of the wolflings' cave, something smaller than the white wolves but taller at the same time, something with a biped's stance. That was all the warning Annie had before Adeline burst into the open, legs churning divots from the ground as she raced to throw her arms around her mother's neck.

Her skin was hot where it pressed against Annie's cheek, and the part of Annie's mind that could never stop monitoring her daughter's health murmured, *she needs her medicine,* before shutting down, unable to process what was happening. She could feel Adeline's breathing, feel her chest expanding with each breath she took. Annie looked up. Hal was looking at her.

"Is that the girl?" he asked.

No, the woods are crawling with children who can't wait to embrace me as their mother, thought Annie nonsensically. Aloud, she said, "Yes. But how . . . ?"

"Martin!" cried Sophia. She took off running, and made it almost five long steps before her wounded ankle buckled and sent her crashing to the ground. The wolflings didn't chase her. Instead, they sat down where they were and watched, looking almost amused by the antics of these strange bipedal creatures.

Martin, who had followed Adeline out of the cave, albeit more slowly, hurried to kneel and lift his lover out of the dirt, his hands under her arms, his eyes fixed on her face. "Sophia," he said, voice warm with longing and relief. "They found you."

"I was so scared," said Sophia, and threw her arms around him, and held him close.

"We found her, and you found my Delly," said Annie, stroking her daughter's hair as she lifted her head and looked at Martin. "How? How did you even *get* here? We left you in the cabin. I thought—it was my belief that you were going to remain there. To wait for us to return."

"Well, ma'am, I—" Martin paused as he caught sight of Hal's expression. The old forester looked grim, resigned even, like he knew exactly why Martin had chosen to leave, and couldn't find it in himself to blame the man. Martin took a breath. "I got worried, ma'am. I thought, what do we really know about this fellow? How do we know he's for the good, and not for the bad? Forgive me, ma'am, it wasn't trusting of me, but you know what Mr. Blackstone says. Never put town over show."

"And by letting me leave with a stranger, you thought you were putting town over show," concluded Annie. She stood, gathering Adeline in her arms as she did, until the girl was bundled against her hip. The weight of it was reassuring, so familiar that Annie felt her tears begin to well up for real. The only thing that could have made the moment more ideal would have been Tranquility pacing out of the woods and standing by her side, all muscle and menace and fur.

Tranquility did not appear. Some things were too much to even hope for, and there has never been a truly perfect world.

"Yes, ma'am," said Martin. He didn't articulate his own fears over Hal's relationship with the wendigo. It would have been petty, with Hal right there and Annie so clearly unharmed. "I left to try to find you. I guess I got turned around, because these big wolf-things found me first, and they brought me here."

"Like they brought us," said Sophia hopefully. "They're *good* wolflings."

"They're man-eaters," said Hal grimly. "They're worse than the wendigo, because they hunt in the summer as well as the snow, and they understand how to function as a pack. They take care of their wounded and their weak. They've killed dozens of men in the time I've lived in Oregon, and I'm sure they'll kill hundreds more before they're burnt from the face of the earth. They don't help lost travelers. Not unless they're helping them into their own bellies."

Adeline leaned back until her body formed almost a right angle from her mother's, trusting Annie to hold her up as she freed her hands and began signing.

'Wrong,' she signed. 'They're my friends.'

"Can they understand you, Delly?" asked Annie.

'They sign, some of them. They don't know many words. Someone needs to teach them more words.' Adeline wrinkled her nose. 'It's hard not to know many words.'

"That's true," said Annie. She looked to Hal. "Adeline says they can communicate with her. They speak with their hands." After everything that had happened, the idea of wolves that spoke with their hands was somehow not unreasonable.

"That's not right," insisted Hal. "They're beasts. They hunt, and they kill. They don't help."

"But they're helping us," said Martin.

"True," said Hal. His eyes were on Adeline. "I wonder why."

Closing up the house had been an easy affair: all it required was some sheets over the furniture in the rooms that would be closed until their return, the donation of the majority of the perishable goods to the temple, where they could be distributed among the deserving poor, and the transfer of the projects Michael had been working on for Hellstromme to other labs, where they could be brought to beneficial fruition.

From the beginning of the process to its conclusion, the whole thing had taken less than three days. It seemed like such a small amount of time, when stacked against the enormity of what was to come next. It should have been impossible.

Helen had long since learned that nothing was impossible when Dr. Murphy willed that it be so. He was no god or monster—only a man—but he was possessed of an iron will and an unshakable belief in his own infallibility. Helen thought, sometimes, that a man convinced that he was doing the right thing might be more dangerous than a monster, which was, after all, only convinced that it should fill its belly and continue on its terrible way. Monsters acted because of the way they were made. Men acted because of the way they chose to be.

Choice was almost always more terrifying than the alternative.

The carriage he had commissioned for the journey sat on the road outside of the house, gleaming with steel plates and polished wood. It was a battleship of a conveyance, capable of standing up to all but the most violent of assaults. A vent at the rear was open to allow a thin, constant trickle of steam to escape. The internal mechanisms were working, then; there was a chance that Annabelle would survive the journey. Only that: a chance. Which meant there was a chance she wouldn't.

"I wish you would let me go with you, sir," said Helen. "With the complications of the road, it's possible that Annabelle will require more care than you will be in a position to provide."

"Are you saying that I can't take care of my own child?" Dr. Murphy's question was mild, but not so mild that she couldn't hear the threat lurking beneath it, like a great worm lurking beneath seemingly calm desert sands. She was walking farther into dangerous territory with every word she spoke.

Still, she pressed on. For Annabelle's sake. "No, sir, only that—"

"Because my *wife* has been able to care for Adeline without me. Without any of the luxuries that Annabelle has been afforded by our life here in the Holy City. She has raised our little girl like a dog in the street, barefoot and profane and surrounded by men who are not of her flesh, not of her blood, not of her faith. Would you really claim that Grace, of all people, is better suited to parenthood than I, who has reordered the world for the sake of my daughter?"

Yes, whispered the traitorous voice of Helen's doubts, deep in the back of her mind, where even Dr. Murphy could not hear or shame her for it.

"No, sir," she said. "You have been the best of fathers, and I am sure you will only continue to grow in your wisdom and experience. I look forward to your returning with Adeline, who has been too long gone and deserves to know her father."

"She will be treated like the princess that she is," said Dr. Murphy stiffly.

"But the road is hard, sir, even for the best of fathers—even for the best of warriors, with nothing but themselves to worry about. I am merely concerned that you might come to harm when you allow your natural concern for Annabelle to distract you from the business of fighting the filthy heathens between you and your goal."

Dr. Murphy's face softened, enough so that Helen thought, for a moment, that he might be listening to reason. He was a brilliant man. Surely he could understand the sense in what she was saying.

"Dear, sweet Helen," he said. "Truly, you are an honor to your father and to your family. I could not take you into the world outside Deseret. Someone as fine and good and unsullied as yourself would never survive there. Annabelle possesses all those qualities, but Annabelle has no choice. If she is to survive, she needs her sister. You understand that, don't you?"

"Yes, sir," Helen whispered.

"Go home to your family. Your wages will continue until I return. If, when I come home, you find that you do not wish to return to my service, we will discuss the matter of your replacement."

"I would never want to leave your service, sir."

"Come now, Helen. You are a young woman in the prime of your life. One day a clever young man will steal you away from me, and I'll be glad to let you go, for what better duty can a woman have than motherhood?" He reached out and touched the top of her head paternally. Helen managed, somehow, not to flinch away. "You have been an excellent helpmeet. I will see you soon."

"Yes, sir," whispered Helen, and ducked her head, so that she wouldn't need to watch him walk away.

As for Dr. Murphy, once he had turned and started for the waiting carriage, he did not look back, not once; did not even feel the urge. Yes, the house he left behind was his home, and the people who stood watching him go were his servants. He felt toward them a casual possessiveness, as he might feel for any of his replaceable tools. Break a hammer, purchase a new one. Fire—or accidentally incapacitate—a servant, hire another. There were always bodies, eager and willing to work in the house of a great man, prepared to risk their own health and safety for the sake of their families. The poor had so many mouths to feed.

(That he classed even those who would have seemed unfathomably wealthy by the standards of Junkyard as "the poor" was perhaps more telling than he intended it to be. In the world of Dr. Michael Murphy, people were either useful, useless, or dangerous. There were few gradations within those categories. The world was either for him, against him, or there to be exploited.)

Three large men stood beside the carriage, waiting for him. Dr. Murphy nodded to each of them in turn as he continued onward toward the front, where a woman in brown leather sat, her feet propped against the running board, the reins held loosely in her hands. A wide-brimmed hat blocked her face from the sun, less out of vanity than practicality. If she couldn't see where she was going, she couldn't shoot, or keep the wagon on the narrow path to their goal.

"Laura," he said stiffly. It was odd, addressing a woman who only technically worked for him without honorific or civility. But it was her preference, and he was not going to go against it: not as long as he needed something from her. "The house is closed. The servants have been sent home. Dr. Hellstromme knows that we're to depart today."

"That's all true," said the woman he called Laura, still lounging with her back against the carriage, shoulders slightly bowed, like she hadn't a care in the world. "Trouble is, he hasn't given me the go yet, and I'm his dogsbody, not yours. Until he drops the hammer, this is where I sit, and since I'm your driver, this is where you sit. Get comfortable, doctor-man."

"Time is of the essence."

"You're not wrong. You're not right, either." Laura sat up, stretching languidly, allowing the reins to drop from her hand. The motion exposed the supple length of her body, forcing Dr. Murphy to turn away, feeling his cheeks flare red. His wife might be a harlot and a Jezebel, running away from her duties, stealing from her husband, but she was still his *wife*. As long as she lived, he was a married man, and looking at another woman—even a stained unbeliever like this Laura—was a sin.

"Explain," he said, voice tight.

"The rattlers are at their most active this time of day. We drive this pretty little rig of yours out there right now, I'd lay even odds that we're devoured before we have time to engage the steam engines—and the house always wins that sort of a gamble, Murphy. The house *always* wins. Wait an hour, let the sun drop a bit, deploy the decoys, and hit the road. We can be out of their range before they realize there was something tasty on that wagon." Laura smiled at the back of his head. "I've made this run before. You haven't. You may be a genius, but part of genius is admitting it when you're not the smartest man in the room."

"We don't have much time. If the passages into Oregon close for the winter before we can get there, we'll never catch them." Annabelle wouldn't survive another winter separated from her sister. She wasn't strong enough. All his efforts, all his treatments, and still she wasn't strong enough. She needed Adeline if she were going to survive.

It was infuriating, how rarely people wanted to listen

to him. How often they *questioned* him, acting as if their own small experiences could make them his equals. Sometimes he wanted to show them just how much damage he could do when he took his own reins off and allowed the monster of his mind to roam free.

But no. Hellstromme would not approve, and this woman, this, this *impertinent girl,* belonged to him.

"An hour, you say," he said tightly.

"No more, no less," said Laura. "Get comfortable. Tell your daughter about what she's going to see. She seems like a nice girl."

"You will not go near my daughter." There was sudden venom in his voice. "You will not touch her; you will not talk to her. You should not have done so in the first place."

"I spoke to her on Hellstromme's orders."

The statement was surprising enough that Dr. Murphy turned back to her, eyes wide. She was leaning forward, elbows resting on her knees, looking at him like he was some sort of insect, barely worth her notice.

"He told me to see the girl, to judge for myself whether she could even survive this little adventure. He's *very* interested in what becomes of her, you know."

"H-he is my mentor and my supervisor," said Dr. Murphy. "He has always been kind to my family."

"He wants to know if you can put something broken back together and make it work," said Laura. "He wants to know if you can *fix* her. Frankly, I don't know why he cares so much, and I don't want to know. It's a waste of his time. He could be doing great things, and instead, he's wasting his attention on you. Your work has never been more than passable. You say you're a genius, but you come up with machines any fool could have assembled. You're a blight on the face of Deseret—and that's funny, when you consider what the rest of the world thinks of us. You stink of ghost rock and despair. So yeah, when your master told me to look at your daughter, I did it. I would have slit her throat if he'd told me to."

"You dare—"

"I do! I do dare. I'm here to babysit you and make sure you don't stray beyond the terms of your release. Hellstromme is happy to help you with your researches, but that doesn't make him a fool, and better men than you have snuck out of Deseret under the cover of going to look at something interesting somewhere else. Bringing your daughter along just makes you more of a chancy proposition." Laura's smile was slow and languid as the sun peeking through the smog, and just as laced with novel, impossible poisons. She was a rattlesnake in a woman's shape, and every move she made only drew the comparison deeper. "She's a pretty thing. Can you imagine how many hearts she'd break if she could go more than a few feet from her bed? There are fathers in the Holy City who'd kill to be in your shoes."

Before he could speak Laura was gone, sliding off the baseboard and vanishing behind the wagon. Dr. Murphy barely had time to register her absence before fingers were threaded through his hair, yanking his head ever so slightly back to make it easier for her to lay the edge of her knife across his throat.

"I dare," she said sweetly. "I do not work for you. I am in Hellstromme's employ, even as you are, and while my science may be a little less clinical than your own, never question that I am a scientist in my own right. I work in blood and bullets and bodies on the floor, and I am at the top of my profession. Do you understand me?"

"Hellstromme will have your hands when I tell him that you put them on me."

"Hellstromme may have your tongue when I tell him that you forced me to do it." Laura withdrew her knife before shoving him forward, hard enough that he had to put out his hands in order to keep from smacking his forehead against the wagon.

Dr. Murphy turned, fury and embarrassment burning in his veins, cheeks flaring red with the realization that his men—*his* men, who were meant to follow his orders without question, to see him as a cruel and absolute commander—had seen his mistreatment at the hands of this slip of a girl. That she was a gunslinger in the direct service of his own master mattered little. It was her place to yield to him, to be subservient to him, and her refusal was a slight in the eyes of God.

She was gone.

He stared for a moment, disbelieving, before he turned and looked back to the wagon. She was seated once more on the boards, the reins back in her hand, looking for all the world like she had never moved in the first place.

"We move in an hour, boss," said Laura easily. "Go see your girl."

Dr. Michael Murphy was a proud man. Some would call him a cruel man. But he had never been a foolish man, nor courted fights he knew he couldn't win. Cheeks still burning from the humiliation of it all, he turned and walked down the length of the wagon to the door.

It was locked. It was always to be locked while they were on the road. He slid the ring from his index finger and pressed it to the keyhole, twisting it sharply to the right. With a click, the lock released, and the door came open under his hand. He stepped up and inside, pulling the door closed behind himself.

The other two wagons that would travel with them were ordinary things: dark, cramped, packed with supplies and weapons to get them to Oregon. The drive would not be long, not when it was to be bolstered by steam across the flat plains and driven by skilled wagoners through the hills and delicate terrain. Most of those between them and their goal would know better than to interfere with a wagon train that traveled under Hell-stromme's banner. There was robbery as a way of life and then there was robbery as a means of suicide. This wagon, though . . .

The inside was white. As white as Annabelle's room, so white that every speck of dust and smudge from the road would show up in stark relief against her gauzy draperies. Dr. Murphy had pledged to clean them himself, showing himself as the humble, devoted father he was. Hellstromme would like that. The great doctor appreciated it when his men were properly devoted to their families, and it wasn't as if Helen could have traveled with them; she was unmarried, unbonded to his household in any way beyond employment, and it would have been the very height of impropriety to drag her outside of Deseret.

(The fact that she had offered was inconsequential. Women rarely knew what was best for them. They needed to be coddled, cared for, and confined, kept from breaking themselves against the harsh realities of the world. Helen thought she wanted to travel with him, to care for Annabelle and prove that she deserved her place in his household. She was wrong. It was a sign of what a good man he was, how gloriously pious, that he would not allow his own desire for the small human comforts to override the need to keep her safe.)

The seats inside the carriage had been removed to make room for Annabelle's bed and the great machines that made up the headboard. They seemed starker here than they had in her room, where he had been able to spend years carefully concealing them behind layers of polished walnut and gauzy linen. They labored, silver sides heaving, as they performed the difficult, essential task of keeping her alive.

Annabelle's eyes were closed. He leaned forward, putting his hand over her own small, cold one.

"Wake up, my pet," he said, voice low and gentle. "Your father would look upon you."

Annabelle opened her eyes. She did not sit up, or even try to; she simply let her head lean forward a bit, lashes fluttering against the pale curve of her cheek. She was so beautiful. She was so perfect. She should have been the crown jewel of Deseret—and would be, of that much he was certain. As soon as he had healed her, undoing the damage dealt by her careless beast of a mother, she would be the finest star in Deseret's crown, and Dr. Hellstromme would see what a good and faithful servant he was, how well he had labored for the goodness and glory of their home.

"Papa?" Her voice was thin as a whisper.

Dr. Murphy made a silent note to adjust the pressure in her breathing tubes. She should have sounded hale, healthy even, regardless of whether she had the strength to put any force into her words. Appearances were as important as realities. When they caught up with Grace, he needed her to see what a good father he had been to the child she'd left behind.

He needed that to be the *last* thing she saw, before he closed her lying eyes forever.

"I'm right here, pet," he said. "How are you feeling?"

Annabelle's pretty face drew into a distinctly unpretty pout. The expression cut deep furrows into the skin to either side of her mouth, making her look like an old woman trapped inside a child's body.

"I want my room," she said. "I want my bed, and my room, and my window. I want Helen. Those men, they *touched* me. They put their hands on me, and they *touched* me. Like they were allowed! They shouldn't even have been looking at me, and they *touched* me." Offense dripped from her words like honey, thick and clinging and viscous.

There had been times—shameful times, for which he

had prayed to be forgiven—when Michael had questioned Annabelle's parentage. She looked so little like him, or like his Grace, and Grace had been unfaithful in mind and spirit both. Who was to say that she hadn't been unfaithful in body as well? But then came moments like this one, when he looked into his daughter's face and knew, beyond the shadow of a doubt, that she was his. There was no one else in this world who could have made her. Not even Dr. Hellstromme had the skill.

"I'm sorry, poppet, but they touched you on my order, and they're not to be punished for what they've done," he said. "You had to be moved from your bedroom to here. I lowered the oxygen in your room to make it easier for you to sleep. Did you sleep?"

"It was like a dream," she admitted. "I thought I was asleep until I woke up and I was here, and I knew that it had all been true. I don't want to be here, Papa. I want to be in my room. Please, can't I be in my room, Papa? I won't even yell when they touch me again, I'll be so good, I'll be like a stone." She looked at him hopefully.

He had asked her to be like a stone before, when he needed to operate on her, or when he needed to refill the reservoirs of ghost rock that powered her cold and clockwork heart. She could maintain her poise through agonies that would have broken a lesser child. Truly, one day, she would be the finest flower in Deseret. All he had to do was fix her.

"No, my dearest," he said. "You must remain here. We're going on a trip."

"A trip?" She frowned again, more delicately this time, so that she still looked like a little girl. "But where would we go? We never go on trips."

"We do today." He leaned forward, smoothing her blankets with the tips of his fingers. "You'll have this whole wagon to yourself, and you have a driver—a real driver—from Dr. Hellstromme himself. Her name is Laura, and she's one of the best drivers in all of Deseret."

"I met her. She seems nice. Are there horses?"

"Yes, on your wagon. We want to avoid using the steam engine if at all possible. It might not get along with your machines. If we have to use it, Laura will tell you first, and she'll ask you to hold your breath, just in case."

"Can I see the horses?" persisted Annabelle.

Surprised, Dr. Murphy smiled. Sometimes it was easy to forget that she was just a little girl. "I'll see about bringing them by your window when we break for the night. You're going to see things you've never seen before, my pet. You're such a lucky little girl."

Annabelle nodded solemnly. She had been told her entire life that she was lucky: that other little girls had things infinitely worse than she did. She had never questioned the people who told her that. They knew more little girls than she did. Surely, they must be correct.

"Where are we going, Papa?"

This was the difficult part. This was the part where everything could come to pieces. It would be possible to make the journey while keeping Annabelle sedated, but it would be difficult, and more, it would require them to travel more slowly, as someone would need to monitor her at all times.

"A man came to see me last week, pet," he said. "He told me that he had found your mother."

Annabelle's eyes widened.

"She is in a far-off territory called 'Oregon,' but we know how to get there. We are clever. We have maps. If we go now, before she has time to move on again, we can find her. We can bring her home."

"Is my sister with her?"

Dr. Murphy nodded. "Yes."

"But . . ." Annabelle frowned. "There aren't any quiet,

clean rooms in places like that. Only in Deseret. Where does she keep Pearl?"

"Outside. With the beasts."

Annabelle's face turned cold, the emotion draining out of it one drop at a time, until she was a statue, pale as marble, cold as summer ice.

"She shouldn't be outside when I'm not," said Annabelle. "It's not fair."

"I know. That's why we're going to get her. We're going to bring her home."

"Good." Annabelle leaned back in her pillows, the machines around her huffing and wheezing. "I need a friend who can't leave me."

"And you shall have it," Dr. Murphy said, and kissed his daughter's hand.

Chapter 18

Adeline danced back and forth between her mother and the wolflings, a child utterly content with her surroundings and her situation. One of the bitches had brought a litter of half-grown pups out into the open, little things that yipped and yelped and chased their own tails when not tumbling over in a tangle of limbs. Adeline scooped one of them up as she ran past, carrying the infant monster over to her mother. Hal tensed, waiting for the wolfling bitch to begin growling, to decide that their temporary peace was done and it was time to kill the human intruders.

The adult wolfling yawned, exposing an impressive array of teeth, and went back to grooming her remaining pups.

Adeline came skidding to a stop in front of Annie, holding up the wolfling pup proudly.

"Er," said Annie, and took the pup from her daughter, cradling it like a baby in the crook of her arm. The pup yawned, much like its mother, and tucked its eerily hand-like paws against the curve of its chest before closing its eyes and apparently going to sleep. "Thank you, Delly, dear. What a charming little creature this is."

Adeline beamed and ran off again.

Martin and Sophia were sitting nearby, him binding her ankle with strips torn off of her skirt, tying them tight enough to keep the swelling down, her watching proudly, one hand resting on her belly. If the girl didn't know that she was pregnant already, she would soon, in Annie's estimation; there was no way she couldn't feel the changes that the baby was making to her body, rearranging the furniture in preparation for its own residence.

Of course, her own pregnancy had involved more changes than the norm, at least according to every woman she had spoken to before or since. Perhaps for some women, it truly was a blessed event, easy and comfortable and bringing them closer to God. For her, it had been agony, all thanks to her husband, who had thought himself higher than the Almighty.

"Miss Pearl."

Annie turned to Hal, still cradling the wolfling. "Yes?"

"You know this isn't right." The old forester's face was set in a mask of cold stoicism. "These are beasts. They don't let children braid their fur and play with their cubs. They should be killing us all right now. That they're not . . . something is wrong here. You'll tell me what it is."

"Or what?" asked Annie. "You're not the only one with a weapon. Martin could stop you if you tried to kill the rest of us. His Sophia is pregnant. Adeline is a child. I am her only family. There's none here you'd threaten for the sake of your precious answers."

"How can you be so sure of that?" Hal demanded. "I might be willing to go farther than you'd think, if it means understanding what's happening here."

"Then do it," she said. "Forget your wife and your daughter; forget that you are meant to be a man of honor. Do what your temper demands and let the wendigo feast on what they find here. Or let our rescuers do it." She tickled the pup's belly. "Monsters they may be, but they're the monsters who saved my little girl. I'd be happy to love them dear for that alone."

"Miss Pearl . . ." He shook his head. "You know this is wrong. Everything about it screams of unnatural perversion, of some cruel trick. The Devil—"

"Walks in Oregon, yes. Of that much I have been absolutely convinced. But it was Adeline who found the wolflings, and the wolflings who went looking for the rest of us, at her request. She met the monsters, and once they had accepted her, she bid them to find the people who mattered to her, the people who were lost in the woods and smelled of circus. Are you telling me that the Devil is in my daughter, sir? Is that truly a conversation you wish to have?"

"If it be true."

Annie looked at him, her eyes locking onto his. For a long moment, neither of them spoke. Neither of them really seemed to breathe. Finally, Annie looked away.

"It might be," she said. Lifting her voice, she called, "Delly? Please come take your friend back to his mother. He looks tired, and I think he'd do better with her than he does with me."

Adeline came trotting obediently back to pluck the infant wolfling from Annie's arms and run back to his mother, placing him among the other snowy pups. Annie sighed. "Her father was a great scientist. He lives still in Deseret, if he hasn't signed his own death warrant with some grand experiment or other. He wanted children, and I wanted to be a good wife to him. Do you understand me?"

"Not as such, no."

"He said he could *make* children, when God did not see fit to bless us with them in the normal manner. He said that if God had not wanted us to force the hand of nature, He would not have equipped His most favored creations so, with clever hands and even more clever minds. I agreed. I was a good wife. I was devoted, pious, willing to yield in all ways to my husband's desires. When he came to me with the needle in his hand, I yielded to that as well."

Hal said nothing. Her words were soft, too quiet for

Martin or Sophia to overhear—although he had no doubt many of the wolflings were listening, with their hearing that exceeded anything known to man. Perhaps telling a tale of a monster bothered her less when her audience was made up of similar creatures.

"Nine months he treated me as an extension of his private laboratory, and when the pain of labor gripped me, I felt only relief. One way or another, this trial was coming to an end. I had been good. I had been faithful. God would reward me with a child, and Michael would lose interest, moving on—as he always did—to some new challenge."

Annie turned to watch Adeline, now rolling on the ground with several of the wolfling pups, her throat convulsing in silent laughter. Sometimes being Adeline's mother was like watching her child through a pane of thick glass, shutting out all sound, forcing her to learn the small refinements of her physicality. It must have been much easier to be the parent to a child that could make wishes known with whimpers and with sighs. She couldn't imagine it would have been any more rewarding.

"It didn't happen that way, did it?" asked Hal. His voice was surprisingly gentle.

"No. I suppose parenthood never does, though, does it? You go in expecting a fairy tale, a perfect family, children that never make messes or disobey, a spouse who adores you and treats you kindly, and instead, you get something real. Good or ill, it exists. It is what it is. It's what you have to live with."

"What happened?"

"I had my daughters." The plural felt like a rock in her throat, something she had to strain to push past her lips. In the end, she spat it out, and she did not look at Hal's face, for fear of what she'd find there. "They were a . . .

a bezoar of flesh, all tangled together, tied so tightly that it seemed like there couldn't possibly be two of them. They were a single child with two heads, somehow, and they were monstrous, and they were mine. I would have kept them as they were. I would have loved them as they were. Truly."

She could say that now, but would she have meant it then, in the long-gone lifetime where she had been a pampered house pet of a woman, kept and cosseted and eternally yielding to her husband? Michael had been the one who yearned for children. Michael had been the one who prepared the treatments, who slid the syringes into the tight skin of her belly, murmuring of heirs and honor. Michael had been the maker of monsters, and she had been nothing more than his lab.

She remembered the sight of her little girls bound together, a roiling ball of kicking legs and wailing mouths. She remembered recoiling, horrified by the thought that this *thing* had been living inside her body, fattening itself like a tick on her blood and marrow. She remembered the relief when Michael had ordered it swept up and toted away, down to his laboratory, where she wouldn't have to look on it.

All the excuses in the world—all the tears, the sleepless nights, the efforts to make amends for the moment when she had first beheld her children—wouldn't make up for the fact that when she had seen them, she had screamed. She had rejected them. The first thing Adeline had ever known from her mother was rejection.

"My husband saw that I was frightened, and he took them from me," she said, voice calm as it had ever been, giving no sign of the turmoil happening beneath the surface. "He said he would fix them. He said he could undo what nature had done—as if nature had any part in what went on in that house. As if nature would *dare*. We were a house of horrors, sir, and nothing that happened under our roof had anything to do with nature, or indeed, with the graces of God."

"Your daughter is hale of body and straight of limb. Save for her silence, I see no outward signs of affliction. Only the kindness of monsters betrays anything of truth in your story."

"He took them," said Annie again. "Down the stairs, into his lab, while I was a prisoner of my own weakness, bound to my bed by the trauma I had endured. Even there, I was more fortunate than some. I had my ladies' maids with me, to care for me and help me recover. I had my own room, no chores to do, no duties but recuperation . . . and he had my daughters. My husband had our children, and there was nothing I could do to save them."

Had she truly wanted to? That was the question that had nagged her for years, would doubtless haunt her until she died. Had she *truly* wanted to rescue the children her eyes had barely recognized as human, or had she been hoping that he would make them disappear, letting them fade quietly into the graveyard occupied by all his failed experiments?

Surely, if she had really wanted them to be saved, she would have stirred from her bed sooner, rather than dreaming away a night and a day in a drug-induced haze while her body struggled to knit itself back together. Surely, if she had truly intended to do right by her children, she would have found the strength to move.

But the sun had gone down on the second night, and she had risen from her bed, and she had gone to the stairs, hadn't she? She had opened the door; she had descended, down into the darkness where her husband's wishes reigned supreme, even more than they did in the house above, into the place where there was no other god but him, save perhaps for Hellstromme, who ruled over all works done in his name. Her legs had still been weak.

Her sex had still been aching like it had been burnt from the friction of giving birth. She had wanted nothing more in the world than to crawl back into her bed and close her eyes against the realities of her life. And still she had descended the stairs, and walked into a nightmare.

Annie took a breath. "I went to confront him, to ask . . . to ask if our children lived. I didn't even know that they were daughters, not then. I expected to be told that they had been too malformed to survive, that God in His wisdom had taken them back to Heaven, where they could rest, untormented by the sins of this world. Instead, I found them laid out upon two separate slabs in his laboratory. He . . ."

She stopped as words failed her. She had never been a particularly loquacious woman, nor was this a story she had told many times aloud. She carried it with her always, the words like stones in her heart, each of them polished by memory, until they shone like terrible jewels denied the light.

Finally, dully, she said, "He had cut them apart. There were two girls contained within the snarl, you see, conjoined, tangled together, but close enough to complete that they would both have lived, had they been left to their own devices. Michael took his scalpels and his ideals, and he used them to slice at our daughters, separating them."

"Is that not what you would have wanted? You said you were afraid."

"Of course I was afraid! Everyone fears what they don't understand. You fear the wolflings. I fear the wood. Fear is *natural*. But I wasn't the only one who was afraid. Michael was afraid, too. Afraid that someone would carry word that his wife had given birth to a monster to someone who might hear it, and relay it to his master. The good Dr. Hellstromme, under whose grace Deseret should flourish." She made no effort to conceal the bitterness in her voice. "Had he taken the time to study our girls, he might still have decided to cut. He was always a proud man. He always thought he knew best, regardless of the situation. He didn't take the time. He simply grabbed his scalpels, and he cut, and cut, and cut, until he had two little girls where one bezoar had been, and he called it good."

Annie watched Adeline playing, watched the way the little girl rolled and jumped, easy within her own body. The scars were barely visible anymore, and only to people—like her mother—who knew where to look for them.

"Miss Pearl?"

"They weren't complete." She turned back to Hal. "Each of them was missing something. The . . . other girl was missing more than Adeline. Perhaps that's why he liked her better. He saw her as something he could perfect and refine, while Adeline was something he could use."

"Use?"

"For spare parts." Annie tilted her head back, until she wasn't looking at Hal, or Adeline, or anything but the distant, uncaring moon. The moon, she was sure, would not judge her. "There's a scar down the middle of her throat. It's barely a hair now. You'd have to get closer than she'd allow to find so much as its ghost. But when she was born, she had the power to scream, and now she has only silence. He gave her voice to her sister as a birthday gift, and never saw that he might be doing either of them ill by slicing them open. They were his children, after all."

"But how—"

"He was a *scientist*." How bitter that word tasted in her mouth; how cruel. How cold. "He had the proper tools, the proper techniques. He delighted in them. Spoke of steam, and mercury, and the miracles of ghost rock, like all those things mattered more than our children. He named the daughter he favored 'Annabelle,' after his mother, and said that he would make her a being without flaw, the final proof that he had been right in his efforts. He named the daughter he didn't favor 'Pearl,' because he intended to cut out her heart and nestle it in her sister's chest like a jewel, as soon as they were both strong enough. I grabbed her and I ran, and I changed her name to something she could keep, that had nothing of him in it."

Hal stared at her for a moment, attempting to formulate his response. Finally, he asked, "What about your other daughter?"

"I'm sorry. I suppose I was less than clear. She had no heart." Annie lowered her eyes from the sky, focusing them on Hal. "They had one between them, and a heart is not a voice, to be so easily cut away and given to another. A heart takes preparation. A heart takes *time*. When I left with my Delly, her sister was being kept alive by a trinket Michael had built in his workshop, some cunning little thing powered by ghost rock and steam and spite."

"I see." Hal shook his head. "This is all more than you should have needed to endure, and you have my sympathies for all of it. But how does this bring us here, to a little girl roiling with beasts as if they were her favorite playmates?"

"He made them. Not with his body: with his science. He had them for days before I realized I needed to run. Adeline has never been well. Her lungs are weak. The incision he made when he took her voice has healed on the outside, but the inside remains raw; sometimes it becomes inflamed, and I must boil water and pray that she spits up all the pus, rather than drowning in it. I took her to a barber once, to have her bled. What came out was blood, yes, and yet. It was laced with strands of silver, like mercury, and it stank like ghost rock. Nothing should be able to live with that in their veins. Adeline does."

"So you think . . ."

"If she is beloved of monsters, it's because they recognize something of themselves in her. She is my little girl. She is her father's daughter. I simply have to pray that I have run far enough, fast enough, for the first to matter more than the second. But whatever else she is or may become, she is a product of the world we've made, and yes. She is a monster." Annie stood, brushing the pine needles from her skirt before she called, "Delly, come here, darling."

Adeline looked up, setting the wolfling pup she had been cradling back on the ground before running to her mother. She looked up, eyes wide and curious, and waited.

"We need to return to the circus," said Annie. "Mr. Blackstone will be terribly worried about us by now, and Sophia is unwell. She needs her bed, and her rest. Do your new friends remember the way back to The Clearing?"

'They don't like people places,' Adeline signed, frowning. 'Too many men.'

"What's she saying?" demanded Hal.

"That the wolflings dislike going too near large settlements, because there are too many people there."

"Too many people with guns, she means," said Hal. "The wolflings are killers."

Adeline frowned at him, signing, 'They eat because they are hungry. Hungry things are allowed to eat. It's not their fault if what they eat is people like you.'

"Adeline, that's no way to speak to someone who's helping us."

Adeline focused her attention back on her mother. 'Why not? He says bad things about my friends. I should be allowed to say what I want. He's stupid anyway. He can't understand me.'

"*Adeline.*" Annie's voice was the crack of a whip. "We do not talk that way about our allies. Apologize at once."

Sensing that she had gone too far, Adeline winced before nodding, turning to Hal, and making a gesture with her right hand.

"That means she's sorry," said Annie.

"No apology needed; I don't even know what she's sorry for," said Hal.

"If the wolflings can understand her, I can't assume you don't," said Annie. "Delly, please, can you ask your friends if they can show us the way home? The woods are too dangerous for us to make the trip alone, but we need to get back. We've already been away too long."

'Yes, Mama,' Adeline signed contritely, and ran off to the wolflings.

Annie sighed, shaking her head with the utmost fondness, and walked to where Sophia and Martin sat, still pressed together like they feared the world wanted nothing more than the chance at cleaving them apart.

"Can you walk, dear?" she asked, focusing on Sophia.

"If she can't walk, I can carry her," said Martin.

"You're injured as well," said Annie. "We have to be realistic."

"Meaning what?" asked Martin. His expression shifted, growing darker, warier.

Annie sighed. "I'm not going to suggest leaving anyone behind. Wipe that thought from your mind. We've already done that tonight, and it's not going to happen again. But if she can't walk, we'll need to cut her a crutch, and we'll need to wait for the sun to rise before we try to navigate these woods."

"How much longer can it be until sunrise?" asked Sophia.

Annie looked up. The moon leered down at her, not seeming to have moved an inch across the sky since she had walked into the woods to find her daughter. "Out here? It seems it could be forever. We cannot count on the morning coming to save us."

"I can walk," said Sophia. She stood, leaning on Martin as he hurried to brace her. "I want to go home."

Home. What a fascinating word that was. Annie smiled a little as she nodded and stepped back, giving them room. "Adeline is negotiating with the wolflings."

Martin hesitated. "Ma'am, you know . . . you know that it's not normal for little girls to talk with monsters like she does."

"We're circus folk, Martin," said Annie. "Nothing about us has ever been normal."

He looked surprised. Then he laughed. "I suppose that's not something I can argue with," he said. "Thank you, ma'am."

"No thanks necessary," she said. "We're family." She turned and walked back to Hal, who watched her approach without comment. When she was close enough, she asked, "Will you come with us?"

"I don't live there anymore," he said. "These woods, they're what I know."

"These woods, and their history," said Annie. "We could be walking into a trap, or worse. If the townspeople know about the wendigo, they may be intending to set the rest of us up as a sacrifice, something to buy them passage through to the other side of the winter."

"Most of those people are already wendigo in their hearts," said Hal. "There's no kindness left there, nor mercy for a traveler. You would be better off striking out for the border. Some soul that still knows what it is to be human would offer you aid along the way, I'm sure."

"And if they didn't? Or even if they did, how could we live with ourselves knowing that we'd left our friends, our loved ones, to be destroyed? This wood has already taken too much from my family. I can't leave anyone else behind." With a pang, Annie realized Adeline didn't know about Tranquility. She had no idea how to tell her daughter that the big cat—her protector since infancy, her nursemaid and playmate—was gone. It would break Adeline's heart, as it had already broken Annie's.

"I'm not your savior."

"I don't need you to be. I just need you to be the man who helps to bring us out of the woods before we're lost forever. Please."

Adeline came running back to her mother, a large wolfling pacing by her side. Hal gave the white-furred creature an uneasy look, which the wolfling met unflinchingly before nudging the girl with its muzzle. She gave one of her soundless giggles, her face contorting in laughter that no one could hear.

"Will they help us, then, dearest?" asked Annie.

Adeline nodded before signing, 'They won't go all the way, but they'll go far enough to be sure the hungry ones don't take us. Mama, what's a hungry one?'

"I'll tell you later," said Annie. She looked back to Hal. "The wolflings—what you would call monsters—will help us. Will you do the same, sir?"

"I owe you a debt," said Hal. "You gave my Poppy peace. That's the only reason I'm doing this. You understand."

"I do, sir," said Annie, and smiled, because everything was going to be all right.

Chapter 19

When they reached the edge of the forest—Annie supporting Sophia, whose leg had given out some time before, while Martin and Hal carried the rifles and watched the woods for signs of trouble— the wolflings melted back into the trees like they had never been there in the first place. Annie looked back, trying to see them through the shadows. They were white, so white it almost hurt her eyes, and yet they were utterly gone, predators to the last.

Adeline, bundled against her mother's hip on the side where Sophia did not rest, raised one hand in a doleful farewell.

"My God," breathed Martin.

They turned, all of them, to face forward, and see what had become of The Clearing in their absence.

The fire that had been threatening to consume part of the circus had been extinguished, although patches of wood still smoked, sending delicate trails curling upward, out of the bowl, like signal flares. There were bonfires down below, set around the edges of the circus. That, too, was strange. Mr. Blackstone usually insisted they intrude as little as possible on the lives of the settlers around them, claiming that a disruptive circus was an unwelcome circus, and an unwelcome circus might as well shut its doors.

"Home," breathed Sophia, who had last seen the circus when she was carried away in the grasp of a terrible beast—and how many others had been taken? How many had the wendigo slaughtered, while sparing only the love of Martin's life?

Annie's stomach was a stone. She knew what Hal had told her, that the wendigo liked to lay traps, and if they had been able to smell the reality of Sophia's delicate condition—the babe that now grew inside her belly, unaware of the turmoil of its parents—then she must have seemed a perfect honeypot. But if they had been unaware of Sophia's pregnancy, why had they spared her, rather than any of the others? What had made her the perfect bait to set their trap?

"Damn," breathed Martin, who had been at the circus when she was gone, and was better prepared to see the damage with clear and open eyes. Perhaps half the wagons were smashed in to one degree or another, from broken roofs to broken axles. Even if they wanted to leave Oregon tonight, there was no possible way. Not without leaving all their supplies and many of their people behind.

Adeline said nothing, and neither did Annie. She merely hoisted her daughter a little higher on her hip and released Sophia, allowing her to move to Martin, who steadied her. Thus prepared, she began the descent down into the shallow bowl, sliding on the sides of her feet when necessary, never quite losing her balance. She felt a steadying hand against her waist once, and looked back to find Hal standing there, a grim expression on his weathered face.

We are going back to the graveyard of your dreams, she thought, and it was perfect, and it was tragic, and they continued to descend.

Someone must have seen them, and no wonder: the shadows in the bowl were once more thin and natural, betraying no trace of the wendigo, and Adeline's pale hair and tattered gown must have shown as clearly as a candle in the fog. By the time their group had reached the bottom, a crowd had formed there, made up entirely of villagers.

"Villains!" shouted the man at the lead—the man Annie recognized as The Clearing's mayor. He lunged before she could react, grabbing her by the wrist. "You return here, after what you've done? The audacity!"

There was a click behind her. The mayor froze, going pale. He did not, sadly, release her wrist.

"Unhand the lady, friend," drawled Hal, voice cold and slow. "She didn't do anything to you or yours, as you damn well know. Stop trying to cover your own crimes by assigning them to her."

"She went into the wood when the moon was full! She *tempted* the demons in the mountain! And now she returns here with *you,* who would have us cosset and tend to them? You prove her villainy more than you could ever hope to deny it!"

There was another click from behind her. Annie didn't need to turn to know that Martin was holding his rifle aimed at the mayor of The Clearing, ready to shoot the man if he didn't let her go. That much was obvious from the way several members of the crowd raised their own guns, creating the sort of standoff that never ended well for any of the participants.

"You are aiming your weapons at two women and a child," she said, voice clear and carrying. "If you fire now, one of us will be hit, no matter how careful you attempt to be. Please, Mr. Mayor, release me. We've had a trying night, and would return to our wagons now."

"Your circus is the reason those monsters attacked us," he spat. He didn't let her go.

Annie frowned. "I think you and I both know that not to be true, sir. I've been to your forgotten town; I've seen what you would rather have unseen. I know things you would rather not be known. If you shoot me, those things might be forgotten, but you will pull the fury of my circus down upon your head. Are you prepared for that? You may believe yourself to be, but I think you'll find that we can rage more brightly than you can."

"You took her there?" The mayor let go of Annie's wrist as if it had changed shape under his hand, becoming horrific to the touch. He turned on Hal, lip twitching in his fury. "That place is a secret and a shame. We do not take outsiders there!"

"What a pity I'm not one of you anymore, to pay attention to your rules." Hal descended a few feet more down the hill, putting himself—and his gun—between Annie, Adeline, and the crowd. He was a comforting blockade, solid and seemingly immovable. "Let us pass, Johnson. You know you have no power here."

"They brought the monsters down on our heads," spat the mayor. There was no strength in his words. It had all been sapped away by the novelty of people actually standing up to him.

"Did we?" Sophia shoved her way forward until she was in front of Hal, until her nose was only inches from the mayor's own. She was a dainty woman, soft of figure and gentle of countenance, but in that moment, she could have been Medusa, rising up from the bowels of the earth to take revenge on the men who wronged her. "I was taken by those things. You think my people called them on ourselves? I saw *none* of yours being snatched up and carried away. When the monsters threw me into their larder to lure my loved ones closer, there were none of your innocents there with me. Could we have counted on your kindness to send you to my rescue, while you had nothing on the line? If anyone summoned those things here to look for sustenance, it was not *us*!"

Her voice had grown louder and louder as she spoke, spiking at the end to a scream. In the woods above

The Clearing, the wolflings howled, sending their voices toward the moon.

The mayor stumbled back, eyes going wide. "Witchcraft!" he accused.

"Hell hath no fury, or so they say," said Annie. She stepped forward, taking Sophia's hand in her own, and walked, with the utmost calm, toward the gathered settlers. There was a moment where the world held its breath, waiting to see what was going to happen next.

The settlers parted and let them pass. Martin and Hal hurried after, guns still at the ready. No one raised a hand to stop them.

"All bark and no bite," murmured Hal, falling into step beside Annie. "That's how they've always been around here. They save their teeth for one another, and for the day the forest takes them."

"Keep walking," said Annie. "We'll be safe once we reach the circus." It was a small lie, but an essential one. She needed to believe that safety was still possible somewhere, even if that safety had been scorched and damaged while she was running through the forest, trying to bring her daughter home. She needed to believe there was a chance, however slim, that they all would live to see the morning.

Adeline leaned back enough to sign something to her mother. Annie smiled despite her weariness.

"She's asking if you intend to run away with the circus, sir," she said, glancing toward Hal. "She thinks you might make a good roustabout."

"I'm too old to change my ways like that," said Hal. "Besides. My Marie is still out there somewhere, and she's alone now, with no daughter to keep her company when the sun is high and she goes to ground. I have to find her. I have to show her peace."

"A pity," said Annie, and walked on.

The bonfires they had seen from above were spaced

around the circus, forming a barrier of heat and light against the townsfolk, ending at the wall of the bowl. As they grew closer to the wagons, bodies appeared through the flames, roustabouts and acrobats, wainwrights and sword dancers, all of them clutching their weapons, keeping watch. Waiting for the people of the town to do something that could not be taken back or forgiven.

They walked on. The firelight touched their faces, tracing their features, revealing them to their friends and loved ones like a magician drawing back a curtain to reveal the hidden lady. Someone gasped. Someone else shouted Adeline's name, bright and jubilant and surprised.

"Sophia!" The seamstress to whom Sophia was apprenticed leapt up from her place by one of the bonfires, letting her rifle fall aside as she ran and flung her arms around the girl, sending her staggering back a foot. "You're alive!"

"Hello, Auntie," whispered Sophia, words almost swallowed by the other woman's shoulder, which pressed against her lips in reassuring solidity.

"You came back," said the seamstress. She looked toward Martin. "You brought her back."

"I promised I would, ma'am," said Martin, with the utmost civility. He tugged on his hair with his free hand, eyes still on Sophia, and said, "I think it might be time for us to have a talk, ma'am, if you don't mind."

"You brought her back to me," said the seamstress. "We can have any talk you like."

"Annie?"

The voice was querulous, trembling; surely it couldn't belong to their ringleader and master of ceremonies. Mr. Blackstone was their unflinching wall against the rest of the world, never frightened, never beaten-down. But when Annie turned toward the sound of her name, it was

Mr. Blackstone she saw, standing in the open space between two bonfires, eyes wide and face slack with shock
and relief.

Adeline tugged on her mother's sleeve. Annie bent and
put the little girl down, smoothing her skirt with the heels
of her hands as she straightened. Nothing could have
mended the tears in her sleeves or undone the tangles in
her hair, but if there had been a way, she would have
witched herself to perfection in that moment.

He deserves nothing less, she thought, and *he already
finds me perfect,* she thought, and she was exactly right,
in both regards.

She took a step forward. So did he, and then they were
running, the both of them, their feet churning against
the sour Oregon earth, to collide in the space between
the fires, his hands going to her waist, hers to his shoulders. He lifted her bodily up into the air, swinging her
around with such joy that it seemed her heart must stop
from the revelation of it all.

Slowly, he lowered her back to the ground. Her toes
touched down first, followed by her heels, and still he
was staring at her, his face gilded by the fire, and she had
never seen anything so beautiful, or so precious, since
beholding her daughter, still alive, in the company of
winter's wolves in the Oregon woods. It was a small distance between those two moments, and yet she had
truly never expected the first to be surpassed.

"Miss Pearl," said Mr. Blackstone.

"Nathanial," said Annie.

His eyes widened a fraction of an inch more in his surprise before he leaned forward and, almost cautiously,
kissed her.

Rare indeed are the kisses that can maintain their
heat—their mystery—through the whooping and applause of circus folk, or the silent cheering of little
girls. If they heard the ruckus being kicked up around

them, neither Annie nor Nathanial gave any indication. He kissed her, and she kissed him, and his hands on her waist had turned into arms encircling her entirely, and her hands on his shoulders had become fingers tangled in his hair, and for a single shining instant, Annie truly understood her daughters as they had been born to her, not as they had been reshaped by science and hubris. She felt as if she and Nathanial were on the verge of becoming a single soul split into two bodies, and those two bodies straining to become one again, to shrug off the petty divisions that had been foisted upon them and fully reunite.

Martin laughed. "This is a good ending for a bad show," he said. "You need that, you know. Nobody comes back if you have a bad ending for a bad show. That's too much badness for anyone to tolerate."

"Hush," said Sophia, and he hushed.

Annie and Nathanial finally pulled apart, separating themselves with a reluctance born as much of hunger as of etiquette. Her cheeks were burning. His skin was darker than hers, but she rather thought his cheeks were burning, too. It seemed only fair that they should be.

"So," she said.

"You found her," he said. "You found both of them."

"Yes, and I found that the people of this town have been keeping rather more secrets from us than I like." She stepped back, away from the safety and promise of his arms, and beckoned for Hal to come and join her. "Hal, I would like you to meet Nathanial Blackstone, the proprietor of this circus. Mr. Blackstone, I would like you to meet Hal, who helped us to survive the woods and the dangers they contained, and who can tell you the truth about The Clearing."

"You should go," said Hal, approaching the pair. Adeline followed close on his heels, silent as ever. "The mayor isn't going to like that you've managed to reclaim some of your people. He's going to see that as an insult to his position, and more, as tempting the wendigo."

"The what?" asked Mr. Blackstone.

"We have a great deal to discuss, and Sophia has been wounded, as has Martin," said Annie. "Are you needed on the watch?"

"No," said Mr. Blackstone. "I've been keeping a watch of my own."

No one said that his watch had been only ever in Annie's name. No one needed to.

Looking flustered once more, Annie said, "Adeline is well past due for her medicine. Does our wagon yet stand?"

"It does," said Mr. Blackstone. He paused then, and said, "Where is—"

That was as far as he got before Annie shook her head, and realization dawned.

"Ah," he said. "Well, then. Come with me, all of you. I'll see what can be done to get some coffee in your hands, and some liniments for your injuries."

He turned and strode into the midnight circus, backlit by the fires, and there had never been a ringleader who looked more proud, or better able to protect his own. Annie followed, with Adeline beside her. Sophia came after them, leaning heavily on her aunt's arm, with Martin and Hal bringing up the rear, their guns once more held defensively, as if they feared attack at any moment.

Perhaps they were not wrong to do so. Many of the windows in the nearest houses were open, and shadows moved beyond the bonfire's reach, shadows that looked suspiciously like settlers with their hats drawn down to hide the glitter of their eyes.

Behind the group, the watchers at the bonfire line shifted back into position, closing the holes in their defenses. When the attack came—and the attack was coming; there was no question of that—it would need to go through as many bodies as the circus could muster.

On the other side of the line, in the circus proper, the smell of char and wet wood hung over everything, eclipsing the usual smells of old velvet and sweat. Annie found herself cleaving closer than her norm to Mr. Blackstone. For his part, Mr. Blackstone stole glance after glance in her direction, drinking her with his eyes.

They passed the wagon of oddities, still closed up and no more damaged than it had been when last she had seen it. Annie heaved a sigh of deep relief.

"We would have burned it ourselves, if it had been further damaged," said Mr. Blackstone. "You would have had my deepest apologies, but the things you keep—"

"I understand," said Annie.

"What do you mean?" demanded Hal, voice rich with suspicion.

"Miss Pearl is our freak mistress," said Martin.

Annie winced a little. "They are oddities, Martin, not freaks. Afford them the dignity nature denied."

"Sorry, ma'am," said Martin, sounding abashed.

"Freaks?" asked Hal. "What manner?"

"All kinds," said Annie. "Some human unfortunates, who will no doubt be at the bonfires or abed at this hour, waiting for their own watch; some natural wonders of this blighted West. If you remain until morning, I can show them to you then."

"Why not tonight?"

"They're strongest at night." Not all of them. The serpents did best in strong sunlight, when the heat could bake through their scales and quicken their torpid blood. But the nibblers, the corn stalker, so many things would find the moonlight rejuvenating.

She had saved them from the fire. She had no desire to lose them to the rightfully horrified.

Hal was quiet for a time before he said, "You frighten people, then. For your profession."

"I suppose you could say as much."

"Fear's a tool of them like the wendigo. It's not for such as us." He looked at her, sorrow and judgment warring for the ownership of his eyes. "You serve the night things when you truck in fear. How much of this do you think you brought down on yourself, by putting your hands so plainly in their service?"

Annie said nothing. It felt like there was nothing to say. A fight would do neither of them any good, and what was done was done: she had frightened people all across the West for the sake of a full belly and a warm fire. All that mattered now was surviving to the morning.

The wagon she shared with Adeline appeared before them, perfect, untouched: as pristine and welcoming as it had been when she had left it behind. Annie blinked back sudden tears, realizing just how much she had come to depend on the constancy of her traveling home. This, not Deseret, not a rich man's private palace, was where she belonged. Was where she should have been from the beginning.

Everything else had just been the world arranging things so that she could have her Delly, and Tranquility, may she rest in whatever peace waited for the best of beasts after their days on Earth were done.

"I'll get the door," she said, and hurried forward, mounting the short steps with a quick, half-mincing stride. It would be a tight fit, getting all seven of them inside, but if they were willing to sit on the beds, and not be too shy about one another, it should work.

The thought of being . . . not too shy . . . about Mr. Blackstone was more appealing than it had been ever before, even just that past morning. She had known herself to be interested in him as a man for quite some time. She had suspected him to be interested in her as a woman.

To have it confirmed was not enough to make the trials of this past night worthwhile, but oh, it soothed the sting. It made the shadows that still clung to everything a little less deep.

Inside the wagon it was dark and cool. The windows had been closed; there was no smell of smoke, only of herbs and tea and Adeline's medicine. Moving quickly, Annie lit the lanterns that remained on their hooks and popped her head out the door, calling, "In you get. There's room for everyone, if you're willing to sit close and be friends."

"We already are," said Mr. Blackstone, with a broad smile, and followed Adeline inside.

The girl stood a little straighter once she was in her own space, looking around with a bright satisfaction that was almost the mirror of Annie's own. Annie hid her smile behind her hand. Sometimes it was impossible to deny the blood between them—not that she would ever have wanted to. While she might have serious doubts as to Michael's place in the conception of their daughters, she had carried them in her own flesh. She knew well whose they were, or whose they had been, in the beginning. Adeline was more her own with every passing day. The same must be true of Annabelle, if the girl had lived. Which she had not, *could* not. Surely there was no possible way.

The seamstress helped Sophia to Annie's bed, coaxing her to sit. Martin sat beside her, and both watched as the seamstress knelt and began fussing with the dressings on her ankle.

"You did a good job, Martin," she said. "This is tied tightly enough to help, but not so tightly as to harm her further. Thank you for bringing her back to me."

"I told you he was a good one, Auntie," said Sophia, practically beaming.

"You did, child, you did, and I have believed you to

the best of my ability." The seamstress bent back over the bandages.

Adeline climbed up onto her own bed and clutched theatrically at her throat. Annie nodded.

"I know, dearest," she said. "You're well past due for your medicine. I'm sure your throat is aching by now. How are your lungs? Good? Or bad?"

Adeline made a "so-so" gesture with one hand. Annie nodded again.

"I'll have to boil water for your tea, then. Hal, can you please tell Mr. Blackstone what you told me in the woods? He'll need to know the whole story." She turned as she spoke, in time to see the surprise and dismay on Hal's face.

"That's no good story for women or children, ma'am," said Hal. "I told you because I had to, not because I had any wish to befoul your innocence."

"My daughter is a friend to beasts; Sophia was kidnapped by monsters; Soleil is of French-Canadian descent and may know more of your wendigo than you think. Any of them will be strong enough to hear your stories, and all of them have good reason to." Annie took her kettle down from its hook. "I'll be right outside."

"I don't like you leaving again so soon," said Mr. Blackstone.

Annie shrugged. "A pity, because I must. My daughter needs her medicine. You understand, don't you?" She looked at him, an open challenge in her eyes. *If you cannot understand that she comes before everything else in this world or the next, we can go no farther than a single kiss by the bonfire's light.*

He nodded, marginally. "I do. But . . . leave the door open. I do not trust the shadows here."

"I will," said Annie, and took the kettle, and stepped outside.

There was something soothing to the process of starting a fire and beginning to boil the water for tea. It was familiar; it was the same, no matter where they were, from Oregon to the Mexican border. Some things endured through everything, even geography.

She could hear Hal inside, beginning to tell his story. She couldn't make out the words, but she didn't need to. They were finally on the track that would take them to morning, and hence to safety, whatever shape that safety had to take.

In the distance, back toward the bonfires, a gun spoke rolling thunder. A woman screamed, and safety was suddenly very far away.

Chapter 20

Annie had the presence of mind to grab her kettle before she spun and ran back into the wagon. The water sloshing inside was only half-warm, but that would have to do; even if the wendigo had returned, God forbid and keep them all, Adeline needed her medicine. The girl was doing surprisingly well for how long she had been without, barefoot and running through the trees like the chill did nothing to distress her. It wouldn't last.

(There had been a time, brief but real, when Annie had considered abandoning Adeline's medicine. All the girl's troubles were a consequence of her father's science: How could science heal science? It seemed better to let nature intervene. Nature's intervention had consisted of Adeline's lungs filling with fluid while her senses departed her, replaced by wild thrashing and nightmares she lacked the physical dexterity to express. The medicine Annie gave her daughter daily was a necessary treatment for the damage Michael had done. Not a cure, no—cures were the stuff of fairy tales—but a treatment that allowed the child to have the closest thing she could ever know to a normal life.)

The others were on their feet when Annie crashed back into the wagon, all save for Adeline, who was sitting cross-legged on her bed, watching the door with huge, dark eyes.

She relaxed when her mother closed the door, and signed, 'It's not the hungry ones.'

"What's that?" Annie grabbed a mug with her free hand, tossing it to Adeline. "Measure your herbs."

Adeline let the cup drop to the cover, keeping her hands free. 'It's not the hungry ones, or my friends. This is people.'

"What's she saying?" asked Mr. Blackstone, moving to the wagon's small window and twitching the curtain aside, peering out into the dark. He shook his head. "I can't see a thing. I need to be out there. Sophia, Soleil, Annie, you stay here."

"She's saying that whatever is attacking is neither wolf nor wendigo, but something human." Annie looked to Hal. "Is there another settlement near here?"

"No." He shook his head. "The Clearing survives alone. We've had a few other villages try to establish themselves, but the wendigo are always waiting, and always hungry. Nothing has been able to take root in this poisoned soil."

Martin grabbed his rifle, kissed Sophia on the temple, and started for the door. "I have to help. I didn't defend the show against the wendigo. Whatever this is, I have to help."

"No, you have to stay here and care for the woman who will be your wife," said Annie. Adeline dropped a handful of herbs into the cup. Annie poured a stream of lukewarm water over them, creating a swampy goo that bubbled and smelled of bitter green. "Sophia needs you as much as the bonfire line does."

"I'll go," said Hal. "Someone has to pay for these people's sins, and it might as well be me."

The gunfire came again, closer and louder this time, so sharp that Annie couldn't imagine the size of the gun or the force of the bullet. It was like listening to a thunderstorm somehow brought to heel and forced to fire at man's whim. It was *terrifying*.

"Drink, dearest," she urged Adeline.

The girl must have been feeling worse than she wanted to let on, because she nodded, hands cupped tight around the mug, and drank its contents without a gesture of protest. She coughed, once, the motion accompanied by the thick, gelatinous sound of things shifting deep inside her lungs. Then she lay back, snuggling down against her pillows, and closed her eyes.

Sophia stared. "She can sleep with this happening?" she demanded, sounding like she was on the border of hysteria.

"She hasn't a choice when she's just been given her medicine," said Annie.

"Maybe I should take some of that," said Sophia.

"It would kill you," said Annie.

Sophia stared. "What?"

"Mugwort and mercury, silk from the terrantulas and threads of stinging nettle, and a dozen things more, all mixed together," said Annie. She gingerly lifted Adeline's abandoned cup and set it back on its shelf, where no one else would accidentally use it. "Ground ghost rock, for the main. It's expensive, but necessary. My daughter has specific needs. Some of them are met by things that would be poison to anyone else."

"My God," breathed Soleil.

"I think we have well established that God has no place in Oregon," said Annie coldly.

"No wonder the wolflings have no quarrel with her," said Hal, and to that, Annie had no answer.

Martin nodded, face grim, and opened the wagon door, stepping foot outside. The night was quiet; the gunfire, loud as it was, was still infrequent. Enough so that it seemed perhaps it had been an error—some hunter, aiming for a fleeing stag, had aimed incorrectly, or some overexcited settler had opened fire on the bonfire without proper cause.

Then someone else screamed, the sound high and shrill and carrying, and the gunfire began anew. Martin leapt down from the wagon's stairs and took off running. Hal was close behind him. Mr. Blackstone lingered long enough to turn to Annie, grabbing her forearms in his long-fingered hands.

"Stay here," he commanded. There was no fury in his words: only fear, stripped naked and allowed into the open for all to see. "I've lost you once tonight. I think I would go mad with worry if I lost you a second time. Stay here, where you can be safe, and guard your daughter."

"I will," she promised.

He kissed her, and he was gone, running out the door after the others, vanishing into the night.

Annie hesitated, fingers going to her lips, before she took a cautious step toward the open door.

"No!" wailed Sophia. "He asked you to stay here, with us! Please stay here, with us! I'm hurt and my aunt is old—we cannot defend ourselves!"

"Hush," whispered Annie, making a "settle" motion with her hands. "I'm going nowhere, but neither am I willing to lock myself in and make of us an easy target for the first fool who comes walking down the center of the boneyard. Stay where you are, stay quiet, and be still."

Sophia quieted, clutching at Soleil's hand so hard that it seemed she must break the other woman's fingers. Soleil bore up silently, unflinching. She had been a seamstress for most of her life. Her hands were the tools of her trade, and while they might not be tender or quick anymore, they could handle any number of shocks.

Silently, Annie walked to the door and stuck her head outside. Mr. Blackstone and the others were already gone, vanishing into the barricade behind the bonfires. Someone fired a shotgun, the sound ringing through the circus. Whether it had been fired by their side or by the other was impossible to say.

There were lights on in The Clearing, bright and unyielding, chasing the shadows away. Men had lit lanterns, opened windows, doing their best to balance out the bonfires started by the circus folk. That, too, was to be expected.

Less expected were the lights around the valley's rim, lights that matched the angle and progression of the winding road down into The Clearing. Annie counted five wagons, all of them lit up like fuel was no object, like they could afford to replace the sun if need be. The shape of them was . . . strange, boxy and familiar at the same time. She had seen these wagons before, or wagons very much like them. If only she could recall where, she was sure this would all start making sense. Every scrap of it, every bead of it would make sense.

A flash of light from the road punctuated another gunshot. Someone returned fire from the town line. The townsfolk and the circus people were shooting at a common enemy, she realized; someone was threatening them both. This might have started as a standoff between enemies, but it had grown into something larger and much more complicated.

Then the wagons on the roadway lit up.

She had thought them illuminated before, bedecked as they were with lanterns that must have been consuming oil and tallow at a prodigious rate. She had been right, in her way; she had also been terribly, horribly wrong. The new lights were clearly steam-powered, so bright and so clean that they were like looking at the sun, somehow taken captive and dragged down to the level of a mundane roadway. They were white and clinical, *cold,* and so unforgiving that they were somehow worse than the shadows, which fled before their onslaught.

Those few shadows that held fast, using some structure or person to anchor themselves, seemed to thicken in the instant that saw their fellows blown away. Annie felt them clutching at her ankles, clinging like living things. She kicked them off, and stared, the blood draining from her face, leaving her pale as paper and trembling. She *did* know those wagons, she *did,* and if there was any shame in that moment, it was that it had taken her so very long to recognize them for what they were, to *understand* what they meant.

It was all in the design. The filigree at their edges, the curve of their roofs, the sharp, austere elegance of their crafting. These were not workhorse wagons, like the ones the circus used, to be repaired by any tinker or wainwright to come along. No. These were show wagons, crafted to complement the households of the wealthy. Their backs bristled with steam tubes and clever attachments, all of them designed to propel the conveyances along the roads without the aid of animals or the fear of becoming mired in mud or untended trail. These wagons could roll across endless desert or through treacherous quicksand and never lose their footing or stall. They could traverse states in hours that would, for anyone else, have been days.

These wagons had been built in Deseret.

As if thinking the name of the land that had once been her home were some sort of summoning spell, cruelly cast and never intended for any loving world, a man emerged from one of the bright-lit wagons. He carried no gun. Instead, he held a long, conical tube, which he raised to his lips.

Annie was too far away to see his face, to see anything more than the slope of his shoulders and the length of his body. That was all she needed to see. She knew who it was before he spoke. After he spoke . . .

Had she ever needed to know what it felt like when the world fell down around her, she would have learned in that moment. She would have learned, and she would never have forgotten.

"My name is Dr. Michael Murphy," said the man—said her husband—said the monster who had driven a good Deseret woman to steal her daughter and run away, across a continent, looking for a place where she could be safe. "I am not here to hurt you, although I will if you force my hand. I am looking for my wife. I am looking for Grace Murphy. She's given you another name, which I will not speak, for she has no right to it, as I did not give it to her. She may have claimed to have the right to set her own course. She lied. She belongs to me."

Annie whirled, running back to the wagon. Adeline was sleeping soundly. Sophia and Soleil were sitting on her bed, their hands still clutched together, like that alone was keeping them from flying off the face of the earth.

"Stay where you are," hissed Annie. "Close the windows. Open the door for no one, no matter how sweetly they ask. *Protect my child.*" She slammed the door, not waiting for them to reply, and turned, and ran for the wagon of oddities.

It was a strange place to seek refuge. It was full of monsters, creatures that would kill her as soon as look at her. With Tranquility gone, there was nothing there that would fight for her. She ran there all the same, fumbling with the lock, while the sound of gunfire spoke from the bonfire and her husband watched impatiently from above.

"All I am asking for is the woman," he said, his voice magnified and bounced off every wall of the bowl surrounding The Clearing. "She is nothing to you. She is my *wife,* bound in the eyes of God to be my helpmeet on this Earth. She is my property, and you must return her to me."

The wagon door was latched. Annie fumbled it open, tumbling head over heels in her haste to get inside. Her head cracked against the wagon floor, and she sprawled there for a moment, struggling to get her breath back.

In the nearest tank, the single pit wasp she had been able to keep alive after separation from its hive shifted, wings buzzing slightly, abdomen pulsing. Its stinger was wet, as always, shiny with the thin venom it secreted as easily as breathing. It would kill her if she gave it the opportunity. It would kill anyone if given the opportunity. Only Adeline had ever been able to come close to handling the thing, and even she could only interact with it safely when she was full of her medicine, when her blood reeked of mercury and ghost rock and silver. Any other time she came close, it would lash out, buzzing death behind a wall of glass.

It buzzed now, listless in the dark, a warning sound more than an actual threat. It had no desire to be forced into a fight, not before the sun was up.

Annie pushed herself onto her hands, fumbling at the lower shelves until she found her emergency lantern, the one she kept low, where Adeline could reach it. A few matches later and she was looking around the wagon, face lit by the lantern's flickering light, searching for an answer to her dilemma—looking for a way out.

She had traveled the continent, collecting monsters everywhere she went, purchasing anything the natives called "unnatural" and locking it away, the way her husband had tried to lock away their daughter. She had allowed Adeline's instincts to lead her to every terrible thing the West had to offer, and when she hadn't been able to tame them, she had kept them anyway. She couldn't aim a gun with more than the roughest accuracy. She couldn't throw a knife or rope a steer. But oh, she could fill her hands with monsters, and she could use them, when no other weapons remained.

Oscar lurked at the bottom of his half-empty tank, turning in the shallow water to watch her with hopeful fishy eyes, waiting for his evening meal. The nibblers tracked her with even more intensity, their toothy jaws chewing at the water until thin lines of blood ran outward from their gums, coloring everything around them.

"You are terrible," she informed them. "Of all the horrible things I've sheltered, you are the worst."

The nibblers swam, all blind hunger and clashing jaws, and Annie knew what she had to do.

Opening the window at the far end of the wagon allowed her to clearly hear the gunfire and screaming from outside. Annie tried to shut it out as best she could, moving through the wagon, shifting exhibits from one place to another, struggling to do so without dropping anything. If she broke a jar . . .

Mr. Blackstone would care for Adeline, of that much she was sure. Assuming Michael didn't burn this circus to the ground for the crime of sheltering her when she ran away from him.

The shots outside were getting more frequent, and closer. The screams were coming closer together. She didn't recognize any of the screamers—all people sound essentially alike when in pain—but she could hear the pain in their voices, and she ached for them. This wasn't their fault. None of this, from the beginning, had been their fault.

"It is not your fault!" declared Michael, his words eerily mirroring her thoughts. It made the skin on her arms rise in goosebumps, hairs standing on end. How dare he? She hadn't seen him in the better part of a decade. He had no right to know her way of thinking. "My wife is a cunning temptress! She is skilled at lying to men, and she has tricked you! Only return her to me, and I promise you, all of this will go away!"

A confused murmur rose from the wagons around her. Annie realized two things in the same terrible moment. First, that much of the boneyard was undefended: the bonfire ring could keep some attackers away, but it would have holes, spans of unwatched ground. There were only so many bodies. There were only so many guns. Even if each able-bodied adult in the circus had gone to watch the border of the boneyard, there would still be places where a clever person could slip through.

They had thought themselves fighting against settlers and monsters, not madmen from Deseret, equipped with whatever new and terrible weapons had been devised in Hellstromme's laboratory.

Second, and perhaps worse, was the realization that Michael had not yet told them *who* his wife was. The people around her, her friends and colleagues and companions on the road, they didn't know Grace Murphy. They had never *met* Grace Murphy, because by the time she had reached them, she had already been calling herself by her daughters' names, Annie in honor of lost Annabelle, Pearl in honor of the child she couldn't save, with Adeline heavy in her arms and her sins weighing heavy on her heart. She was Annie Pearl to them, had always been Annie Pearl, and Michael might as well have been demanding they hand him the moon.

They weren't leaving her to prepare for the onslaught because they believed in her ability to defend herself. They were doing it because they didn't realize, yet, that she was the key to making this new problem go away. They let her work because they didn't know they had an alternative.

Once they did know—and they *would* know; Michael would tell them, sooner or later, once he realized why no one was leaping to obey him—would they still be willing to protect her? Would she still be one of them, part of the family, once they understood what she'd done? That she was a fallen woman, unfaithful, a kidnapper and a deserter of children in the same action? She didn't deserve this good place. She never had.

The door was heavy, designed to stay in place even when the wagon hit bad spots on the road. Annie put her shoulder to it, shoving it into the position she needed. She left it propped just enough to form an angle between itself and the frame. When she was sure that it was good, she grabbed a bucket and went back to work.

Outside, the gunfire, and Michael's cold narration, went on.

"You may not know my wife by name. She may have lied to you. If that is the case, there is no need to feel ashamed, and I will not hold her deceit against you. She was always an excellent liar. A better liar than I had any idea. She may have given you a false name, a false history. She may have told you that she was the daughter of a robber baron or a banker, or the sister of some wanted criminal. But she is none of those things. She is Grace Murphy of Deseret, and she is my wife, and I would have her back again. Return her to me, or know that you have made an enemy."

The night was loud enough to cover almost any sound. Annie was sure that the people who had come to The Clearing with Michael were counting on that. She knew her husband; knew how he thought and how he planned. A frontal assault, such as the one she could hear through the open window, was contrary to his nature. He wouldn't want to endanger himself if there were any possible way to avoid it.

So: Assume that he had come to The Clearing expecting to find a sleepy little forest settlement, the sort of place that greeted visitors with open hands and open doors, putting up no resistance. The sort of place, more, where no one would hear the residents screaming if he allowed his goons to do what goons did best.

There was no way he was traveling without goons. Even if he had wanted to, Hellstromme would never have allowed it. In a way, Annie thought she had more in common with Hellstromme than she would ever have wanted to admit. They both kept dangerous pets. It was just that, in his case, the dangerous pets were human, while hers at least had the decency to reveal themselves openly as the monsters they were.

Moreover, there was no way Michael was here without Hellstromme's blessing. Her husband never did anything without the full consent of the man he called master, the man who had lifted a brilliant but brittle boy out of the Holy City and elevated him to the position of scientist, untouchable, irrefutable. She knew little about her husband's past, but she knew that he had no family; that his family name was, in fact, worth little to nothing in the temple, where bloodline and social position were everything. Their marriage had been predicated largely on what she brought to the table: her name, her position in society, and the legitimacy it endowed. Without her, he would have been nothing but another flunky as far as most of Deseret was concerned.

When Hellstromme told him to jump, he replied by asking how high he should aim. Hellstromme had approved this. Hellstromme had *dispatched* him, to bring back something he believed should be the property of Deseret.

Had Michael sent men to retrieve her, Annie would have had no trouble believing that she was the target. Now, however . . . he was calling her name, he was speaking of her betrayal, but he was doing it himself. Even her husband's science couldn't be so advanced as to allow him to duplicate himself so perfectly well. This was him. This was the man himself. And that meant that he had been sent to bring back something so precious that Hellstromme would risk his right-hand man for the sake of having it.

He was here for Adeline.

Annie moved the tank containing her largest, most

aggressive snakes into position on the floor, feeling a strange serenity steal over her. There was nothing else that made sense. Michael was here to reclaim their daughter, whom he had always considered to be his property. Perhaps Annabelle had finally died, and he felt compelled to prove to Hellstromme that he could produce an heir. Perhaps Deseret was running low on the hearts of little girls. It didn't matter. Michael was here for her daughter. Michael was here for her *child*.

Michael wasn't going to have her.

Annie looked around the wagon, now reduced to a maze of dangers and potential booby-traps. Anyone who wasn't her would have a hard time walking from one end to the other in full daylight without releasing an oddity and possibly killing themselves in the process. It wasn't enough.

It would have to do.

Calmly, she hung her lantern in the window, marking the wagon as open, and occupied. Then she took a step back, until her calves hit the chair she kept for the long afternoons, when the sun was hot and the wagon was full, and it felt like she might die if she didn't have the chance to sit down. She sat, spine as straight as it had been when she was a girl, learning the ways of etiquette and Deseret womanhood from the nursemaids and instructors her parents hired. She folded her hands in her lap, eyes fixed on the partially open door.

Annie took a deep breath and settled in to wait for her husband's people to come and try to take her home.

Chapter 21

The first iteration of The Clearing had been built by people who didn't understand the land, not yet: who didn't know what it would hit them with, or how it would struggle to destroy them. They had looked at the shallow bowl in the earth and seen, not a killing jar, not a place for rain to pool and snow to gather, but fertile soil that wouldn't need to be cleared before it could be built upon. They'd believed the strange fingerprints driven into the ground by some unseen hand were a blessing to them, and when the wendigo had come, there had been nowhere for them to run.

The sensible thing would have been to leave Oregon with the first thaw—or, if that was somehow not possible, to build their new settlement on high ground, someplace where the advantage would always be theirs to claim, where they could see the dark coming and turn it aside. The survivors of the first settlement had not been sensible. Or maybe Hal was right when he said that they were already wendigo in their hearts, already hungry and planning for the future when they would be tall and strong and vicious. They had constructed their second home in mirror to the first, and when Dr. Michael Murphy had moved his wagons into place along the line of the road that circled the bowl, they had had no chance to run.

Seven wagons, six of them filled with armed men who wanted nothing more than to impress him, and through him, Hellstromme: that was all it had taken for Dr. Murphy to take the town. There were still people below him with guns, people who thought that they could fight their way out of this, but they were all behind the bright glare of the firelight, and from what his scouts had said, they were members of the circus to a man. The townsfolk were outside their houses, watching, some with weapons in their hands. That didn't mean that they had fired a single shot.

Indeed, there was something almost eerie about the way the townsfolk stood there, not hiding, not shouting, and not leveling their guns. It was a standoff that made no sense, and it might have concerned him, had he not had other dangers on his mind. Like those damned circus folk, who huddled behind their fires—as if fire had protected anyone from anything since humanity crawled out of the caves—and aimed their rifles, and tried to keep him from what was his.

There was a flicker of motion at his elbow. Michael turned, lowering the cone he was using to amplify his voice for the edification of the fools below. Laura looked at him calmly, waiting for his attention to be devoted solely to her.

It burned him, how this woman assumed she had any authority, any *right* to command his actions. She'd been like this all the way across the country, calm as a rattlesnake coiled in the sun, ready to strike at the slightest provocation. She was his babysitter, assigned by Hellstromme to make sure he came back, and that burned, too, because it spoke of a world where he would have considered doing differently. He was loyal. He had always been loyal. He would be loyal until the day he died. To suggest anything else was not just inaccurate, it was cruel.

That others might consider him cruel—might consider

what he was doing in this very moment to be nothing short of monstrous—had never crossed his mind.

"What?" he demanded.

Laura smirked. She had put her hat aside when the sun went down. Somehow, that little change had made her more difficult to see. She was darkly tanned, dressed in brown leathers, with hair only a few shades lighter than her skin. In the shadows that clung to The Clearing, she stood just to the side of invisibility.

"It's the right circus," she said. "One of my boys made it down and back while we were drawing their fire, and he saw the sign on their big tent, clear as anything. These people don't know how to hide."

"That's not my concern," he said. "Did your man see my wife?" *Did he see my daughter?* Adeline would not be perfectly identical to her sister, not after all her years of running in the sun and scraping her knees on wagon floors. Grace had been unforgivably negligent, risking his property in such a manner.

"No," said Laura. "But then, how would he have known if he had? It's not as if you've provided any pictures. I need your permission to descend." The corner of her mouth curved into a hooked smile, reminiscent of the curve of a rattlesnake's tail.

Everything about the woman was reptilian and terrible, repugnant in the extreme. How she hid her nature behind smooth skin and a woman's curves was beyond even his genius to explain. Had she revealed that she was born in Hellstromme's labs, crafted from the flesh of a hundred such snakes, he would almost have been relieved. At least then she would have made sense.

(Her origin was nowhere near so flashy, or so fabulous: Laura was a daughter of Junkyard, shaped by her environment, refined by her own fight to survive, until she was a killing blow walking in the shape of a gunslinger, selling her services to the highest bidder to keep her belly full and her shelter secure. Michael Murphy was an essentially immoral man. Laura was something different. Like the snake she so reminded him of, she was essentially amoral, willing to do whatever was required to keep herself alive.)

"I thought my permission was not required for your mission," he said stiffly.

"Hellstromme told me to get you here safely, and then to afford you any assistance you required," she said. "I don't leave without you, but while we're here, I'm to do what I can to aid you. I assumed you wanted the woman."

"I do," he said. "But I want the girl more."

Laura tilted her head slightly to the side, so that a lock of hair fell across her cheek in a disarmingly feminine manner. It made his flesh crawl. Nothing as terrible as she should have been permitted to feign womanhood in a believable fashion.

"So the woman," she said. "If she resists, you don't mind my killing her?"

Michael paused. He and Grace were still married in the eyes of God: he had loved her as much as he was able when she had been faithful, and once she had proven false, he had been unable to entertain remarriage. Not with Annabelle still needing him so direly; not with the city ready to forgive him for losing one wife, but poised to judge him if he lost two. It had been too great a risk to take.

"Only if you must," he said finally. "You can damage her as much as you like. She can be repaired. Women are like wagons. Break a few wheels, splinter a few axles, but you'll still be able to find a way to put them back together if necessary."

Laura nodded. "So may I descend?"

"You may."

Her smile was swift and sharp, making his heart clench

with the sudden conviction that he had given her the wrong instruction: that he had somehow condemned himself and his daughter both with his words.

"As you like," she said, and turned, placing two fingers in her mouth and giving one short, sharp whistle. Two of the men hired to accompany their caravan separated themselves from the shadows and moved to stand beside her, flanking her. They were both so much taller than she that it should have made her look small, even comic. It didn't. Instead, she seemed all the more dangerous for being so obviously overpowered. If she weren't dangerous, how else could she have survived?

Michael watched as Laura and the two men walked to the edge of the road, where the land dropped off and rejoined the gentle slope of the basin's walls. She looked back once, winked, and vanished into the gloom, leaving Michael standing on the road, the amplifier in his hands.

After a long moment's hesitation, he raised it to his lips and began speaking again. "You have stolen something that belongs to me. The rules of the sovereign nation of Deseret state that a man may do as he likes with his wife. I would like to have my wife returned. If you do not—"

His words faded into so much background nonsense as Laura and her men slid down the curve of the hill, using the sides of their feet to control their rate of descent. Dust and pebbles spilled in their wake, the small, scuffling sound covered by the gunfire and shouting. Michael Murphy might be a useless rotter of a man, Laura observed, but he sure could kick up a distraction when he needed to.

In a matter of seconds, they were on level ground, stepping away from the hill and onto the territory claimed by the settlers. Laura motioned her men to silence as she looked around, waiting for some sign that they had been seen. She'd seen better killers than her taken down when they failed to account for some local kid sending up the alarm. Better to go slow, and be sure that they went unseen.

Nothing moved. They were secure.

When the settlers had chosen the location of their new home, they had probably celebrated finding something as perfect for their needs as a natural bowl in the earth, surrounded on all sides by gently sloping hillside, keeping them safe from surprise attack. They wouldn't have thought about situations like this one, where they would need to defend themselves against a smaller force with better weapons and higher ground. That was the trouble with some people. They set themselves up to feel like the world couldn't touch them, and then they didn't know what to do when it touched them anyway.

Maybe. The townsfolk didn't seem to be *doing* much. They were just standing there, slack-jawed and staring, while Murphy's men fired on the circus, and the circus fired back. A few of the circus folk had already gone down, swallowing dirt like the corpses they had always been destined to become, and still the townsfolk were standing in silent witness, rather than moving to defend their homes. It was unsettling.

It was none of her concern. She was here for the brat, and for the woman, if she could get her without compromising herself. The spot she'd chosen for their descent was well behind the line of bonfires—and that, too, was a sign of the shortsightedness of the average person. The circus had created a barricade in fire and light, drawing it between itself and the settlers, but hadn't thought to protect its rear flank. Anyone could slide down the side of the hill and take them from behind.

A few slit throats would have been educational for them. Let her ghost up to their fires, grab their sentries by the hair, and show them what it was to smile from ear to ear. The survivors would thank her. Well, the survivors would curse her name, if they ever learned it. But they would go on to build better walls, to draw circles with no weak spots, to protect themselves properly. Really, it was almost a shame that she didn't have the time to teach them how to do that.

Regretfully, she shook her head. Nice as it would have been to educate these people—and they damn well needed education—this wasn't the time, or the place. If she ever met any of them again, she could show them then what it meant to protect yourself. She turned back to her men, motioning quickly to show them where to go. Three people would be enough to search this circus. Especially when the bulk of their able-bodied adults were at the bonfires, trying to protect the boneyard from a frontal assault.

One of the men drew his finger across his throat before looking at her hopefully. She nodded. If they needed to kill to fulfill their mission, that was fine by her—and by Murphy as well, she was quite sure. The man was still too wrapped up in his own fancy ideas of dignity and ethicality to be a proper killer, but he could take a body apart when the need arose. She'd done her research before agreeing to sign on with him. She knew how many drifters and never-do-wells had been reported missing on or near the Murphy land. All of them had been forgiven by Hellstromme, and thus by Deseret. The two might as well have been one and the same in the eyes of the law, and a man like Murphy, well. He had no reason to restrain himself, not when there was something to be learned from the wet red treasures inside a man.

Laura pointed to the far end of the circus. The first of the men started in that direction, moving quickly, stepping light. She pointed to the center. The second of the men nodded and went where she had indicated, following the first for no more than a few yards before he veered off. She turned, squinting into the dark in front of her. Then she smiled, and slunk into the shadows.

Time to get to work.

There were those in Deseret who knew her by name, or by reputation, if nothing more than that. She was one of Hellstromme's throwing knives. Less efficient than a bullet, which would kill whatever stood between it and its target, but more reliable in the long run. She could always come back to his hand and be flung again, while a bullet, once fired, was fired forever.

Murphy was a bullet. He had been sitting in the chamber of Hellstromme's plans for years, and he might never feel the hammer come down, propelling him to his fate. Or he might find himself fired the second he returned to Deseret. Hellstromme wanted to see Murphy's work completed, she knew that much. It mattered to him.

If it mattered to him, it mattered to her, at least as long as he was filling her pockets. Laura slipped between the wagons like a shadow, pausing at each one to listen to the sounds from inside.

Some were silent.

Some were filled with the sounds of people hiding from the world outside, the little scuffs and scrapes that betrayed the presence of the living. But none of them sounded properly terrified. They sounded scared, yes, like they didn't know what was going on outside and didn't know what they could do to help, but they didn't sound *terrified*.

Grace Murphy would be terrified.

Grace Murphy would be shitting herself with the realization that this was it: she had reached the limit of her long and winding road to freedom, and was now pinned between the Oregon woods and the end of the world. She had to have known that she was always running on borrowed time: that short of finding a way off the continent,

Murphy's agents would catch up with her eventually and bring her back to Deseret to pay for what she'd done. It was a cold vendetta to draw against a woman with no resources of her own, but she should have expected it. She was Murphy's property, and he was Hellstromme's property, and that meant she had never had a prayer.

Laura couldn't feel sorry for the woman. She had been given every opportunity Deseret had to offer. If she'd wanted a life of luxury, she could have stayed. If she'd wanted her freedom, she could have left the little girl. By refusing to do either, she had signed her own death warrant.

The shadows around the wagon wheels seemed thick as taffy. They tangled at her feet and clung to her ankles, until it was like they were trying to slow her progress through the circus—which was just silly. Shadows didn't have minds. They couldn't decide to do something like that.

A wolf howled from the forest above the town. Laura stopped, waiting for the echoes of the sound to pass before she resumed walking slowly forward, eyes darting from wagon to wagon.

The Blackstone Family Circus was a mid-sized show, smaller than the ones she'd seen outside the Holy City, but large for a production without a patron. They were beholden to no one save themselves. That must have been nice for them, to roll down the roads without worrying that they'd somehow offend their masters and find themselves called back.

At the same time, with no master, no patron, there was also no one who would come to save them if something happened.

Laura was very good at being something that happened.

A light caught her eye, shining as it did through the blackness of the boneyard. She shifted positions and saw that it was a lantern, hanging in an open wagon window. Laura frowned. Lanterns, placed like that, usually signified that there was someone inside. All the other wagons were walled up tight. So what did this one mean . . . ?

Placing two fingers in her mouth, she whistled, long and low and sad, like the cry of a desert bird. The wolves were still howling up above; anyone who heard her and didn't live here was likely to take the sound for just one more piece of the local landscape. She stepped back into the shadow of the nearest wagon, and waited.

It wasn't a long wait. The nearer of her two helpers came trotting out of the shadows, his hands already clenched, ready to punch whatever she aimed him at. She stepped forward, enough for him to see her through the gloom, and waved him over.

"What is it?" he whispered, once he was close enough. Hand signals could only get them so far.

A pity. Speech was so *loud*. "Look," she replied, and pointed to the lit wagon.

He turned, and his eyes widened. "Oh," he said.

"Go," she said.

He nodded, and went.

Part of being a throwing knife was understanding that some targets were better hit by other people. As long as she was the one who always returned, Hellstromme would continue to think of her as the truly useful one, the one who could accomplish whatever tasks he set for her. Every mission, every kill served to increase her reputation among the kind of people who could afford to pay her fees. Eventually, she'd be in a position to make demands of her own, and when that happened . . .

She did understand Grace Murphy's desire to put Deseret behind her. She shared it. She was just going about it in a much, much smarter way.

Slinking back into the shadows, she let her hand rest on the stock of the pistol she had belted to her right hip and waited for the screaming to begin. One way or another, she was sure there would be screaming. All she had to do was stand back.

Her man—Hellstromme's man, really, one of the great unwashed mass who teemed in Junkyard, waiting for the chance to prove themselves worthy of becoming something better than they were—approached the wagon slowly, cautiously, like he expected it to strike at any moment. There was something almost comic about watching a grown man stalk a wagon. Laura turned away. He would call if he needed help, and there was more boneyard to search.

Hand still resting on her pistol, she resumed her slow passage through the boneyard, pausing at each wagon. At the fourth wagon, her pause became a stop.

Someone was inside. They were crying. No: they were weeping, a soft, constant sound that reminded her uncomfortably of her childhood.

Laura drew her pistol, steadied her hand, and swung herself up onto the wagon steps, nudging the door open with her toe. The woman who had been crying lowered her hands and turned to stare.

There were three people inside the wagon: the crying woman—girl, really, barely out of her teens, still half-finished, with the ghosts of the pox living on the skin of her face like a brand—and the older woman who sat beside her, rubbing her back with one hand. There was a certain similarity between their faces and figures. They were family.

The same couldn't be seen for the little girl who lay in the bed across from them, her white-blonde hair fanned out across the pillow, her eyes closed and her breath coming easy. She was wearing a tattered white gown, and her feet were muddy, but apart from those small details, she could almost have been Annabelle Murphy, the scientist's lovely, dying daughter.

"Well, well," said Laura, with a slow smile. "What have I got here?"

The older woman made as if to stand. Laura raised her gun, aiming the barrel square at the woman's forehead. The woman froze.

"No," said Laura, calm as anything. "I don't think you want to do that. I'll shoot you, don't see if I won't, but Dr. Murphy might be a little put out if I bring his daughter back to him all covered in your brains. That's his girl, isn't it?"

"You stay away from Adeline," said the younger woman. Tears still streamed down her pocked face, but she looked ready to get to her feet and fight for the sake of the child. Interesting. "She's not some Dr. Murphy's daughter. She's Miss Pearl's little girl, and she's not yours to take."

"Either of you have a weapon on you? No? Then she's mine to do with as I please." Laura took another step into the wagon. The little girl hadn't so much as stirred. Her mother must have drugged her before running away again. Made sense. It was easier to leave a child when they couldn't beg for you to stay.

Unless she'd poisoned the girl, and that was why the younger woman had been weeping. Fear—a rare emotion for her—uncurled in Laura's breast. If the girl was dead, this had all been for naught. The journey back to Deseret would kill Annabelle, of that there was no question. Hell-stromme would be angry if she returned with Murphy and neither of his children. The thought of his anger . . .

If the girl was dead, maybe this was when she would do her own cut and run. Some things were worse than being on her own in potentially hostile territory. Hell-stromme's wrath was among them.

"Wake her up," Laura commanded.

"It's her medicine," said the older woman. "She needs to sleep in order to heal."

"Her father's here now. He'll see to healing her. Now wake her up, or I'll do it."

"We can't," said the older woman. "It's not—"

The bullet between her eyes stopped her in the middle of her sentence, painting a red punctuation across the wagon wall. The younger woman began to scream, high and shrill, putting her hands over her mouth like they could somehow hold the sound inside.

In her bed, the little girl rolled onto her side, and kept sleeping.

"She's alive, then," said Laura. "Good—oh, stop your screaming. If you don't, I'll have to shoot you, too, and that would be a wasted bullet." The sound of Murphy's voice drifted from outside. It was far from quiet out there. The woman's screams might go overlooked for a while.

Not forever. Screams had a nasty tendency to attract attention. Laura stepped closer to Adeline's bed, raising her gun so that the barrel was pointed at the screaming woman.

"Sorry," she said.

Something snarled behind her. She began to turn. Heavy paws, bristling with claws, impacted with her shoulders and drove her to the ground. The screaming continued.

Chapter 22

Annie sat perfectly still in the back of the wagon of oddities, her hands clenched in her lap until she could feel the bones shifting under her skin, forced into stiff new positions by the pressure she was putting them under. It wasn't painful, not quite, but it would be if she didn't move soon.

Michael was out there, baying for her return. She knew him—she had married him—and she knew if he was yelling, it was only to draw and hold the attention of the people who might defend her. He would send his minions down into the boneyard through other channels, and they would be looking for her, that she might lead them to her little girl. No. She would not move. She would wait, taking the lesson from her oddities, and let them come to her.

The heavy tread of a boot on the back step of her wagon put steel into her spine, pulling her that fraction of an inch farther upright. She held her breath, still waiting.

A gunshot came from somewhere outside—somewhere closer than the bonfire line. A woman screamed, high and shrill and terrified. Annie's hands clenched down harder, until she felt her nails break the skin on her palms. Still, she did not move.

Every instinct she had told her to go back to Adeline, to stand between her little girl and the world. But Adeline was sleeping. Adeline was drugged into blissful unconsciousness, locked safely in a dark wagon with Sophia

DEADLANDS: BONEYARD   321

and Soleil to watch over her. The only thing Adeline needed more than her mother was the opportunity to survive—to wake in a world where no one was looking for her, where she could be left alone to grow up and become the woman she was meant to be.

Annie could buy her that opportunity. She would pay for it with blood and with bone, but she *could* pay for it. Wasn't that a mother's burden? If she could make the world a better place for her daughter, she had to do it.

The wagon door eased open. The lantern light caught on the barrel of a pistol as it slid into the room ahead of the man who held it. So many men did that, entered a room gun-first, as if the trigger could pull itself when it sensed danger. This was a man of Deseret, land of scientific wonders. Maybe his gun *could* sense danger, could cock and aim itself. Annie doubted that. Hellstromme would one day make the men who thronged to follow him obsolete, but not yet, not until he had finished sucking the goodness out of them, one crime and one sin at a time. He still needed to be served.

The door opened farther. The bucket she had so carefully balanced there teetered.

(She had played that trick before, when she was a little girl, when dousing a housemaid with soapy water had been the absolute height of hilarity. Even her father hadn't been able to be angry with her when he had come around the corner and seen little Grace laughing, while the long-suffering maid was flicking bubbles out of her ear. Sometimes children's pranks were the best solution to adult problems.)

The door opened farther. The bucket fell.

The man with the gun abruptly became the man without a gun: it fell to the floor, landing harmlessly on its side, as he screamed and clawed at the fish that were biting at his face and throat. The nibblers, for all that they might not be able to survive long outside of water, had more hunger than survival instinct—rather than flopping away, looking for the safety of their bucket, they clung to his flesh, chomping and tearing with their terrible jaws, filling their bellies while their gills starved.

The man kept screaming and clawing at his face, even though some of the fish were now clinging to his hands, stripping his fingers to the bone. They ate with incredible efficiency. The nibblers still confined in their tank thrashed and beat their bodies against the glass, jealous of their dying companions, who were *eating,* they were *eating,* they were filling their bellies and they were *eating.* Fish weren't intelligent, but they knew envy. Annie was sure of that.

Still, she did not move, but only watched as the screaming man ventured farther into the wagon, staggering more than walking, and kicked the side of the tank that contained her pit wasp. The lid was off. The night was cool and the sun was down, rendering this particular monster sluggish, but even a sluggish beast could be roused to anger by the right stimuli.

Wings buzzing, the pit wasp rose slowly into the air. The man, still flailing, didn't seem to notice it. His hand, swinging wildly, brushed the tip of one fast-moving wing.

The pit wasp struck.

It was a worker, small as pit wasps went, separated from the body of its hive. That didn't seem to matter much. Maybe its venom was less potent than a queen's, but it was still fully capable of burying its stinger in human flesh and pumping out poison. The intruder stopped screaming as he collapsed to the floor of the wagon, seizing wildly. The smell of urine filled the air, hot and acrid.

The nibblers that were still alive continued to burrow and chew, working their way deeper into his flesh, until Annie had to wonder whether they were able to use his blood like water, continuing to breathe as long as it was flowing over their gills.

The man stopped thrashing. Annie remained motionless, and not only because the pit wasp was loose now, and had no loyalty: like the nibblers, it would destroy her as quickly as it would anyone else. Loyalty was for mammals, and she had few of those.

"Noah?" The door slammed open as a second man charged inside. He kicked the bucket as he came, sending it spinning across the floor to slam into the side of another tank. He didn't seem to notice. Without the nibblers to fall on him from above, the entrance was harmless, ordinary even.

His attention was all for the man sprawling in the center of the wagon, and for the giant wasp that stood athwart his softly swelling neck. The first man—Noah—was quickly coming to resemble someone suffering from a terrible case of mumps, save for the almost total absence of his face.

"Noah!" the second man repeated, and dropped to his knees, nibblers squishing under the impact. He still didn't seem to have noticed Annie.

It was interesting, she reflected, feeling oddly removed from the scene, like she was watching it through a pane of thick glass. Men liked to talk about how women were the centers of their worlds, how everything they did, they did for love, or for the sake of the women who waited for them at home, but when the time came to make those ideals real, women faded into the furniture. As long as she didn't move, she didn't matter. She was a prize to be won or a disobedient possession to be punished. She wasn't *real*.

The newcomer reached for the dead man. The pit wasp, sensing danger, pulled its stinger free and rose again, wings beating so fast that they were a silver shimmer in the air, transcendently, terribly beautiful, too fine to exist in this world or any other.

The man shouted incoherently and grabbed the hat off his head, swatting at the wasp. Perhaps he could be forgiven for assuming that the thing was dangerous only to the already-distracted, like the unfortunate Noah, who had been consigned to death even before the pit wasp had become involved: few men thrive without their faces.

His hat brushed the wasp's wing, knocking it off-balance. It spun in the air, soft buzz becoming a loud whine as it beat its wings even faster, struggling to stay aloft. He swung at it again. This time, it wasn't there to hit. It had already moved, darting toward his face at an impossible speed, stinger curved around so that it was the first thing to impact with the surface of his left eye.

The man screamed, clawing the wasp off his face and beginning to stagger around the wagon, howling. Unlike the unfortunate Noah, he didn't kick a tank: he stuck his foot straight through the lid of the tank containing the terrantulas.

The skull-backed spiders swarmed up his leg, biting as they went, and he fell, howling, to join his friend on the floor.

Annie stood.

It was only a few feet to the back door. She crossed them quickly, pausing to look into the corn stalker's cage. It looked back at her, orange eyes solemn in its impassive pumpkin face. She smiled.

"Go, then, monster," she murmured, and undid the latch. "Do what you like to them. They've *earned* you."

She didn't wait to see whether the little manikin climbed out to find its way to fertile soil. It was no longer her concern. Instead, she walked on, reaching the door in seconds, and let herself out into the night.

The shouts and gunfire continued, and the voice of her husband droned over it all. How had she ever taken him for anything other than a distraction? He was keeping the roustabouts and acrobats focused on the bonfire line, on the threat of a frontal assault. Maybe he had even killed a few of them. The soldiers allowed outside of Deseret were among the best she had ever known, because they had to be. Anything less would have dishonored the Holy City and, by extension, Hellstromme. They could shoot a man at that distance, if they had time to lay their aim and be sure of what they were doing.

There were no more screams from inside the wagon of oddities. She hoped the man hadn't crushed all her spiders when he fell. They were terrible beasts, and they would die quickly in these cold woods, but the people of The Clearing deserved a few monsters not of their own making. They were too accustomed to the wendigo. They didn't fear them anymore.

They needed to be reminded that some monsters were worth fearing.

Annie hurried back toward her own wagon, feet light on the uneven ground. Every boneyard was different. In some respects, every boneyard was the same. This was her home territory, and if Michael wanted to face her here, he could learn the error of his ways.

She was almost there when she heard an unfamiliar woman's scream. She broke into a run.

Stupid, stupid, she thought. Michael wouldn't stop with two goons. He would send a battalion, an army, to take back what he thought of as his own. He would have her, and he would have Adeline, and he would keep coming until he felt her slights against him had been avenged. Yes, she had drawn some number of his goons to her, but so what? It hadn't been everything. It hadn't been *enough*.

The door to her wagon was open. She grabbed the poker from the fire she had built around her kettle stand and all but leapt up the stairs, ready to beat in the brains of whoever was intruding on her home. Then she froze, eyes going wide at the sight before her.

Soleil sprawled in Annie's bed, a bullet hole between her eyes, no longer of this world. Sophia was beside her, feet kicking ripples into the duvet as she struggled to press herself against the wall, away from the battle now being played out on the wagon floor.

The strange woman—the woman who had screamed before—was there, dressed all in brown, face a mask of blood. Her teeth were bared in a hateful grimace, and she held one arm up, across her face and neck, blocking the furious lynx that had her pinned to the floor from ripping her throat out.

Tranquility looked to be in worse shape than the woman she was attacking. There were deep gouges cut into her sides, so wide that the blood and shocking whiteness of bone showed even through the thick fur. No human hands had made those cuts. They were too widely set, too deep, the work of a bear—or of a wendigo. If there was any question of whether the loyal cat had saved her mistress and Martin in the woods, her wounds answered it. Anything that could have done that to Tranquility would have had a human in pieces in an instant.

Adeline was still asleep, despite the screams and the snarls and the hot smell of gunpowder hanging in the air, left over from the bullet that had killed Soleil. Her medicine was strong.

The woman's gun was on the floor. Annie lunged for it, trusting Tranquility not to hurt her. Her faith was not misplaced: the lynx snarled, biting down on the woman's raised arm, and continued in her attack until Annie had the gun in her hands and had backed up against the wagon door, aiming it as carefully as she could.

"Tranquility," she said in a clear, carrying voice, "release."

Tranquility snarled.

"*Release.*"

Tranquility let go. She snarled one last time, saliva dripping from her blunted fangs and onto the woman's face, before she retreated to press herself against Annie's leg, panting. Blood coated her muzzle. Most of it wasn't hers, but too much was; her wounds were deep.

"Good girl," murmured Annie, looking down the barrel of her stolen gun at the stranger. "Brave girl." More loudly, she demanded, "Who are you, and why am I not shooting you where you lie?"

"She killed Auntie, and said she was going to take Adeline away," wailed Sophia. She made no move to uncurl from her position against the wall. She was starting to shake. Shock was setting in, and soon she would be no use at all.

That wouldn't do. "Stop your weeping," snapped Annie. "Get the rope from my chest and tie her hands. I know you can tie a knot. You wouldn't have been apprenticed to your aunt if you couldn't." Invoking Soleil was a calculated risk. With the woman's body still cooling on the bed, saying her name could make Sophia freeze.

Or it could enrage her. Sophia's expression went dead. Slowly, she pushed herself to the edge of the bed and crossed the wagon to the chest, opening it and beginning to rummage.

Tranquility growled, the sound seeming to vibrate all the way up through Annie's leg. She snapped her attention back to the stranger, who had been pushing herself into a sitting position.

"Don't do that," said Annie. It was marvelous, how calm she could sound. That, and not her private menagerie of monsters, should have been the show's star attraction. "Stay still, and maybe I don't put a bullet through your throat."

"I'm bleeding and beat," said the woman. She had a

Deseret accent. No surprise there. Michael might be willing to go to the gutter for the people he hired to help him, but he would never look outside the Holy City. Not while he still cared for his reputation. "What do you think I'm going to do to you?"

"You broke into my wagon, shot my friend, and threatened my daughter," said Annie, voice cool. "It doesn't matter what I think you're going to do to me. What you have done already is more than sufficient to earn you your current treatment."

To her surprise, the stranger smiled. The gesture pulled at the claw marks gashing down the left side of her face, making them weep blood. "You must be Grace Murphy."

"What makes you say that?"

"If the brat's your daughter, there's no one else you could be. Children are not transitive. But beyond that, you still stink of the Holy City. Ghost rock in your skin, mercury in your blood—the things that don't wash away so easy."

"Annie?" asked Sophia.

"I knew you'd change your name, but you can't change who you are, or where you came from." The stranger kept smiling. "They call me Laura. Your husband sent me to bring you home. You've been a very naughty girl, Grace. You've run out on your holy duty to house and husband. Dr. Murphy will probably be forgiving, though, if I tell him you came willingly. Will you come willingly?"

"If you're stalling because you're hoping the men who accompanied you will come to your rescue, I'm afraid I've some terrible news for you," said Annie. She crouched, putting herself more on a level with Laura, the gun still aimed square at the other woman's face. "They're dead."

Something flashed in Laura's eyes. Something dark and dangerous. "You're lying."

"I'm not. You see, being married to Michael Murphy

left me equipped for little in the world outside Deseret—
but I am, it seems, a wonderful mistress of monsters.
Your men came after me in my wagon. One of them met
his death at the teeth of my nibblers, terrible river fish
that can reduce an adult to skeletal form in a matter of
seconds. He didn't suffer much. He enraged my pit wasp,
and it handled the rest. As for the other, he seemed very
concerned for your first worker—Noah, I believe he
called him—and he didn't look where he was stepping.
He found my terrantulas. Nasty things. I never could
teach them not to bite the hand that fed them."

Tranquility continued growling. The cat looked like
something out of a nightmare, all blood and bone and
anger. That, more than anything, seemed to make Annie's words believable. Laura's eyes widened again, and
this time there was no doubt in her expression at all.

"You killed them."

"My creatures killed them. Or perhaps they killed
themselves, by forcing their way into a place where they
had no business. It doesn't matter. Splitting hairs will
make them no less dead. Sophia?"

"I'm getting it." Sophia pulled the rope from the chest
and moved to kneel next to Laura, reaching for her
hands.

"No," said Annie sharply. Sophia froze. Laura scowled.
"Put them behind her back. We want to take her captive,
not allow her to lull us into believing her subdued."

"Bitch," Laura said pleasantly.

"Such language," said Annie. "I'm surprised they allow you to remain in Deseret."

"I have my uses," said Laura. "More than you do. You
couldn't even stay and honor your marriage vows."

"I pledged myself to a man, not a monster." Annie
stood, keeping the gun on Laura the whole time. "Why
are you here?"

"Because your husband needed a guide. He's a soft

man. Scientists always are. They think of themselves as hard because they can take things apart in their safe little labs, but you put them out in the world and they're as lost as the next fool. He wants his daughter back. He wants what rightfully belongs to him. Who was I to refuse such an earnest, well-paying request?"

Annie's eyes narrowed. "Michael hired you? Don't lie to me. Lie, and it's a bullet in your gut."

"What, so I can bleed out a little faster? Your damned cat already has me split open and leaking." Laura scowled. "If you want me to survive, you'll worry more about patching me up and less about tying me down."

"That's an interesting assumption," said Annie.

"That you'd want me alive? If you wanted me dead, you'd have pulled the trigger. You don't seem to care that you've killed two of my men, which tells me you're not sparing me out of soft-heartedness or some concern for human life. You *want* something from me. Whatever it is, I assure you that I'll be less good at doing it once I'm dead." Laura moved her glare to Tranquility, who was leaning more and more against Annie's leg. "A goddamned lynx. Who keeps a lynx in a wagon with a small child?"

"The lucky and the blessed," said Annie. "You're right that if I wanted you to die quickly, I would pull the trigger. You're wrong about why I haven't done it. You *threatened* my child. You are here at the bidding of a man I never wanted to see again. I haven't shot you because that would be too kind. I don't care if you bleed to death. You deserve it for what you've done."

"Big words from a woman who kidnapped her own daughter and left her other child behind."

Sophia gasped softly.

Laura smiled. "She didn't tell you, did she? Adeline isn't an only child. Never was. She has a sister."

Annie froze. "Has?"

"Oh, did you think she was dead? That by running away, you'd killed the child you didn't want? Dr. Murphy was a better parent than you could ever hope to be. While you were running around with circus performers and animals, he was nursing your sick daughter through the worst of her illness. He was keeping her *alive*. You couldn't even do that. You should never have been allowed to be a mother. You don't deserve your children. You don't—"

Laura yelped, stopping midsentence as Sophia drew the rope tight around her wrists. Annie stood frozen, staring.

"That's enough of that," said Sophia primly. She looped the rope around Laura's wrists again. "You went too far. Miss Pearl is not a bad mother. She could never be a bad mother. If she left a little girl behind when she left Deseret, she had good reason."

"You don't know that," Laura said through gritted teeth.

"Maybe not, but I'm not believing the things you say about her." Sophia looked up. "Shall I tie her feet?"

"Please," said Annie. "As for my good reason, my bastard of a husband planned to chop Adeline up for spare parts. I ran because I had no choice."

"She wasn't yours to steal," said Laura.

"She wasn't his to keep," replied Annie. She lowered the gun, finally shifting her attention to Tranquility. "Oh, my poor girl. My poor darling girl. What have they done to you?"

Tranquility made a deep chuffing noise in the back of her throat, bowing her head. Annie knelt.

The lynx had been grievously wounded, that much was clear: the damage Annie had seen upon entering was not the whole of it. Her fur was thick enough to have stuck together when she bled, forming seals over the wounds, stopping her from bleeding out entirely. It wasn't enough.

It could never have been enough. Even as Annie got her hands under the big cat's head, the light in Tranquility's eyes was going dim, flickering on the verge of going out.

Tranquility attempted to purr. The sound turned into a wheeze.

"Oh, my poor girl," said Annie again. She leaned forward and kissed Tranquility on the nose, ignoring the blood clotted there. Tranquility closed her eyes. "You did so well. You were so brave. You saved us both, you did. You saved your people. You can rest now."

"It's just an animal," said Laura, and was rewarded with a cuff upside the head from Sophia.

"Be quiet," she snapped. "That animal saved me from you. You don't get to talk to her."

"My poor girl," said Annie, for the third time. She lowered Tranquility's head slowly toward the floor. The rest of the cat's body followed, until Tranquility was lying on her side, chest moving shallowly up and down.

The lynx wheezed again, cracking her eyes open just enough to be sure that Annie was still there, watching over her. Then, with no fanfare or thrashing, she closed her eyes, and stopped breathing.

"Ah," said Annie. "My girl." She stroked Tranquility one last time. The big cat's fur was still warm.

Annie stood.

"Watch my daughter, Sophia," she said. "I have to go see my husband."

Chapter 23

Bullets had been peppering the bonfire line for quite some time, most passing through the fires before they could reach their targets. It was a small thing, but enough to throw some of the shots ever so slightly to the left of true, leaving them to whiz harmlessly by.

Or perhaps the people shooting at them from above were not truly interested in killing them all, just in pinning them down. Nathanial had to allow that this was possible, even probable, especially since the screams had come from the circus behind him, where the children and the people who weren't equipped to handle a fight like this were hiding in their wagons, waiting to be saved. Counting on *him* to do the saving.

There wasn't a single person in this show who didn't trust him to keep them safe. That was what it meant to sign on with a circus with no patron, no backing, no powerful ties to some permanent place: it meant accepting that the ringleader would be the one to protect you. But he was the one who had decided that they should come to Oregon, following tales of prosperity and plenty that bore no resemblance to this green and dangerous land. He was the one who had told them he would protect them if they followed him into the woods.

He had to keep them safe. He had to keep *all* of them safe. If he failed to do that, he might as well sell his wagon and settle in the first town they passed, because he was no longer equipped to serve the circus.

Martin stood, firing at the men on the ridge before dropping back down into the shelter of the fire. "I'm running low on bullets, Mr. Blackstone," he said, with an anxious glance at the only man who had ever been willing to tell him he had value. "I think we all are. What should we do?"

They couldn't run; the lit-up wagons were blocking the road, effectively pinning circus and settlers alike inside The Clearing. Whatever would have possessed people to make it all the way to Oregon before building their homes inside a pit where anyone who came along could turn them into targets? It didn't make sense. It was like the settlers had been *trying* to get themselves slaughtered.

They couldn't take the fight to the ridge. There was no cover there. Even if they could manage to climb the soft walls of the bowl without sliding back down to level ground, they'd be picked off one by one as they walked.

They couldn't surrender. Those people . . .

Most of the circus didn't know that Annie had changed her name upon joining the show, or that she had worked for years to strip the Deseret influence from her voice, shaping and flattening her vowels for the sake of sounding like she came from the same amorphous West as everyone else. There was a circus accent, a mashed-up mix of a dozen territories, and she had learned it one careful word at a time, gradually erasing the woman she had been. But when she was tired or under stress, she sometimes slipped, and the Deseret would come out, written clear as anything in every word she said.

Nathanial had never known her as "Grace," but there was no question of who the madman on the hill was demanding be returned to him. He was here for Annie. If it was her or the circus . . .

Maybe it made him a terrible person, or maybe it made him a man in love, but Nathanial thought that he would let the whole damned show burn to the ground before he handed her over to the man on the hill. Deseret had failed her once. There was no other reason for a woman to run with a baby on her hip and a wildcat wrapped around her shoulders. He wasn't going to be the one to fail her again.

"Who's injured?" he asked, voice tight.

People murmured from either side of him, whispering their names into the night air like secrets. They were all on edge, terrified of what was yet to come, but aware that they had passed the point of no return. They had nowhere to run. All they could do was stand, and fight.

"Who's dead?" he asked.

"Caleb, and Roland," said Martin. "Roland was done in by one of our own. A bullet bounced back when it struck the wall. Caleb went out from behind the fires. They saw him too clearly, and they shot him dead."

"So we stay behind the fire and we hope for a miracle," said Nathanial.

"A miracle?" asked Martin.

"Morning." Nathanial frowned through the flames at the bright-lit shapes up on the ridge. The cocky bastards were making no effort to hide themselves. Why should they? There was no way for the people on the ground to reach them.

Had the settlers been joining the fight—in either direction—things might have been different. Between The Clearing and the circus, the people on the ridge were well outnumbered. There would have been casualties, yes, but they would have been an overwhelming wave. They could have won. And if the settlers had set themselves against the circus, which they had seemed determined to do before the wagon train had shown up, the bonfire line would have been gunned down in minutes. Instead, the settlers stood in silent clumps between the two parties, some of them holding weapons, none of them opening fire.

It was strange. It was *wrong*. It was, like everything else they had experienced since reaching Oregon, barely this side of incomprehensible.

"We can't stay like this forever," said Martin, almost as if he had read Nathanial's mind.

"I don't know what else to do."

"I do."

Nathanial went cold. He turned, and there was Annie, walking up behind them. She had bloodstains on her dress. Not dainty drops; great streaks of blood, drying to a dirty brown. Another streak bisected her face, running along the bridge of her nose and onto her right cheek. She didn't appear to be injured. Whoever had bled to bring her here, the blood was not her own.

"Annie," he said, half-standing. "You need to get down and get back. It isn't safe."

"They won't shoot me," she said.

"Annie—"

"They might shoot Annie Pearl. But they won't shoot Grace Murphy." Annie lifted her head a little higher, the firelight playing off skin and blood alike. "My husband has come too far to shoot me."

Nathanial stopped in the act of reaching for her, going silent before he finally said, "I wish you wouldn't do this."

"I know," she said. Then she smiled, the expression faded and wan. "I intend to be a widow when I come back down that hill, Mr. Blackstone. If you'd like to make an honest woman out of me, we can talk about it then. In the meantime, if I don't come back, take care of Adeline for me. Tell her that I'm sorry."

"I'll raise her as my own," said Nathanial. He started to reach for her and stopped himself mid-motion, leaving his hand hanging lonely in the air, the gulf between them unbridged. "Be careful, Annie. Come back to us."

"I will," she said, and walked on, out of the firelight,

into the no-man's-land between the bonfires and the hill. The settlers watched her go. Any one of them could have drawn on her and shot her dead where she stood, but they did no such thing. It was as if the world had been encased in amber, cast in firelight and shadows like molasses, and no one could break free.

A bullet whizzed past her cheek as one of the men on the hill fired again. She felt the breeze from its passage. That confirmed, as much as anything could, that Michael had never been intending to kill the people down below: not until he had her, and Adeline, back in his clutches. The Clearing and the circus would become expendable once she and her daughter had been returned to him. Until then, killing the people who might know where they were would have been counterproductive.

If he had come in quietly, sending his little helpers to slit throats and burn bodies, she could have slipped away in the chaos. She could have freed herself. Instead, he had come in like thunder and made it impossible for her to run. She could admire that, even as it drove home precisely how little he had ever understood her. He thought that because she had run away from him, she was the sort of person who ran away from everything.

He'd never been able to understand that in the end, he had been the only thing she needed to flee. Everything else could be faced, but him . . .

Well, she was going to face him now, and may God have mercy on her soul.

Someone must have seen her, must have recognized her from Michael's description, because the gunfire stopped after that. Maybe it was even Michael himself, although she doubted that. She was older than his blushing bride, harder, with fewer soft curves and more jutting angles. Grace Murphy had never gone out into the woods and come back with a woman rescued from the jaws of monsters; had never killed a man, or held a lynx while it breathed its last, beloved breath. Grace Murphy was the skeleton Annie Pearl had built herself upon, and while she could still feel Grace moving beneath her skin, she wasn't that woman anymore. Try as she might, she could never be that woman again.

Foot by foot, Annie climbed the soft side of the hill, sometimes sliding backward when her feet failed to find the proper purchase, other times grabbing scrubby little bushes or jutting roots to pull herself a little closer to the top. No one came to help her. That, too, made her believe that it had been one of Michael's men, and not Michael himself, who had spotted her. He might not have helped her, but he would have come to taunt her as she climbed, reminding her of all the luxuries she had cast aside when she had chosen to run from him.

Finally, her questing hand found the hard soil of the road, and Annie pulled herself up onto it, standing. Three men with guns were already there, weapons drawn and aimed at her, like they thought one woman would be enough to bring their entire operation tumbling down.

It would. Please, God, it would. Annie straightened, pulling herself up until she felt as tall as any pine in the forest. Tall as a wendigo, and equally as terrible.

"Take me to my husband," she said.

The men moved to flank her. One stood behind her, digging the barrel of his gun into her spine, so that the metal bit into her flesh and made her shudder. She refused to allow herself to slump or shy away. If she showed weakness, they would forget that they needed to respect her as a woman of Deseret and start treating her like one of the faithless. That would be . . . bad.

The trouble with dividing the world into the Saved and the unsaved was that eventually you began to think that something must be wrong with those who had not been found worthy of salvation. There was no one kinder than a man of Deseret to one of his own, nor was there anyone crueler than that same man when faced with an outsider.

"You're Grace Murphy?" demanded one of the men.

"*Mrs.* Grace Murphy," she replied coldly, stressing her title. Let them remember who she was, in Deseret. Let them remember who owned her.

He had certainly never forgotten.

The man behind her dug his gun in a bit more harshly, urging her forward. She walked, head held high, refusing to let him knock her off-balance. Let *them* be the ones unsure of their footing. It was already working. They were casting confused glances between themselves, unable to reconcile their ideas about the kind of woman who would run away from a wealthy, loving, respected husband with this proud, blood-streaked creature before them.

I was always a person, she thought, putting one foot in front of the other, trying not to think about her daughter sleeping down below, unaware that her mother had left her, possibly for the last time. *The fact that I was once for sale to the highest bidder did nothing to reduce my humanity, and that which is human is also complex. That is the cost of humanity.*

The wagons were even brighter from this close, spangled with lights and humming from the strain of their steam engines. Michael must have drained his coffers to buy this much equipment—or else he had been funded entirely by Hellstromme, a thought that made her skin crawl. There were few people, even in Deseret, with this much ghost rock to waste in the recovery of a single runaway bride. For Hellstromme to be this extravagant . . . he truly wanted her little girl.

They kept walking, and suddenly, with no fanfare at all, there was Michael, and for a moment, Annie felt as if she couldn't breathe.

He had been a handsome man when they had married,

and he was still a handsome man now, straight of back and long of limb, with a face that verged on beautiful when he smiled. But if the years had stolen away her softness and replaced it with the strength to survive, they had peeled away some ineffable quality of his humanity, leaving behind a man who looked as if he had been crafted from a flesh-colored stone. Michael Murphy had always been hard, had always been cold, and yet. The man who turned to face her as she walked along the road was to that long-gone scientist as a tree was to an acorn.

We are all built on the skeletons of those who came before us, Annie thought, and for the first time she realized that she could feel sorrow for Michael, who had been as much a prisoner as she was, in his own way. Once.

"Grace," he said, and smiled. The expression did nothing to chase the cold calculation from his eyes: he was taking her measure with every second that stretched between them, and he was finding her infinitely wanting. "I knew you would come back to me."

"You sent people into my home to kill my friends and steal my daughter," said Annie. "I thought it best for me to come and tell you to your face why I needed you to stop. There's nothing for you here, Michael. Take your wagons and your weapons, and go back to Deseret."

"There's you," he said. "There's Pearl. That's two pieces of my property in this Godforsaken place, and I'll have both of them back again before I turn and head for home." He took a step toward her.

It took everything she had and more not to answer with a step back. "I am not your property," she said. "I am a free woman, and I am no more of Deseret. Two of your men are dead below, by my hand. Let that be enough to tell you that I am not your wife, and that you should leave me be. I would bring nothing but disgrace onto your house."

"I would have made you a princess. I would have made you a *queen*."

"I was already a princess, as Deseret measures such things, and even you lacked the power to make me a queen. Dr. Hellstromme could have done it, but he didn't want me. I know, because he didn't have me. He left me to you, to warm your bed, to soothe your flesh, and he told you what he wanted of you. He ordered you to create life. Did you ever think to ask what I wanted? Whether I wanted to be a princess, or a queen, or anything more than a beloved wife? I could have learned to be content, if only you had learned to love me."

"I did love you," snapped Michael. "I gave you everything, and you stole from me."

"You were going to kill our daughter."

"*I made her!*" He lunged forward, grabbing her forearms before she could flinch away. "She wouldn't exist without me! You would be nothing without me! I have the right to do as I please with my own things, and what I pleased was to take her apart! Now where is she? The girl needs her father!"

"The girl needs to be protected from her father," said Annie. She had to fight to keep her voice level. If she let him see how frightened she was . . .

No. This ended here. Tonight. It had already gone on for far too long.

"Liar," Michael hissed, and yanked her closer to him. "I have you back now. I will keep you. And you will see what you've done."

Letting go of her right arm, he dragged her by the left, fingers clamped down so hard that they were sure to bruise, until they had reached the largest and most elaborately lit of the wagons. He turned to glare at her.

"You're filthy," he said. "I shouldn't allow you this. You leave me no choice. If you're to understand what you've done to me, you need to know what you've done to *her*."

He jerked open the wagon door with his free hand. Annie had time to see the billowing white curtains inside before he shoved her through, slamming the door behind her.

She landed facedown in a pile of bedding. The smell of sweet wine vinegar hung thick in the air, barely masking something darker and sourer, like the taste of rotting meat.

"Hello?"

Annie froze.

The voice was not familiar. It was female, and young, but those attributes were almost outweighed by the faintness of it: it was a sigh masquerading as a little girl's voice, pushed out into the world despite the protests of the flesh around it. None of that mattered. Annie recognized it instantly. Even with all the years and miles between them, there was no way she could fail to recognize the voice of her own daughter.

"Who's there?" The voice sounded peevish now, like Annie was violating some sacred script. "Come where I can see you."

Annie sat up, pulling her face out of the bedclothes. White netting hung over everything, even here, inside the wagon. It would keep mosquitoes at bay during the summer months, but now, with winter coming, it seemed oddly excessive. She swept the netting aside with her arm, moving to kneel on the mattress beneath her—

And there she was. A little girl who could have been Adeline, were it not for the scars. One slashed across her throat like a permanent crucifix, arms climbing toward her chin and reaching for her spine. Another peeked above the collar of her frilly white nightgown, hinting at something more extreme slicing across the meat of her chest. Her white-blonde hair hung prettily over her shoulders, pulled forward into two pigtails, presumably to keep it from getting tangled with the thick black tubes that connected her to the machine behind her.

It chugged constantly, adding a soft whine to the sounds inside the wagon. The tubes connecting Annabelle—because it had to be Annabelle, it *had* to be; Annie had no other daughters—to the machine were attached to the flesh of her back and shoulders, driven into her body like railroad spikes into the earth.

Annabelle blinked, mouth curving downward in a confused frown. That, too, was exactly like her sister: Adeline frowned in just the same way when she was unhappy.

"Who are you?" she demanded. "Are you my new nanny? I don't need a new nanny. I want to go home. I want Helen."

Helen. Annie remembered Helen. She had been a timid, tidy girl, working at the fringes of the household, bringing bowls of apple slices floating in sugary lemon water when Annie—when *Grace,* she had still been Grace then, taking service and sweetness as her due—when the pregnancy was too hard on her. Helen had always been a good girl.

She supposed she should be glad that Helen had managed to weather the upsets in Michael's household that had no doubt followed the disappearance of the lady of the house. All she could feel was jealousy, burning in her breast like acid, that she could finally meet the daughter she had been forced to leave behind, and the first name from her child's lips belonged to another woman.

"I'm not your new nanny," Annie said through numb lips. "I'm your . . . Annabelle, I'm your mother."

Annabelle looked at her with cool, dark eyes, and there was no love in them, nor kindness, nor joy at the reunion. "He found you."

"Yes."

"You left us."

"Yes."

"You left *me*."

"I didn't—I never meant to harm you," said Annie. "I didn't know you had lived past infancy. I'm sorry. I'm so, so sorry."

"You took my sister, and you left me." Annabelle's small frown had become an outright scowl, distorting the planes of her face, making her look ancient and cruel. "Why?"

"I'm so sorry," said Annie again. "I couldn't take you both."

To her surprise, Annabelle laughed. The sound was thin, brittle, and almost drowned out by the steady wheeze of the machines. "I would never have gone with you," she said. "Even if I were a baby, I would have fought. But you took my sister. She was supposed to fix me, and you took her. I won't forgive you for that."

"Annabelle—"

The wagon door swung open. Strong hands grasped Annie, hauling her back out into the night, where the shadows surged thickly around her ankles, seeming to pin her in place. Michael was standing impassively by, face a mask as he watched his goons restrain his wife.

"You've met our daughter," he said. "Isn't it nice to see your own flesh and blood with your own eyes? It's a joy I haven't felt in years, thanks to you. I wanted you to understand what you walked away from."

The image of black tubes and a strange machine flashed through Annie's mind. She began to struggle. "What have you done to her? Can she even get out of bed?"

"She will," said Michael. "I'm no monster. I have been healing her, perfecting her, making her into the woman she should always have been—*would* always have been, if you hadn't stolen her sister from me and disrupted my work. I've had to settle for nonfamily donors, for piecemeal repairs, and why? Because you couldn't accept that we had the makings of one perfect child between the two."

"You had no right."

"I am your husband. I am their father. That gives me all the rights I could ever have wanted, in the eyes of both God and the law. I will make a perfect child. I will show the world that Deseret is the perfect country, so great that even our babies are without flaw. I will do it with you or without you. My Grace." Michael took a step forward, reaching up to caress her cheek.

Annie writhed, trying to break free, to no avail. "Don't touch me."

"Love, honor, and obey," he said. "Remember? Alive or dead, you're coming home with me. I would much prefer alive. You need to be disciplined for what you've done. You need to be *forgiven*."

Annie spat. Michael smirked.

On the bluff above them, the wolflings began to howl. It was a chilling sound, like moonlight made manifest. Michael took a step back, eyes widening.

"What is that?" he demanded.

This time, it was Annie who smirked.

"The monsters heard you wanted to join them," she said. "I suppose they're coming to test your mettle."

Chapter 24

Michael whirled, eyes scanning the ridge for the source of the howling. Annie went very still, offering no resistance to the men who held her. If she fought them, if she resisted them in any way, they might forget that they weren't supposed to harm her. But if she could hold her peace for a few seconds longer—

White bodies began to appear around the curve of the bowl, flickering out of the darkness like lanterns being lit by some terrible and unseen hand. They resolved into the bodies of creatures that were wolves and more than wolves, too large to be the creatures they so resembled, too white to be truly of this world. They were so white that they burned, and the thickened shadows swirled around them, unable to touch them or dim that brightness.

The shadows and the wolflings were cut from the same cloth: Annie saw that now. They were part and parcel of the same terrible West, neither moral nor amoral, as wild as the weather and as deadly as the desert. They did not judge. They did not forgive. They did not forget. They simply *were,* and they would do as they would.

Remember me, she prayed—and if it was blasphemy to direct her prayers to white wolves out of nightmares, she was fine with being blasphemous. They had been kind to her Adeline. That was all she required in this world, to make something acceptable. To make something kind. *Remember me, and spare me when you descend.*

"What madness is this?" demanded Michael. "Kill them! Bring me their pelts!"

The men along the lighted wagon train opened fire. They were no longer the ones with the higher ground. The wolflings shied back from the sound of gunshots, dancing along the ridge, and no red blood fell to stain white fur. Michael's men were burning their ammunition on nothing. Annie's heart sang. Bullets were a limited resource. No matter how many they had, they could run out. They *would* run out.

There was no more gunfire from below. She risked a glance at the bowl containing the town. She could see her friends and traveling companions clustering together, lit by the bonfire line, preparing for the next stage in the siege.

A bellow split the air, freezing the fingers of the gunmen on their triggers, echoing through the forest and The Clearing alike. Annie lifted her eyes, starting to quake as dread clutched at her heart and joints, seeming to turn them into stone.

On the other side of the bowl, blocking all hope of retreat, stood the wendigo.

There were less than a dozen of them. Somehow, that seemed like more than enough. Enough to destroy everything below them; enough to send this night straight to the depths of Hell. The townsfolk down in The Clearing pointed and ran, descending into panic. The circus folk grouped even closer together, like they thought the firelight would be enough to keep them safe.

Maybe it would. Faced with a choice between well-armed, well-protected people and the villagers who had been their prey for so long, why would the wendigo spare the townsfolk? The bargain between them was easy to see, even without hearing it stated aloud: The Clearing lured in travelers, circuses and vaudeville shows and tinkers, and gave them to the wendigo in exchange for their own survival. But this time, the travelers had fought back. This time, the travelers had taken back one of their own, and killed one of the wendigo in the process. The compact had been broken.

The compact was between the wendigo and the settlers. Who were they going to punish?

The men on the ridge were running low on ammunition. More and more, they were glancing at Michael before they pulled the trigger, waiting for him to give the command to run. They had half of what they'd come for: they had his wayward wife, finally back where she belonged, ready to be dragged home to Deseret and punished for the temerity of thinking that she could ever get away.

Did they even know that they were supposed to stay long enough to retrieve his little girl as well? Or did they think their job was done, and wonder why he hadn't given the order already? The trouble with the kind of loyalty that had to be bought and paid for was that it was never as strong as you wanted it to be. In the end, it was always loyalty to the money, and not to the person who paid the bills.

"What are they?" Michael spun on Annie, face contorted in rage and fear. "Did you do this? Tell me how to be rid of them!"

"This is their place, not yours," said Annie. She felt surprisingly calm. Terrified, yes, but she was accustomed to terror. She had been a wife in Deseret and a mother running through the West with a silent child bundled at her hip. She knew fear in all its shades, all its subtle flavors, and while she had the utmost respect for it, it could no longer command her. "The wolflings and the wendigo, they had things divided between them. You've thrown off the balance. They'll have your head for that."

Roaring—sounding half-wendigo himself in his rage—Michael ripped her out of the arms of the two men who had been holding her in place. He jerked her forward until their noses almost touched, until she was afraid, for one dizzy second, that he was going to kiss her, to wipe the memory of Nathanial's lips away.

Do not let me die with you the last man I have kissed, she thought, and did not struggle, because struggling would no longer do her any good.

"Slut," he hissed. "Consort of monsters. *Demon bride.*"

"All those things and more," she replied, in the sweetest tone she could muster, and brought up her knee, and slammed it as hard as she could into Michael's manhood.

His eyes went wide and round, matching the perfect circle of his mouth as the blood drained slowly from his face. Then he collapsed, falling into a heap at her feet, hands scrabbling uselessly at his crotch, like he thought he could somehow undo the damage she had done.

Annie turned to flee, and was unsurprised when strong hands grasped her shoulders. The men who had been ordered to hold her hadn't gone far. She closed her eyes, waiting for the bullet to pierce her skull. Instead, she felt her feet leave the ground, and she opened her eyes to find herself plummeting down, down, down into the bowl that contained The Clearing, flung so hard and so far that she seemed to be on a direct course with the ground.

Only seemed: her shoulder slammed into the side of the bowl, striking hard enough that she heard something inside her body snap, and then she was rolling end over end, scrabbling frantically for a handhold on the scrubby soil. Bits and pieces of the scene around her flashed by as she tumbled: wolflings leaping from the ridge down to the path, still unbloodied, fangs already bared; wendigo racing down the side of the bowl as if it were nothing, as if gravity were of no concern; muzzle flashes from both above and below, as the people with guns suddenly snapped out of their temporary truce and realized how much danger they were all in. And at the top of the bowl, far from the fight that was to come, two wendigo who had traded the fight for a feast, their teeth and claws red with Michael's blood, her marriage finally dissolved in the covenant of their hunger. A rush of hot, vindictive joy raced through her.

Thank you, she thought. That was all she had the time for before she hit the ground hard, landing in a heap well outside the shelter of the bonfires.

Get up, she commanded herself, to no avail. Her body refused to listen to her orders, refused to even entertain the idea that they might be important: her body was perfectly content to remain where it was, beaten and bruised and waiting for the aches to die down.

A wolfling howled, the sound too loud for the creature to be more than a few feet away. It was answered by the snarl of a wendigo, and then, almost as ominously, by the report of a rifle. The wolfling yelped. A man screamed. One of Michael's men.

Good, she thought. *You get what you deserve.*

But what did she deserve? She had left one daughter behind for the sake of saving the other: did that mean she deserved to die here, on the cold hillside, while everything she had ever loved burned around her?

She had run away from a man who had claimed to love her, who had put a ring on her finger and a roof over her head: she had left him to be devoured, and rejoiced at the fact of his death. Did that mean she deserved to lie helpless while the man who might have come to love her died at the hands of men and monsters who had once been men?

The question of the deserving and the undeserving was a difficult one to answer. It pained her even to try.

Then a familiar voice screamed, and she suddenly found the strength to climb to her feet and run, despite the ache in her thighs and the arm that dangled, limp and no doubt broken, against her side. She raced for the bonfires, pausing only to grab a burning brand from the edge of one of the stone circles, and when she saw the wendigo poised to rip Nathanial's throat out with its talons, she did not hesitate. She leapt between them, swinging her makeshift weapon wildly, heedless of the blisters rising on her palm.

The wendigo roared and stepped back, more puzzled than pained, and was hence off-balance when three wolflings slammed into it from the side, their teeth tearing, their hand-like paws scrabbling for a better grip on the creature's rank fur. The wendigo howled. Annie hit it again, careful to avoid the wolflings. They might be monsters, might be man-eaters in their own right, but the enemy of her enemy was her friend, now as much as ever.

Nathanial swung his gun around and shot the wendigo, five times in the chest. It howled again before turning to run, shedding wolflings as it went. More fell in behind it, chasing it into the darkness.

"Annie." Nathanial grasped her uninjured arm with his free hand. "I thought we'd lost you."

"We may yet have lost ourselves."

The chaos was continuing to unfold all around them. As Annie watched, the wolflings took down a man from The Clearing, while two wendigo fought over the body of a circus roustabout. The largest of her snakes—a diamondback rattler as pale as bone and as thick as her arm—coiled on the chest of a dead man, heavy head resting against its coils, seeming content. The night was alive with screams, and with monsters.

Through the thick of it, Adeline came.

The little girl was still barefoot, still pale as the world. She walked between the fires, stopping right next to her mother and looking up at her with wide, weary eyes.

"Delly . . ." whispered Annie.

Adeline walked on.

She walked until she reached the midpoint between the settlers and the circus. The largest of the wendigo was waiting for her there. She looked up at it. It looked down at her. Monster and monster's greatest creation stared at each other, across a gulf as wide as all the West, unfordable, unbroken.

The wendigo snarled.

Adeline shook her head.

'No,' she signed.

The wendigo snarled again.

'Not my family,' she signed. 'Take yours. Go.'

There was a long pause, split only by the screams coming from the ridge above. Finally, the wendigo nodded its vast, shaggy head, and turned to the settlers.

The sky was brighter with screams than with stars, and the night went on.

Chapter 25

Morning dawned upon a ghost town.

Not a single house in The Clearing was occupied: not a single store was opened, save for those which had been broken into in the hours before sunrise, stripped of provisions and of the materials needed to repair the broken circus wagons. Half the wainwrights were dead, killed by gunfire or by the claws of wendigo; those who remained were coaxing apprentices and acrobats through the process of putting things back together. Hal worked alongside them, unflagging, saving what could yet be saved.

They could, if they worked hard and fast and never faltered, be on the road again before the sun went down. Those who had survived the night wanted nothing more. Those who hadn't . . .

Every able body not occupied in repairing the wagons, looting the town, or minding the children was busy burying the dead. The wendigo would likely have them out again by the next dawn, but it was the principle of the thing. The idea that, perhaps, a little goodness could be brought to this dark place.

The wendigo had gone after taking their fill of the townsfolk, leaving no survivors. The Clearing was done. The wolflings had done the same, after filling their jaws with the men of Deseret. All the monsters had been missing by morning—even Laura, who had slipped her bonds, or been untied, and had vanished into the night without any further damage done.

There would be damage, one day. Adeline might have spared the woman, but Annie was sure that Deseret would hear of what had happened in The Clearing, and Deseret did not forgive. That was one holy attribute which had never reached the Holy City.

Annie walked up the road to the ridge, a shovel over her shoulder and Adeline walking beside her, silent. Her injuries were such that it might take her hours to dig the grave, but some things were necessary. Some things were part of remaining human.

Annabelle was still inside her wagon. The wagon was on its side. The tubes connecting her to the machinery had come loose at some point; her body had long since turned cold.

Annie pulled her out and laid her on the road. Adeline looked at her in silence for a long moment before touching the scar on her throat and turning to her mother.

'I remember her,' she signed.

"Good," said Annie. "Sisters should remember each other."

Down below, in The Clearing, Nathanial was overseeing the reconstruction of his circus. Somewhere nearby, in the woods, the wendigo waited to feast, and the wolflings prowled. Hal would return to the trees before nightfall, to the long, slow vigil for his wife, who had yet to find her own rest. But here, and now, there was a grave to dig, and the forest stretched from here to Heaven, and soon the circus would roll on, seeking something better, something brighter, something, in the end, to believe in.

TOR

Award-winning authors
Compelling stories

Please join us at the website
below for more information
about this author and other great
Tor selections, and to sign up for
our monthly newsletter!